ON WINDS OF DESIRE

We seemed to fly: across meadows; over streams; through the thorny heath to soar, finally, to the crest of Smugglers' Peak. I slid from the mare's back. Dark, empty clouds taunted the sky and sly gusts of wind tossed the sea.

Suddenly I heard the thunder of hoofbeats. I swung around, exultant. He was there. His flying hair blacker than the sky. His horse an ebony streak daring the horizon.

He lifted me high in his arms and our lips clung as if forever . . .

"You came," I gasped.

"I could not stay away."

"Love me. Now."

We sank to the harsh ground. Wild as the day itself, our bodies heaved under the tempestuous sky . . .

Mistress of Wynds

Meg Haviland

A DELL BOOK

Published by
Dell Publishing Co., Inc.
1 Dag Hammarskjold Plaza
New York, New York 10017

Dell ® TM 681510, Dell Publishing Co., Inc.

ISBN: 0-440-15707-2

Printed in the United States of America
First printing—October 1981

Part I

Chapter 1

"Knowlton!"

"Y-yes, ma'am."

"You have not, as yet, miss, joined that simple piece of lace?"

"Ah, n-no, Mrs. Walsh," I stammered. "But it is nearly finished, I think."

"You think?" Mrs. Walsh moved closer. "How is it, pray, that you do not know?"

"Well, y-yes, then—I know," I murmured, "ma'am."

"Perhaps your skill is such that your place is properly in the shirtroom, miss, rather than amongst the finer dresses."

"Mrs. Walsh—please, no!"

"It was the sacred credo of the Reverend Walsh, my late, lamented husband, that one should never nurture expectations in life beyond one's obvious limitations."

"I can manage this, Mrs. Walsh. Truly, I can."

"The Reverend Walsh strongly maintained, also, that it can be considered scarcely Christian, on the part of one in authority, to demand achievement from his subordinates greater than that of which they are eminently capable." The woman crossed heavy arms over stiffly encased breasts. "I trust you follow, Knowlton."

"Y-yes," I nodded miserably, "ma'am."

"In that case, miss, I shall expect to find your task accomplished well before tea."

"Certainly, Mrs. Walsh."

"And not a stitch in evidence, mind."

"N-no. Of course n-not, ma'am."

"Else"—her sigh was deliberately pronounced—"I shall be obliged to give serious consideration to a modification of your position."

"Y-yes, Mrs. Walsh."

"And of what possible concern can this conversation be

to you, Baker?" Mrs. Walsh rasped at the dressmaker sharing my bench. "You had best keep those wandering eyes applied to their own work."

"Yes, ma'am," the girl replied easily.

Mrs. Walsh's gaze raked the crowded room. "Attend me, ladies," she announced, loudly imperious. "My admonition to Miss Knowlton embraces you all." She drew herself to fullest height. "Each and every one." There ensued an immediate burst of exaggerated industry. Apparently satisfied, Mrs. Walsh, back rigid in its constraints and with an air of determination, sailed importantly from the room.

"The old harridan," muttered Molly Baker.

"Hush," I cautioned.

"Off to pester another room," sneered the girl, "and welcome to her!"

"Molly!"

"Ah! I've naught to fear from her," she boasted, tossing lively red curls. "I'll not be under her nose much longer."

"Whatever do you mean by that?" Bea Foster leaned across the worktable.

"I am being considered for the shop," Molly confided.

"La te da!" giggled Ada Humphreys, neighbor to Bea on the bench opposite.

" 'Tis no fairy tale," retorted Molly. "I heard the First Hand and Walsh discussing me yesterday."

"And just when is the great occasion?" Ada smirked.

"Any day now," Molly said airily. "Any day!"

"While I am off to the shirtroom!" I wailed.

Molly laid a comforting hand on my arm. "You fret overmuch. Walsh will not hide the likes of you in there."

"But," I protested, "I can never satisfy her, it seems."

Molly teased, "Ah, the lot of the apprentice!" She grinned, her blue eyes sparkling. "The witch'll ease off some, once you move up to improver."

"An age," I groaned.

"It's not much longer until your rise, Elizabeth," consoled Bea kindly, "only lacking but a few months of your two years now, as you are. . . . And, truly, it gets better." She sighed, "Or is it that one simply becomes more tired. . . ."

Noting the girl's pinched face, eyes pale—lost in their

deep shadows—I asked in quick concern, "Whatever is the matter, Bea, dear? You are not ill?"

"Gracious, no," the girl smiled wanly, returning truant strands of lank hair that had strayed from the thick coil based at a neck seeming too frail, suddenly, to support its heavy burden.

"My word, yes, Bea! You are a bit peaky!" observed Molly.

"The heat, I expect," Bea hastened to reassure us, "it is stifling in here . . ."

My eyes then swept the room: past sightless windows, spilling their sluggish dusty sunstreams onto the web of lint that choked the floor below; rose to smoky flames, nervous in their spitting jets; fled the cavern of the blackened hearth, only to be tripped by random bolts of colored fabric splashed against somber walls; resting here on ashen cheek, there on sagging shoulder; caught finally by skillful fingers, orchestrating nimbly, inexorably, the tabled clutter beneath. Pervasive over all: the air of resignation.

"Bea is right," I reflected, "the atmosphere is really quite oppressive. There is certainly little provided in the way of ventilation—"

"Do tell," gibed Ada.

"Couldn't one window be opened at least?" I asked.

"What?" scoffed Ada, "and dare to let in a breeze to extinguish a precious gas jet in the process?"

"In the words of Madam Walsh," mimicked Molly, " 'Ladies: To work well, one must see well!' "

Ada giggled.

"It's a miracle we don't all suffocate," I complained.

"Cheer up, luv," comforted Molly, "it'll be time for tea, soon enough."

"Tea," I gasped, "and my work not yet done!"

"Here, give over," Molly offered, "let's have a look. . . . Oh, dear . . ."

"What is it?" I asked in alarm.

"Your stitches are not nearly fine enough," Molly judged. "See—this one here, for example . . . and there . . . that will never do. Dear heaven! These are fit for the neck of an elephant, hardly a lady's skinny wrist!"

Ada tittered.

"My skill with a needle has never been remarkable, I fear," I confessed ruefully.

"Amen to that!" Molly agreed promptly.

"You would have learned betimes, Elizabeth, had you been shipped from one boarding school to the next, like the rest of us," Ada remarked sourly.

"Aye," seconded Molly.

"Day and night, night and day," droned Ada, "pin this, sew that, put it in, rip it out. . . . I recall, in particular, one scold—head smooth as polished marble under that false piece of hair sticking out every which way like a bloomin' shrub—and just as hard, I'll swear. That one would mosey over, nice and easy, and stare at my work— every ruddy stitch of it, through a glass, mind—and chant, the while: 'A stitch in sight is poised for flight. . . .' "

Molly nodded. "Sounds uncannily like my Mrs. Dillon: 'Any stitch I see, must flee!' "

"Bloody old fools!" Ada said contemptuously.

"Your language, Ada, dear," reproved Bea gently.

"Mastered plenty of that, too, I'll vow," Ada giggled. "Eh, Molly?"

"Don't mind if I do," Molly allowed, chuckling.

"However, girls, I am sure that Elizabeth did not," warned Bea, "living as she did—at home."

Home . . . so far away . . .

. . . Home . . . Number 32 Leicester Square . . . with its arches—gabled spires—tall square chimneys, thrusting proudly—spear-tipped railing, entry soldier guarding the great door where the bronzed knocker hung high . . . Home . . .

. . . Golden times . . . far away now . . . but never lost from memory . . .

. . . Leicester Square . . . Although never quite equaling the supreme classical elegance achieved by the sumptuous columned residences of Belgrave Square (near neighbor and commonly adjudged the most fashionable in the quarter), Leicester Square could claim as occupants families of substantial wealth and solid respectability. Number 32, a house rising to four storys (including an attic) and offering an indecisive façade mingling both Tudor and Gothic design, was withal beautiful to me: It had been my place of birth and until now my only home.

I was the single child to survive of the brief union of my parents, James and Isabella Knowlton, my mother having died attempting to deliver a male child some two years after my own birth. The heir, long-awaited, proved stillborn and my mother succumbed some few weeks later, exhausted by the ordeal and, I have been told, lost in the throes of deepest melancholy. Deprived thus at such an early age, I remember virtually nothing of my mother, and any recollections (I think I may have realized even then) were spawned by childish fantasy or garnered through offerings divulged by kindly servants sympathetic to my loss, and, on occasion, a sentimental reminiscence—contribution of my father. Even so, my mother's strongest presence could be felt in her portrait, life-size and hanging in state above the huge marble fireplace, which dominated easily the spacious drawing room. Truly she was a glorious, golden creature, from that wonderful cloud of hair and tone of skin to the arresting, rich amber color of her eyes. I resemble her, but palely.

Immediately after my mother's death Auntie Maude, maiden sister to my father's mother (deceased), came to live with us and assume, in addition to the duties of governess to me, the practical position of mistress over an establishment large and liberally staffed, demanding, therefore, explicit supervision. And although I was made to understand the distant relationship early on, I nonetheless regarded Auntie Maude, almost at once, as my real maternal parent and looked to her for solace and advice. Short of stature and so plump as to be almost rotund, my Auntie Maude saw the world through a pair of mild eyes, their gray color matching perfectly the knot of hair wisping untidily above a broad face, which was dimpled rather than lined; the world saw Auntie Maude as the epitome of a gentle nature with purest heart. We were constant companions, she and I, both at home and on holiday, and ever did the sweet disposition and even temper prevail, despite any recalcitrance exhibited by a young and willful child. She attempted to impart to me her not insufficient knowledge of domestic affairs, but since I was infinitely happier at

the pianoforte and easel, or immersed in the pages of a book,
she did not fret or scold, even when my conscious lack of
effort warranted reproof, or when the lesson seemed
doomed to failure from the start.

With my father I had little real contact. Much of his
business activity was conducted at night, Auntie Maude explained, although rather vaguely. Through my earliest and
fondest memories, I can relive those glorious times when
my father, after a stay away, arrived home with great fan-
fare, creating a flurry of excitement and all but buried under a mountain of gaily colored bundles containing gifts for
one and all. I can see him now, standing tall in the doorway to the nursery, reaching into his pocket to extract a
packet of bills, pressing them then in astonished Auntie
Maude's hand as he announced: "The child is pale,
Maude. Why not ship her off to Bath for a spell—or
Brighton for some sea air!" I can remember how he
stooped from his great height to pat my head absently.
"Run along now, sweet, and let your Auntie Maude pack
you both up for a nice holiday . . . there's a good girl . . ."
How I adored him! What enchantment was there in
that lithe figure, those roguish eyes, and the romantically
curling hair! Not before his laughing mouth had kissed my
cheek did I trot off to inspect my newest treasures and
bask in the knowledge that my father was not only the
handsomest of men, but the dearest and most generous in
the world!

Often, and increasingly so as the years passed, I recall
that his absences began to extend both in duration and frequency and that my father's return became strangely sober
and was accomplished without so much as an advance
word. Always now he looked worn and ill. Once at home
he did not stir from his room even to take his meals, except
on those occasions on which he rose before noon to confer
in his private study with gentlemen of a surprisingly rough,
even sinister, aspect. At these times Auntie Maude fluttered about, wild of eye, suggesting that nothing would do
but that she and I must pay an immediate visit to the shops
on Charles or Pont streets—better still, instruct Brooks to
hitch up the phaeton and head for Regent and Oxford and

have a look at the materials there. Once lost in the mayhem of the city, beguiled by velvet mantles, lured by graceful silks and flimsy gauzes beckoning from shop windows, I was able in the callous manner of the young to erase the disturbing image of my father, to put aside the haunted look in his eyes, the trembling of his hands, dismiss his now habitual air of troubled preoccupation . . . forget all these until my return, when I was informed that he had again left the house. For how long now?

Years spent trying vainly to penetrate her patent evasions and interpret her feeble explanations, I resigned myself eventually to accept Auntie Maude's reticence regarding the nature of my father's occupation. Questions on the matter merely occasioned her eyes to shift uneasily and her soft mouth to bunch in disapproval. I could not, in fact, determine whether her aversion to such discussion was prompted by my interrogation or by the manner itself in which he conducted his affairs; I, however, forbore. Whatever my father's mode of business transaction, I was well supported in the luxuries of life customarily enjoyed by the young ladies of my station: riding, when I became of an age proper to the pursuit, on the Ladies' Mile, perched high atop a sleek mount selected from our own stables, and they perfectly equipped; privy to a wardrobe that was both extensive and varied; permitted unblemished entry into the finest establishments through an easy acquaintanceship with the daughters of the rich and prominent set of London; treated to frequent and capricious visits to elegant resorts deep in the country or at seaside; complemented by surroundings, exquisitely appointed, in which to entertain properly those guests deemed suitably of my class.

The golden days of my life, then, passed in comfort and luxury, their wonders shared by a joyous companion of unfailing good humor: Auntie Maude. She, true to her obligation, dutifully set forth my regular morning lessons; these, however, could be intruded upon whenever the fancy so suited one of us or, as it usually developed, both. Such interruptions might take the form of an excursion to Regent Street, a picnic hastily decreed, or even the arrival of Miss Hattie Wyler's most recent novel, deliciously unexpected and delivered by hand, a courtesy extended by the little bookstore off Pont Street. Auntie Maude gave more serious attention to my prowess at the pianoforte, even so far as to engage a Master, appointed to determine weekly my continuing progress. That Monsieur Raggot was skillful at his craft remained without dispute; his breath, propelled by a pair of enormous bellows, raged as fire from a dragon—so much so that I took conspicuous pains always to move as far as possible from him on the tapestried piano stool without offense to him and at a real hazard to my own person. Supporting such an unnatural posture at the keys, it was a mark of dedication and fortitude that I managed the simplest scales. Entirely cognizant of my plight, Auntie Maude derived hilarity from the scene: Seated strategically in a discreet corner of the room and well removed, that lady was barely able to conceal her rollicking mirth behind a fan that fluttered too rapidly and quite without grace.

Despite such unprecedented odds I became reasonably proficient at the keyboard, to both Auntie Maude's delight and, I must confess, my own; music became important to me, and I reveled in all of the selections assigned, especially those of my acknowledged favorite, Scarlatti. Too, although I could boast no real prowess as a painter, I contrived to set down several creditable watercolors; these Auntie Maude lovingly and tastefully framed and hung in prominent positions throughout the house. Reading, even the mandatory and often laborious passages of the Bible, was a gorgeous pastime; but in needlepoint and similar pursuits, I evinced little interest and dramatically less ability. Regularly attended by an army of dress designers and never obliged to suffer mended garments, I could not for the life of me recognize the need for perfect refinement in that quarter; Auntie Maude, devoted as always to my immediate desires, did not press the issue.

At the age of twelve or thereabouts I began to notice a subtle alteration in the household arrangements, commencing with the unexpected and abrupt dismissal of my father's valet, a man advanced in years and one whom I regarded as a fixture in the house. I inquired of Auntie Maude as to the possible reasons for his removal; she murmured some inanity about insufficient need for his services with my father so often absent, which occasioned the man to beg release from his duties . . . and then, as usual, she adroitly changed the subject. Moments later found us bouncing off to Oxford Street to inspect the exciting new arrivals in the shop windows, the valet forgotten in the sharp slap of the horse's hooves against the dusty cobbles.

Not long thereafter Mary, one of the upstairs maids, followed suit. She was always an agreeable and industrious servant; I could not fathom why, indeed, she had lost her position. Again Auntie Maude diverted me with vague and troubled mumblings, and suddenly we were off, boarding the brightly painted phaeton, headed for Hove, our bags hastily packed and our anticipations high for a fortnight of light-hearted fun and heady sea air. . . .

Nor did the stables escape unscathed: I was horrified to learn that all of the saddle horses save two had disappeared (their stalls never to be replenished), as had the large carriage and all grooms but one. The phaeton remained, and my own mount, Bathsheba, and for their reprieve I was truly thankful. Auntie Maude made no serious attempt at explanation but, rather, assumed an air of studied carelessness that, while not convincing, was stubbornly maintained.

The ensuing years saw individual interior furnishings gradually vanish, particularly those stunning items in the drawing room, customarily the greatest source of beauty and monetary value in any establishment. Gone: a vase here, a silver box there, until even some heavy pieces were carted away one by one. I was startled to observe, for example, during what was to be my terminal lesson at piano with Monsieur, that the massive standing lamps whose curved and gilded stems supported large illuminated balls, and that had always framed the stolid mahogany sideboard, were no longer at their station. I played badly that session, waiting as I did for it to end so that I might question Auntie Maude concerning their disappearance; my reward, as usual, was an imprecise, confusing revelation: The lamps were off to be repaired . . . no, to be cleaned . . . no . . . "Oh, well, darling, it is really of no great consequence, now is it, dear."

Suddenly too the delicate contours and subtle hues of the

oft-admired Coalport vases continued no more to grace the
stern marble fireplace. Gone besides, the end tables fashioned of papier-mâché, which I had privately loathed for
years. I did regret the absence of the monopodium table set
in the bow window, curve for curve a perfect fit, and the
round ebony tea table whose mother-of-pearl inlay shimmered as a rainbow. I knew that I should certainly not
grieve for the departure of the Parian statuary—its gods
and goddesses, viewing overly plump offspring at unnaturally languid play, were themselves so passive and fleshy as
to negate any claim to either interest or charm—and like-
wise good riddance to the pedestal table with its grotesque
carvings of yawning gargoyles intertwined with acorn
groupings—an incongruous marriage, surely.

The bulk of the sideboard, sustained by enormous paw-
like supports that clutched the floor before working upward to create, ultimately, sphinx figures flat of face and
oddly winged, appeared stark now without the mitigating
effect projected by the stirring red-gold tapestry that had
until recently hung in dramatic contrast on the wall directly above. A pity that the sideboard could not have been
the one to go and the tapestry spared! Gilded mirrors were
stripped from the walls, clocks, elaborate with floral de-
signs or detailed country scenes, plucked from now-naked
mantels, followed by heavy silver candelabra, or cunning
snuffboxes snatched from shiny tabletops.

My determination grew that the gradual depletion of our
temple's treasures must be connected somehow with my father's private, intermittent audiences with his ruffian-
visitors; it was usually after an interview of this nature that
the reduction of our possessions accelerated perceptibly, to
subside until the next visit, when the cycle was again renewed. I wondered briefly if these "gentlemen" might not
be removing our valuables by stealth—but dismissed the
idea as frivolous and fanciful.

One by one, doors to spare bedchambers were closed, my
Auntie Maude carefully pocketing their keys, reasoning
aloud to me that since the numbers serving the household
had diminished, surely it was no longer desirable, or practical, to keep idle rooms in a state of readiness. She explained further that the rooms had been placed in a waiting

condition merely, and that everything remained intact, appropriately under protective dust covers. This last was a patent lie: Permitted an unguarded, telltale glimpse into the interior of what had been the suite reserved for the guest of state and lavishly decorated as such, furnished as it was with many pieces of beauty and value—including for one an enormous richly draped half tester, intricately carved with precious cupids clutching spectacular roses in their chubby fingers, for another (and my favorite) a dainty conversation chair covered in yellow satin delicately patterned— I saw that the room had been completely emptied of its contents.

Confronting Auntie Maude, I was put off with fumbling assurances that the room was being prepared for painting and general refurbishing and that the furniture and trappings were simply in storage elsewhere, until the work had been completed and order restored. I will confess that I did not give any real credence to her protestations here, any more than to those regarding the lessening of visits from the dressmakers; Auntie Maude, taking considerable pains to disparage the newest styles as being uncommonly awkward, decreed that my present wardrobe was far and away more becoming than anything currently featured. Not that I was denied new apparel; it was simply that the lavish sums previously expended on my wardrobe, as well as those assigned to other niceties, were now markedly reduced. "When the time arrives for you to be presented," Auntie Maude declared, "I suppose we shall have to relent and subscribe, however unwillingly, to the ugliness of the latest fads. . . . Until then"—her sigh was tremulous—"I can enjoy my girl in prettier and more flattering garb." Privately I viewed the tiny bonnets and improbable crinolines featured in the smartest shop windows and adorning fashionable ladies as they glided along a busy city street, or emerged (revealing a splash of colored petticoat) from shiny liveried carriages, to be most intriguing indeed. . . .

Meanwhile a slow deletion of the staff continued—a maid here, a busboy there; next, perhaps, a footman—until ultimately only a skeleton force remained in residence. Visitors to the house dwindled in number and regularity and were welcomed in turn by a hostess noticeably ill at ease.

Auntie Maude no longer made social overtures, issued invitations, or invented excuses for informal gatherings—suitably planned or delightfully impromptu—as had been her wont. Although I did not deem solitude one of Auntie Maude's outstanding inclinations, I did not question her hesitancy to entertain: The drawing room bore the unhappy air of inelegance, bereft as it was of all its finer pieces. And of the two small sitting rooms, one was not now in use; the other seemed forlorn, even a little shabby.

On the very afternoon I had recorded the disappearance from honored heights in the entry hall of the globe gas chandelier (an ornate, impressive fixture), Miriam Longwell, an unexpected caller and no favorite acquaintance, asked in pretended innocence, "Elizabeth, when are you planning to engage your lady's maid?"

"Oh, ah—well—" I hedged.

"You know, we are *all* getting them this year," she confided deliciously.

"Is that so?" I parried.

"Surely you *are* fifteen?" goaded the girl.

"I—ah, yes . . ." I admitted grudgingly.

"That is the proper age," Miriam said airily. "*Mine* is coming next week. Of course," she was delighted to confess, "I shall not reach fifteen until midsummer, but Papa feels that I should learn to adapt fully to the world of society I shall be entering."

I nodded absently.

"When does yours arrive?" Miriam persisted.

"Perhaps when we return from holiday," I lied. "I really could not answer. . . . Auntie Maude takes care of such tiresome arrangements. . . ." I rose, indicating dismissal. "Now, if you will be so good as to excuse me, Miriam, I am expected in town for tea within the hour and must fly if I am to bathe and change. . . ."

The culling of little luxuries neither offended nor disturbed me for their own loss, but rather for the implications therein. That I was not provided a lady's maid in no way troubled me and certainly did not justify Auntie Maude's gushing rationalization: "After all, *my* girl, with her lissom figure, has no need for one—not requiring the cumbersome stays and corsets many young ladies in her circle, not so fortunate, are obliged to wear." Our life continued, then, deprived of a frill here, an extravagance there, and with a tacit understanding that those delight-filled spontaneous trips to the sea or countryside must be, of necessity, curtailed. Auntie Maude's spirits remained high, at least outwardly, and we enjoyed life and one another much as before. More often than not my father remained away. No longer cause for celebration, his homecoming meant not pageantry but a sustained seclusion in his room, permitting social invasion by none save the suspicious-looking callers, who seemed to cut short his awaited stay by their intrusion. Predictably, after consultation with his visitors my father would fling himself frantically from the house, and another of his extended absences would begin.

Chapter 2

Shortly before the advent of my sixteenth birthday my father was ushered hurriedly into the house by the butler, Chambers, and in a sorry sodden condition. It was late afternoon of a cold November day. A sharp wind had moved in from the river, bringing with it a stabbing rain, which carried a chill to penetrate the bones of even one enjoying robust health and dressed perfectly against the harsh exposure. My father could claim neither. Visibly shivering, he all but stumbled through the entry hall and into Chambers's arms, appearing, in fact, dazed. "Feverish!" I heard Auntie Maude gasp as, suddenly activated, she hastened to the kitchen, issuing a barrage of orders for hot packs and warming pans and a "Toddy. Strong and steaming!"

The night passed, jarred by constant activity. Doors opened and closed repeatedly, footsteps whispered; presiding over all, Auntie Maude, suddenly shrill guardian of the sick.

Early morning found the octogenarian Dr. Crofts pulling his way with enormous difficulty up the broad staircase. His face livid with the exertion and perspiring unnaturally, the doctor paused in his labored progress frequently to ease his breathing and clear his congested throat; after a few noisy moments he began again the slow ascent. Chambers, respectfully carrying the physician's bag, hovered close by in the event that his services were required. He too was of such an age that I wondered idly what would happen if his inconsiderable strength were actually called upon. I am ashamed to say I almost giggled.

The doctor remained closeted with my father for a suitable interval, while Auntie Maude paced nervously outside the closed door. Upon completion of his examination the doctor emerged for the customary consultation with the family. "Well," he announced cheerfully, "I have bled 'im!"

"How is he?" Auntie Maude asked anxiously.

"He? Who?"

"Er—Mr. Knowlton."

"Mr. Knowlton? Oh, quite so. . . . Yes, well now, let me see. . . ." Dr. Crofts scratched his shaggy head. "What did I say was the precise nature of the ailment?"

"Er—you didn't," reminded Auntie Maude.

"I didn't? Hmmm . . . oh, quite so. . . . Hmmm. Well, ah—the patient is suffering from a severe cold, is all. And," he declared triumphantly, "I have attended to her first stage of treatment."

"Her? You mean his," corrected Auntie Maude.

"His? Ah, quite so. . . . Yes, indeed, his." The doctor cleared his throat vigorously. "Now, as I have indicated, I have administered the first dose . . ." His voice trailed away.

"Yes?"

"Yes. Ah, let me see, what was it exactly that I prescribed . . . let me try to remember . . ." The old man rubbed his chin in deepest concentration. "It quite eludes me. . . . No, now . . . I have it now! Emetic tartar and ipecacuanha!"

"Have you any instructions for me?" asked Auntie Maude.

"How's that?"

"Is there something that I should do?"

"Something you should do . . . What should you do . . . let me see now. . . . Ah—yes, I believe I have hit on the answer. Quite so. If the fever persists," he recited, "you are to take this dose three times, m'dear."

"You mean my nephew."

"Your nephew? Er, quite so. Your nephew . . ."

Auntie Maude nodded.

"Let me think, now—there is something I was to remember to remind you . . ."

"About the emetic tartar and ipecacuanha?"

"Ah! Quite so!" His blue eyes wandered thoughtfully beyond Auntie Maude, seeking an obscure location some distance down the long hallway. "The ingredients must be mixed with water!" He was triumphant. "*Salt* water!"

"Salt water," parroted Auntie Maude.

"Quite so! Salt water. 'Pon my soul, salt water!"

"What then, doctor?"

"What then? What then . . . oh, yes . . . Now, if I recollect . . . Ah, quite so . . . if your stomach should not be satisfactorily purged by then, I would prescribe a mild aperient."

"My nephew's stomach," Auntie Maude prompted weakly.

"Er—forgive me, m'dear. Quite so! *His* stomach!" The old man chuckled in huge enjoyment. "*His* stomach. Quite so!"

"May I ask, Doctor, what is an aperient?"

"An aperient? Did I say that?"

Auntie Maude inclined her head miserably.

"Why, yes—so I did. Quite so!" the doctor admitted. "An aperient. Now, m'dear, an aperient is nothing more complicated than a mixture of Epsom and Bruber—er, no—that is not correct—Grumber—no, Gauper—no. Always get that confounded name confused, somehow." His smile was sheepish. "Glauber's! That's it: Glauber's salt!" Exultant, he snapped his fingers. "Glauber's! Add a small amount of tincture of senna and presto! An aperient!"

"Oh, dear!" sighed Auntie Maude.

"Simple procedure, my dear. Childishly simple." He rocked on his heels proudly.

"Yes?" prodded Auntie Maude. "And?"

"And what? Oh, I see . . . quite so. . . . One must make certain that the mixture is dissolved in antimonial wine."

"Antimonial . . . oh, my," breathed Auntie Maude.

"Fret not, m'dear," the doctor smiled, "I have left . . . at least I *think* I . . ." he mumbled vaguely.

"Yes?" Auntie Maude pursued, "you have left—what?"

"Oh . . . A preparation on the shelf in the bath . . . near the WC, as a matter of fact. . . . Now, then," he frowned, "I hope that I did not put it *in* the WC . . ." He moved toward the door to my father's room. "Perhaps I had best go and have a look."

"Oh, no!" shrieked Auntie Maude. "You couldn't have!"

"No? I couldn't? Good . . . Good . . . No, I couldn't," he grinned. "How, then . . . bottle needs only a brisk snap of the wrist before administration"—he paused—"or is that the thermometer . . ."

"Doctor," Auntie Maude asked fearfully, "will he be all right?"

"Er, who?"

"Mr. Knowlton, my nephew . . ."

"What did I say was wrong with him?"

"A c-cold," ventured Auntie Maude.

"A cold? Bah! M'dear, this is the season for colds," the doctor exclaimed, his mood jocular. "None of us mortals is safe from the filthy little beggars in this miserable climate!" Waggling a teasing arthritic finger under my aunt's nose, he laughed a shade too enthusiastically, causing him to cough richly. When the distressing spasm finally passed, the doctor mopped at his brow and blew his nose with surprising energy. "Good day, m'dear. Lovely party . . . lovely . . ."

"Er—Doctor—should he be kept in bed?"

"In bed?" The doctor considered carefully. "In bed? What did I say was his affliction again?"

"A cold."

"A cold? Quite so. Of course . . . In bed . . . Bed rest. Only sensible precaution . . . He should rise for normal bodily functions only, and for the periodic cold bath to bring down his fever. Routine . . ." He rubbed his nose in indecision. "I did say he had a fever . . ."

"I—I don't know."

"Probably does. Stands to reason. . . . Now, let me know, m'dear, if any change should develop," Dr. Crofts directed and, eyeing the long staircase dubiously, added, "I can be here quick as a hare. Although"—he placed a kindly hand on Auntie Maude's plump shoulder—"I seldom anticipate any complications with the chicken pox."

"Cold," whispered Auntie Maude.

"Cold? Er, quite so. Cold . . ."

The day progressed. The melancholy fog that hugged the earth's sodden surface, pressing ever closer in its grim determination to seep through the very walls of the house, was no match for the pall of gloom that had settled firmly within. An endless parade of buckets—this one emitting wavering wisps of steam; that, sloshing drops of frigid wa-

ter—were hefted up and down the broad staircase first by
an exhausted footman, next by a faltering housemaid. Covered pans, pitchers, were removed hastily from the sick-
room and returned promptly. Fresh supples of linens and
towels were carried in, wicker baskets, overflowing with
their soiled burdens, out, dispatched to the laundry for immediate cleansing.

From time to time throughout the day, escaping even the
heavy panels of double doors, the agony of painful, convulsive retching. Then: silence, broken only by the whimpering sounds of the very weak and helpless. I became uneasy,
despite Auntie Maude's attempts at reassurance. "It will be
a busy day here," she said, folding a batch of fresh toweling on the walnut table in the upper hallway. "Why not
plan to go calling, this afternoon?"

"Oh, no, I couldn't," I shuddered.

"Perhaps you could ask Brooks to harness the phaeton
and escort you to Regent Street."

"No."

"On second thought," Auntie Maude decided, "that
might not be wise, should the phaeton be needed
here. . . ."

Sudden sounds of movement and violent distress, erupt-
ing from behind my father's door, caused Auntie Maude to
turn quickly to me. "Run along to the music room, dear,
and practice for a bit," she suggested. "I am sure your father would enjoy a little concert." At my hesitation she patted my cheek, "Run along, love. . . ."

I sat at the piano, fingering the keys—softly at first,
then with an increasing vigor that matched the turbulence
of my thoughts. This brought Auntie Maude to the doorway, a pudgy finger placed across her lips. "Shh, dear,"
she cautioned, "I think that perhaps you should not be
playing, after all. Your father's rheumatic pains are making it difficult enough for his much-needed rest."

"Rheumatic pains?" I asked, frightened.

"Yes, dear. They commenced a short while ago. . . .
Now, now, there is no need for alarm, I have sent Brooks
to Dr. Crofts' dispensary for some extract of hemlock. Relief should be forthcoming soon."

Shortly before dusk rude knocking abruptly shattered the awed hush of the house and interrupted its quiet industry: my father's sinister callers. Above the feeble protestations of the aged Chambers that the master was ill and could not be disturbed, a rough voice laughed, "He will see us."

"Perhaps tomorrow, sir," suggested Chambers politely.

"Just tell him we are here, old man."

"But, sir—"

"Now!"

My father appeared at the head of the stairs then, his face ravaged and his hand, trembling, seeking support from the sturdy iron banister. "Instruct them to wait in my study," he ordered Chambers. "I shall be down directly."

"But, sir—" the old man began.

"Please, Chambers," my father sighed, "if you will be so kind as to help me dress." Later, ignoring Auntie Maude's objections as she fluttered helplessly about, my father slowly descended the stairs; moments later the door to his study clicked shut and the murmur of voices commenced, rising and falling in pitch, until at last the visitors took leave, my father in their company.

"Oh, no!" gasped Auntie Maude. "He is not going out?"

For hours afterward Auntie Maude roamed the house, restless hands pulling aside heavy drapes, anxious eyes peering through empty windows, seeking to pierce the hungry fog that had devoured the darkened streets. There was no sign of my father that night. And no word. Midmorning of the day following, a commotion at the door signaled his return, and that in a state of near collapse.

"Merciful heavens!" cried Auntie Maude.

"I am all right, Aunt," my father managed, "just call someone to help me up the stairs, if you will—"

"Oh, James," wailed Auntie Maude.

"Please, Aunt—"

Toward twilight Dr. Crofts was again summoned. The visit proved of greater length than the one previous. A change in the medication was indicated—a tonic of muriatic acid combined with cinchona—calculated to remedy any debility caused by my father's incautious exertion and exposure.

Throughout the night I was aroused by my father's inter-mittent pacing up and down the length of the hall, tracked by Auntie Maude, wild by now with anxiety, urging him to return to his bed. "James, dear, be sensible. You must not move around like this . . ."

"I cannot sleep, Aunt," was my father's peevish re-sponse.

"Pray, then, rest," she pleaded.

"My legs ache so," he sighed, "I cannot keep them still."

"Perhaps more hemlock," she suggested.

"It is useless."

"Some tonic, then."

"Bah!" my father sneered. "My tongue is dry and leath-ery now. I vow it is that damned medicine that has turned my mouth so foul!"

"Surely not, James," she cried.

"Cease, Aunt," he groaned wearily. "I beg you . . . leave me in peace."

Nearly a week passed and still my father continued his fretful wanderings about the house, trailed closely by Aun-tie Maude, imploring him to lie down, "Or at least partake of some nourishment, dear."

"I am not hungry."

"Your stomach is empty," she insisted. "Katie has made some fresh chicken broth—your favorite. . . . Come, James . . ."

"You know I cannot eat," he moaned. "I implore you, Aunt, desist."

By the tenth day of his illness my father displayed marked deterioration, both physical and, alas, mental: Woe-fully weak and wracked by a troublesome cough, he moved listlessly about the house in a near stupor of delirium. Aun-tie Maude, that morning almost beside herself with fatigue and in an agony of fear, sent for Dr. Crofts, who this time prescribed pills of spider webs (for the fever and restless-ness) and left instructions for an emergency treatment of brandy and ammonia should my father sink lower in his illness. His expression grave, the doctor informed my aunt in solemnest tones that he determined, now, my father's complaint to be gastric bowel fever.

"Typhoid!" Ashen, my aunt dropped into a chair and buried her face in her hands.

As day closed, my father's breathing became difficult, so much so that he was at last persuaded to take to his bed. Around midnight Auntie Maude, terrified, dispatched Brooks in the phaeton for Dr. Crofts, who, himself incapacitated by a sudden ugly flare-up of the gout with which he had been plagued for some years, sent in his stead a colleague, Dr. Smithson by name, a youngish man with jaunty step and confident mien, who arrived at Leicester Square promptly despite the lateness of the hour. Upon completion of the examination the doctor assured my aunt that the course of treatment already prescribed in the case was certainly proper and indicated and, he declared further, there was really nothing more the medical world could do. He went on to warn Auntie Maude of the dangerous complication of lung congestion, possibly even now developing. "Madam," the doctor concluded gravely, "time alone will reveal the outcome. It rests with the Almighty. . . ."

Auntie Maude burst into tears. I shrank from the sound and sight by hiding, shivering, in my room.

From that awful moment a malignant silence at once deadly and vibrantly alive fell on the house, which, in turn, watched and waited. Waited for my father to die. . . . Huddled next to my bed I crouched, my body shaking with terrible spasms of fear and cold. Alert now to every sound, I jerked to immediate attention at the slightest suggestion of activity in the corridor. . . . I thought then about my father . . . projected my life into a world without him . . . I remembered the charm of the young man, vigorous, triumphantly returned, eager to swing his tiny daughter high in his arms by way of greeting. . . . I recalled too the later years: My father, sequestered in his study, secluded in his bedroom, little time remaining for his child, who had yearned so for his homecoming, for his love. . . . I would weep at his passing, sorrow at my loss: That, I knew. But had I really known the man, really touched his life—even in those early days of joy and laughter?

When a pale, fluid dawn began to lighten the sky, thoroughly spent and afraid I ventured out into the hall. Auntie

Maude, face blotchy and lids swollen above reddened eyes, was emerging from my father's room.

"Auntie Maude?" I asked timidly.

"Oh, child." She shook her head.

My eyes filled suddenly and Auntie Maude gathered me in her arms. "He is alive, dear. But . . ."

"You mean—he will d-die?" I blurted, weeping softly.

"I don't know, child. . . . His condition rests with God. But," she added, "I think you should go in and see him. Perhaps he might rally with you there."

Ashamed of my reluctance, I allowed Auntie Maude to lead me to my father's bedside: I looked down into the strange waxen mask that was my father's face. "Father," I whispered.

His once bright eyes, now glazed, gazed past me, as if on objects unseen and far beyond me. "Elizabeth . . ." he murmured.

"I am here, Father," I said softly.

"Isabella?"

"No. Elizabeth," I repeated.

"Isabella," he smiled.

"Yes," I said, "Isabella."

"My hand, Isabella. My hand . . ."

Hour after hour that day I sat near him, holding tight his limp, fever-parched fingers in my own. Over his face had spread a queer dusky color, and his labored breathing became troubled by peculiar guttural sounds. Dr. Smithson, shaking his head sorrowfully, had come and gone, offering little or no hope, and Auntie Maude, hunched in a far corner of the room, snuffled audibly. The clock, perched high on the carved walnut chest, seemed to be ticking away inexorably the hours of my father's life.

Suddenly, struggling to raise his head from the pillow, my father addressed me directly. "Elizabeth, why are you not out enoying the Ladies' Mile on such a fair day?"

"I would rather be with you, Father," I replied, tears streaming unheeded down my face.

He sank back abruptly. "Elizabeth?"

"Yes, Father?"

"Elizabeth? Isabella . . ."

"Yes?"

"Isabella . . ." He sighed deeply, trembled, then was silent.

He was dead.

I remember few details of the next days, except that the house, so silent during illness, was now thrown into hideous confusion. Visitors, connected mainly with the clergy, kept an intermittent vigil, eating prodigious amounts of food, contributing prayers, subdued whisperings, and much clucking over the bereaved. Benumbed, I managed to endure the ordeal only by slipping away and hiding in my room whenever it was feasible to do so.

The day of the funeral dawned gray with rain, raw as if to threaten snow. The service itself, conducted in Christ's Holy Anglican Church, Belgravia's most fashionable, was a nightmare of cloying floral scent and the unmistakable and vile reek of wet wool. The Very Reverend Thomas J. Wickwire intoned endlessly, I thought, particularly since the affair was conspicuously ill-attended: My father, absent much of the time, had retained few contacts in the area. The bulk of the mourners, then, consisted of young ladies from amongst my social circle, who appeared by parental injunction alone or in idle interest; many of them until now had enjoyed limited experience with death and wore their natural curiosity self-consciously.

The prayers delivered at graveside, adhering to the pagan practice furthered sadistically to insure the clergy additional moments of glory at the expense of the grieving, provided the most painful time of all. Auntie Maude and I, sobbing, clutched at each other for support and, when the final chant had droned to a close, left the sodden cemetery grounds under the protective umbrella held by the faithful Chambers, himself frankly weeping.

Chapter 3

I do not know whether or not I expected my life to continue as before—as though merely interrupted, and briefly, by the death of my only remaining parent; I was, however, in no way prepared for what was to prove the real portent of my loss. Suitable time had elapsed (perhaps the period of a week) before Auntie Maude and I were visited by a Mr. Wilkes, my father's personal barrister and long a friend of the family; Auntie Maude had been distantly acquainted with the man since girlhood. His manner grave and his voice hushed, Mr. Wilkes sat before us in the much-depleted drawing room and informed me, as kindly as he could, that I was, in actuality, not only orphaned but a pauper as well. . . .

The considerable fortune brought to the marriage of Isabella and James Knowlton had been as a dowry from my mother, her family being people of substantial wealth and position. My maternal grandfather had been more than generous, conferring upon his only daughter a sizable fortune to insure that his Isabella might continue to enjoy the standard of luxury wherein she had been raised. The house, its lavish furnishings, the veritable army of servants—all had been acquired through my mother's personal funds. My father's good looks and easy charm had earned him early in life an enviable social stature, which embraced select circles; these in turn enabled him to win the hand of a woman glorious in appearance as well as wealthy in her own right. A bon vivant of no little reputation, my father had neither expressed the desire nor felt the need to pursue a conventional profession or even seek out a respectable trade; thus at the death of my mother, my father, unoccupied and privy—easily and unopposed—to a seemingly endless supply of money, began to gamble to excess. At first the playing of cards, the throwing of dice, remained simply casual, accepted adventure. As time went on my father moved up to the sophisticated professional gaming tables and the spinning wheel of chance.

He enjoyed, of course, moments of triumph, coming away from the casinos with impressive winnings: easy money, spent quickly, and carrying with it that undeniable enticement to play again. Win or lose, soon the impulse to gamble for its own sake had become the force, uncontrollable, governing my father's every waking moment. More often than not the losses well outnumbered any occasional profit-taking, and the time inevitably arrived when his monetary sources were exhausted and he must look to liquidate other assets in order to meet his heavy gambling debts.

"The furniture . . ." I breathed.

Auntie Maude nodded.

At first it must have been relatively painless to part with a trinket here, a knickknack there; with demands for restitution, once courteous, now rudely insistent—even threatening—in the persons of hired henchmen, pressures mounted, undermining my father's physical and mental well-being. Cutting old family ties and avoiding past friends, except for contact with individuals frequenting the tables, he became a virtual recluse, a stranger—even in his own house.

Mr. Wilkes sighed deeply. "It is the oldest story in the world. Elizabeth, my dear," he turned to me, "it is my unpleasant duty to inform you that this house and all its contents must be sold immediately, to satisfy the creditors who have made legal claims against your father's estate."

"The h-house?" I stammered.

"The house. All. He has left you nothing."

Auntie Maude gasped.

"My dear Elizabeth," Mr. Wilkes sighed again, "your father was a charming man—witty, urbane—but improvident, I fear. Most unwise in the cruel ways of the world."

"Merciful heavens!" cried Auntie Maude. "Whatever is the poor child to do?"

"That is, of course, my first concern, Miss Treadway," Mr. Wilkes answered. "And I have taken the liberty of pursuing some arrangements in that regard." He cleared his throat. "I have initiated preliminary inquiries as to possible situations suitable to the present needs of both you ladies."

I sat dazed.

"Miss Treadway," the barrister went on, "I am in contact at present with a family newly settled in the Bayswater district. There are, I believe, a number of small children, and the head of house is seeking a governess who is qualified as well as socially acceptable, if you follow me." He coughed slightly. "I have indicated to the gentleman that I might well provide him with an appropriate candidate in the near future."

"Elizabeth will not want that responsibility," Auntie Maude said promptly.

"I had, actually, Miss Treadway, you in mind for the post."

"But—what of Elizabeth?"

"Ah! A more difficult consideration—but I feel that I have devised a scheme that might prove agreeable to her and one that would afford her the companionship of young ladies of her own age, if not entirely of her own station." He crossed his legs elaborately. "A position in the dress trade," he announced proudly.

"The dress trade!" shrieked Auntie Maude. "Never!"

"Pray, hear me out," he begged. "Miss Treadway, I have conducted considerable research on the subject and find that for the delicately reared young lady finding herself in a—well, penurious condition, the dress trade proves remarkably satisfactory."

"Humph!"

"The young ladies employed in these establishments, I am assured, are eminently respectable, as daughters of the clergy or teaching profession and the like, suddenly on hard times. They are offered an opportunity for employment in decent surroundings amongst decent people and are, thus, not forced to jeopardize their gentility or subject themselves to the vulgarities of a coarse, untenable mode of living." Mr. Wilkes rummaged in his leather valise. "I have jotted down some information gleaned from a personal visit I made to a firm such as this, operated by a Mr. Hiram Miller, who was kind enough to escort me on an extensive tour of the premises himself. Now . . . let me see if I can find . . ." He examined a sheaf of papers. "Ah here we are! Now, if I can only decipher my own writing," he said in an attempt at levity. "As far as I could determine, the young ladies who 'live in' "—he coughed—"there seems to be a conspicuous disparity between the ladies who 'live in' and those who do not . . ."

"Incredible!" sneered Auntie Maude.

"The young ladies who 'live in' at Miller's," Mr. Wilkes explained, "occupy a building separate from the workhouse proper and are entitled to certain privileges. . . . They are," he recited from his notations, "permitted to walk out in the mornings or evenings (with a curfew imposed, naturally, for purposes of their safety). Sitting rooms are provided for their use—"

"Preposterous!" sputtered Auntie Maude.

"A cuisine," continued Mr. Wilkes, unruffled, "well-prepared and abundant, supplying meat and vegetables daily and served in a dining area completely apart from the young men of the establishment. They may also"—he rubbed dry hands together noisily—"avail themselves of the services—free of cost—of a physician, engaged on a retainer basis, who calls every day as a matter of routine. . . . Each young lady has her own bed . . ."

"I should hope so!" snorted a scowling Auntie Maude.

Mr. Wilkes ignored Auntie Maude's rude commentary. "And the workroom has a high ceiling, permitting excellent ventilation—which is vital, of course; there are a few water closets and limited apparatus for washing. All in all"—Mr. Wilkes made his final summation—"hardly luxurious accommodations, but adequate. And what is of inestimable worth—the means to earn a respectable livelihood in respectable surroundings!"

"I can't sew," I whispered.

"Ho! Ho!" laughed Mr. Wilkes, "have no fears on that score! Many young ladies enter as apprentices and are trained on the job."

"How much would my girl actually earn?" demanded Auntie Maude, who was by this time openly furious.

"Well—ah—" There, Mr. Wilkes became evasive. "I—ah—was quoted no specific figures . . . but, as I under-

stand the—er—process—the, er, ah, apprentice—usually—
ah—normally—is not, er—compensated."

"Not compensated!" shrilled Auntie Maude.

"Not in terms of physical currency—as such," the barrister amended quickly. "But, madam, payment starts as a
roof over her head and healthful food served on a regular
basis. More, much more, than Elizabeth can claim in her
present situation."

"Over my dead body!" declared Auntie Maude.

"Madam." Mr. Wilkes settled back in his chair. "Can
you offer an alternative?"

Auntie Maude was silent.

"Can you suggest another course to follow?" His challenge was confident. "If so, name it, pray, and I shall be
more than happy to pursue it in Elizabeth's behalf."

Miserable, Auntie Maude shook her head.

"Well, then." Mr. Wilkes's smile was smug. "It is settled."

"But I hate to sew," I murmured.

Mr. Wilkes chose not to hear. "I shall be in touch with
Mr. Miller this very afternoon and make the arrangements
necessary to enroll Elizabeth into his service."

"I hate to sew," I repeated numbly.

The barrister replaced the papers inside his valise, rose,
and addressed Auntie Maude formally. "Miss Treadway, I
shall confirm your appointment with Mr. Jensen at Bayswater. He will send the carriage for you at the end of the
week, I doubt not." Mr. Wilkes bowed to Auntie Maude
and patted my hand awkwardly. "Good day, ladies."

I was to be the first to go. . . . Shortly before dusk a
clerk from the offices of Albert Hawkins Wilkes, Esquire,
called at the house, bearing the message that Mr. Miller
was most anxious that I commence my new position the
day after next and that accommodations were being readied against my arrival.

I have no clear recollection of the next day. Auntie
Maude and I squandered its precious hours in a mindless
state of suspension, roaming through the house almost wit-
lessly, lost in an agony too deep for tears.

Chapter 4

The morning of my departure dawned bleak to suit my mood and the start of my new life. Dun-colored clouds hung low in the sky, seeming to touch the tops of the leafless trees. I made my farewells to the few remaining servants, who were themselves packing in preparation against new circumstances. Chambers broke down openly as he pressed my hand in his; I think he might have kissed me had he not been trained in the Proper Old School. The phaeton, polished and sparkling, awaited us by the iron railing at the curb in front of the house. Brooks, dressed in fullest livery, I observed, leapt down from his seat and took from me my one small valise and handed Auntie Maude and me inside, settling the fur rug snugly around our knees.

I looked back at the house. . . . Already it seemed a million miles away.

It was eight o'clock.

The phaeton made its way on this, my last journey, slowly in implied deference to the solemnity of the occasion; more likely it was simply impeded by congestion heretofore unknown in my experience. I watched as an endless cortege of young women, poorly dressed, listless of manner, formed a living column, filling the splendid promenade of the park, passing the formal elegance of the dazzling mansions that housed the nobility, still sleeping . . . The sluggish pilgrimage, unseeing and unseen . . . onward . . . toward Vanity Fair . . . bound for the West End—and— the dress houses . . .

"Oh, God," I whispered.

Auntie Maude squeezed my hand tightly.

From under one dreary bonnet I could glimpse a cheek, pale, drawn . . . escaping another, a pair of reddened eyes . . . now, a sullen mouth . . . the tilt of a resentful chin . . . perhaps a saucy swagger . . . the slope of a tired shoulder . . .

The phaeton halted before a tasteless square-shaped building of dingy brownish stone, disfigured further by vacant, staring windows, none too clean. "I think this is it, miss," Brooks said apologetically.

The interior of the building proved no more appetizing than its dismal façade. The entry hall, if one might elevate the shabby passageway by such definition, was quite devoid of furnishings, even lacking carpeting, so that our shoes clacked as we moved, self-conscious and resigned, in the direction of the only light visible along the dusty corridor. It led to a small, airless room.

"Oh, my!" gasped Auntie Maude.

A woman of formidable dimensions was sitting at a rolltop desk of dark, scarred wood. Cold eyes scanned me with disfavor. "Miss Knowlton?" she inquired.

"Y-yes," I replied.

"You are, miss, precisely eleven minutes tardy," the woman announced, consulting a diminutive lapel watch, whose size was swallowed up in the immense expanse on which it rested.

"Ah—forgive me," I made my excuses, "but we had some difficulty getting through the crowds—"

"At what hour did you leave your place of disembarkment?"

"I—I am not entirely sure—" I began.

"I believe it was eight o'clock, dear," Auntie Maude intervened helpfully.

"Madam," the woman interrupted, "I suggest that you permit Miss Knowlton to reply, herself, to my inquiries."

"W-well—" Auntie Maude stammered.

"Yes," I concurred in my aunt's defense, "it was eight o'clock."

"Did it not occur to you, miss, at any time previous to departure," the woman remarked, "to allow for eventualities or possible impediments, so that you might strive to be prompt on at least this, your first day of employment in our establishment?"

I blushed hotly.

"In future," the woman continued, "I would strongly advise the adoption of a brisker gait when walking, thus guarding against tardiness, which, in the words of my late, lamented husband, the Reverend Walsh, 'Constitutes a mortal sin!' "

"Oh, but we did not walk," offered Auntie Maude innocently.

"Did not walk?" repeated the woman. "How interesting. By what means, then, did you arrive?"

"By phaeton," Auntie Maude murmured.

"By phaeton!" the woman exclaimed. "May I ask, Miss Knowlton, if you had planned to employ the services of a phaeton during your stay at Miller's?" she inquired with heavy sarcasm.

"N-no," I whispered.

"No?" The woman smiled. "No. I did not suppose you had." She rose then, and circled about, examining me minutely. "Have you other clothes to wear?" she inquired bluntly.

"Y-yes, a few gowns," I responded uncertainly.

"We do not allow the girls to wear silk," she declared flatly.

"B-but—"

"Only the girls in the showroom claim that privilege."

"I—ah—only—"

"You own nothing but silk?" the woman asked, incredulous.

"No—y-yes—I mean—I am afraid s-so," I admitted lamely.

"Then you shall be obliged to borrow from one of the other girls until you can make up a cotton dress for yourself."

"Make up a dress for myself?" I cried, stricken. My expression of horror was halted by the sudden warning glint in Auntie Maude's eye. Fortunately the woman failed to observe the tacit signal, choosing instead to introduce herself to me formally and with not a little show of pride. "I am Mrs. Walsh, Superintendent of this distinguished establishment. In my capacity as Superintendent, I answer only to Mr. Peckham, General Manager, who in turn answers only to Mr. Miller himself." She cleared her throat to permit me to digest fully this impressive declaration. "A very responsible position here, Miss Knowlton, would you not agree?"

I nodded politely.

"Before I escort you upstairs to your assigned quarters—so that there will be no confusion or misunderstanding in the future, I shall endeavor to explain in some detail the procedure to which we at Miller's adhere explicitly. I shall repeat that, Miss Knowlton: explicitly!"

I shifted my feet uncomfortably.

She began, "The schedule is as follows: breakfast is partaken of at precisely eight of the clock in the morning and is terminated in one half hour, at which time work commences. Dinner is served at one of the clock in the afternoon and work recommences exactly one half hour later. Tea is served at five of the clock, to be of a twenty-minute duration, after which time work begins again, to end at nine of the clock in the evening. Is that clear?"

I stared at her blindly.

"Of course, from April until mid-July we here at Miller's are at our most hectic, accommodating the rush of Spring Season. Naturally, at that time we are obliged to extend the working hours."

"E-extend them?" I gaped.

"The time is not without compensation," Mrs. Walsh explained. "Supper is served at nine of the clock at night, or if one finds oneself too busy to repair to the dining hall, a tray of sandwiches is graciously provided and set in a place of convenience at the sewing table. Obviously," she confided, "no spirits can be tolerated during the day, but beer is occasionally allowed at the supper hour—but," she added, "never during Season."

I swallowed.

"Now, the Winter Season we consider not nearly so important—although it can prove, some years, to be surprisingly frantic, at that. The girls are expected to work longer hours then, as well. . . . During the slack season," the woman recited, "Mr. Miller graciously permits the girls to visit friends, or travel for a fortnight—even, in some situations, for as long as an entire month!" She smiled. "There can be, as you might have already surmised, no financial compensation awarded on holiday."

My frightened eyes sought Auntie Maude's horrified ones.

"We heartily encourage our girls to seek the air and engage in healthful exercise," Mrs. Walsh maintained. "They may walk in the morning before breakfast—or in the evenings when the workday is over. Note, Miss Knowlton," she smirked, "I indicated the practice of walking—not the use of a phaeton. . . . A word of caution." She edged closer. "The ten-thirty curfew is strictly enforced. Any infringement thereof results in the offender being locked out on the street at night and mandates dismissal in the morning." She paused to allow me to assimilate her pronouncement. "If you have no questions, I shall guide you to your quarters without further delay." She eyed my valise. "Is this your only luggage?"

I nodded.

"Sensible, at least," she complimented, then, turning first to Auntie Maude, she remarked, "I will ask you to take your leave at this time, madam," and next, to me, directed, "Miss Knowlton, if you will be so good as to follow me . . ."

Standing forlorn, Auntie Maude hesitated, her eyes brimming with tears.

"Come along, Miss Knowlton," urged Mrs. Walsh, grasping my arm roughly, "the workday has commenced and I must be in attendance forthwith!"

"Auntie Maude—" I began, looking back.

"Pray, do not tarry, Miss Knowlton. I must not be absent from the floor overlong." Impatiently Mrs. Walsh drew me from the room.

Numbly, then, I followed the superintendent down the long, darkened passageway to the end of the corridor, outside across a muddy courtyard, and into a neighboring building, somewhat smaller in size but of identical design. She led the way down a shadowed hallway and preceded me up three flights of stairs, steep and badly scuffed, onto another floor of equal dimensions and as dimly lit. She chose one from amongst a series of doors, opened it wide, and announced: "These are your accommodations, Miss Knowlton."

I stared: Lined squarely against a wall of yellowed,

shredding paper were jammed four narrow cots. At one end of the small, crowded room stood a costumer, awkwardly suspending its clutter of bedraggled articles of clothing, there being no wardrobe; at the other crouched a low washstand, supporting two clay pitchers and four basins, unmatched, their surfaces severely cracked and plainly discolored, and speared by a smattering of hooks on which were carelessly draped four towels, worn so thin as to be sheeting. There was no rug on the floor. The starkness of the room's solitary window was unrelieved by either drape or frivolous curtain but was emphasized, rather—and to my dismay—by a lacy overlay of iron grillwork. *A prison,* I thought.

"There will not be adequate time, at present, for you to unpack your belongings," Mrs. Walsh decided. "Simply drop your valise next to your bed"—she indicated the cot on the farthest wall—"and come along with me." She stopped suddenly. "On second thought, you cannot enter the workroom dressed thus." Drawing a limp garment from the costumer, she offered, "You may wear this until you have procured your own proper attire."

"Th-this?" I asked in horror. From its original color—a dismal and serviceable gray—the dress had failed to fade uniformly, creating a disturbing effect of random blotches; strongly pervasive through the material itself was the acrid reek of perspiration. "I cannot wear this," I protested.

"No?" smiled Mrs. Walsh, unperturbed. "I rather think, Miss Knowlton, that you have no other choice."

"P-perhaps it won't fit," I countered helplessly.

"Then we shall simply have to find something that will."

In startling contrast to the meager illumination permitted other areas of the establishment, the workrooms were almost savagely ablaze. Dotted along the walls at frequent intervals were gas lamps, fired at full volume, and each room hosted a large central fireplace serving the multiple functions of heat, light, and, in the summer months, ventilation, I was informed. The workrooms numbered three: one reserved for designing, cutting, and the arrangement of fabrics; another used as a showroom for customer reception; and the last to handle the actual sewing, to which I was assigned.

Mrs. Walsh prodded me toward a long table surrounded by backless wooden benches presently occupied by three industrious young women who stared quite without embarrassment. "Take a seat, Miss Knowlton, and prepare to earn, in the words of my late lamented husband, the Reverend Walsh: 'A day's wage for a day's work.' "

"What wage?" someone muttered.

"Ladies," Mrs. Walsh formally addressed the group. "I should like now to introduce Miss Elizabeth Knowlton, who will be joining your table as an apprentice. I can assume, I trust, that you—one and all—will offer her any needed assistance until that time when she is fully acclimated to her new surroundings and our routine?"

"Lor!" one hissed, "she's got on my ruddy dress!"

"Miss Knowlton has no other suitable attire at present." Mrs. Walsh stiffened. "I was positive that you would find no objection to the slight inconvenience, as it is only temporary." She smiled. "Miss Humphreys . . ."

Miss Humphreys glowered but refrained from further comment.

"Now then, Miss Knowlton—Miss Baker, here, will furnish you with any materials necessary to begin your duties. Which," she added smoothly, "will begin forthwith."

"Yes, Mrs. Walsh." Bobbing a head of bouncing red curls, Miss Baker directed a pair of dazzling blue eyes and a warm smile in my direction. "Elizabeth, is it?" She turned to me. "Have a seat and I shall get you started."

Mrs. Walsh beamed. "Very well, Miss Knowlton," she declared importantly, "I leave you in Miss Baker's charge. I am already far in arrears for rounds and, as my late, lamented husband, the Reverend Walsh, sternly maintained: 'Punctuality is akin to godliness.' " She sailed off, a proud ship.

"I thought it went: 'Tardiness is a mortal sin!' " sneered Miss Humphreys.

Miss Baker giggled; I confess that even I, drowning in despair, had to smile . . .

My first day at Miller's remains, in memory, as only a horror show of vague impressions. . . . I wandered through the hours in a haze of disbelief, numbed kindly by a sense of unreality. . . . It was not until I lay huddled on that little wretched bed, all but smothering in the stagnant, airless room, my nostrils plagued by the clinging tang of the sweat-stained dress in which I had been forced to spend the day, that the real implications of my surroundings struck with fullest force. Sudden, scalding tears spurted down my cheeks and I began to sob convulsively and with a sense of helplessness greater even than the desolation I had experienced at my father's death. I felt a comforting hand on my head, then, and heard the whispered words: "Aye, Elizabeth, let it out, luv. . . . Cry. . . . We—all of us—have."

"I wish I were home," I whimpered.

"I know," said Molly Baker, "we all do. . . ."

. . . Home . . . those golden days . . . lost to me forever . . .

"What ails our Elizabeth," teased Ada, "there she sits, placid as a besotted cow and the tea bell about to sound . . ."

"Tea!" I shrieked. "The piece of lace! Mrs. Walsh will be here any minute!"

"Any minute?" grinned Ada. "The nasty viper is slitherin' her way across the floor right now."

"Slitherin'—our Mrs. W? Impossible!" giggled Molly.

"Whatever shall I do?" I wailed.

"Here, look sharp!" Deftly, Molly pushed the garment toward my hand. "Pick it up and act as though you have just got through putting in the last stitch," she hissed.

"Knowlton!" bellowed the familiar voice.

"Y-yes, ma'am," I gulped.

"Have you something to show me, miss?"

"Ah, no—"

Molly glowered.

"Ah—that is to say, y-yes, ma'am." I swallowed.

"Well?"

"H-here—"

"Hmmm." Mrs. Walsh stared in disbelief. "Knowlton, did you do this work?"

"Ah—"

"Of course she did," offered Molly easily, nudging me under the table with the sharp point of her shoe.

"I did not inquire of you, miss," Mrs. Walsh reminded the girl. "Well, Knowlton?"

"Uh—of c-course, ma'am . . ."

"Either your work is improving with remarkable alacrity, or someone has—" Mrs. Walsh's head swiveled toward Molly. "Do you deny, Baker, that this work is yours?"

"Mine?" repeated Molly, feigning astonishment. "And why should I be takin' on the task of another and puttin' my own self behind, will you tell me the logic of that?"

"Less sass, miss."

"Yes, ma'am," said Molly demurely.

A bell pealed thinly in the distance.

"Very well, Knowlton, run along," Mrs. Walsh relented, "this time . . ."

Chapter 5

Sunday was a day without peer, beginning a week of drudgery, or ending it, depending upon one's view of the order of the calendar. The dawning of a Sabbath morning bright with sunshine—even one cloudy but free from rain—gave a lift to my heart and mind quite unprecedented in my experience, promising reprieve, however brief, from this near servitude which had become abruptly the style of my life. Molly Baker, confirmed leader and strategist unexcelled, presiding over our group, planned our Sabbath outings, striving always to inject variety into our weekly activities. That she assumed a task wherein achievement was impossible never discouraged her efforts or dimmed her natural enthusiasm. "Our Group" consisted of: Molly Baker, Ada Humphreys, Bea Foster, and myself, sharing bedroom as well as worktable. An unlikely assemblage, we managed to get along remarkably well without, thankfully, disagreeable bickering and petty jealousies. There were some moments of stress, to be sure; it would be quite absurd to suppose that four young women of divergent personalities could manage to spend every waking and sleeping moment in each other's company without suffering an occasional break in unity. Perhaps it was the dissimilar nature of our temperaments that contributed in large measure to our success: Molly—ebullient; the dour Ada; Bea—gentle peacemaker; myself, alas, hopeless innocent.

Despite Molly's dogged efforts and eternal optimism, our Sunday jaunts routinely consisted of extended walks the length of the park, staring in awe and envy at the stately mansions shielding their noble occupants from any less pleasing aspects of city life. Characteristically, Ada, ever querulous, would be sure to proclaim, and loudly so: "I'd just like to know why the hell we can't live in palaces like that! We're every bit as good as those bloody buggers!" A gentle reproof from Bea usually tempered Ada's mood and language—that is, on the days Bea accompanied us on our promenade; often, of late, she did not choose to come along, indicating a preference to rest or read.

Although it was only through the anticipation of our Sabbath expeditions that I managed to survive, with any degree of equanimity, the week of dispiriting labor in the dreary, enervating atmosphere that was Miller's, I could not dismiss a certain sense of unease (even moments of direct anxiety) in the contemplation of our tours abroad. Lest I be spied in my fallen state by any amongst my former circle of acquaintance, nearing Mayfair or approaching the Ladies' Mile, I drew my faded bonnet close to my face and dropped my head low against the possibility of a dreaded chance encounter. I might have spared myself the mental anguish and unnatural posture: How could anyone possibly equate this indigent waif with that elegant, pampered creature of a bygone day. . . .

I much preferred, then, the chaotic trips by steamer up and down the Thames River, assured there of absolute anonymity as I mingled with the pushing, shoving hordes of coarsened working people, to whom I unaccountably belonged now, and who, in turn, regarded me as one of their own.

Generally, boating on the Thames offered a predictable excursion: the initial struggle to board; the ensuing scuffle to secure a place on deck promising an unobstructed view of the scenery; the harsh reek of close-packed humanity mixing with the fetid waft from the river—all routine, expected. There did occur moments of heightened adventure: someone falling acutely ill, engendering panic and a presentiment of disaster; another leaning too close to the railing and slipping, squawking, over the side, to be fished out forthwith, a sodden mass of redolent greenish slime and eschewed at all costs for the remainder of the trip. Any abrupt descent of mist was quick to dampen the high level of jollity present on board, holding with its advent the hint of mishap and negating any possibility of sight-seeing. Caught in the fog's soft, cottony web, the passenger became suddenly an unsmiling mask above a figure that was shadowy and subtly restless. The hilarity provided by the faulty performance en route of a defective engine, however, extended to the passenger more value realized for his money than he dared hope in the increased pleasure afforded by the unadvertised diversion and the outing's necessarily prolonged duration. Derogatory remarks flew, questioning the abilities of those in charge and the innate worth of the equipment utilized; along with the innocent banter, a lusty songfest was sure to begin, as well might have dancing, had there been room.

I can recall one trip vividly, undertaken on a fine day in early spring; can see still the dazzling blue of the sky overhead, reproduced perfectly in the smooth water lapping quietly beneath. The ride began as a particularly pleasant affair because of the balmy air and the sun's rays, warm now after the damp of the winter months preceding. Of a sudden the engine seemed fairly to explode: A quick gust of smoke catapulted straight up to the sky, followed by a cloud, propelled less vigorously, spurting white steam. The boat rocked a little, then stopped altogether. There was a great commotion: Some of the ladies shrieked; others fell to the deck in graceful swoons, which I thought privately were certainly unwarranted—we were scarcely on the high seas. I turned to convey my impressions to Bea, only to discover to my dismay that she had left my side. I looked around. Reveling in her moment of glory, Ada, arms akimbo, was regaling her audience with a good-naturedly acerbic treatise on the deficiencies of the steamer's managerial staff. Molly was entertaining a mild flirtation with an equally mild young man who focused on her with pale eyes, openly admiring. But where was our Bea? I tugged at Molly's sleeve, only to be tossed the casual quip that Bea certainly had not jumped overboard. "After all, ninny, she can't swim, you know!"

The damage to the engine, it developed, was beyond immediate repair; from the dock rowed a hurried little fleet of skiffs, which had been pressed into service to remove the stranded passengers from the disabled vessel back to the nearest shore. Those to be "rescued" were transported in groups of not more than six, women and children and the physically infirm selected first. When it was our turn to disembark, Ada was frankly disappointed to step down from her impromptu dais, and I overheard her lament with considerable irritation: "Just because we happen to be women, we miss all the bloody fun!" Molly waved a cheery, impersonal farewell to her swain of the day. I, dutiful to the instruction, "Get along, please, miss," complied without argument. Still no Bea. "Molly," I said, "where on earth?"

"You fret overmuch, luv. Bea'll show. You'll see."

It was not, however, until the last skiff had deposited its burden on land that we caught sight of our missing companion as she was being handed from the boat by an undistinguished, if pleasant-looking, youngish man with light brown hair and a slight build. Their farewell did not seem cheery, or impersonal.

"Stop gawking," hissed Molly, "we had best get a move on if we are not to be late for tea. And as for me: I am positively starving!"

"Probably stale bread and rancid butter," complained Ada. "Sabbath tea is notorious!"

"It could be rats' tails boiled in lard, for all of me," declared Molly happily. "I am that famished!" She shouted, "Come along, Bea. We daren't be late, you know."

Bea nodded absently.

"All that fresh air does give one an appetite," I remarked to Bea as we all strolled homeward. "Don't you agree?"

Bea, a faint flush tinting her cheeks, smiled. "Oh, I don't know, dear. I am not the least bit hungry. . . ."

On those occasions when the boats proved already too crowded for boarding, naught would do but that we must visit the neighboring beershops and inns to dull our disappointment with some much-needed refreshment. Any uncertainties expressed on my part concerning the wisdom of patronizing establishments such as these were put aside promptly by a casual toss of Molly's red curls and a churlish expletive from Ada. I found myself, if reluctantly, seated in a dimly lighted room, observing with amazement Molly as she scrambled for the attentions of a busy, blowsy barmaid and listening with horror to Ada's noisy enjoyment of the dubious utterances of the boisterous mob in attendance. Vaguely I wondered what Auntie Maude would think to find me in such surroundings.

As the foaming beakers were thumped ungraciously on the tables before us, Molly poked Ada. "What wouldn't the old witch say if she saw us in here!" she giggled.

"Hag Walsh is probably in the next room," Ada snorted, "cavortin' on some poor bugger's lap."

"And that flattened like a johnnycake in the process!" laughed Molly.

Ada hooted.

"Hush, girls," Bea remonstrated, looking anxiously around the room.

"Have a beer, hon," offered Molly, pushing a tankard across the table toward me.

"I have no money—" I protested.

"So—you can return the favor one day."

"Drink up, Elizabeth," encouraged Ada. "Let's all have a bit of fun!"

As I raised the foaming mug to my lips I asked myself again: *What has happened to my life . . .*

On a particularly raw, blustery weekday afternoon in late June, some three months after my "settling in" at Miller's, Auntie Maude paid a call and was awarded an equally chill reception, courtesy of Mrs. Walsh, who proclaimed in her customarily ungracious manner: "Madam, since this is not a leisure hour, your request to see Miss Knowlton is untenable!"

"I have come a fair distance by public conveyance," Auntie Maude explained.

"What?" Mrs. Walsh's smile was devilish. "No phaeton?"

Auntie Maude ignored the cruel barb and asked quietly, "If you would be so kind, Mrs. Walsh—"

"Madam," was the tart response, "how in conscience can I extend privileges to Miss Knowlton exceeding those I offer her fellow workers?"

"I simply wish to see how she is," said Auntie Maude wearily.

"She is perfectly well."

"I should prefer to see for myself," Auntie Maude persisted.

"Madam, I trust I may not find your inference insulting?"

"Please!"

"Tea will commence at five of the clock," Mrs. Walsh advised. "You may be permitted audience at that time."

"I cannot remain away for that long a period."

"Plan a visit for the Sabbath, if you like." Mrs. Walsh shrugged. "Surely your needs are not so pressing that they will not wait until the proper time and the circumstances allowed?"

"I am never free on the Sabbath," said Auntie Maude softly.

"Never free on the Sabbath!" parroted Mrs. Walsh. "Preposterous!"

"But," Auntie Maude sighed, "true."

"Very well," Mrs. Walsh relented, "just this once—and for five minutes only!"

"I am most grateful," Auntie Maude thanked her humbly.

Mrs. Walsh recorded our tearful reunion with a loud grunt of disapproval and a clucking tongue, prompting Auntie Maude to request politely, "Do you suppose, Mrs. Walsh, that Miss Knowlton and I might have a moment alone?"

Leaving a trail of sour invective, Mrs. Walsh quitted the room, suffering us what seemed, indeed, precious stolen moments.

"You look tired," Auntie Maude observed sadly.

"I am in good health," I was quick to reassure her.

"Do they feed you properly?"

"Oh, yes."

"And the food is decently prepared and of wholesome quality?"

"Truly, Auntie Maude, everything is satisfactory. Now," I inquired of her, "how do you fare at Bayswater?"

Auntie Maude's strangely narrowed eyes evaded mine. "I shall survive," she said.

It was not until that moment that I fully sensed my aunt's total desolation. Dismayed, I asked, "Auntie Maude, whatever is wrong?"

"Your five minutes were exhausted more than thirty seconds ago," Mrs. Walsh gloated, poking her head into the room. "Time for Miss Knowlton to resume her duties!"

Auntie Maude drew me close and I kissed her cheek, which felt parched even to my own dry lips. I wished, suddenly, that she had not come at all; I was afraid to remember her thus. . . .

Chapter 6

The arrival of spring, with its subtle breezes and brightening sun, prepares the sluggish land for its wondrous rebirth and sows in the flagging wintry spirit a stirring resurgence of hope; to those of us in the dress trade the arrival of spring merely ushers in: The Season. Commencing in the latter part of March, the Spring Season continues, inexorably and without cessation, until sometime in mid-July; its anniversary is inevitable and dreaded, like death. . . .

It had been during my fourth month of employment at Miller's (having entered the establishment in early December) that I, unprepared, was introduced to my first Spring Season; now, after an interminable year and a half of service and squeezing in, between, an appalling Winter Season, I was reminded, and to my horror, that this incredible practice was approaching, if not already at hand. One morning Ada, peering through the iron grillwork that disfigured our bedroom window, remarked sourly, "The trees are sporting a bud or two . . . it's that time, again."

"What time?" I asked idly, yawning.

"Time for another bloody Spring Season."

Pressing my nose hard into my flat pillow, I croaked, "I refuse to get up."

"Perhaps it won't be nearly so hectic in the shop," Molly posed hopefully.

"You and that bloody shop!" sneered Ada. "There's been a flood of fancy talk, but I've not seen a sign of you there yet."

Molly stretched and smiled languidly. "Never you mind, the dragon promised me the shop at the onset of Spring Season."

Lying still, Bea moaned softly, "I don't think I can endure another Season."

"Nor do I," I agreed.

"Oh, God," Bea whimpered.

"Whatever is the matter, Bea?" I asked, alarmed. "You are ill."

She patted my hand. "No dear, I am fine." Her smile wavered.

"You surely do not give that appearance," I argued. "Why—look at you—pale, worn—and the day not begun!"

"I am simply remembering the evils of the Season, that's all!" Bea bounded from the bed. "You see, Elizabeth? I am up and about—which is more than I can say for you!"

"Yes! For pity's sake, Elizabeth, leave the poor girl alone!" Molly laughed. "Most probably she is a bit run down." Turning to Bea, she suggested, "Why not ask Dr. Wells for a packet of Jonas Tonic Powders?"

"No!"

Molly shrugged.

"A spring tonic for the Spring Season!" mocked Ada bitterly. "That may be all right for you girls, but I for one do not intend to be buried from this place!" Her eyes hardened. "I've done naught in my life but the bidding of others. My father, to start: schoolmaster—from morning to night! Schoolmaster! Hell, even the dinner table was the classroom arena!"

"My father was a country parson—from morning until night," Bea murmured distantly.

"Next," Ada continued, "my mother—until she tired of the whole thing and chucked me over to the school and bade me fend for myself." She laughed bitterly. "Three years there, bent over, receiving the switch of grinning matron . . . and now here—harnessed to Madam Late-Lamented . . ." Ada's tone was mutinous. "I came to Miller's when I was scarcely a hair beyond fifteen; I will turn twenty in exactly three months' time—and what, just what, have I to show for the years? Money? Ha!" she snorted, "two years as a drudge apprentice and another miserable six months as an improver before a farthing, even a bloody tuppence, for my pains. . . ." Her voice was flat, deadly. "Hell, I have better things to do with my life than to wear it away in a place like this, I can tell you that!"

"Like what, pray?" goaded Molly.

"At this precise moment," Ada considered thoughtfully,

"I lack the proper answer. But I mean to have it by the end of the Season—if not before."

"Ta la la," teased Molly.

Ada ignored the taunt and continued, speaking in rapid and serious tones. "First of all, I shall be realistic. For instance, with my ugly face and scraggly shape—"

"And snide personality," giggled Molly.

"I could not hope to make the shop, even here," Ada confessed humbly. "Admitting that, it is not practical to waste my time trying—or regretting . . ."

"Continue, Socrates," chuckled Molly.

"There is no future here—shop or no shop—so, the logical consideration: Find a way out."

"Find a way out . . ." Bea repeated softly.

"What can I do to get by?" Ada frowned in concentration.

"Sew," prompted Molly.

"Exactly: sew. Do I, then, head for another Miller's? Run straight to another establishment?" She clenched her fists. "No! No! These places are all the same. . . . Some worse, some better. But, basically the same . . . So—I resign. I resign from the whole bloody sewing trade. Just like that!" Ada snapped her fingers crisply.

"Just like that," Bea sighed tremulously.

"But"—Ada's murmur was disconsolate—"what the hell do I do then?"

"You could get married," I said brightly.

Abruptly Bea burst into tears.

The breakfast gong sent us scrambling to bathe and dress quickly and head for the dining hall before its doors were locked against us, tardiness constituting a mortal sin at Miller's. . . .

Ada's doleful prognostication brought its bitter yield. Much as a general—sounding the heightened cry for battle; charging his troops to assemble for the march; girding his forces for the invasion; exhorting his army to seize their weapons and fell the loathed foe—Mrs. Walsh stood her ground bravely at her command post in the dining hall. Head erect, back stiffened with fortitude (and a heroic framework of metal stays), and sheathed in a mail of delicious anticipation, she trumpeted: "Eat with heart! Nour-

ish the inner spirit! Gather ye your strength! We face a
challenge to be met and won!"

"Jesus," Ada muttered, her face dark with gloom, "I was
right!"

"Today is March twenty-third!" Mrs. Walsh reveled in
the declaration. "Can anyone tell me what is the signifi-
cance of this date, marked on our calendar as March
twenty-third?"

"What a windbag," snarled Ada. "Gets worse every
year."

Mrs. Walsh's eager eyes swept the room. "No?" she
asked in surprise. "Then it will be my duty—nay, my privilege—to inform!"

Bea sighed softly.

"Today," Mrs. Walsh announced, a wave of profound
emotion swelling her voice, "today, ladies, we are purposed
to meet the force opposing . . . to deny a would-be con-
querer . . . to violate new territories and make them
ours . . . allies together in this, our yearly struggle!" Noble head bowed in noble dedication, she added, "And, ladies, to do honor for our honorable profession!" In order to
savor the moment fully, she paused.

"This is ridiculous," hissed Molly.

Ada snorted.

"On this day we are directed to launch an offensive,
moving as a company—united, one and all—be she Superintendent"—Mrs. Walsh inclined her head graciously to accept recognition due, before continuing—"First Hand, Second Hand, Designer, Cutter, Improver . . . or lowly
Apprentice . . ."

"There you go, Elizabeth," Molly snickered.

"My word." Ada poked Molly. "She's left out the shop-
girls."

"There may be days—and nights," Mrs. Walsh conceded, "that your deepest reserves of energy will seem
sorely taxed. Some of you may even feel momentarily unable to carry on for the cause. . . . But in every valiant
soldier lies a vein of strength as yet untapped. And you,
ladies, are as soldiers, proud of your allegiance to your
craft, your trade . . ."

"Days and nights," Bea murmured.

"Of course, in consideration of those evening sessions which may extend far beyond the hours of the morn— when hands may reach around to embrace the clock . . ."

"Oh, God." Bea passed a trembling hand across her eyes.

"The House of Miller will do its part, you may be sure, to see that its army is well fed, properly equipped to do battle on those, the front lines of fashion. . . ."

"Hell," Ada groaned.

Mrs. Walsh's voice fell, now hushed. "When the war is delivered and we leave the field victorious, can we—each and every one—look back in satisfaction at a job well done, a fight well fought? Will that answer be: Yes?" Her head bowed reverentially, she concluded, "I shall leave you now, bearing abroad the words of my late, lamented husband, the Reverend Walsh, as your talisman: 'A minute spent in honest toil brings the wayward sinner an hour closer to the Kingdom of Heaven!'" Then, hesitating as if in sudden afterthought, she smiled. "Ladies, ladies, I have neglected to mention a procedure idiosyncratic to the dress trade . . ." Her smile was brilliant. "It is perhaps useful to remember that any young woman dismissed from one establishment in the trade will, unfortunately, find it difficult— if not entirely impossible—to procure employment at another . . ." Pausing before she negotiated a grand exit from the hushed room, Mrs. Walsh raised fleshy arms high in salute and a voice still higher in the ringing chant: "In March, *we* march—for Miller's. . . ."

Chapter 7

And the season began; true to her word Mrs. Walsh freed Molly from her sewing tasks and ordered her to repair promptly to the shop. "Of course, Baker," she exhorted, "it goes quite without question that your black glacé silk has been prepared in advance of your assignment."

"Yes, ma'am."

"Very well, then, you are awaited in the shop room, properly costumed and ready to assume your position within—precisely—the next ten minutes." Pointedly Mrs. Walsh consulted her miniature timepiece. "An appropriate reminder, Baker, spoken in the words of my late, lamented husband, the Reverend Walsh: 'Tardiness is the subtle pickpocket of time.'" Head held patrician-high, eyes direct, course duly charted, Mrs. Walsh sailed resolutely from our table, the starch of many petticoats bristling in her wake.

"Well, I'm off," grinned Molly, her eyes wide with excitement.

"I wish I were going with you." I felt unaccountably downcast at the sudden realization that Molly would be no longer working beside me.

"Aye. And so do I." Molly patted my hand. "Sure, you've the face and figure for the shop, but not that bit of sauce that goes with the job." She put aside my protestations by adding, "You do come over, luv, prudish-like." Turning to go, she called over a retreating shoulder, "With any luck we'll get the same dining shift. . . . Whatever, I shall see you back in the room at bedtime tonight." She waved cheerily, "Ta!"

"Ta!" growled Ada. "If there is a bedtime tonight . . ."

Molly's replacement, a fourteen-year-old girl, contributed little to the table but astonishing girth, questionable hygiene, and a sullen, petulant nature. A middle child of an enormous progeny (eleven offspring living), she had been pressed into service, looking to learn a trade, probably—for daily sustenance, certainly—the penurious family happily relieved to have one less mouth to fill. Privately I wondered that they had not severely curtailed the girl's intake some years earlier.

Proving an unwelcome addition to our group, Jennie, as she was named, was a stolid, humorless creature, grimly defensive, and—making camaraderie impossible and conversation difficult—an ardent *religieuse*. Although hired on as a mere apprentice, the girl was already an expert needle-woman and delighted in flaunting her considerable skills and pointing up my own ineptitude and continued low estate. "I shall certainly not follow your lead, Elizabeth," the loutish Jenny boasted loud and often, "an apprentice for almost two years!" Snipping an offending thread with uneven, discolored teeth, she brayed, "I plan to become improver in six months!"

"Do tell," gibed Ada, who had loathed the girl on sight and made no effort to hide her feelings.

"Just see if I don't, smartie."

"Why don't you try for the shop?" Ada sniggered.

"Ada—" admonished Bea.

"I don't care," Ada snapped. "I am tired of her constant bragging!"

"Mrs. Walsh ordered you girls to treat me nicely," Jenny bleated. "I think you're mean—each and every one of you!"

"Now, Jenny . . ." Smothering my growing irritation, I made a tepid effort at conciliation.

"And *her*." Jenny indicated Bea. *"She*'s done almost nothing in the way of work since we sat down this morning. . . . I've a mind to tell Mrs. Walsh."

"Oh, God." Bea's face crumpled.

"You do—and I'll—" threatened Ada uselessly.

"Do what?" taunted Jenny. "You may not be my friends, but Mrs. Walsh is. . . ."

"Am I being summoned?" boomed the lady herself as she sidled up to the table. "I do believe I heard my name mentioned!" Mrs. Walsh was grotesquely coy.

Ada glowered a warning at Jenny, who, ever ingratiating, bubbled—her enthusiasm earnest, girlish—"see, Mrs.

Walsh, see how much I have managed to accomplish already—and the day scarcely begun!"

"Admirable, Miss Connors, admirable! You set an enviable example for the other ladies here!"

Under Mrs. Walsh's starry approbation Jenny fairly glowed. "Thank you, Mrs. Walsh," she said demurely. "I hope I shall never shirk *my* duties," she added obliquely, casting a meaningful glance in Bea's direction.

"You ladies would do well to emulate our Miss Connors, here. I trust that you recognize her worth and are determined to achieve a measure of her success. . . ."

Jenny beamed, her monstrous corpulence jiggling its delight.

"Oh, indubitably," said Ada with heavy sarcasm.

"Spendid. Splendid." A frantic signal from the doorway drew Mrs. Walsh scurrying across the littered floor and away from our table.

"You almost did it that time!" Ada's mood was dangerous.

"I didn't—but I always can," Jenny challenged. "Just try me!"

"God! You miserable bitch!" sputtered Ada.

"Best not to swear and call names, Ada," Jenny parried. "Father Brennan of St. Timothy's says that you can go straight to hell for blasphemy!"

"Father Brennan!" Ada spat.

"Why, Bea, what is it?" I asked, observing suddenly the fine, glistening film that moistened the girl's face, heightening the sickly greenish pallor of her skin and accentuating the deep wound of her eyes; seeing her lips tremble.

"Ah—headache," Bea murmured weakly. "All this bickering . . ." her voice trailed away.

"Bea, see the doctor," I begged.

"No!"

"Bea!"

"I shall be all right—need a little air, s'all . . ." Bea rose from the table abruptly and walked with unsteady gait from the room.

"I am distraught about Bea," I confided to Ada. "She seems poorly indeed."

"Probably her stays are too tight," decided Jennie with little interest and even less concern.

"She had best return before Walsh discovers her absence," Ada frowned.

"You mean *Mrs*. Walsh, Ada," Jenny corrected primly.

"Here she comes now!" I hissed.

"Goody!" smirked Jenny.

"One, two, three," counted Mrs. Walsh elaborately, "am I deluding myself—or are there not customarily four ladies assigned to this table. . . ."

"Oh, yes, there should be four," Jenny supplied promptly.

Smiling, Mrs. Walsh suggested, "Let me try again . . . one, two . . ."

"That will not be necessary," purred Jenny. "One of the group is missing. . . ."

"Missing!" Mrs. Walsh was shocked. "Missing! From a work session and in the height of Season!" Mrs. Walsh was incredulous. "And what, pray tell, is the reason for such unorthodox behavior?"

"Bea claimed to be ill," came the immediate unsolicited reply. Clearly Jenny was enjoying the little exchange.

"No," Bea contradicted, sliding into her chair. "I am fine, really."

"You are not indisposed?" inquired Mrs. Walsh coldly.

"No." Bea managed a shaky laugh. "My stays were a trifle tight, I discovered."

Jenny's small, buried eyes swept the table in delicious triumph. "I told you so . . ."

Mrs. Walsh addressed Bea directly. "I trust in the future, miss, that you will predetermine the range of your undergarments so as to avoid the loss of precious working time and needless anxiety on the part of those of us in charge."

"Yes, ma'am," Bea assured her hastily.

"On what costume are you currently engaged?" asked Mrs. Walsh, suddenly curious.

"Ah—"

"I shall be happy to show you," Jenny offered helpfully. The gong proclaiming the midday meal shattered the atmosphere of harried industry as the workers rose, en masse, from their benches and streamed eagerly from the room. Thus Mrs. Walsh's captious inquisition was diverted, as was Jenny's pettish harassment; customarily Jenny was the first one out the door.

Chapter 8

To her chagrin Molly discovered that the shop offered not the rewards anticipated, but rather a new set of aggravations. "Starting," she exploded, "with the customers themselves! What a fat lot of spoiled brats! Must have everything now—this minute—cannot wait—no, not them. . . . Even if it means the poor dress slavey sews the whole night through. . . . Miss Throckmorton-Throckmorton simply *must* have her satin gown for the Great Ball. 'Yes, Miss Windsor-Windsor, we shall have your outfit ready, never fear. . . . Oh, yes, we are aware, dear Miss Windsor-Windsor, that the Hunt is *tomorrow*' . . ." She flailed her arms. "And contemptuous! Rude! They are positively outrageous! And what is even more outrageous—we take it! We suffer these incredible indignities! Do we tell these gawks to go jump in the Thames? No . . . No . . . We smile . . . Bowing and scraping low, as though we were slops on the street. 'Yes, ma'am . . . Certainly, sir . . . Whatever you say.' " She grimaced. " 'Smile, Miss Baker . . . Smile . . .' And," she ranted, "meals! We don't take meals—we snatch 'em. A bite here, a taste there . . . always on the run . . . can't keep the blessed customer waiting. Heavens, no! 'Don't eat, Miss Baker . . . Smile. You were not hired to eat—you were hired to smile. . . . Smile, Miss Baker' . . . I could scream!" Molly plucked fiercely at the black silk of her dress. "See this? I must wear this every day. *Every day!* And how long do you think this silk is going to last . . . a month? Perhaps . . . Six weeks—with luck . . . Two months? Never! And when, finally, a useless rag, it peels in ugly shreds off my aching back—who replaces it? Answer me that. Who buys me a nice new one? Ha!" she shrilled. "*I* do! That's who! And with what? *My wages*—that's what!" She dropped down on the bed heavily. "Smile, Miss Baker . . . *Smile* . . ."

"I am truly sorry, Molly," consoled Bea.

"Simply request a transfer," I reasoned.

"Why not!" agreed Ada, brightening. "Chuck the shop and come back to the table!" She grinned in delicious anticipation. "Then we could give that grotesque glutton the boot—and good riddance!"

"Can't." Molly was suddenly spent. "The shop is understaffed now as it is. The Season promises to be more feverish than even last year's circus. . . ."

Bea sighed deeply. . . .

By early May (and midway into the Season) the working hours, extending as they did—habitually and without exception until eleven (the earliest) at night—and those brutal, if occasional, sessions round the clock, seemed almost too cruel a price to pay for the doubtful privilege of eating and staying alive. Heads bent; pale, dry hands flying; shoulders sunk low, red eyes sore and staring; lips sere and thin; nostrils glutted with the tiresome reek of the febrile gas jets that jerked their smoke blackly overhead; senses plagued unmercifully by the rank, sickly odor of bodies only hurriedly washed and drained often to the limit of endurance: thus we worked. . . .

The gong sounding the call for meals became now the symbol of freedom, proffering a moment of rest (even evanescent) and the opportunity for solid sustenance to mend the fraying fibers of our beings. Never allowed was the prolonged and tantalizing anticipation of the dining hour: no clocks on the walls or timepieces on the persons of the workers were suffered at Miller's, as per the rigid and unalterable instructions from the head office, a practice ascribed to, without reservation, by Mrs. Walsh, who announced with tireless enthusiasm and annoying repetition, "In the words of my late, lamented husband, the Reverend Walsh: 'To watch the hands of a clock, rather than your own hands at their honest toil, is time spent in the hands of the Devil himself!' "

"I wonder how soon we eat," whined Jenny, "I am ever so hungry!"

"I thought the food was supposed to improve during the Season," Ada loudly complained. "Yesterday's offering was a gelatinous horror, if I ever saw one. That beast couldn't have walked through life—it slid."

"I thought it very tasty," contradicted Jenny.

"Flavor and texture may be missing," Molly observed fairly, "but the meals have been more than generous, you must admit—haricots—puddings—stews—"

"The stews are abominable," Ada remarked.

"But, hearty . . . In fact, if we are not soon privy to some vigorous exercise—we shall all be as outsized as—" Molly stopped short.

"As Jenny," supplied Ada happily.

"I hope you choke on a bone," Jenny sulked, "a diseased bone."

Ada laughed. "Just so long as it's dead."

On a morning in late June when the air, heavy with haze even in the early hours, promised a sultry, oppressive day, I became conscious suddenly of Bea moving about restlessly on her cot next to mine. The pallor in her cheeks was no less than that of the sweat-dampened sheets on which she twisted. "All right, Bea?" I asked lightly, making a conscious effort to appear offhand so as not to reveal my steadily growing anxiety concerning her perceptibly failing health.

"It is so hot," she sighed.

"Going to be another rough one," observed Ada grimly, squinting through the iron mesh. "I vow, not a breeze to ruffle so much as a leaf!"

"I don't think I can bear it if today turns into another all-night push," Bea said, her voice quavering.

"Oh, I think not." I tried to dismiss Bea's worries with an airy, "It is close on to Saturday and, therefore, not at all likely."

"I wish it were the Sabbath," the girl breathed, "then I could stay in this bed all the long day."

"Perhaps that is what you should do in any case," I suggested tentatively.

"Oh, no!" Bea sat up. "I couldn't. Not possibly." She coughed slightly.

"Bea, that cough! Have you had it long? Do you have pains in the chest besides?" I asked, really frightened now.

"No." Bea smiled wanly. "A little indigestion, that's all."

"A common enough affliction," snorted Ada, "considering the quality of our daily rations!"

"Summer complaint is rampant," offered Molly sleepily. "Thought yesterday that I might be in for a bout myself. But it passed."

Relieved, I stated with finality, "That's Bea's difficulty, then: summer complaint!"

"Yes," Bea agreed wanly. "Most assuredly . . . summer complaint . . ."

The airless workroom was stifling that day, and the sulky Miss Jenny Connors more quarrelsome than usual, making the atmosphere at our table thoroughly disagreeable. Too, Ada seemed cruelly perverse, goading the girl unmercifully until her sharp thrusts and Jenny's peevish retaliation became impossible to tolerate. "Heavens, this constant bickering! Ada, do let up," Bea implored. "Jenny, please!"

"I must defend myself," Jenny said querulously.

"Oh, rubbish!" retorted Ada.

"I never do anything—it's you girls—you are all hateful and mean!" Jenny pouted.

"Jenny," Bea flared, "if you don't stop your eternal whining—just this once, I think that I shall scream!"

"I haven't done anything—it's you girls," she sniveled.

"Oh, for pity's sake!" Jumping up, Bea slammed a balled fist ineffectually on the table. "This continuous harangue!" Abruptly then, as if melting, she slipped quietly to the floor.

"Bea!" I gasped, hastening to her side. "Ada, quickly! Bea has fainted!"

"The doctor!" Ada rushed from the room.

"Help me, Jenny!" I cried. "Help me to loosen her stays!"

"That won't do any good," objected Jenny even as she knelt beside me.

"Never you mind about that—just set to, now."

"I don't know where you girls get to be so bossy," Jenny grumbled.

Once alerted, Mrs. Walsh came running. "Well, Knowlton," she bawled, "what's amiss?"

"B-Bea is indisposed," I stammered.

"I can see that."

"She only fainted," Jenny said.

At that moment Dr. Wells made his unhurried appearance, trailed by an anxious, frowning Ada. With a confident, preemptive air he inquired, "Here, here. What seems to be the matter?"

"Bea fainted," Jenny supplied.

"Fainted. So I see. Fainted . . ." Lazily the physician's eyes scanned the room. "Anyone else so afflicted?"

"Mercy!" shrieked Mrs. Walsh, her nervous glance leaping after his. "You cannot be intimating an"—she aimed the dread word confidentially at his ear—"epidemic . . ."

Dr. Wells shrugged. "Always that possibility."

"She must be removed from this workroom at once!" Mrs. Walsh decreed without hesitation.

"One moment, madam," the doctor said stiffly.

"Contagion!" she hissed in a frantic aside.

"Madam," Dr. Wells asked, his tone icy, his manner insolent, "are you, pray tell, the physician in this case, or am I?" Livid spotches traveled irregularly over Mrs. Walsh's wildly perspiring face—much, I observed, to Dr. Wells's evident satisfaction. He turned then to me and inquired smoothly and, I thought, in view of Bea's unconscious state, demonstrating neither interest nor a sense of urgency, "You, miss, share living quarters with the deceas—er—patient?"

I nodded.

"Tell me, then, since you are in the enviable position to record such pertinent information—did you observe the patient enter into a spasm of coughing—or exhibit indication of catarrh at any time?"

"She did cough once, I think—this morning—" I began uncertainly.

"Predictable." The doctor smiled smugly.

"Not consumption!" screeched Mrs. Walsh.

"Madam!" boomed the doctor, "I have every intention of making my own diagnosis; I do not solicit yours." As Mrs. Walsh's already raddled face once again flamed unbecomingly, Dr. Wells continued, "Has the patient displayed signs of indigestion?"

"Why, yes," I confirmed, "she acknowledged some distress—yes—"

"I thought so."

"Typhus!" wailed Mrs. Walsh.

"Miss," Dr. Wells queried me further, "have her—ah—stays been released?"

"Y-yes." I could feel the color swamp my cheeks.

"Splendid! Now, if you will be so kind as to stand back," he instructed, "I wish to administer smelling salts. The patient should revive momentarily." Bea's lids fluttered briefly, permitting her gray eyes to open; they closed again immediately. "I shall assist you in rising, miss," Dr. Wells informed her, "and I shall conduct a proper examination in the dispensary. If you please," he urged gruffly, pulling the girl to her feet. She leaned against him for support.

"Come along," Mrs. Walsh ordered crisply, propelling Bea's limp arm.

"Madam!" thundered the doctor. "You dare to commandeer my patient?" Incredulous, he glared at Mrs. Walsh. "I shall myself escort this young lady to my examining room without your assistance—or interference . . ." He turned to Bea. "Shall we go?" His bow was exaggerated, almost comic.

"That man is insufferable!" Helpless, Mrs. Walsh watched the doctor guide Bea's slow progress from the room. "Playing a fast and easy game with what could well prove an incipient disaster—a lethal epidemic, capable ultimately of ravaging this revered establishment! Riffraff!" she raged. "Unconscionable boor! Obvious incompetent! Exposing my workers unnecessarily to contagion of perhaps epic proportions! And in such a cavalier manner!"

"Aw," said Jenny carelessly, "we can't catch nothing."

"What do you know, Jenny," sneered Ada.

"I know what's wrong with her," the girl maintained, "I surely seen my mum enough."

"What are you saying?" Mrs. Walsh questioned sharply.

"Bea's 'that way,' " smirked Jenny.

"How dare you!" Ada lunged forward.

"You just see if I'm not right, smartie," Jenny bragged.

"Damaged goods!" Shaking her head in tragic disbelief, Mrs. Walsh sagged weakly into the chair so recently vacated by Bea. "And in *my* workroom! After all these years—in *my* workroom!"

"What does she mean, Ada?" I asked, frightened.

"There's something in the oven," Jenny quipped.

"She thinks Bea is going to have a—baby," Ada explained with difficulty.

"A baby!" I cried. "Oh, no! Not our Bea! There must be some mistake!"

"In *my* workroom . . ."

Jenny was right. Suspecting for some months the true nature of her condition, Bea found it increasingly awkward to minimize the spells of acute nausea and prolonged periods of fatigue, classifying them as natural appendages to the trade, as it were. Not only was her physical indisposition enervating and a real impediment to her working efficiency, the haunting uncertainties indicated in the circumstances of an illegitimate birth provided an emotional stress that was distressful beyond all imagining . . .

Miserably Molly, Ada, and I watched as Bea carefully folded and placed her meager belongings in a small, light-brown hand trunk, its leather shabby and badly scuffed. Tears sliding unheeded and without shame down my cheeks, I blubbered, "But, Bea—where will you go?"

"Don't fret, Elizabeth, I can stay with my cousin," she replied easily and without, I felt, conviction.

"Where?"

"Oh—ah—Merchant Street. Not an elegant neighborhood, but substantial and respectable enough."

"What is your cousin's name?" I persisted.

"Ah—Conrad. Conrad Fletcher."

"You will write, Bea?" Molly asked, almost shyly.

"Of course."

"And—tell us what the—the baby is?"

"Of c-course."

"And—when?"

Bea nodded.

"Perhaps we can visit you on a Sabbath!" I suggested, brightening.

Bea smiled sadly. "We'll see, dear."

"The dirty bloke should marry you," Ada muttered fiercely.

Bea shook her head. "No," she whispered, "he is already married. . . ."

Heartbroken, we huddled in the sweltering, mud-dried courtyard, Molly, Ada, and I, and watched as the forlorn, beloved figure, clutching its clumsy burden, passed slowly down the broken path, onto the cobbled street, and out of our lives. . . .

"You missed dinner," observed Jenny gleefully as our mournful little band resumed its appointed place at the worktable. "We had a delicious joint," she gloated, pointedly licking her lips, "a scrumptious pudding with clotted cream, and ever so many other tasty goodies—too numerous to mention."

Unhearing, I sat benumbed, my agonized thoughts roiled without mercy by questions unanswered and wild, improbable imaginings; even Ada seemed too disconsolate to return Jenny's tiresome, petty barbs.

Bea. Our Bea . . .

"But who is the—er—man?" I had asked Ada.

"Evidently someone she met aboard the steamer."

"The steamer! When? Were—were we there?"

Ada had nodded.

"We must have seen him, then."

"Yes."

"How—was there ever opportunity for Bea to see him—after?"

"On the Sabbath," Ada had replied curtly.

The Sabbath: I had recalled, then, Bea's frequent refusals to accompany us on our weekly outings, pleading a headache, or correspondence lamentably in arrears . . . the book that simply must be read . . . or a "little sit-down in peace and quiet . . . but, you girls run along and make a splendid day of it." . . . I remembered now . . . "But, Ada," I had persisted, "how—"

"Oh, God," Ada had sighed, "how can anyone be so bloody unworldly?"

Color now uniformly if unnaturally high, eyes ablaze, and breathing emphatic, Mrs. Walsh strode purposefully into the room and, as if unseeing, headed without hesitation straight for our table. Grasping a pair of cutting shears by their blades, she proceeded to rap the handles on the tabletop, wielding them in such an excess of energy and rage as to gouge severly the solid oak beneath. "Ladies!" she bawled, her voice bruising the very walls, "Ladies! Your attention! Ladies, I must have your unmitigated and unqualified attention!" Her ruthless gaze penetrated deep into each corner, opened every crevice in the crowded, airless room, which was made uneasy, even frightened, by her fiery presence. "There has been," she declared, "an unholy and heretofore unheard-of occurrence in our establishment. One which concerns us all—profoundly!"

Instinctively titillated, little sounds rippled through the aggregation.

"Silence!" commanded Mrs. Walsh. "The House of Miller, revered seat of our beloved trade—our very home, in fact—has been cruelly tainted, invaded, sickened, by the Devil himself! Ah, yes, ladies, I said by the Devil himself, sowing the seeds of evil, planting the roots of the most heinous sin of all: *adultery!*"

The subtle murmurings recommenced; Mrs. Walsh paused, permitting the group to savor each implication, every nuance of that delicious word.

"Yes, ladies: *adultery!*" It rolled smoothly over her tongue. "Adultery, corrupter supreme, without peer on this mortal sphere of raw temptation. . . In my late, lamented husband's finest hour he spoke of adultery, exposed it for the plague, the infestation it is as it assaults the structure of our lives, contaminates the purity of our very souls. It was his firm, unshakable belief that she who doth lust and who seeks to satisfy lascivious bodily cravings shall enter a world of eternal damnation—cast adrift by her people, barred from the Kingdom of Heaven, forfeiting the love of the Almighty—and shall bear but bitter fruit. For she is Eve, seductress. Wanton. Loathed excrescence, turning man from his path of good and righteousness by her tempting, taunting ways. She: siren, destroyer, dragging helpless, hapless men down, down, down to ruin and degradation. She must be vilified. Set forth and destroyed . . . In the Reverend Walsh's exact words: 'The woe of the world is a wanton woman!' "

Mrs. Walsh's bright stare stabbed the hushed room. "Hiding within our group, slithering like the snake, plying her wares was one such wanton. You may inquire the identity of this jade, this harlot . . ." She smiled sadly. "I

shall forbear. Refrain from such divulgence. Perhaps you
have already divined the truth by the sudden, unexpected
absence of one from amongst your company. . . . For, ladies, Eve has been plucked out, banished—sent forth to
bear her bitter fruit!"

Necks craned; whispers were audible. Mrs. Walsh indulged their natural curiosity for a generous moment; then,
drawing a lacy handkerchief across her saddened eyes, she
continued. "Never in all of my productive years of responsible service, conducted with perfect dignity and impeccable taste, has such a misfortune been visited upon my
realm. Ever had I remained scrupulous in the selection of
my workers—tirelessly demanding respectability, good
grace and—unblemished virtue. I have not been content to
engage idly—to chance the mongrel—to court those of inferior breeding who might fare better in lesser situations—
in lower station, among the coarser dayworkers. Always,
my choice of live-in girls has been beyond reproach. Has
proved worthy. Until," she proclaimed, "until this day
when that slut—that strumpet, carrying her deceitful seed,
her tainted bloom, in full view of us all—tarnished a spotless, luminous reputation." Her eyes narrowed, "Ladies
. . . this, I forgive not! For this I grant no reprieve!
Never! Never! Never!"

Her voice rose, high and shrill. "And, ladies, lest you
think that this sly abuse of my good name and smirch of
my record will suffer repetition—let me disabuse you of
any thoughts of that nature, forthwith. I shall be on guard:
watchful, as never before!" A thread of fear wrapped itself
tightly around the room. "And, ladies, never will there be
exception . . . extenuating circumstance—or ameliora-
tion!"

She crossed heavily fleshed arms over her breasts,
guarded by their network of steel. "Miss ——— walks
alone: friendless, unemployable; no house will hire her, I
shall see to that!" Mrs. Walsh smiled. "Our Eve treads a
rocky path. . . . I pray that none of you ladies shall be
tempted to follow in those mired footsteps." She turned
then, prow setting a firm course, and sailed forth magnifi-
cently from the room.

Chapter 9

At long last the Season ended. Its passing was not feted with elaborate ceremony; simply, it was a cessation of work, longer awaited and more welcome than any festivity in my remembered experience, however elegant. A blessed fortnight of blissful freedom, unfettered by needle, thread, cluttered worktable . . . or Mrs. Walsh. The prospect was delicious! On the part of many there was an immediate scramble to quit the premises, as the girls were permitted to take leave for the purposes of visiting friends, heading for resort areas, or pursuing individual inclinations at will. The sanctioned absences specified, for the most part, a fortnight; there were some, however, that, by reason of lengthy service or some prior arrangement, were extended for as long as a month. Since Molly, Ada, and I found ourselves without similar destinations and, in my case, quite devoid of resources as well, we were able to make no plans to enjoy such expansive excursions to far-off places. We were, then, to remain at the establishment, which (and for this I, completely penurious, was suddenly and abundantly grateful) continued to supply meals. There were additional compensations: Jenny, thankfully, had gone home to help "mum" prepare for the new child evidently expected momentarily, so that we were spared, for a time at least, her disagreeable presence. There were times, I suspected, however, that Ada missed her daily target practice and was mentally stockpiling new and varied weaponry in advance of the girl's return.

Secondly, our new roommate, Hattie Corcoran, had been invited, at no expenditure to herself, by an affluent and childless aunt and uncle to pass her holiday in Lancaster, thus freeing us from the discouraging burden of her perpetual attitude of affront and disapproval. Hattie was a timorous, chill creature: Remarkably plain of feature, her prickly person was rendered even less endearing by the consistently dolorous droop to her lips and eyes (ever downcast), as if nothing lay in her environs that was not distasteful to contemplate. In particular Ada's language provided Hattie with the greatest cause for distress, eliciting a reaction in the piteous manner of a wounded dog sorely afflicted and abused; seldom verbal, her objections to Ada's coarse expletives came in the form of eyes closed against severe pain, accompanied by those irritating sibilant sounds of an offended clucking tongue. I must confess that I, too, had been somewhat startled by Ada's unique mode of speech at first; but since most of the words were both alien to my vocabulary and thus quite without meaning and so much a part of Ada herself, I soon became accustomed to their use. Not so Miss Hattie. It was then a happy moment when we waved a genuinely cheery farewell to the girl, wishing, each, that she might remain in Lancaster—or wherever—permanently privy to the bounties of her uncle's generous table . . . and prepared to formulate our own joint activities for the holidays.

Thoroughly exhausted by the rigors of the Season and unused as we were to protracted leisure, we seemed to drift the first few days, wandering about aimlessly, simply savoring inactivity. "We must not waste another precious moment!" decided Molly firmly as we finally awoke one bright summer morning.

"Where shall we go?" asked Ada, stretching.

"Anywhere," shrugged Molly.

"We could visit Bea," I suggested, "and see the baby."

"The baby!" shrieked Molly.

"Lor!" chortled Ada. "What a bloody innocent!"

"Elizabeth, luv," explained Molly patiently, "she shan't have had it yet." She and Ada exchanged knowing mirthful glances.

"Well, then, we could see *her*," I said.

"That's going to take a bit of doing, I fear," Ada frowned. "I've no idea where Bea's Merchant Street is. Have you, Molly?"

"Not the slightest."

"I suppose we could have a go-round and see what there is," posed Ada.

"I suppose."

"Then, while we're about it, introduce our Elizabeth to some real sights of the city. I fear she is not acquainted with much else but Regent Street or Mayfair." They both laughed. "Bea would never let us take her last year. . . ."

Thus the search for Merchant Street and Bea began, both deviated from and heightened by the heady promise of the guided tour, so prescribed. The weather proved benign; most of the days dawned softly sunny and without the unbearable heat usually associated with mid-July: conditions, then, ideal for on-foot exploration and sufficient to entice us from our beds, excited at the prospect of adventure. . . . We witnessed with fascination the daily—almost ceremonial—removal of the great shutters that served as protection for the plate glass, shielding fashionable shop windows, unveiling in the process the splendor and magnificence therein. . . . On street corners of less substantial neighborhoods we listened with awed amusement to the cacophony of vendors as they hawked loudly, and in chantlike regularity, their wares: "Get your Epping sausage 'ere . . . fresh today . . . Get your Epping sausage 'ere . . . fresh today . . . Get your . . ." We clocked the lordly financiers moving in solemnity abreast of the commercial giants as they strode with brisk importance down Grand and Fleet streets, gold-tipped walking sticks wielded to precise style and with infinite flair—or observed, some time later, these same dignitaries as they strolled in studied carelessness toward St. James's to relax or dine in the exclusive clubs there, amidst select peers.

Entering one day a stunningly seamy district, Ada nudged me and cautioned, "Best keep a tight rein on your reticule, Elizabeth."

I laughed. "There is naught in here for the taking."

"These buggers would slice your head in half for the mere pleasure of making that determination," she muttered.

Puzzled, I asked uneasily, "Whatever are you saying, Ada?"

"You'll see soon enough."

It was not long before I discerned, peeking out from behind a house here, derelict and crumbling, a building there, all but tottering—children, nay, what proved to be a pack of children: lawless, certainly; neglected, obviously; some naked; all filthy; roaming at will and seeming to fix their intently staring eyes on us as we passed. "What on earth is this place?" I inquired of Molly.

"Bethnal Green."

"And these children?"

"The news sheets describe them as, 'Hatching in the incubator of crime,' " Molly quoted.

"They are—criminals?" I was aghast. "That little fellow?" I indicated a scrawny urchin with a grimy balled fist busily wiping at the ribbons of mucus suspended thickly from his nose, which was small but thoroughly encrusted. Even through the many layers of caked dirt gleamed a pair of impish blue eyes and a puckish pink mouth spread wide in an irrepressibly engaging grin. His front teeth were badly chipped. "Impossible!"

"Bah!" scoffed Ada. "That rogue's probably the keenest lift of the lot!"

"Impossible!" I repeated.

"Why?" asked Molly reasonably. "They all start as sneak thieves, pickpockets—then move up in the trade and become housebreakers—or some such."

"Children?" I was horrified. "But what of their mothers?"

"Their mothers!" Molly dismissed the idea with an amused wave of her hand. "Don't think that these mites are nurtured at fond mum's gouty knee and learn this on their own—mercy!"

"Hell, no," agreed Ada promptly. "These babies are coached. And by experts."

"Coached!"

"Coached, and by the best: thief-trainers—knaves who earn their livelihood teaching children how to steal, and to their own considerable profit, too, it would seem."

"Incredible!" I cried.

"Easy," corrected Ada. "A clever pickpocket can raise his station in life by simply moving his trade to better surroundings—more fashionable circles—where the money is.

He poses as a banker today—and tomorrow—" she shrugged. "Pulls in a respectable haul, to boot."

"And," added Molly, "if he is truly accomplished: on to Jago's with him!"

"Jago's?"

"The lair of the flourishing high-mobsmen."

"Isn't there anything ever done to help them—the children?"

"Sure," Ada replied, "there's always Devil's Acre."

"Ever heard of it, Elizabeth?" questioned Molly.

I shook my head.

"A house of correction—stands right behind the Houses of Parliament," Ada supplied, "filled to the walls with the young of the poor. . . . Hell, mites jailed on charges of pea-shooting or robbing birds' nests—or the awful crime, perhaps, of stringing a couple of lines at night for fish. . . . Some of the tenants of Devil's Acre are as ancient as six or seven!"

"Years old?" I was aghast.

"Years old."

"Horrible!" I shuddered.

"But," said Ada, "true."

"Enough of this grim talk!" cried Molly. "We're on holiday, remember? Let's treat ourselves to a nice fresh Epping sausage—what say?"

"I have no money," I objected, hiding my disappointment.

"I have."

"Good idea," applauded Ada immediately. "I've had enough of this sewer to last a bloody lifetime!"

We marched then, arm in arm, turning away from the squalor and its heartbreak, toward a pleasanter quarter of the city, our appetites—healthy and young—titillated by the prospect of addressing a succulent sausage. I realized suddenly that my reticule was missing; I did not mention its loss. . . .

The long days and nights spent in endless exploration continued in their peculiar fascination for me, still not so far removed, in time at least, from the perfect shelter from all sights, disagreeable, and smells, noisome, afforded by the horse-drawn phaeton and under the protective aegis of my Auntie Maude, duenna. I stood on a street corner now in helpless awe as a German band bawled: blaring, brassy, lusty; watched, enraptured, as men and women, suddenly giddy in the softness of a summer night, clapped hands broadly and stamped the lively steps of a polka, some faltering, others quite expert; listened, smiling, as a trio—with huge enjoyment—lifted spirited voices high in a jolly glee; daring to venture abroad on a lonely city street, feeling the frightening chill of the fog as it settled, rendering passersby headless and fading tall buildings to dingy shadows that swayed slightly against their wispy background.

The eleven o'clock curfew was still rigidly enforced; in the late evening, then, we played heated games of whist or Pope Joan or, better still, planned elaborately our next day's itinerary.

"We still have not found Merchant Street," I declared one night as we were preparing for bed.

"Tomorrow," promised Ada. "Tomorrow . . ."

Chapter 10

"Tomorrow" dawned bleak, burdened with heavy clouds, hanging gray and low from a glowering sky. Ada, rising, squinted through the iron grill. "Perhaps we had best save Merchant Street for still another day." Her tone was doubtful.

"You promised!"

"Perhaps it will burn off after a bit," compromised Molly. "Let's have a go at it anyway. We can always make a dash for home if it really starts to pour."

After a breakfast of remarkably pale, tepid tea and glue-like porridge, more filling than tasty, we set forth to find Merchant Street and our Bea. Although actual rain forbore, the dark clouds persisted, chilling the air.

"I really haven't the least notion where to start," Ada confessed.

"Perhaps we should ask directions of someone," I suggested.

"That can be a trifle dangerous," warned Ada.

"Surely not in the business district," Molly judged reasonably. "Look here, we're getting onto St. Paul's now . . . we could inquire of the rector or sexton—we should be safe enough with them, certainly," she giggled.

"I say," I queried slowly, "what is all the straw on the road?"

"Lor," breathed Ada, "must be going to have a bloody trial."

"A trial?"

"Over there, my dear girl—as any good Londoner should know—stands Newgate Prison." Ada indicated a harsh building, its dark stone wrapped in eternal gloom by the long, imposing shadow cast by the reaching, thrusting cathedral.

"I do believe you're right about the trial, Ada," said Molly. "There seems a crowd gathering now."

"Not just for the trial," muttered Ada grimly. "See—the Debtor's Door is opening . . ."

Two men, thickset, their unkempt uniforms hardly suitable attire to grace the distinguished arm of the law, emerged, dragging a man who was bareheaded, bootless, his scraggy limbs covered only by a shredding shirt and a pair of pitifully ragged trousers. His was a cruel, agonized struggle.

"Perhaps he's being transferred to one of the convict barges," Molly posed hopefully.

"In the Thames?" Ada said. "Not likely, with this mob."

The growing crowd of restless men and women became still more agitated at his sorry appearance; ranging about, pacing in poorly contained excitement, pushing, shoving, they began to scream obscenities at the victim and his plight.

" 'Ang the bloody barsted!"

"Swing 'im 'igh!" came a bawdy laugh.

"We wants 'is feet to dance—what say, gang?"

The crowd bawled, "Aye! A ruddy jiggy polka!"

"On with it, blokes, 'ang the rotten pauper!"

"Aye," squawked an aged crone, "drinkin', 'orin'—"

" 'angin's too quick for the goddamned cheat!" shrilled a young woman, holding high her tiny child so that he might see.

"They're not going to hang that man?" I asked in terror.

"Aw—'angin's too good for the likes of 'im," railed a mountain of a woman, waggling a dirty finger in the direction of the prisoner. "Drinkin', gamblin', robbin' his family blind . . ."

" 'Ang the bloody gambler 'igh!" brayed another.

Gambler! My eyes filled; my throat constricted. Gambler! My father! This could have happened to my father . . . Stripped thus of all dignity, abused, reviled, his life and being reduced to a single rabble-incited moment of entertainment, of sick enjoyment enacted for this surly, thirsty human scum . . . This could have been my father . . .

"What is it, Elizabeth?" gasped Molly. "Ada, quick, she looks about to faint!"

"There's still time before it's done," muttered Ada, grabbing my arm roughly. "Come along . . . let's be off . . ."

Flanking me on either side, the two girls propelled me forward; blindly, woodenly, I obeyed their urgings and frantic exhortations. "That's it, luv," encouraged Molly, pulling at my arm.

"A little faster now . . ." implored Ada.

Suddenly, at our backs: the single, thunderous roar of an ecstatic crowd; in unison, as if orchestrated.

Unseeing, I knew.

I vomited at the curb . . .

We made inquiries at what was obviously an establishment of unblemished respectability as to the location of Merchant Street and the easiest route by which our destination might be reached. It was through the efforts of an orderly, sympathetic gentleman, very much middle-class, who on our behalf, consulting a detailed, confusing map of the city and its network of streets, presented us with the most direct course possible. The distance was nonetheless much greater than we had anticipated. Regarding us with a quizzical, troubled expression, the man remarked with undisguised concern that Merchant Street and its environs did not constitute the most desirable section of the city and, coughing discreetly, advised us that perhaps it might be prudent to forgo the trip altogether. Seeing the disappointment plain in our faces, he hastened to add, "Or, ladies, at least postpone your activities until a day when you might better venture on the premises in a driven conveyance."

After thanking our benefactor profusely for his pains and knowing that we had no intentions whatever of taking his advice, however well-meaning or justified, we began the journey.

"A driven conveyance!" spluttered Ada, once out on the street. "Bloody old fool!"

"But," Molly cautioned, "we shall have to walk quickly. " 'Tis a fair way . . ."

Despite the chill wind and a brooding sky our spirits began to lift, both as the acute horror of the scene played before Newgate Prison began to fade and as the delights projected in once again seeing our Bea grew stronger. As the man in the shop had promised, neighborhood after neighborhood became increasingly less presentable, assuming at first only a careless, untended aspect, finally parading an air of total dereliction. . . . And then: Merchant Street.

"Lor!" exclaimed Ada. "This is naught but a slum!"

"Our Bea cannot live here!" I protested.

"Are you quite certain it was Merchant Street she said, Ada?" asked Molly, frowning.

"Positive."

"Did she give the number?"

Ada shook her head, "We shall have to ask."

It was not easy to select what might conceivably pass for the most prosperous and more reasonably maintained dwelling on the street; the slattern answering our tentative knock eyed us suspiciously and after some moments of hesitation grudgingly released the information: "I don't know no Conrad Fletcher. That don't mean much, leastwise, ain't been here more'n a 'alf year." She smoothed her creased wrapper with the palm of a fleshy soiled hand. "Try Number 28. Bloke there seems to know most of what goes on 'ere. Can't promise nothin'—but," she shrugged, "can't 'urt nothin' to try, neither." Peering inquisitively from under thinly plucked brows, she asked, "What'll ye be wantin' with them buggers, anywise?"

"To give them the Queen's grace," answered Ada levelly.

Molly tittered.

Number 28 Merchant Street proved an abhorrence beyond all imagining: Framed of decaying wood above a crumbling cement slab, the house now listed precariously to one side, freeing the paint—a stained white, which peeled frankly and in huge chunks from bucking clapboards—to wave without constriction in the mild summer breeze. Those windows lacking glass were covered with jagged pieces of tar paper, nailed in obvious haste and without visible attention to accuracy. Its receding entry rotted uninvitingly, aped by a pair of steps serving as hazardous access. From deep within a crevice in the foundation's rubble crawled a large yellow dog. His coat was thickly matted;

clumps of dead fur swayed suggestively as he lumbered toward us, paused, and snarled a surly greeting.

"What say, old boy . . . Rover . . . Spot . . ." Ada
reached out a tentative hand; her awkward gesture of
friendship was awarded immediately with a still deeper
growl and a show of impressively sharp white teeth.

"You certainly have a way with dogs," giggled Molly
nervously.

"Chesterfield!" bawled a strong male voice, "get over
'ere, you bloody arse!"

"Chesterfield!" snorted Ada.

From behind the house sauntered a man of average
height, well into his middle years and molded on generally
lean lines, save for an oddly protruding pouch that hung
lazily over a pair of filthy ill-fitting trousers, calling provocative attention to the mat of wildly curling hair escaping from his half-buttoned rag of a shirt. Noticeably greasy,
even from a distance, the hair on his head grew thick and
gray-black, falling forward in a long untidy shock that
could not begin to conceal the insinuating leer lurking in
his dark eyes. As he neared his malodorousness became
almost overwhelming. With a mud-caked boot he took a
cruel swipe at the dog, who whimpered pitifully and slunk
off, seeking doubtful haven once more under the sagging
house. Drawing a grimy hand over a beard that straggled
intermittently over his jutting jaw, the man wetted full red
lips and asked, "What can I do for you girlies?"

"Ah—" Ada began uneasily, "we are looking for a—
er—Mr. Conrad Fletcher—"

"Mister!" howled the man, slapping at his thigh. "Mister
Conrad Fletcher! I like that!"

"Are you Mr. Fletcher?" she asked.

"Who might be axin'?" he grinned, exposing brownish
decayed teeth.

"We are trying to find his cousin—a Miss Bea Foster,"
put in Molly.

"That so?"

"We wondered if perhaps she might be here." Ada
looked beyond the man toward the house.

"You ain't messin' in with the p'lice?" He peered at Ada
through suddenly wary eyes.

"The police!" repeated Ada, stunned. "Of course not!"

"Jest so's you ain't lyin'."

"Let's go," decided Ada, turning away. "There is no use here."

"What about Bea?" I protested, hanging back.

"Wait 'alf a mo, girlies," the man said slowly, "since you seem on the ups, I'll tell you what you wanna know. First, I ain't *Mister*"—he underscored the word—"Conrad Fletcher. Ain't never 'eard of the bloke, neither."

"This is not Merchant Street?" Ada asked.

The man nodded. "Sure is. Every bloody stick and stone of it!" He threw back his head and laughed broadly.

"Are you acquainted with a family, then, by the name of Fletcher living on this block?"

"Ain't nowise. And I grew up 'ere. Right there"—flicking a brief, backward glance toward the house, he grinned—"me old family 'omestead, you might say!"

Turning to Molly, Ada shrugged, "Well, I guess that's all we can do."

" 'Old on there, girlies." The man made a move toward Ada's arm; she withdrew it quickly. "Maybe your friend there meant Merchand Street."

"Merchand Street?"

"Yeah. Some five blocks over," he said, pointing.

"Why," exclaimed Molly, "that's the way we came!"

"Merchand Street!" the man spat. "Think they're some kinda toffs," he sneered. "Hitchin' and pantin' to put on the brass, they don't take no time out for livin'!" Vigorously he stabbed his armpits. "Now, take us over 'ere," he chuckled coarsely, "that's another deal altogether . . ."

"Is there a Conrad Fletcher on Merchand Street?" inquired Ada with renewed hope.

"Tole ya, girlie, ain't no idea."

"We could try, though." Molly looked anxiously at Ada.

"There's a good idea—and I can 'elp ya some. . . . Tell ya what," the man proposed, his voice low now and syrupy, "why not leave your little playmate 'ere"—he jerked his head in my direction. "Seems kina peaky—so quiet 'n'all . . . Let 'er stay 'ere and relax over a nice cuppa—maybe a little nip . . . After a bit you girlies could come back and . . ." He sidled slyly toward me.

I was frozen with fear.

With the sharp command "Come along! Now!" and a fiercely determined palm shoved against my back, Ada forced me down the scrubby path and out onto the street proper, Molly hurrying after. Our retreat was pursued by a burst of coarse laughter and a string of ribald epithets, accompanied by the hollow sounds of a barking dog.

"Bloody bugger!" swore Ada.

"We'd best keep running," Molly panted, looking anxiously behind, "lest that dreadful creature take it into his head to follow. . . ."

Although they were similar in name, the resemblance between Merchand and Merchant streets therein ended. A far cry from the squalid neighborhood we had so narrowly escaped, Merchand Street stood as the aggressive model of social conservatism, oozing respectability and nervously aspiring to that elusive aura of gentility universally coveted by the ungenteel. Our inquiries as to the location of the Fletcher ménage were meet with civility. I was relieved to note, by what appeared to be this household's maid of all work, a rosy young thing newly from the farm, smelling of lye soap and beeswax, who managed, it would seem, to survive nicely under what probably constituted a workload suited to a staff of twenty. "The house be across the way, miss," the girl directed Molly pleasantly, "the one all over flowers . . ."

One could easily discern that Conrad Fletcher's residence had sprung up from a more humble construction than that of the establishment we had visited only moments before; it was far more pretentious. Conspicuously smaller in actual size and boasting fewer accoutrements, the indication nonetheless was clear: Mr. Fletcher was on the move, or desperately trying to prove so. The front lawn passed as a patchwork of variegated color, staggering under a frenzied assortment of floral profusion cataloguing, I was sure, a hundred different species: The effect created was comedic. Relentlessly scaling its light gray stone, sturdy ivy successfully eclipsed the square-shaped building, so much so that one could not help but count it a blessing that the creeper failed to bloom. Those portions of the lawn not smothering beneath their bunting of flowers emerged as a grotesque formal garden area, where plucky shrubs, cut and pruned as bizarre statuary—depicting crouching animals and feeding birds—writhed. At curbside, suspended from a slender wrought-iron stand, swung gently a small, discreet sign: "Millinery Creations by Miss Alice."

We were met at the door this time not by a servant but by the daughter of the house herself, a whey-faced lass in her earliest teens, painfully thin and of indeterminate coloring as to hair and eyes. In fact her manner as well as her appearance was lusterless, a defect the mother, or whoever might be responsible for the girl's choice of wardrobe, tried to offset by a plethora of ribbons and bows and doubtful inserts of lace that peeked out indiscriminately and without justification from a too-brightly-colored gown. So shy as to be almost tongue-tied, the girl nonetheless made a strained effort at cordiality, her eyes the while flying behind her, anxious, it seemed, that someone in the household other than herself assume the responsibility for three uninvited guests. We explained the nature of our intrusion and the girl bade us, albeit reluctantly, to wait in the small parlor; she withdrew.

"My God!" sniggered Ada. "Put that one out on the lawn and she'd disappear from sight straightaway!"

"Ssh, Ada," admonished Molly, swallowing a giggle. "Did you ever see such an outfit!"

I nodded absently, my attention fixed on our immediate surroundings: The room was a study in fussy frippery. And lace. Nothing escaped it. Strips of intricate lace were draped over, pinned to, drawn stiffly across, or lying loosely on any object that stood or squatted, be it table, chest, settee, or chair—the latter carrying the enormous burden of protective antimacassars spectacular in breadth and length. No area of flooring was left to chance: If it was not actively occupied by a stray piece of furniture, then a wild scattering of rugs was introduced, each patterned more frenetically than the last.

I could not help but remember the drawing room at Leicester Square: a cruel comparison . . .

It was not many minutes before Conrad Fletcher made his hurried, nervous entrance. A man still in his late thir-

ties only, he bore the too-high forehead that presages early
baldness, carried the merest excess of weight, promising
that his insinuating tendency toward stoutness today would
lead to real corpulence tomorrow, and dressed in attire im-
peccably neat and properly subdued but certainly not Regent Street. His manner was unctuous; his eyes, guarded.
"Ah, ladies," he greeted us, rubbing his hands scratchily
together. "How may I be of assistance?" His voice was
newly cultured.

"May we sit down?" asked Ada.

"Oh, certainly. Certainly!" Conrad Fletcher coughed in
instant apology. "Forgive me! Heh! Heh!" He settled himself cautiously on a dainty velvet chair. "Now, then,
ladies . . ."

"We have come about our friend Bea Foster," Molly began without preamble.

"Oh?" The man lifted a noncommittal eyebrow.

"We understand her to be your cousin," Molly continued.

His eyes dropped. "Ah—ah, that is—ah—correct . . ."

"Bea informed us that she would be living with you—for
a—while," Ada interjected.

"Oh, my!" Conrad Fletcher's eyes shifted uneasily. "Oh,
dear. What I mean to say is—ah—no."

"You mean that she is not here?" I asked.

"Ah—" The man wetted his lips. "Well, no—she is
not—here . . ."

"Has she been here, then?" persisted Ada.

"Well—ah—as a matter of fact, come to think of it—"
he replied vaguely, "she did pay us a brief call . . ." His
words trailed away.

"When?" pounced Molly.

"Ah—let me see now." In pointed deliberation Conrad
Fletcher's wary eyes sought the ceiling. "Ah—perhaps two
months ago—I can't be expected to recall the precise date,
after all." A petulant edge crept into his voice.

"She did not stay with you, then?"

"Oh, dear." He fidgeted in his chair. "No. As a matter
of fact—she did not."

"Why not?" Ada asked directly.

"It was—ah—not convenient at—the time . . ."

"Not convenient!"

"Ah—that is—not appropriate, I should have better said . . ." Conrad Fletcher's moist hands restlessly fingered the sword-sharp crease of his dark trousers.

"Appropriate!" cried Ada.

"Now, miss," he parried, "you know how them—these—things are—what with the little gel here, and all." Conrad Fletcher's manner became defensive. "And with the missus havin' clients to the house—all nice respectable ladies, and all."

"My God!" sputtered Ada.

"Now, miss—easy on—I can't have no scandal in this house . . ."

Ada glowered dangerously.

Conrad Fletcher flashed her a sickly smile. "Can't 'ardly afford it with the new business jest takin' 'old, now—can I? Ladies don't 'old with scandal . . ." Flustered, he cleared his throat harshly. "I'm a family man, first thing off. A man's got to think of his family straightaway in this 'ere cruel world. . . . Now, I'm right, ain't I?" His coarse face was sweating profusely.

"You would not let Bea stay here?" Molly was incredulous.

"N-now, miss—hit's not that I'm a 'ard and selfish man—leastwise, hit's never been my nature, you might say, and all. . . . But there comes a time in a man's life when 'e's got to think practical. For 'imself and 'is precious family." Conrad Fletcher paused to take an uncomfortable breath. "A wayward gel ain't got no place in a nice respectable 'ouse like this—nowise." He coughed. "Not with the little gel and the ladies visitin' the house and all, nice and respectable like—for the business, and all . . ." he finished lamely.

"She had nowhere else to go," whispered Molly.

Conrad Fletcher struggled to his feet; his stance was uncertain. "Oh, don't get me wrong, I give 'er a few pence, you know. . . . I ain't 'ardly a 'ard man . . ."

"W-where did she go?" I asked.

"Ah—well, now, miss . . ."

"Where the hell is Bea now?" demanded a hostile Ada.

Elaborately Conrad Fletcher drew a handkerchief from his pocket: predictably it was lace-bordered. "I am afraid I've got some bad news for you young ladies," he sniffed.

"B-bad news?" Suddenly I was afraid.

"I—can't 'ardly find the words to tell you, and all . . . but . . ." He blew his nose emphatically. "I'm sorry to say—but: Bea is no longer with us . . ."

"What?" rasped Ada.

"Bea is—" Conrad Fletcher's voice broke—"dead."

"Dead!" cried Molly. "When?"

"H-how?" I was trembling.

"I'll jest say it right out. Clean," Conrad Fletcher declared bravely. "Drowned, she is. In the Thames. Almost a month ago, now."

He had answered all of our questions.

"But," Ada said, her voice ominously low, "I don't see how that could have happened, Mr. Fletcher."

"Well—ah," he evaded.

Ada stood. "Mr. Fletcher."

"Aye," he shook his head sadly, "by 'er own 'and . . ."

Benumbed, we filed one by one—a pitiful processional—out of that cloying, muddled room and away from the dreadful presence of Mr. Conrad Fletcher. As he held the door politely his invitation was jolly: "Come back any time, ladies. Any time!" His smile, ingratiating. "Any time. The missus will be pleased to sew up anything for you . . ."

"Sew! For us?" I shrieked and began to laugh. "Sew! For us!" Caught helplessly in the grip of hysteria, I zigzagged drunkenly across the lawn, collapsing finally in a heap on the ground. As Ada and Molly pulled me, sobbing convulsively, to my feet the low but distinct exhortation of our host trailed after: "Leave off the goddamned flowers, ye bloody drabs . . ."

Chapter 11

As August began, our holiday came to an end. On that first Monday of the month, drawn up at our table, already hard at work, was Jenny. "Hell," Ada groaned audibly, "I was hoping she'd got married."

"Hush, Ada." I suppressed a giggle. "She'll hear . . ."

Ada shrugged. "Who cares . . . My God," she grumbled, "Jenny all day and Hattie all night."

"It would have been nice," I admitted wistfully, "if Hattie had stayed on with her uncle in Lancaster."

"He probably couldn't abide her either."

"Wish we had Molly back . . ."

"And Bea . . ."

. . . And Bea . . .

We were treated to Mrs. Walsh's customary ceremonial homecoming speech, which, true to form, was tiresome in length, repetitive in content, and predictably spiced at lagging intervals by admonitions stern and axioms inspiring—courtesy of the late, lamented Reverend Walsh. Petticoats billowing, she sailed majestically into the workroom, head high, prow pressing ever forward, and, beaming broadly, addressed the crowded room, "Ah, ladies, it is most gratifying indeed to see your faces thus: happy and flushed . . . those busy, clever, skillful hands eager to be put back in harness once again." She smiled, her manner musing . . . "Back in harness . . . The horse come home from the hills . . . to pull the plow . . . furrow the fallow field . . . harvest the awaiting land . . . For, ladies, a day spent at work in the Trade is a harvest . . . your fulfillment . . . your yield . . ." She paused.

Ada poked me. "Here we go . . ."

"In the words of . . ."

Ada jiggled my arm. "Told you so," she hissed.

I tittered.

". . . my late, lamented husband, the Reverend Walsh: 'Let the sweat from the brow at honest toil fill the golden goblets of the gods . . .' "

And so they went: the days . . .

Molly, Ada, and I pursued our Sabbath outings, assiduously avoiding by tacit understanding, however, the steamer excursions—in memory of Bea and with a new aversion to the activity that had provoked her downfall. I think, too, we feared that we might, by sheerest happenstance, recognize the person of Bea's "young man."

Molly continued at the shop; Jenny at the table; and Hattie in the room.

Summer faded; autumn fled before chill rains and bleak skies; it was November, and time once again for the Winter Season.

"At least the goddamned thing is not as long as that ruddy hell we suffer in the spring," growled Ada one morning as she peered through the iron mesh and grimaced at the lowering fog grayly swaddling the earth. "We'll be in for it soon," was her dour prediction. "Mark my bloody words!"

"Your words! Your language, Ada!" Hattie shuddered delicately. "Our minister says that cursing and blaspheming are merely a means employed by the ignorant to conceal the fact that the refinements of vocabulary are singularly lacking," she quoted priggishly.

"Oh, is that so!" Ada sparred. "You want some refinements . . ."

"I think you are boorish and unladylike," Hattie accused pettishly. "My mamma always said that real ladies never, never swear!"

"Oh, come along, you two." I leapt from the bed. "It is going to be dreary enough around here without your constant squabbling!"

"Amen," yawned Molly . . .

Close on to teatime on a dismal day in mid-December, a solemn Mrs. Walsh, cloaked in the unrelieved black of mourning, paraded into the room. Her stately progress was slow, befitting one cruelly bereft, one whose sorrowing heart is locked eternally in the jaws of deepest grief. Even her handkerchief was black.

"My God!" Ada's foot stabbed mine under the table. "Whatever have we here?"

A bewildered hush gradually claimed the group at large as Mrs. Walsh, step measured, head bowed, moved bravely into the middle of the room. There, center stage, she held sway: the tragic queen. With regal delicacy she fluttered the ebony linen, carefully aimed to encompass each in the waiting crowd, offering brief but gracious acknowledgment. "Ladies," she began, voice low and throbbing with powerful emotion. "Ladies, I come to you this day with the weight of sadness lying heavy on my soul and in my deepest heart." She pressed the handkerchief under an enormous breast.

Ada snickered.

"Perhaps far better and more intimately than any of you, I know, have felt the wrench, the complete eternal despair that accompanies the loss of one's love, one's mate, one's dearest companion, sharing delight and woe, wandering—my hand in his hand—down the twisting, turning corridor of life . . ." She sniffed, the black handkerchief traveling artfully to one side and then the other of her protuberant nose.

"Jesus!" snorted Ada.

"In the words of my partner, my own departed liege," Mrs. Walsh's voice quavered pitifully, " 'To pass a few moments of his darkest hour in dedication to one bereaved is not a task, surely, but a privilege, God-given . . . a sacred obligation.' " She lifted misty eyes. "A privilege . . . God-given . . . sacred obligation . . . to add, each in her small way, to the comfort and tranquillity of one who lies prostrate in weeping for her beloved who has gone on—and long ere his time . . . God rest his immortal soul. . . ." She bent her head. "We all in the family of Miller's pledge proudly our time and energies to this pursuit—if that should mean working every day and night, every night and day—to provide our fair city—nay, our beloved nation, if so decreed, that attire traditionally prescribed to conduct, with proper grace, the solemn period of mourning. . . . Then, so be it!" Eyes downcast, she whispered, "We can do no less for our Queen!"

"The Queen is dead!" came a shocked gasp from another table.

"No." Smiling sadly, Mrs. Walsh shook her head. "No. The Almighty, in his infinite wisdom and generosity, has spared our treasured monarch . . . Why, it is her sovereign lord—Albert, Prince Consort—who has flown to the gates of Paradise and has left his Queen, his partner, to rule alone . . . much as my own prince, the late, lamented Reverend Walsh, left me. . . ." Mrs. Walsh pressed the handkerchief to her now streaming eyes.

Jenny was blubbering noisily; many of the girls had followed suit, some weeping loudly for the departed prince, others softly, in pity for their little queen. "Ah, she loved him so," sobbed one. "Fair worshiped him," gargled another. "'Twas a marriage made in heaven," bawled still another.

"What I want to know," Ada remarked practically, "is what the hell Walsh means by the 'every day and every night' business . . ."

"D-don't you have *any* feelings *at all,* Ada!" snuffled Jenny. "This is *tragic!*"

"Ladies!" Mrs. Walsh's eye was suddenly clear; her voice, strong. *"Ladies!"* she boomed, "even now, when England's shocking loss is only hours old, Miller's has been besieged with orders for mourning raiment. Men, women—young, old—have come to our establishment seeking to be outfitted for the festiv—er, solemn occasions already scheduled and those yet to be announced. It will take all of our combined efforts and perfect cooperation to meet these orders. . . . This challenge . . . I have been tossed the gauntlet, ladies. The battle is mine . . . I am confident that it will be yours as well. . . ." Meaningfully her narrowed eyes traversed the room. "Each and every one . . ."

"Oh, God!" Ada sagged against the table.

"And, ladies, before I pass the torch of combat on to your eagerly waiting hands, I leave with you the following exhortation: Until further notice it will be mandatory for all employed by the House of Miller to be carefully attired in black. In the event that some may not possess, immediately, such appropriate apparel, they will be given exactly two days in which to secure—or make—same. Failure to comply with this regulation—er, request—will result in severe reprimand." Her eyes scoured the room. "Or—dismissal . . ." She smiled. "Now, ladies, I shall leave you to your industry, mindful always that any slight additional effort on your part here will be recorded as respect due Her Imperial Majesty . . ." Mrs. Walsh bowed her head with becoming grace. "Your little tribute to our Queen . . ."

"And to the coffers of Miller's," Ada muttered sourly.

"Knowlton!" Mrs. Walsh squawked from across the room.

I jumped. "Yes, ma'am?"

"You have a black silk gown in your wardrobe, I presume?"

"Er—yes, ma'am. It is a number of years old by now."

"No matter. I have a mind to transfer you to the shop—at least during this present crisis," Mrs. Walsh announced doubtfully. Then, looking me over with minute care, she declared, "You are scarcely an optimum consideration but, after all, presentable . . . and the department is desperately shorthanded. Furthermore," she added, her gaze baleful, "heaven knows you are not of a great value here."

Jenny glowed.

"I shall expect you, then, fully attired and prepared for service in exactly ten minutes," Mrs. Walsh decided firmly. "I advise you not to be tardy. In the words of my late, lamented husband, the Reverend Walsh: 'A messenger bringing God's work to lowly man is never late . . .'" Turning abruptly, she strode out of the room, the black silk of her gown whispering softly in her wake.

Ada's wounded eyes traveled toward Jenny. "Oh, God!" she moaned, "Oh, God . . ."

True to Molly's description, rather than the respite one might have rightfully supposed, the shop proved naught but a penance and the black silk dress a veritable hair shirt. I was further troubled by a useless resentment steadily growing within myself against the customers who invaded the premises for their fashionable wardrobes and richly designed coiffures, evoking a style of life all but forgotten in the shabby confines of the workroom . . .

And so the nightmare began. I can never remember such fatigue. And frightening to contemplate: After only a few weeks of inhuman, grueling abuse, the delicate fabric of my silk gown was showing alarming signs of fraying. "Whatever shall I do when this gives out?" I asked Molly frantically.

She tapped me under the chin, "You'll have to get a replacement then, luv."

"You know I haven't so much as a farthing," I wailed.

"Perhaps," she winked, "someone will treat you to a new one."

"Who?" I demanded.

"A gentleman," she teased, "like, for example, that young chap who has been back to the shop three times so far this week and can't seem to keep his eyes off you."

My face flamed. "No such thing," I protested.

"Best not to accept his offer, though," she advised. "He'll be after payment, you know." At my puzzled expression Molly laughed. "Just take my word for it, Elizabeth, luv . . ."

To my consternation, then, I became slowly aware of the increasingly expressive—even ardent—glances cast (and quite deliberately so) in my direction by a young gentleman whose visits to the shop were now of daily regularity and of unwarranted duration. His eyes were direct in an even-featured face; his tailoring was impeccable; his smile, engaging—but I was uneasy in his presence and went to exaggerated lengths to evade his unsolicited attentions. My inexpert efforts to extricate myself from an improper entanglement seemed to amuse rather than discourage; tantalize, not weaken, his inclinations. I knew nothing of men or their drives and desires—less of their methods of acquisition; thus it was with flaming face and palpitating heart that I fingered the note he had managed to slip into my trembling hands only moments before. Molly, witnessing the transaction, hissed, "Give that here! They catch you with a note from a man and you'll get the boot for sure!"

"What would be in the note?" I asked, suddenly afraid.

"Hell!" Molly borrowed the expletive from Ada. "What does it matter? What matters is for you to watch your step and mind your manners, luv, or they'll sack you as quick as that!" She snapped her fingers briskly.

Late on a dreary afternoon in January shortly before tea break and during my third dismal week assigned to the shop, I was attending a customer—an old woman, querulous, myopic, and disconcertingly redolent with the musty odor emanating from the very old and not altogether clean—I was halted midsentence by a gleeful screech reaching from across the room. "Elizabeth! Elizabeth! Elizabeth Knowlton! My dear! Is that really *you*!" I froze: Miriam Longwell rushed to my side, an expression of malicious triumph alight on her broadly smiling face. "*Darling* Elizabeth! How utterly *perfect* to see you! Why, we all thought you had simply dropped from the earth!" Her delighted eyes raked my appearance. "We have missed you *so*, dear! And now to have found you, *at last*!" She looked around the room. "*Here!*" Her enjoyment was devilishly complete . . .

The scene was oft replayed: After her initial delectable discovery Miriam managed neatly to maneuver a constant and varied parade of chums, one by delirious one, through Miller's salon, each *so* surprised and *so* happy to find her *old, old* playmate once again, after such a *long, long* time. . . . Dear heart . . . Darling . . . Sweet . . . Angel . . .

Thus, another year "in the Trade" . . . Winter melted into spring . . . spring blossomed into summer . . . and summer faded into autumn . . . another year, plagued by unrelieved fatigue; the troublesome advances of designing men; an appalling sense of shame engendered by the devoted Miriam and her unrelenting entourage. There were good times, yes—in the company of Molly and Ada; but hovering over all, a growing sense of futility and defeat . . .

I stood one gray morning in mid-November, lost in gloom, when I felt Mary O'Hara, a Second Hand, tug at my sleeve. "Mrs. Walsh would have you in her office, right away."

"What's this?" asked Molly anxiously as Mary, message

delivered, had bustled from the room. "You've not been accepting notes from gentlemen, Elizabeth!"

"Of course not . . ."

She sat, dwarfed by the colossus of Mrs. Walsh, whose shadow, even in the dimly-lighted room, stretched to embrace her across the scrabbled desk. I recognized at once the dear familiar figure: older; a little grayer, perhaps; with no lifting smile gracing the pale face . . . still, well known to me. My beloved Auntie Maude. She sat stiffly, hands prim in her lap, and eyed Mrs. Walsh with undisguised distaste. "If you will be so good as to advise Miss Knowlton to pack her belongings forthwith, Mrs. Walsh, I shall be in your debt." Auntie Maude sniffed pointedly. "And, since there is no substantive monetary compensation forthcoming, the cumbersome, time-consuming burden of formal discharge is thereby negated. If I am correct?"

"C-certainly. Of c-course—" stammered Mrs. Walsh.

Auntie Maude rose. "If the circumstances are perfectly clear then, Mrs. Walsh, I shall await Miss Knowlton in the confines of the cab which attends me at the curb, as"—her glance passed lightly over the room—"I prefer less doleful surroundings." Her manner was insulting. "Pray, see to it that my niece is released without delay. Our schedule is precise; our departure, immediate."

Despite the affront Mrs. Walsh managed to recover. "Never fear, Miss Treadway . . . In the words of my late, lamented husband—"

"Madam," interrupted Auntie Maude rudely, "I have neither the time to hear nor the slightest interest in determining the nature of your late, lamented husband's personal observations. . . ." With that impertinent disclosure Auntie Maude turned, inclined her head in mock civility, and swept grandly out of the room, leaving me with my jaws frankly agape and Mrs. Walsh to suffer the torment of the random, disfiguring blotches of humiliation that were rapidly traversing her rather large, perspiring face. . . .

A tearful farewell to Ada and Molly, much hugging and promising to write faithfully from wherever I might be . . . then a tearful reunion with Auntie Maude, much hugging and promising faithfully to explain all, and we settled back at last, aboard a stagecoach that, at whirlwind speed, was spiriting us farther and farther away from London and Miller's . . . and racing us ever nearer the rugged coast of Devon and Wynds . . . and a new life . . .

Part II

Chapter 12

A milky sky hung low and there was a keen edge to the air, presage of a winter storm. Auntie Maude and I, wrapped warmly in our thick woolen rug, ignored with lazy indifference any threat of snow or icy rain, so absorbed were we in ourselves and our sudden shift in situation. Our breath, in little cloudlike swirls, wafted around us, fogging the windows of the carriage as, oblivious, we chattered and giggled much as any two giddy school girls freed on unexpected holiday. Although we conducted ourselves as if still enjoying the privileged privacy of the phaeton, with only the discreet Brooks in attendance, we did not have the conveyance (public, after all) to ourselves. The vehicle itself, while not overly luxurious, appeared nearly new: Well-upholstered, with snugly fitted glass windows, the accommodations provided ample room indeed for the six passengers within to sit comfortably, untroubled by an overcrowded condition.

Auntie Maude occupied a middle seat, wedged easily in between myself, at the window, and a man of indeterminate years and intermediate corpulence who was engrossed unrelievedly, even from the onset of the journey, in an enormous sheaf of impressive-looking documents; these he consulted industriously, making periodic notations in the margins or lifting his eyes momentarily from the page in an attitude of intense concentration. I do not believe he uttered one word while on the road, a reticence reflecting not surliness, as one might project: merely preoccupation. Across from him, head resting in the lap of a companion who bore the cautious mien of governess or nursemaid, lay a small girl drifting in and out of an uneasy sleep. She was surely mortally ill. Even in repose the child was drawn, almost wasted, in appearance, stirring (and then only weakly) when her forehead was smoothed lightly by the tender hand of the nurse, who herself seemed close to complete exhaustion. Directly opposite me a woman, well-advanced in years, perched stiffly on her edge of the seat. Although of diminutive proportions—and these markedly shriveled—her unusually lengthy facial structure was whimsically emphasized by a heavy knot of tormented hair rigidly skewered at the crown, the effect insinuating, if one were to be cruelly fanciful, a hooded merganser. Her clothing was of deep, unaccented black, from petite footgear to tiny bonnet riding saucer-like atop that extraordinary abundance of hair; on another the jaunty angle of the hat might have suggested rakish good humor. Spare, wrinkled, and unyielding, her demeanor published perpetual disapproval, Auntie Maude and I the immediate objects of her baleful eye and condemnation. Pursed lips denounced our abandoned prattle: "Simply disgraceful . . . Outrageous . . ." Narrowed eyes deprecated our appearance. All commentary—visual or vocal—frequently punctuated by a distressed and clucking tongue.

Suddenly put in memory of Hattie, I giggled, "The Great Dowager . . ."

As the creaking stage bounced and swayed, Auntie Maude confessed, "I suppose we might better have resorted to the rails. But this is rather more fun—don't you think?"

I nodded, responding instinctively to the romance of the stagecoach, awakening to the provocative music of jingling harness and magical ringing hooves; my senses quickened by constant danger from footpads abroad; charmed by the flamboyant livery of the driver, equaled by that of his colorful guards . . .

"I know of a luscious little inn in Dreyfoot, along our route." Auntie Maude's sigh was wistful. "A stay there would be delightful—but out of the question, naturally, as we are expected—and—obligated . . ."

Obligated! I straightened in my seat. To whom? Or to what? "Auntie Maude! You must tell me . . ."

While in her position of governess in the Bayswater district, Auntie Maude was, it seems, contacted unexpectedly by Mr. Albert Wilkes, barrister to my late father and long-time friend to the Knowltons. In his capacity as attorney, handling my father's ravaged estate (actually, a task of single dimension, consisting mainly of satisfying rapacious creditors) Mr. Wilkes had received an elaborate communication from a Sir Robert Wyndham of Wynds, Drewsby, concerning the disposal of some objects d'art that had for generations been in the possession of his family: to wit, a frieze depicting a grouping of gods and goddesses and a tapestry in religious motif, employing in sensitive treatment only the colors red and gold. The articles in question had been brought to Sir Robert's attention, initially, as featured and highly touted offerings at a recent public auction conducted on the outskirts of Mayfair. After his immediate procurement of the pieces Sir Robert was able to confirm positively that they had been indeed included in his family's treasured legacy, the proof lying in the clear representation of the Wyndham crest (a raven devouring a mouse) sculpted, in the case of the frieze, unmistakably on the rather fully developed right breast of Ceres, and, pertaining to the tapestry, manifestly woven on Saint Paul's freely displayed reproductive mechanism (Auntie Maude blushed hotly).

It was Sir Robert's best information that the items purchased had been described with pride by the auctioneer as priceless relics belonging to the distinguished Knowlton estate, late of Leicester Square. Aware, too, of the affiliation between his distant cousin, Isabella Wyndham (my mother), and James Knowlton (my father), Sir Robert made further inquiries that led him to Mr. Wilkes. From the barrister Sir Robert sought information pertaining to the location of possible additional artifacts or household items relevant to the Wyndham lineage, since the Knowlton acquisition of such properties must have by necessity come from the Wyndham-Knowlton marriage, and through that connection alone.

Sir Robert, himself something of a self-styled antiquarian, went on to indicate that historically the Wyndham name had enjoyed a consistent reputation of solvency; he was sorely troubled, then, to learn that belongings cherished by the Wyndham line should find themselves on the crass public scene—more worrisome still, to contemplate the financial disaster implicit in making such sacrifices necessary.

A lengthy correspondence followed, Mr. Wilkes describing with some reticence the lamentable state of the Knowlton holdings, passing along the practical suggestion that any protracted search for Wyndham memorabilia would be frivolous, to say the least. After these many years of dissipation the bulk of the articles must be strewn about widely throughout the city (certainly) and the empire (possibly) as well. Mr. Wilkes went into some detail then, concerning my own impecunious situation necessitating employment in the dress trade. Sir Robert found the latter a fruitless pursuit, not worthy of a Wyndham, however distantly connected, and advised Mr. Wilkes that he was prepared to offer me a position in his home in some capacity or other. Really intent on the acquisition of a competent housekeeper, Sir Robert realized sensibly and at once that someone of my youth and inexperience would be totally inappropriate to the responsibility. He was, however, agreeable to the consideration of my suitability as a companion to his wife, who was temporarily suffering from failing health. He informed Mr. Wilkes that he felt it prudent that my presence in the household be established at the onset as one of a purely business nature, thus obviating any possible insinuation that I might be there on sufferance as an object of pity or charity. Mr. Wilkes, in thorough agreement, complimented Sir Robert on his wise decision and judged him then as a man of sound reason and unusual sensitivity. And—as to the housekeeper—Sir Robert need look no farther: Mr. Wilkes could enthusiastically and without reservation recommend Auntie Maude as a woman of spotless character and in possession of those capabilities equal to the administration of any ménage, large or small.

"And that is how it all developed," declared Auntie Maude happily. "When Mr. Wilkes arrived in Bayswater with the news, I just packed my bags and left." She giggled. "I did not even give those people notice: just packed my bags and left!"

"What were they like, Auntie Maude—those people?"

Immediately her face closed. "I survived," she said. Nothing more . . .

As daylight faded, the bright glare from two coach

lamps cut through the darkness, bedazzling the intermittent spit of snow that lightly sprayed the rocky road ahead, softening the click of the horses' feet with its gentle cover. Suddenly from atop the carriage sounded the cheery blat of a horn, causing me to rub quickly my gloved hand across the window to clear its filmed pane: I could make out a faint but unmistakable band of lights winking unsteadily in the distance. "A hostelry," I decided, much gratified, for by this time I was ravenous.

We slowed gradually, and once the bridles of the horses were secured by the waiting pikesmen, one on either side, we pulled to a complete stop.

"Whoa," a rough voice called.

"Steady there, lads," cautioned another, "there's hay aplenty in the stable. And from the looks of ye, you're entitled!"

"Aye, they've been travelin' a clip," observed his partner, who then called up to the driver, "Whatever, Charlie, boy? Are ye tryin' hard to fly?"

Escaping through the open door, the welcome haze of woodsmoke and the tantalizing aroma of steak and kidney pie promised warmth and sustenance to the cold and hungry traveler. As we alighted from the carriage I observed with dismay that the nurse was obliged to half-carry her charge from the cab into the way station, seating her then carefully at an unoccupied table. Despite the cajolings and gentle, if insistent, urgings on the part of the nurse that the girl eat, "At least a little something, lovey," the child shook her head in weak but firm refusal, although finally consenting to accept a glass of tea, and that guided by the nurse's patient hand. The man ate hurriedly and alone. The Great Dowager pecked, much as would a bird, at her food, eyeing the tankard of ale placed politely at her elbow as a serious affront.

"This is simple fare," remarked Auntie Maude, "but certainly tasty."

I nodded wholeheartedly. "Nothing whatever like Miller's . . ."

We rode all night. Lulled by the sway of the carriage and the steady rhythm of the pounding hooves, one by one the passengers dropped off to sleep in the dark, close con-

fines of the cab: Auntie Maude snoring gently but with
determination; the man coughing once or twice; the child
whimpering fitfully on occasion, hushed quickly by the
soothing tones of her anxious nurse; and the Great Dowager, again in the manner of a bird, resting with one suspicious eye conspicuously open and wary; while I, snuggling
against the comfortable warmth of Auntie Maude and the
woolen robe, indulged in fantasies of my new life, yet won-
dering, a little sadly, what Ada and Molly might be doing
at that moment . . .

Close on to midnight the quiet sounds exploded into wild
notes blared by the guard's horn as we approached another
hostelry. "Awake, ye bloody buggers!" shouted the guard
good-naturedly.

"Hell! Ye be enough to wake the dead!" protested a
yawning pikesman as he went to gentle the horses.

The carriage door was opened then, and the passengers
advised that they might wish to alight to seek relief in the
accommodations provided and take advantage of the hot
coffee awaiting their pleasure inside.

"I don't know when anything has tasted so good," I declared, sipping from an enormous mug.

"And I, for one, am delighted to feel some sensation returning to my toes," confessed Auntie Maude, stamping
her feet energetically. "I was beginning to think they were
lost to me forever . . ."

. . . Light, filtering unevenly through the misty pane,
shone gently on my eyelids, prodding them awake. I looked
out: moving its soft light over rolling empty ground,
flecked casually with blinking snow crystals, a great golden
disk was lifting itself slowly above the rise of a hill far in
the distance. . . . Dawn . . . The birth of a new day
. . . Dawn . . . The beginning of a new life for me . . .

After a sumptuous breakfast of sausages, herring, and
kidneys, served at a quaint but inelegant inn located in a
tiny village near Exeter, and safely aboard the coach,
which was making extraordinary progress (I overheard the
driver inform our taciturn male passenger), I asked Auntie
Maude, "Whatever does a companion do?"

Auntie Maude remained thoughtful as she gave my
question full consideration before answering. "Why, dear—

accompanies, I should imagine." Her foolish rejoinder sent us promptly into paroxysms of laughter, earning further contempt from the Inimical Presence who sat mouth bunched and eyes snapping. After we had quite collected ourselves, I reflected with some disappointment, "Sir Robert must be rather elderly."

"What makes you say that, dear?" queried Auntie Maude, still wiping her eyes.

"For his wife to ail to such a degree that she has need of a companion."

"I would suspect the contrary," Auntie Maude assured me. "Well," she amended, "I supposed his wife, at any rate, to be young indeed."

"Young?"

"The—er—nature of her—er—disability, after all," she hedged neatly.

"And what is that?"

"She is—er—" Auntie Maude's face became suffused pinkly with painful embarrassment.

"Well?" I prompted.

"She is—ah—well, er—" Auntie Maude confided heroically at last, "well into her—confinement." The last word was whispered.

We were three days into the journey before subtle but definitive changes in the character of the landscape became markedly apparent: The innocent rolling face of the countryside was being refashioned to present a harsher, more sullen countenance. The lazy white feathers of snow had given way long since to a driving, chilling rain. . . . We were nearing the sea . . .

The group of passengers remained intact. At each hostelry or inn visited, I could not help but pray that the little girl and her nurse would disembark there. At the passage of each day on the road I wondered, with increasing concern, whether the child could continue to endure the rigors of such a lengthy journey, taxing the strength of one enjoying the best of health. Daily, it seemed, she noticeably faded. For naught could she be tempted to eat; since the menu was childishly plain and simply prepared, one would have supposed that by now, even ill, she might have acquired the beginnings of appetite. Only a sip of tea, and that hardly substantial. The nurse looked to be reaching the end of her own reserves as well.

Our lone male passenger remained faithful to his bookish pursuits and the Great Dowager to hers: the untiring, almost ritualistic censure of Auntie Maude and me. Although she might be indefatigable, I was not: My body grew stiff and felt acutely the discomfort attendant in the black glacé silk into which I had been all but sewn for the past long weeks, gummy as it was now in its still more soiled state. "I shall be grateful for a change," I admitted.

Auntie Maude's nose wrinkled delicately. "I, too," she agreed vehemently. "I intend to burn—personally—that disreputable rag as soon as we arrive at Wynds."

"Wynds . . ." I mused. "Name comes from Wyndham, naturally."

"I expect so," Auntie Maude replied absently.

"Do you suppose it is so-called for only Wyndham, or because of the actual wind itself?"

"A bit of both, I should suspect," judged Auntie Maude. "Wynds stands, after all, directly on the coast."

"A castle?"

My aunt laughed. "I hardly think so. More likely a manor house."

"Oh."

"But it should prove adequate. Sir Robert is a man of substantial means, or so Mr. Wilkes has led me to believe."

"What is his livelihood?"

"One does not speak of men of his station as having 'livelihoods' as such, dear," Auntie Maude reproved gently.

"He must do something."

"Sir Robert is a landowner . . ."

Rich stands of tall trees proudly lifting empty arms to a glowering winter sky were thinned now to random shrunken gnomes, struggling across a churlish and barren land. A stunted shrublike growth, yield of a stingy soil, bent low, twisted to grotesque shapes by unrelenting winds. . . . We were coming ever nearer the sea. . . .

"One more hostelry," Auntie Maude announced, consulting our itinerary, "and we arrive in Drewsby—there to be met by Sir Robert's personal carriage . . . and then—

home . . ." She sighed happily. "Sir Robert has certainly provided detailed information, as well as a generous allowance for our journey, I must say. . . ."

As the now-familiar blast of the guard's horn rent the air, I looked out: We were fast approaching a village of such diminutive size that it seemed to consist of only a scattering of modest houses flanking either side of a main dirt road, and that narrow to the extreme. . . . Our last way station . . .

"Auntie Maude, what does a landowner do?" I asked suddenly.

"Why, dear," she pondered carefully, "I really couldn't say. . . . Owns land, I guess. . . ."

I laughed aloud.

"Young woman!" snapped the Great Dowager. It was the first time she had addressed me directly. "Young woman, you have conducted yourself in a vulgar, raucous manner since precisely the commencement of this journey. Need I remind you, miss, that the whole of England is plunged into deepest sorrow for the death of her monarch's sovereign prince?" Her eyes scoured my person. "I suggest if you possess sensibilities at all, then they are less than frivolous! You betray yourself a social dullard! Immature! Impudent! A product of vastly inferior tutelage!" Here she glared at Auntie Maude. "Or," continued the woman grandly, "is it due to sheer ignorance that you remain unaware of the great tragedy which has befallen our leader, who lies grieving, inconsolable? Is it that you are unaware of the state of mourning that she, as our anointed Queen, has every right to expect her people, as respectful and loyal subjects, to observe and honor?"

"Why, I never!" bristled an affronted Auntie Maude.

"Madam," I regarded my critic coldly, "I doubt that there is anyone in the whole of England who has not been made more keenly aware of the state of mourning than I." Inwardly seething, I forced my gaze to the window. . . . Oh, if only Ada were here . . . she would put that one to rights fast enough. . . . Ada . . . I sat straight in my seat, suddenly aflutter with excitement. "Auntie Maude, why couldn't Ada and Molly come to work at Wynds?"

"Well." Auntie Maude was doubtful. "I don't know, dear."

"Why not? They are both clever—"

"But, dear, remember we will be as servants here."

"Surely not!"

"Perhaps not yourself," Auntie Maude conceded, "but I am formally engaged in the capacity of housekeeper." Her smile was wry. "A position most certainly categorized as that of servant."

"No more than mine as companion."

"Ah—but you are a blood relation . . ."

"Only faintly so, it seems," I countered hotly. "Besides, you are my aunt."

"Dear—technically your great-aunt—and then only on your father's side—not the Wyndhams'." Cognizant then of my intense disappointment, Auntie Maude offered by way of consolation, "We shall have to see how things go. . . . Perhaps suitable openings will present themselves." She patted my hand, "Best to wait a bit, love. . . . Wait a bit . . ."

We were relieved, thankfully, of the Great Presence at our final way station. With studied hauteur and mounting ire, the Dowager stepped down from the stage, scorning rudely all efforts of the hostelry staff to assist her in her descent, and disappeared into the little inn at which we were to partake of our last refreshment on the road. As usual our male traveler rushed from the carriage in a great flap, anxious to get the nuisance of food over and done so that he might return to his work, I supposed. The others made no move this time to disembark; the little girl lay heavily asleep and the nurse, I presumed, thought better than to disturb her rest.

Close on midafternoon the guard's horn sounded, now with still stronger exuberance, heralding as it did the end of the journey. My heart thumping wildly, I rubbed to clear the glass: The Village of Drewsby spread before my eager eyes. "It is quaint, certainly," I observed aloud, betraying some little disappointment. "But I thought you said, Auntie, that we would be on the coast. I find nothing of the sea here."

"Drewsby is not directly on the sea, dear. Wynds is."

"It seems so tiny after London!" I exclaimed.

"I shouldn't wonder," laughed Auntie Maude.

"I wish we would actually stop so that I could have a real look round."

The coach was halted at last; the horses safely secured; and the carriage door flung open: I alighted. The wind-whipped air, teasing my skirts, was penetrating and raw; suddenly I yearned for the thick woolen rug that had warmed us on the stage. Auntie Maude instructed me to stand and wait for our belongings to be removed from the baggage rack, while she made a few discreet inquiries at a shop that, offering compensation for its unimpressive size, sported an enormous sign affecting the lofty title and accompanying boastful caption: "Mortimer's: All Goods for All Purposes." My aunt was eyed as she bustled importantly away, cautiously by some and with open curiosity by others.

The village was unpretentious, to be sure. A cluster of rustic stores, fronting on the main street, made up the modest commercial area—and these aimed at a rural clientele exclusively. "Cole's" stood as the largest shop and as such enjoyed a prominent location. Mr. Cole, obviously an enlightened, ambitious merchant, displayed his merchandise aggressively and with a flair: In full view were great bins of grain and feed as well as a staggering collection of farm tools and equipment. Ever versatile, the management further claimed facilities for the professional sharpening of saw, plow, and ax, as well as vowing: "Restorations, General and Specific." Through the windows of the only visible dry goods store, I could glimpse the awkward and disheartening exhibition of materials; even at a distance I recognized the fabrics to be sturdy stuffs, drab and serviceable; nothing frivolous there. The blacksmith's shop and attached livery seemed prosperous enough, actually buzzing with activity. An extravagant number of signs attested to the variety of services extended, such as wagon maintenance and harness repair; the availability of drawn vehicles and horses for hire or trade as well as for sale; advertising stock suitable for saddle or plow. A wooden sign depicting a rooster-like form, so crudely carved as to be almost a caricature, swung crookedly and with noisy abandon on rusty hinges directly above the well-worn entrance to what was patently—even at midafternoon—the most popular establishment of the lot: "The Golden Cock, Public House."

This, then, was Drewsby . . .

Thoroughly chilled by now—sufficiently so as to set my teeth achatter, I realized that I was acutely tired—and growing a little cross. Oh, where was that carriage! Auntie Maude reappeared, aglow with a new confidence; in tow, an aged, desiccated man garbed in formal livery, whose manner even from a distance away seemed completely servile: our driver, unmistakably.

The carriage was handsome. Drawn by a perfectly matched team, its interior was upholstered with rich leather of a subtle shade of yellow. Its exterior was painted a pearly gray, flawed only by the faint outline suggesting the Wyndham crest: a raven devouring a mouse. The raven's eye was yellow. . . .

"Ah!" Auntie Maude settled back in complete contentment. "This is like old times!"

"Papa's carriage was not so grand as this," I reminded her.

"Did you ever see such elegance!" Auntie Maude rubbed an appreciative hand across the soft, plump leather. "Why, the horses' coats are the exact gray of the carriage!" Her smile wide, Auntie Maude cocked her head skyward. "Even old Angus up there on the box is handily turned out!"

"I expected, after one look round Drewsby," I giggled, "to be hauled in a feed cart!"

"Hush!" Auntie Maude whispered. "Angus will hear. . . ."

As the carriage pulled away from the more congested mercantile section of the village, it took us past a broad, unblemished stretch of green presided over by a dainty, towered church fashioned of stone the soft color of honey. Juxtaposed on one side, the churchyard, its population of gravestones unassuming, if venerable, was frankly dominated by an ornamented mausoleum rising over all; on the other side was the vicarage, duplicate in miniature of the church itself. The traces of an enchanting garden, now dormant, surrounding the manse remained, dotted picturesquely here and there with a beehive or bench, carved from the same warm stone as the church and house.

"How utterly charming!" sighed Auntie Maude.

We were traveling at a smooth, comfortable pace, permitting a leisurely view of the countryside as we moved along a dirt road, which for all its humble surface was remarkably well maintained and seemingly free of ruts and annoying potholes. A field here, now harsh and withered in the grip of winter's death, betrayed dried evidence of the seed and plow, lying fallow only until the gentle touch of spring and its faithful promise of rebirth; another sprawled intact, preserved as pastureland for lazily grazing sheep or cattle. What trees there were in evidence, shade or fruit, were misshapen, grizzled growths, suggesting a meager yield in either function.

Now and then along the route a cottage, creeper-grown or washed a dazzling white, its thatched roof imitating the brown of the fields, faced the roadway. Close by, its roof topped by a jaunty weathercock, stood the barn, far larger than the cottage it served proudly, hoarding the precious harvest. At more frequent intervals, sprung as if from the soil itself, low, squalid hut-like structures, almost listing in their decrepitude, dirtied the landscape. A frail tendril of smoke, rising hesitantly from a careening clay chimney, gave indication that, despite a state of blatant disrepair, these hovels were inhabited still.

"Do you mean that people actually live in those disreputable shacks!" I remarked, aghast. "They seem in such a desperate state, it is a wonder to me that they even stand—much less provide shelter! Not unlike Merchant Street," I murmured.

"What's that, dear?" Auntie Maude was conspicuously inattentive, preoccupied as she was by the sights on review. . . .

We had driven some miles before I realized that the scenic flavor had begun a marked shift in emphasis. Gone now the homestead, the cultivated field; great tracts of sterile land spread untouched, the lonely expanse challenged weakly by a scattering of stunted trees bowed in timeless resignation or viewed with scorn by random outcroppings of rugged, lifeless rock. Striving vainly to cover all: the sly, rapacious scrub.

"It feels as though we might be climbing," observed Auntie Maude.

We were indeed: The road began to twist and turn across an incline, gradual but perceptible. Overhead, swept aloft to touch the stark backdrop of dusky clouds, a pair of gulls dipped and soared before the wind. "Sea birds!" I exclaimed. "Surely, then, Wynds must be close by!"

The carriage negotiated a sharp turn as the roadway narrowed abruptly, banked now on either side by sprawling masses of jagged rock. "They must have had to chisel their way through," I commented. Suddenly the rock yielded; the passage yawned wide. Before us unfolded a vista that rendered us both speechless: Across an open fen, pierced north and south by two formidable arched gateways, one barred, the other served by a gatehouse resembling a miniature fortress, spread a great castellated wall. Beyond it, in chiaroscuro, its golden stone struck by a single shaft of sunlight escaping the web of clouds, loomed a tower, sovereign over all.

"Oh, my!" Auntie Maude had found her voice.

Chapter 13

After a brief pause at the gatehouse the carriage breezed through an archway and into a courtyard, permitting us then our first glimpse of Wynds: Wrought of the same honey-colored stone as the buffering wall, the house erupted from an outcropping of rocks, rising to great heights on one side and dropping down precipitously on the other three. Down to the sea, I supposed. Massive abutments of undressed stone supported the tower, which upon closer scrutiny proved a more dramatic sight still than when merely etched against the bleak winter sky.

Wynds was magnificent.

"I had no idea!" breathed Auntie Maude.

We came at last to a full stop before the main entrance, itself imposing with its carvings done in vigorous masculine scroll. Assisted by Angus, we alighted then and carefully mounted the stone stairway, penetrating the deep, vaulted entry. Pausing before the nailed door, which was flanked by elaborate stained-glass windows, I reached for the ornate bronze knocker; the door swung open lazily and I stared into a pair of supercilious inquiring eyes. "Yes?"

"Er—ah—" I sent a beseeching sidelong glance in the direction of Auntie Maude; frankly overwhelmed, she did not seem able to return it. Nervously I addressed a tall, spare man who regarded me without interest from the doorway: "Please, er—we are expected . . . I—believe?"

Thin eyebrows lifted delicately before the man coolly stepped aside to let us pass into the great hall. Visible above its height of two storys, the timber roof arched majestically; the walls were rich with panelings of the most exquisite colors imaginable, serving as eloquent background for a sideboard of mammoth proportions that supported with casual ease a pair of branching candelabra fashioned of weighted, filigreed silver. Auntie Maude, plainly overcome by all this splendor, seemed to wander about in an aimless daze, lighting finally in the cozy inglenook before the huge bulk of a fireplace already comfortably ablaze against the chill of a winter's twilight. As she walked her heels sounded a provocative echo on the picturesque encaustic tile.

"May I ask who is calling?" came the indifferent inquiry. Sober uniform faultless; mien subtly insolent—these attested to the lofty status of "butler," shamelessly coveted in any establishment of note.

"Er—I am Miss Knowlton and this is my aunt, on my father's side—Miss—ah—Treadway . . ." To my complete horror I found myself almost gushing. "Sir Robert has engaged—er—"

"Yes," the man drawled, "I am aware of the arrangements."

"Ah—do you suppose—would it be possible to have someone show us to our rooms?" I requested meekly.

"Certainly." His bow was condescending. A command issued by means of the barest inclination of his arrogant head summoned a young girl, who materialized as if by magic. "Yes, Mr. Judd?" She was breathless.

"This is Annie, who will direct you without delay."

Annie's round body bobbed a hasty curtsy and her plump cheeks bulged in a cheery smile. "If you would come this way, miss."

"Come along, Auntie Maude," I prompted over my shoulder.

"I beg pardon, miss," the man called Judd intervened, his manner too polite. "Miss Treadway is to follow me."

I stopped, puzzled. "I-I don't understand."

"Miss Treadway has been engaged to fill the position of housekeeper, if I am not mistaken?"

"Y-yes."

"Then, she will occupy those quarters assigned to that position."

"But," I protested, "Miss Treadway is my—"

"Elizabeth!" Auntie Maude silenced me quickly. "Very well, Judd—"

"*Mr.* Judd," he corrected stiffly.

Auntie Maude bit her lip. "Mr. Judd," she sighed. "If you will be so kind . . ."

With a vague feeling of disloyalty I followed the energetic Annie up the broad, curving staircase to the many-arched balcony, whose screened passage was of a dark wood, ornately carved, along the main upper corridor some little distance before stopping outside what was to be my suite of rooms at Wynds. . . . The suite was demarcated with a gracious sitting room opening onto a modest but airy bedchamber (both rooms overlooking a contained formal garden that could boast in winter only lifeless statuary and an inactive fountain) and beyond to a dressing nook, fitted with an armoire of generous proportions and a washstand invitingly equipped. One complete wall of the alcove was banked with floor-to-ceiling mirrors. The suite in its entirety was pristine: furniture, draped; bed—even floor coverings—were uniformly dressed in a fragile shade of yellow. A welcome fire lent the warm reflections of its variegated flames to the pale blue patterned tile that sparkled on the chimney piece, providing the decor its only contrasting color.

"Is everything all right, miss?" Annie asked, troubled by my silence.

"Positively enchanting!" I said sincerely.

The girl dimpled. "May I unpack for you, then?" She made a move toward my shabby valise, which had somehow preceded me into the room.

I was loath to reveal the threadbare condition of my wardrobe; but to refuse the service would have constituted a breach of etiquette. "That will be f-fine," I lied bravely, and attempted then to draw the girl into idle conversation so as to distract her fullest attention from my pitiful belongings. "Is—Lady—er—" I blurted, not giving an idea what to call my new mistress, "at home?"

"Madam is not seeing anyone, this day."

"But—Lady—er—she is at home?"

"I believe so. Yes, miss."

"Do you suppose I might have audience with—er—Sir Robert, then?"

"Oh, he be away, the now, miss."

"Then—what—"

"I have me orders, miss, to bring your supper to your rooms, this night." At my look of dismay, she amended, "If it be all right, miss . . ."

"Oh, yes," I agreed lamely. "It will be f-fine."

. . . Annie was certainly agreeable enough, I thought to myself as I luxuriated in the tub she had obligingly filled only moments before. I had not experienced a proper bath in a proper tub in two years; I had almost forgotten the utter delectation of it: almost, but not quite. And no skimpy hip-bath this: full-sized; soapy; and steaming! I scrubbed my skin until it tingled and scoured my hair until my scalp stung in protest, splashing all the while with the hilarity of a small, delighted child. At last, when the water had cooled, I climbed out reluctantly and, dripping, enveloped myself in an enormous towel. Suddenly, not remembering that this was to be a moment of personal gratification for Auntie Maude, I seized the black glacé silk from its place of low discard on the floor and heaved it gleefully and with some show of force into the hungry flames. The fireplace sputtered dangerously; objecting further, it gave off a noisome reek that permeated the room with a peculiar dusky haze. "Dear heaven!" I gasped, horrified, quickly flinging wide the windows, "this will never suit on my first day here!" When I had fully aired the room and set it to rights once again, it was with not a moment to spare: Annie was at the door, tapping discreetly, my supper tray held in her chubby hands.

The simple meal was tasty, plentiful, and perfectly prepared: The soup was hot to scald; the breast of chicken tender and succulent; the bread fresh and thickly spread with sweet butter, topped by a generous dollop of wild strawberry jam; finally, a serving of clotted cream, spilling richly over its deep dish. It was a delicious feast . . . I had almost forgotten the feel of heavy silverware—the curve of delicate china against my lip—the texture of fine old damask . . . tangible evidence indeed that this was Wynds and not Miller's. . . . My thoughts strayed to Ada and Molly, and I wondered what they would be doing now and if the incredible rigors of the mourning siege had abated, even somewhat. Yawning, I climbed onto the bed, which was wide and soft (truly indecent after the narrow, unyielding cot supplied at Miller's) and sank my still-damp head into the unresisting reaches of the feather pillow. . . .

Where was Auntie Maude? In her quarters? Where and what were they? Nothing so fine as my accommodations, I was sure. . . . If only I could do something . . . work a miracle for Auntie Maude—for Ada and Molly . . .

If only . . .

I must have fallen asleep immediately; I did not hear Annie when she came to retrieve the tray . . .

Chapter 14

The pungent scent of wood smoke gently nudged me awake; I opened my eyes to find Annie kneeling by the hearth, vigorously prodding the flames. "Good morning, miss," she smiled, "and a glowering morning outside it is!"

I stretched languidly. "I must have slept a week! What time is it, Annie?"

"It be close on to ten of the clock, the now, miss."

"Ten o'clock!" I sat up abruptly. "Oh dear! Whatever will Lady—er—say to my laziness."

Annie shrugged. "Nor can I say, miss, for she has not stirred from her room as yet this day."

"Has—she sent for me?" I asked fearfully.

"No, miss."

"Should I simply knock on her door—or wait until she requests my appearance?"

"Nor can I say for sure, miss."

"Oh—but—" I was disappointed.

Annie chuckled. "It's that anxious to get to work y'are?"

I giggled.

"Meantimes, breakfast be waitin' downstairs—at yer convenience, miss. And later, if wantin', you could roam the house a bit, miss—" She dimpled. "You know, explore, like."

"Can you go with me?"

She laughed, "And sure not, miss! Mr. Judd'd sack me for fair, for lolly gaggin' and wastin' my workin' time!"

"My aunt—Miss Treadway?"

"Been up and about since six of the clock, miss." Annie opened the armoire. "If you please to dress, miss, I can take you to the dinin' hall before I go on with my chores."

My enthusiasm that morning ranged somewhere between those of a healthy lackey and a young field hand; I sampled a little of everything steaming under the aegis of

an assortment of silver chafing dishes lined up on the sideboard, and not until after the initial edge of my appetite
was dulled did I inspect my surroundings, which were—
and not surprisingly—sumptuous. . . . The wood of the
wainscoting, deeply chocolate brown in color, reached from
floor to ceiling, its glowing patina interrupted only by a
handsome, expansive bay window that paraded its unobstructed view of sea and sky almost as would a merchant
peddling his finest wares. The vaulted ceiling was dominated
by a spectacular lachrymose chandelier, which drooped
its graceful droplets of crystal tears over the appreciable
length of the dining table, itself seeming to extend miles and
to be capable of seating, I did not doubt, at least forty in
complete comfort. The strict formality of the room was
spared a possible attitude of desperate gloom by the enormity
of the window's tableau and by the gaily colored floor, which
was worked of yellow, red, and blue scagliola. . . .

After breakfast, then, designating the great hall as arbitrary touchstone, I initiated my trial peregrinations about
the house, which reigned supreme, far exceeding anything
in my experience, even transcending those sentimental recollections of Belgravia, which, while itself splendid, suffered now and again from the awkward ostentation displayed by the nouveau riche. Not so Wynds. Never
Wynds: Here was tradition cherished; heritage revered,
spiced, when indicated, with a yield from the modern
craftsman offering perhaps an advantage in comfort, possibly a concession to convenience. A healthy union of the old
and the new. A lavish showcase? Perhaps. Nonetheless
Wynds, behind its glorious expression, conveyed an attitude
of understated elegance: without dispute, the emblem of
the true aristocrat.

It was, I confess, with a feeling of humility that I undertook my explorations. . . .

. . . beginning with the drawing room . . . whose astonishing dimensions were further dramatized by the characteristic vaulted ceiling and the broad bay window, twin to
that found in the dining hall, opening the outside wall to
permit the panoramic ocean scene, dismal now with the
ominous threat of rain. Although avowedly less cluttered,

the decor here, on superficial examination, might have seemed reminiscent of the house in Leicester Square; closer viewing revealed that the furnishings comprised finer pieces, more gracious for their simplicity and selectivity. I could sense a treatment of lightness and femininity overall, probably due to the floral colors prominent in the floor covering and also to the rather delicate Spitalfields silk with which the room had been hung. . . .

. . . I found the music room to be a delight, juxtaposed to the chapel and almost identical to its religious counterpart in atmosphere with its walls of dark, seasoned paneling; its solitary, narrow, cathedral-like window of exquisite stained glass; and, of course, its vaulted ceiling. No carpeting marred the rich velvet of the floor's old and polished wood. Across the room from the grand piano, which was protected by a tapestry cloth woven in muted earth tones, stood a majestic golden harp; these were the only pieces of furniture in the room.

The chapel was similarly sparsely appointed, save for a smattering of religious artifacts set on a rude raised altar, looking over a few plump red cushions, tasseled in gold, that were strewn in casual readiness on the floor below.

Neither room seemed to be in regular use.

I had not touched a piano in two years. Drawing my fingers gently over the keyboard, I found the instrument to be in perfect tune. I wondered idly who in the family played, and if I would be given permission to do so. I was anxious, suddenly, to have audience with Lady Whoever so that I could determine my status in the household and to identify precisely my privileges and, if any, my constraints. . . .

Unused for so long to any protracted period of aimlessness, I became acutely restive, anxious now for another activity quite apart from poking through the house, grand though it might be. There was too much to absorb at one time; I would have welcomed at this moment a visit to the stables, perhaps the gardens . . . a search for a path to the sea, which I could hear flinging itself crazily against the rocks below; today's inclement weather precluded outdoor exploration. . . . I sighed.

Unaccountably I was hungry again. This was truly ridiculous, considering the enormity of the meal I had consumed not two hours before. . . . Perhaps there would soon sound a gong, summoning me to luncheon. I giggled. . . . Gong indeed! You are not at Miller's, silly, silly girl . . . . Miller's: Molly, Ada. What were they doing now? I experienced suddenly a keen longing for their companionship.

Always about, individually or bustling in numbers, hurried troops from what must have constituted a veritable army of servants: men, women; every age, size, and description. Each in turn nodded courteously, but carefully aloof—as if to discourage an attempt on my part at conversation. I had not glimpsed Annie since she had guided me to the dining hall. Or Auntie Maude . . .

Auntie Maude . . . How did she fare? What were her accommodations? The pangs of my guilt persisted. I was, it seemed, to reside at Wynds, assigned to conspicuously greater comfort and style, as well as to enjoy a position infinitely more prestigious than that of my aunt, although we had both been placed in service. The quarters to which Judd had so pointedly referred must have pertained to the servants' wing of the house. Was I to be treated to trays served in my elaborate suite of rooms, while Auntie Maude was to be relegated to the backstairs?

Lost in thought, I found that I had wandered back into the great hall—actually, into the inglenook, attracted, probably, by the inviting hearth fire. What a charming niche, I thought absently as I looked around. . . . It can't be . . . I wonder, is it? The frieze? The frieze from Leicester Square . . . I looked this way and that. . . . Yes . . . No . . . I really could not be sure from this angle . . . or that . . . I stretched and strained, tiptoed and half-jumped. . . . Yes . . . and then again . . . I dragged a bench forward, climbed up and stared . . . I found myself coloring vividly: carved (and quite plainly) on the bared breast of a sparsely garbed deity was the Wyndham crest—the raven devouring a mouse . . . "But," I murmured softly, "Sir Robert is wrong: This is Aphrodite, not Ceres . . ."

"Is there something you require?" rapped a frozen voice behind me.

Turning sharply, I tottered for a moment before slipping backward and landing directly on the unsuspecting Judd. He eyed me coldly. Next to him, assuming a posture of real suffering, stood my Auntie Maude. "Er—ah—" I grinned foolishly.

"I can see the bench to be impossibly out of line with the other furniture in the room," the butler observed tartly. "I shall remedy the situation forthwith. If you will be so good as to stand back . . ."

I blushed.

Pained, Auntie Maude shook her head helplessly. . . . Overnight, it seemed, her appearance had subtly—but perceptibly—changed. Around her thick waist dangled a ring clogged with keys; they jangled at her slightest movement. On the point of inquiring if she had seen my rooms and when I might, in turn, visit hers, my questions were preempted by Judd's authoritative, "Now, Miss Treadway, shall we continue with our little tour?" His face was stony. "If you please . . ."

They withdrew. Auntie Maude did not look back; it was simply, I think, that she did not dare. . . .

Face still burning, I found the courage to ascertain from a timid maidservant the location of the house library. Her expression doubtful and her manner hesitant, she informed me emphatically that the library was really Sir Robert's personal domain, but she supposed I might avail myself of some reading materials if I were careful to return them promptly and in undamaged condition. "Lor, I don't want no trouble, miss," she pleaded. I took great pains to assure the girl that I was completely trustworthy and even prevailed upon her good nature to lead the way.

The maid proved quite literal in her assessment: The library was, indeed, masculine in flavor—obviously dedicated to the habits and individual preferences of its master. The room was aggressively comfortable, lavish as it was in its assortment of well-seasoned leather chairs and conveniently placed tables, also bearing the casual scars of age. Above the plain chimneypiece (the fireplace itself, wrought of jagged stone) was displayed a generous arsenal of long guns and pistols, horns, and other paraphernalia pertaining to the Hunt. In undisputed dominance, however, stood the book stacks, reaching from floor to ceiling, filled to capacity, and encircling the entire room, breaking briefly for an area of mullioned windows—and that situated well above eye level, so as not to distract the reader with unwanted interruptions from the outside world. . . .

It was perfect.

I discovered the reading material to follow disappointingly the natural inclination of a man's intellectual bias: One glance disclosed an intense interest in biography and history and only a little less devotion to geography and science, leaving my own rather romantic taste in literature sadly unappeased. But I did uncover, to my enormous delight, a complete collection of the works of Mr. Thackeray, who was, in the words of my Auntie Maude: "Hardly appropriate exposure for the delicate female mind . . ."

With my trophy under my arm and a prudent look around the door to see if I were observed by that lady in question, I dashed from the room, clattered through the great hall and up the broad staircase to the sanctuary of my rooms and many hours of illicit, and therefore delicious, reading . . .

My new mistress (Lady Frances, by name—I was so informed by Annie) did not seek my attendance that day. Or the next. Nor did she, it developed, once stir from her own quarters. And since the storm continued of moderate severity and was disposed to linger overlong, I spent most of the daylight hours sprawled before a luxuriously glowing fire, happily absorbed in my inappropriate, jealously guarded novels.

Sir Robert remained in absentia, evidently delayed on some business matter or other. In view of the fact that my appearance at table was not required, my supper was served nightly in my private rooms, courtesy of the industrious Annie. All in all, a highly gratifying arrangement.

Auntie Maude had not approached my suite, nor had I expected her to do so. I imagined that she was still experiencing a rigorous indoctrination period at the finicky hands of Judd. Perhaps I should say Mr. Judd. I made no overtures in her direction; I felt that careless attentions on my part at this time might jeopardize her new position. . . .

And so, basking under a torrid literary sun with Mr. Thackeray and Company, I sought to indulge my own immediate sense of well-being rather than pursue any vague concerns for the welfare of my aging relative. . . .

Chapter 15

Nearly a week passed thus. Annie convinced Sarah, personal maid to Lady Frances, that it was high time I was sent about my duties. "The young miss has now't to occupy her time," Annie had explained. "Aye, there's that," Sarah had agreed. "Have your Miss Knowlton come to Lady Frances's sittin' room at ten of the clock this mornin' . . ."

Annie, realizing that I was nervous contemplating the interview, stayed to help me put the finishing touches to my modest toilet and to conduct me to the location specified. Oddly, the girl seemed to be plagued by a greater sense of anxiety even than I; so excessive was her concern that I be prompt, she all but propelled me down the corridor. My arrival, then, was breathless and accomplished with more than fifteen minutes to spare, providing me additional moments to nurture my already considerable discomfiture but also affording opportunity to assess my surroundings at enforced leisure. The room was softly feminine—demure, actually—with its decor of pink and white furnishings, extending even to the floor cover and a wallpaper patterned in diminutive pink and white floral sprays. It was discreet, pleasant, and cloying.

If I had considered myself discomposed in anticipation of an introductory audience with a new employer, that lady herself was no more convincing. I had been fully prepared for the rather blowsy, inflated aspect traditionally presented by women in her delicate condition; Lady Frances, leaning heavily on Sarah's arm, proved so slight as to be wraithlike, with a pallor more indicative of the last stages of a wasting illness than of a conventional female indisposition. She was young, no older than her mid-twenties. Her hair was of a rich brown color, although immediately somewhat dimmed and dressed only perfunctorily as well as in haste. Stunningly garbed and enjoying the full bloom of good health, hers

might have been a dazzling, provocative presence; a sallow
complexion and ashen lips robbed her face of the dramatic
testimony it deserved, and her gown, deplorably drab and
frankly shapeless, was unbecoming to the extreme. Movements listless, manner so languid as to appear uninterested,
she could have been a somnambulist. Except for her eyes:
They were terrified.

Sarah guided her mistress into a chair; after an awkward
moment I followed suit. The woman clutched her hands in
her lap, willing them, I think, to remain calm; I could see,
even at some little distance, that the nails had been chewed
thoroughly—as far down as to the quick—and that the
flesh surrounding the ends of the fingers was spatulate and
sore. Sitting with downcast eyes, she might have been
asleep, were it not for the betraying sounds of her breathing, which was shallow and rapid, and the restless movement of her hands.

The unbroken silence of the room grew increasingly uncomfortable, and although it could hardly be considered my
obligation to initiate the conversation, I began, "Ah—
Lady—er, Frances . . ." Self-consciously I cleared my
throat. "My name is — Elizabeth Knowlton . . ."

She did not stir.

"I—ah—have been engaged by Sir Robert—"

Her eyes flew open.

"I have been here for several days, now . . ."

She stared.

"I am anxious to commence—er—serving you in—ah—
whatever . . ." My words limped away.

The woman seemed frozen with fright.

"Perhaps," I tried again, "perhaps you would like me
to—read to you . . ." I smiled brightly. "Or I could help
you—dress?"

She shook her head violently. "No!" she whispered.

"Ah—that is, what, then—" I asked helplessly. "What
may I do for you, Lady Frances?"

"N-nothing," she said, her voice low; I had to strain to
hear the words. "N-nothing."

"Ah—surely . . ." This was incredible.

Lady Frances sat gazing fixedly on her uneasy hands.

"I know!" I suggested gaily, "we could take a stroll around the garden—"

She made no sound.

"Perhaps I could bring your trays . . . sit with you while—"

She looked startled.

"My room is delightful!" I became absurdly fulsome then, in an effort to shift the emphasis of the conversation, hoping to reach her instead with aimless chatter. "Lady Frances, it is done completely in pale yellow—the room, that is!" I giggled girlishly. "The walls, furniture . . ."

She shrank back in terror; wild hands grabbed at her throat.

Sarah gasped.

Fearing that Lady Frances was on the point of seizure, I rose quickly.

The woman recoiled, her eyes maniacal with fright.

"Lady Frances—"

"No!" she shrieked, and pitched drunkenly out of the room, an anxious Sarah flying after.

Plainly the interview was over. . . .

My knees buckled and I sat down abruptly. . . . I must, before all else, collect my wits. . . . Whatever was I to do? I had been engaged to perform the service of companion to the mistress of the house, obedient to whatever ministrations constitute the role. I had come prepared to execute my duties exactly as charged. That the lady, however, would have nothing to do with what seemed amiable suggestions was clear; that she would have nothing to do with me was more accurate still. Sir Robert had every right to expect absolute compliance with his instructions; after all, he had gone to some trouble and expense to bring me to Wynds, had he not?

What was I to do? How could I proceed. . . . It had been my cherished hope to earn my own place here, to preclude the pitiable image of the poor relation begging for a kind word from her benefactor, groveling as would a starved stray dog . . .

There was also, I thought suddenly, the destroying possibility that Sir Robert might feel inclined to withdraw his generous provision if I could not provide substantive benefits for payment received. . . . Without his patronage, what was I to do?

The woman must be insane, surely; how else would she act so peculiarly? Could confinement alone account for that sickly aspect . . . justify the lunatic behavior . . . explain her obvious fear? . . . Admittedly I was conspicuously devoid of worldly considerations; I could claim intimate acquaintanceship with only one other similarly afflicted: my beloved Bea, also demonstrating fatigue and despair. But a mutual infirmity and its accompanying malaise was all that could be remotely compared here: Bea had been quite destitute, lacking financial security, family considerations—even a husband; Lady Frances resided in regal estate, attended by a regiment of servants—all under the protection of a wealthy and aristocratic marriage.

Marriage . . . the husband: Sir Robert . . . When would he return? I must wait. Wait for the return to Wynds of its master. Surely, with such a troubled wife, my duties would necessarily be described by Sir Robert himself. Wait, then, I would. I had no other choice.

I felt a keen sense of loss: Until these last disheartening moments my scheme had been to acquit myself handsomely, to prove so valuable an addition to the household that it would not be long before I commanded a position strong enough to request situations for both Molly and Ada.

Molly and Ada . . . How I missed them: Molly's ebullience; Ada's dour wit . . . Even Miller's was included in my new nostalgia . . . its dismal aura, inhuman expectations . . . Mrs. Walsh—that preposterous buffoon, parading up and down the airless room, corseted, expostulating . . . Jenny—fractious . . . Hattie, dreadful . . . Were they ridiculous? No question. But—rational.

Auntie Maude. Perhaps she could offer advice—solace, anyway. I shrugged. I had not held private audience with Auntie Maude at any point since our arrival. In fact I had not caught sight of her save under the aegis of the ubiquitous Judd. Mr. Judd . . .

No. There was no one.

Slowly I walked back to my room, hoping to find Annie there awaiting my return, anxious for a report on the outcome of the interview. All traces of our earlier frenzied preparations had been cleared away; the room was immaculate. Except for a lazy fire making idle overtures toward warmth and light, I was alone. And lonely.

Chapter 16

A shaft of sunlight breaking through the window invaded my gloomy thoughts: Consumed by apprehension before the appointment and frozen in the aftermath of despair following, I had not stopped to realize that the storm had broken at last, and that the sun rose high in a sky whipped free of clouds. A fresh-washed world awaited me. Rummaging through the armoire for my cloak, I observed idly that although it appeared a massive closet on the outside, the actual storage allotment was meager indeed. No matter: My garments were few in number and frankly passé; an overcrowded condition could scarcely work appreciable damage. My cloak, once an extravagant, dramatic piece, was now merely a shabby relic, annoyingly declarative in its fall from glory. Never mind: I was naught but a servant at Wynds, one whose usefulness remained doubtful and projected length of service certainly held in question. Besides, I reflected, my new mistress herself could hardly be dubbed as aspiring to the heights of fashion, judging from her unfortunate costume only this morning. Her near-dishabille indicated either an inherent lack of flair or the discouraging insinuation that social activity here at Wynds was itself deficient. Then, again, the trials of the lady's indisposition may have diminished the energies required for routine grooming as well as lessened its importance.

I escaped the confines of the house through the main door leading from the great hall, soliciting as I did so a thin frown from Judd and a questioning arch to Auntie Maude's frankly worried brow. It seemed that they were ever together, these two: now he was taking great pains to outline some formal procedure or other; self-conscious, Auntie Maude merely fingered her ring of keys. With a quick smile and a breezy greeting I retreated hastily into the crisp December air to find that the storm had playfully splashed the courtyard with random puddles, some of a surprising depth, causing me to lift my skirts high as I walked. Turning finally before the gatehouse, I looked back at Wynds. Only then did I taste its real flavor. Haphazard rivulets of moisture, remnants of the storm, slithered lazily down the tawny stone, capturing a rainbow of color from the winter sun. The castellated wall, seeming modestly to point the way, the tower thrust then arrogantly skyward, defying clouds and the plaguing winds from the sea. Sparking like little jewels, the myriad windowpanes, perhaps emboldened by their number, tossed back the sun's dazzling rays. The sight was breathtaking.

I passed through a small, arched doorway cut through the wall, stepping into an exquisite miniature garden. A tiny statue of Pan stood aloof, intent upon his pipe and none other; an even smaller Narcissus stared obliquely into a now empty fish pond, measuring itself not more than two feet in diameter. *This must be the view from my window,* I thought. Despite a placid pastoral setting the garden pulsed with excitement, as the sounds of the restless sea penetrated deep into the idyllic enclosure. A heavy wooden door set into the far wall creaked slightly, vexed by the teasing wind. It was with difficulty that I lifted the rusted latch; the door protested noisily but gave way with a final sigh. Before my eyes spread a scene of primordial magnificence: far out into the distance reached a coaxing sky; below, colliding against the massive, jagged rocks, a roiling, insistent sea. A lonely gull, pinned against the endless blue, shrieked, its urgent cry lost in the whine of the wind's lament. . . .

The abrupt slamming of the gate, directly at my back, jerked my return to reality. Pray God it had not locked, thus preventing my reentry into the safety of the garden. The sheer drop to the rocks below was staggering in its implications: death, surely . . .

Once secure again within the walls, I sank onto a small marble bench to ease the sudden nervous thudding of my heart.

Another arched doorway led from the main courtyard into the kitchen court with its utilitarian garden, and into the coach house and stables beyond. The familiar equine sights and smells drew me closer: The stalls were roomy and numerous and their occupants spirited, impatient beasts eager to trample the wild, spiny gorse, perhaps, or race the savage waves along a narrow stretch of beach. In sight were three stableboys currying their charges' sleek coats, the touch of their rough, expert hands motions in artistry.

"Damme, if this mare don't need another shoe," one grumbled. "Always throwin' 'em, seems like," he complained. "Means another trek afoot to the village with Spangles, here, to the bloody blacksmith."

"Why can't the lazy bugger come here?" inquired another, his voice indolent.

The first boy sneered, " 'Cause Hartley's too goddamned close-fisted's why."

"Aw," reasoned the second, "Hartley wants Sir Robert to look at he's some kind of big. Save the master a few coppers—it don't matter us works like hell."

"Wa," observed the third, a tall youth, an untidy nest of incredibly yellow hair escaping from his dirt-encrusted cap, "that un's gone stock buyin' with Wade, this day. So's he won't be nosin' round here for a bit."

"Wade!" the first boy snarled, "that barsted! I'd like to peel his arse, I would."

"You'd be a long time at that, I vow," sniggered the second. "Him's built like a ruddy teapot!" he bellowed, slapping his thigh in huge enjoyment.

"Aw," scoffed the first, "him's ain't got that big a pecker!"

"More the fool, you," argued the second. "I seen 'm bulgin' at the wench over yonder servin' the pub." He jerked his head. "An him with that ole hawk on the perch at home!"

"She's worse nor him," growled the first, "always sniffin' round, axin' fool questions—and it ain't even her place, nowise. It be supposed to go to the mistress."

"Aw," the second spat neatly. "That 'un don't do nothin'!"

"Some says she's sick," remarked the tall one.

"Jest so's she don't come smellin' round's all I care," shrugged the first.

"We don't want nothin' from they," offered the second.

"Naw, now us wouldn't get it if us did," agreed the first hotly.

A horse nickering sharply at my approach caused the tall youth to turn abruptly. He colored. "We dint see you, miss."

"Do you suppose I might have a mount today?" I asked.

"Er—I dunno, miss," he demurred.

"I am staying at Wynds," I hastened to explain.

"Yes, miss, but—" His feet shifted uneasily.

I wondered if his hesitation might in great part be due to the fact that I was not properly attired for riding; one, however, does not discuss the propriety of wardrobe with the stable help. "I assure you, it will be all right," I asserted blandly, not sure in the least if my liberties extended to the arbitrary use of the equestrian facilities afforded at Wynds.

The youth was miserable. "Excuse me, miss, for axin'— but—do you know anything of the land abouts?"

"No."

"All's that means is you'll get lost out there." He made a vague, sweeping motion with his hand.

"Then perhaps you could escort me." My smile was bright.

His face flamed. "Ah—I—I guess I can, miss . . ."

The first stableboy tittered.

"Shut up, you." The tall youth mouthed a warning to his fellow.

His name was Ian, and he was to be my constant companion in those early days as I explored this new world, mounted on the back of Smoke, a gentle gelding with mournful eyes, an easy gait, and a coat of cathedral gray. During the time that followed and with Ian as guide I urged Smoke down the rocky, ribboned road to the village, along the narrow strip of beach, up and down hilly meadows—now winter-lean—through shadowy woodlands; dodged the scabrous branches bent low in orchard fields; leapt over foamy, swollen streams; clattered across a wind-scoured moor, parting the furze with pounding hooves. . . .

Sir Robert's holdings, I was to learn, were prodigious—

nay, boundless; Auntie Maude's innocent description of him as landowner was, at best, quite without imagination. Land, extending for miles; prosperous farmhouses; shacks, mean, derelict; barns, spilling the summer's bright yield; plump livestock; the village proper, including stores, church, school—everything was under his domain. Even the bees in the scattered hives, it seemed, buzzed for Sir Robert.

And the people: the runty, degenerate—filthy of dress, profligate of conduct, scurrilous of speech—gathering to 'have their daffies' under the twitching sign of the Golden Cock; the defeated, slouching on the decayed crumbling stoops of decayed crumbling shacks, scanning the horizon with the almost sightless eyes of indifference, the freed, marked only by modest stones in the neat little churchyard . . . they, too, belonged to him. . . .

I soon became aware that Ian differed most perceptibly from the other youths I observed loitering on village streets or idling in front of dilapidated dwellings. Remarkably, he was tall—not typically undersized—and, while lean, did not fall to that underfed aspect so prevalent here; a head of springy yellow hair, ruddy cheeks, and eyes blue as the vinca flower attested to radiant health; and while his manner of address was far from cultured, it was relatively free from the inarticulate guttural sounds of speech lamentably common to his peers. Most notable was his motivating ambition: cynical, outspoken. "I ain't lyin' hereabouts," he confided to me later. "There's more to livin' than wipin' someone else's spills. No," he maintained, "what coppers I gets goes into me sock, against the day I leave here." His soft young mouth thinned. "Not like me da," he muttered.

Suddenly I was mindful of Ada . . .

Ian, the guide, proved proficient and unconsciously charming, as on that first day he conducted me on what I discovered was the accepted tour for the guest of the household, newly arrived. Laughing, I accused him of an unnatural obsession with the moor—stopping frequently as he did to point out this or explain that; I was to learn that he was merely following the prescribed itinerary designed specifically for the recent initiate, including much detailed landmark identification and a lengthy litany of sensible precautions. Contained on the tour also, I suspected, was a

tactful assessment of the visitor's riding prowess; Ian
adroitly managed to put me through a series of subtle
equestrian maneuverings before, openly admiring, he remarked: "You'll do, miss."

I could feel my own cheeks flame.

I could have gone on riding forever, breathing in the
spicy tang of the sea and reveling in the raw freedom of
the barren heath extending its uncivil, grudging welcome.
But the winter sun drops quickly; Ian, reining in, informed
me with a reluctance equal to my own that it was now long
past the hour that we should have returned to Wynds.
"We'll take the shortcut to the main lane," he decided,
casting a look at the rapidly darkening sky. "That'll be
some quicker than goin' back through the furze."

It was not long before we intruded upon land that
showed harsh evidence of the plow and the till and the
cruel scars wrought by the wretched hovels scattered pitifully about. Before one hut, a fine line of smoke, pencil-
thin, ascending at right angles from its tilting chimney,
stood a man, his horned hands resting on an ancient scythe.
His pale face was deeply lined; graying hair escaped a
grimed cap; mouth hung slack; frame hunched, stooped,
eroded by fatigue. As we passed, his eyes—vacant, staring—came alive suddenly: hooded, watchful; unmoving.

Owl's eyes.

Unaccountably, I shivered. Glancing at Ian, I observed
that his face bore no expression. "Let's be off," he said
abruptly and dug the heel of his boot roughly into his
horse's soft piebald flesh.

As we parted company I extracted a pledge from Ian
that he accompany me again the following day, of course
weather permitting. "Wade's permittin's more like it," he
pronounced grimly.

"Wade?" I asked.

"General Overseer, he calls hisself," Ian declared. "More
likely a big farmer with a bigger head and a mouth to
match." I think had I not been there, he would have spat.

Chapter 17

As had been the custom since my arrival at Wynds, I ate a solitary supper in my sitting room before a lively fire. This had become a highlight of my day, actually: a pleasure further heightened by the delicious promise of another unsanctioned romp with the illustrious Miss Becky Sharp, whom I found flagrantly fascinating indeed. The intense heat of the fire transferred itself to my wind-whipped cheeks, so that when Auntie Maude made her belated visit to inspect my rooms, I must have radiated a state of pure euphoria; she smiled in approval at my obviously thriving condition before she dropped wearily into a waiting chair and sighed: "Ah, Elizabeth, it has been a long few days!" Her tired gaze flicked about the room. "This is lovely, dear," she nodded, "lovely."

"The bedroom is beyond and the dressing nook," I explained, "come and have a look—"

"Wait a bit, dear," Auntie Maude begged, "allow me to rest for a moment longer."

"Are your duties that strenuous?" I asked, alarmed.

"No," she hastened to assure me, "it is merely Mr. Judd. He can be a trifle tiresome, you know. But," she added, "my indoctrination period is almost at an end, thank kind Providence! And I shall then be able to proceed on my own with little supervision from him."

"He sounds a demon!" I shuddered.

Auntie Maude leaned back and closed her eyes. "How may I best describe the man," she paused, thinking. Her decision came slowly, "Mr. Judd is faintly reminiscent of Mrs. Walsh."

"Oh, Auntie Maude!" I could not help but laugh.

"He claims no late, lamented husband," she qualified.

"I should hope not!" I tittered.

"*His* credo is: 'The Accepted Wynds Method'."

"What on earth is that?"

" 'Miss Treadway,' " Auntie Maude mimicked, " 'The Accepted Wynds Method suggests that one, for example, count the bed linens, commencing from the bottom of the stack and not the top, as your average lesser household is wont to proceed. You will find, Miss Treadway, that employing The Accepted Wynds Method will prove infinitely more accurate and will diminish that time expended on lowly duties appreciably. Remember, Miss Treadway, The Accepted Wynds Method. At all times. At all chores. In all situations . . .' "

I was giggling helplessly.

"But," she despaired, "I seriously wonder if I shall ever learn the code and master all these keys." She indicated the key ring bulging at her waist. "Here, dear girl, you will find the key to every conceivable room that serves any (even minor) household function: the scullery; the pantry; the meat larder; the game larder; the fish larder; the dairy; the bakery; the brewery; the——"

"Stop!" I pleaded. "What about your living quarters?"

"My quarters . . . they are reasonable, I suppose. Spotless, in accordance with The Accepted Wynds Method. And utilitarian, mostly. I find that my room is squeezed in between the stillroom and the china closet."

"How awful!" I breathed.

"No," my aunt said reasonably, "the location as such is designed merely to insure the safety of the china and cakes, I gather."

"Cakes? You'll be getting fat!" I teased. "When can I come and have a look round?" I asked.

"Sunday. I think that Sunday will be the best day. Mr. Judd will be on leave for a bit to see his ailing sister, I believe it is."

"Good. Then perhaps we can have dinner together," I suggested brightly, "in your room."

"Oh, no!" Auntie Maude demurred. "I doubt it would be prudent, dear."

"Then—why not join me—here."

"Here? Mercy, child," she shook her head vehemently. "I can't think that a suitable arrangement at all."

"Why not? You are my aunt—"

"Not here. Dear Elizabeth, not here." My aunt patted my hand sadly. "Now, tell me about Lady Frances."

"She is dotty," I said promptly.

"Ssh, Elizabeth," Auntie Maude hissed, "someone may hear."

"All right, then, I shall whisper: She is dotty."

"Whatever do you mean?"

"The woman is simply a lunatic. That's all."

"She is not—er—restrained?" Auntie Maude gasped.

"No. But perhaps she should be."

"She is—dangerous?" Auntie was horrified.

"No," I chuckled, and proceeded to outline the peculiar interview with my new employer and its startling termination.

"Perhaps she became suddenly unwell—her condition . . . you know, dear . . ." my aunt ventured delicately.

"I even went so far as to offer to help her dress," I snickered, "just as if I were back at Miller's in the shop."

Auntie Maude suppressed a smile.

"And then I asked if I might at least attend her while she ate!" I laughed. "That made her noticeably uneasy. But," I hooted, "it was my flattering description of my quarters that all but unhinged her and propelled her from the room!"

But Auntie Maude's eyes were wide with concern. Soberly she asked whatever was I going to do, to which I replied airily that I would wait until Sir Robert's return and then receive any and all instructions from him directly.

"Oh, my!"

"I rode out today and plan to do the same, tomorrow—"

"Oh, my!" Taking her leave at last, Auntie Maude turned to me and cautioned solemnly, "Elizabeth, guard your actions well. This is a privileged establishment. And," she added with meaning, "it will not be so easy to find another such. . . ."

After her departure I retrieved my precious contraband (Mr. Thackeray) from his cache behind a stack of dainty satin cushions and became blissfully immersed once again in Miss Sharp's daring escapades. Sleep overtook me early that evening: The day's brisk outing and the contrasting warmth of the hearth had placed an impossible burden on my eyelids. The print dimmed; I closed the book and climbed up into the big feathery bed, snuggling in contentment against the plump pillows. Auntie Maude was right: This was indeed a privileged establishment.

My return to full consciousness was gradual; my acute awareness, abrupt: Someone was whispering my name. Gently. Softly insistent. "Yes?" I called automatically. There was no answer other than my name, repeated over and over. My eyes, wide open now, were drawn to a path of glorious light. It was coming from a far corner of the room. "Elizabeth . . . Elizabeth . . ." The whispering, too, seemed to emanate from, or was a part of, that same rich luminosity. "Elizabeth . . . Elizabeth . . ." Beckoning: "Elizabeth . . ." Enticing: "Elizabeth . . ." Urgent: "Elizabeth . . . Elizabeth . . ." The glow deepened; the path widened. "Elizabeth . . ."

I rose obediently and made my way across the night-chilled floor. My feet, as they touched the gilded strip that spread temptingly before me, were oddly warmed. The lustrous stream spilled down a flight of stone stairs: narrow, winding . . . Compelled, I followed. Down one step and then another until I reached the landing. There I paused. From behind a door standing partially open came unintelligible murmuring sounds . . . Without thinking I gave a gentle nudge; after initial resistance it moved smoothly on its hinges, revealing then a small intimate chamber, heavily draped and washed from floor to ceiling in a wonderful flood of golden light. A man and woman were engaged in earnest conversation, his head cocked slightly to capture each softly uttered word. Involuntarily I caught my breath; before me stood the most strongly handsome man I had ever seen. His features, above a tall and slender figure and framed by thick black hair that curled crisply at the neck, were placed in perfect arrangement: a firm if arrogant chin; sharply angular nose; and, under roguish, mocking brows, eyes fiercely dark, yielding now to the woman almost in his arms. He was carelessly attired in a lounging coat of royal crimson velvet, matching precisely the drape of her own sleeve resting on his as she laid her hand with gentle grace on his arm. Her gown, cut low, allowed the milky tones of her skin to radiate the warm light that pervaded the room. Her hair flowed unrestrained to her waist: a shimmering golden cloud. I was not able to see her face, which was turned away from me.

The few distinguishable words that passed between them were honeyed, caressing . . . "Sweet . . . Love . . ." The woman's hand traveled from his arm to trace tenderly the line of his chin; he imprisoned it playfully in his own and she protested against his affectionate teasing with a low, sensual chuckle. "Come," he said, threading her arm through his as if to draw her from the room, "come . . ."

She laughed softly, then moved provocatively in his embrace. As she turned I saw her face.

It was mine . . .

Transfixed, I stared, watching them withdraw, becoming aware at last that the golden glow, too, had faded from the chamber, leaving only the path that illuminated the curving staircase . . . As a witless marionette, one foot tracking the other, up, up, upward and into my room, mechanically I crossed the cold floor, clambered onto the high broad bed and settled the quilted coverlet around my quaking shoulders. . . . Without conscious volition my eyes were pulled to the corner of the room, seeking again that glorious golden path: The light had fled; I was in darkness again.

Benumbed, I retreated into the farthest recesses of the bed to comfort my limbs and still their wild trembling and to conceal from view my cheeks, scorched as they were from unknown fires. Shame? Guilt? Or some illusory untried yearning unleashed within me? My body rocked in the harsh grip of a raging, relentless fever: parched; coldly, wetly chilled; waxing, waning . . . Helpless . . . Behind closed lids flamed the image of that handsome face . . . Attentive ears strained for his words, caressing . . . coaxing . . . My body reveled in his nearness—in our almost embrace . . .

Towards dawn, I slept, awakening finally to find full sunlight invading my room; it was late in the morning indeed. I stretched languidly, then remembered . . . Dream . . . The dream . . . If in fact it had been a dream . . . My eyes flew to the corner of the room, now innocent, coolly indifferent, betraying no sign of the elusive beckoning path . . .

Annie found me on my hands and knees, deeply absorbed in poking and prodding, tapping a wall here, the floor there. "Whatever are you up to, miss?" she asked more in surprise than actual curiosity.

"Annie," I asked, "was there ever a door here?"

"A door?"

"Yes. Here. In this corner."

"No, miss, not that I can remember."

"No secret paneling—no hidden latch. Nothing of that nature?"

"No, miss," the girl giggled, "that be kinda silly, like. Besides," she reasoned, "where could a door go to—there's nowt out that corner but a great drop to the garden."

"I suppose you are right," I said uncertainly.

"Come along with ye," she scolded, "traipsin' round the room in your nightdress only, and it near to freezing outside!" She took my elbow. "I've brought your breakfast, seein's how you're too late for the dinin' room."

My eyebrows flew.

"Ten past eleven, 'tis."

"Lady Frances has summoned me?" I cried.

"No, miss."

"Not that I think she will," I murmured. "Annie," I began carefully. "Lady Frances . . ."

"What did ye say, miss?" The girl avoided my eyes.

"Lady Frances—what is she like?"

"Don't be askin' me to tell no tales of the mistress, miss," she reproved stiffly.

I blushed. "No, of course not. Forgive me."

"Best eat up whilst it be hot." Annie withdrew quickly.

Even while I ate, my eyes were drawn to the corner of the room. Could Annie be right? Was there no secret passage hollowed there—no false panel, masking a sharply curving staircase? Where then had I been? What had I seen? Was I still simply in the grip of a particularly vivid dream? Ensnared in its lingering web long after full restoration of a conscious state?

Had I been sleepwalking? Although somnambulism had never before been one of my peculiarities, this was no as-the idiosyncrasy could not develop at any time. woman: face identical to my own . . . What urely such precise resemblance alone suggested a essence: Were not in dreams identities routinely confused, even plagiarized, so as not to be remotely reconcilable to the world as it really exists?

But what of—him? My cheeks burned in remembrance . . . Easily explained. Were not flights of fantasy commonplace in the febrile longings of young and untouched womanhood? . . .

I could have reached out and touched them both; yet neither seemed to know that I was there . . .

Perhaps Auntie Maude had been wise, after all, to forbid the introduction of Becky Sharp et al into my innocent experience. Perhaps Mr. Thackeray had nudged me toward a precipice born of fancy that was ill-conceived in taste and attitude. Nonsense, I told myself flatly: There were no concealed stairways, no secret panels, no gimmickry in that gentleman's writings. No. This was a dream. Remarkably lifelike and disturbing, unquestionably. But a dream nonetheless . . .

Foolishness, at any rate, to be put aside promptly on this day that had dawned bright and sunny, perfect for another outing, courtesy of Smoke and Ian; a fine morning to explore my new environs . . . not one to waste dwelling on the absurdities of a girlish reverie . . .

Chapter 18

It was apparent that Ian had been waiting for me with some impatience; although too well trained to express overt disappointment at the lateness of my arrival, he made an elaborate show of scanning the sky to assess the position of the sun. "We'd best get a move on," he announced, "if us is to see somethin'."

We trotted along at a companionable pace, teased by capricious gusting winds that slapped deliciously at our cheeks. "Oh," I sighed, "this is heavenly!"

"Aye, looks all right, I guess," Ian acknowledged dourly.

"How can you bear to leave all this someday?"

"All what?"

"This beautiful country!"

"Oh, I can bear it, seems so . . ."

"But—why?"

"Ain't no future here," he said flatly. "Me was licked afore I was ever birthed!"

"Surely not!"

"Hell, miss. I ain't no farmer's son!" His voice grew harsh. "Sure, if my name was Wade 'stead of Childer, I'd be ridin' some higher nor this. . . ."

"Wade—he's the bailiff, overseer," I prompted.

He nodded. "Him's got the best farm hereabouts—well as to go runnin' to Sir Robert on every other thing."

"What of this Wade—"

"I hate the air the bugger breathes," Ian snarled. "But he's climbin' bigger mountains nor the rest of us," he added grudgingly.

"Is Wade the only farmer?"

"Naw. There's a good dozen in Drewsby asides of him. They ain't fallin' short neither," Ian pronounced bitterly. "And if I was Ditman, or Schneider, Whitfield . . . Hell, I'd be doin' some better'n I am now."

"You don't like stable work?"

ed. "It be a wage, leastwise." The youth thrust
defiantly. "But I ain't rottin' in no horse's stall
. No, ma'am! Nowise! Not me!"

, then," I suggested brightly, "why not invest your
earnings in a piece of land and start your own farm."

Ian's laugh was sharp, disagreeable. "Like I said, miss,
me was finished here afore I was birthed. . . . Farms is
handed down. Ain't no other way. And like I said, I got the
wrong name. " 'Sides"—he looked around—"can't buy
none of this land, leastwise. It don't even belong to them
farmers. Land's all Sir Robert's. Hell," he snorted, "them
farmers is so high and mighty! Them's jest foolin' on livin'
theirselves, s'all's I can see!"

"Sir Robert leases the land to the farmers, then?"

"Every speck on it."

"And the houses, too—and the barns . . ."

"Every stick."

"Those shacks up ahead?"

"Them, too. Although they ain't much." His tone was
sour.

"Do people really live in them?"

"Seems so."

"Who?"

"Them poor buggers what works for the farmers." His
mouth grew hard. "Them's not so much as the dropped
pies lyin' flat in the fields." He sneered. "Nor even the fly
what sits on 'em . . ."

The sun's rays were dimming rapidly now. Ian drew
rein, signaling that we should turn our horses and head
back for Wynds, as night was fast approaching. "Us had
better take the main route," he decided, "it be quicker and
surer."

Pulling away now from the cultivated fields and heading
into the vast reach of untouched fen that led up to Wynds
proper, we passed once again the listing hut before which a
man stood, knotted hands kneading an aged scythe. Once
again vacant, staring eyes sprang to life: wary, fixed. Owl's
eyes. Again Ian ruthlessly urged his mount forward; again
I shivered.

Clattering finally into the courtyard, we came upon a
brindle gelding tethered to a ringed post stationed just out-

side the main entrance. I looked questioningly at Ian, who shrugged. "Ain't none of our'n."

At that moment, with a flourish more elaborate and a sense of ceremony I had not deemed possible, Judd ushered from the deep confines of the entryway and out onto the stone steps a young man carrying a small black leather satchel. Beside me Ian murmured, "Doctor," and touched his cap.

"Doctor?" I looked from Ian to the young man. "Is someone ill?" I asked, dismounting immediately.

Judd glowered.

"Ill? No," the doctor replied. He regarded me steadily. "Who, may I ask—"

"Ah." I blushed. "I am Elizabeth Knowlton, companion to Lady Frances."

Skeptical eyebrows rose.

Judd scowled.

"Recently arrived," I swallowed.

"Mine was merely a routine visit," the doctor declared decisively, "in accordance with Sir Robert's instruction while he is himself absent from the hall."

"I am glad that she is not unwell, Doctor—" I finished lamely.

"Briggs. Jonathan Briggs." The doctor turned then to Judd and announced peremptorily, "That will be all, my good man. I shall have no need of further attention."

Quite without thinking I smirked; my expression was, unfortunately, not lost on Judd. "Yes, sir." The butler bowed stiffly, flicked an angry glance in my direction, and withdrew.

Ignoring the impatient nickering of his waiting horse, Dr. Briggs, stride long, approached me. I had a clear view now of dusty hair, a shade lighter than the rakish brows that jutted out over hazel eyes flecked with green chips; a mouth lifting sardonically; and a nose that might have been broken at one time, so irregular was its disposition. Of greater than moderate height and solid in build, his entire aspect was more that of a cocky sportsman than a dedicated physician. "Lady Frances did not speak of you," he declared without preamble. "I wonder that she did not confide that Sir Robert had engaged someone in her behalf."

impression," I began and stopped, recalling
embarrassment Annie's cold disapproval only
     ng at the hint of criticism as regards her mis-

impression of what, pray," he pursued with some
insistence.

"That—well—"

"Come, come, Miss Knowlton. Let us not mince about,
the shy schoolgirl around me, for pity's sake. I am Lady
Frances's formal physician, after all, not a traveling medicine man."

"I—sensed that she wished no part of me."

"When was this?"

"In our first—and only—audience." Ashamed, I lowered my gaze.

"Were you rude, or forward?"

"N-no."

"Did you venture indiscreet commentary on her appearance?"

"N-no."

"Imply an investigatory interest in her pregnancy?"

I gasped, "No!"

"Express exaggerated sympathy for her impaired
health?"

"Of course not!"

"Attempt to pry information concerning her personal relationship with her husband?"

"Certainly not!"

"Did you speak in tones as shrill as those you are currently employing?"

"Why!"

"There is no need for a display of temper, Miss Knowlton," the overbearing Dr. Briggs remarked with a condescension I found infuriating. "Lady Frances is patently under some severe strain that I cannot fully comprehend,
myself. She is, I observe, inordinately sensitive to anything
that is loud, or harsh."

I bridled. "I am hardly that—Doctor!"

"Nor did I imply that you were—Miss Knowlton."

I moved away, about to withdraw, when I was stopped
by the doctor's officious: "Miss Knowlton! In your position

of companion"—he made the term itself questionable—"I am presuming that you intend to report to me any and all observations or reflections relevant to my patient's feelings of unease. . . ."

My words squeezed themselves through a clamped jaw: "To be sure, Doctor . . . Although, since Lady Frances's infirmity and its accompanying peculiarities are admittedly far beyond the reach of even your profound scope of professional understanding, I can hardly be expected to advance information valuable in, or even pertinent to, your learned diagnosis . . . If you will be good enough to excuse me now . . ." Head high, I turned, prepared to flounce away with an insouciance the equal of any sovereign liege, only to be so unnerved by both this caustic oaf and my own unprecedented outburst that my heel caught in the trailing hem of my skirt: I stumbled and fell onto the hard, cold cobblestones.

The echo of his loud laughter resounded in the enclosed courtyard. In a fury I glanced back. Dr. Briggs was almost beside himself, slapping his thigh in unabashed enjoyment. "My God!" he roared, completely delighted. "That was magnificent!"

"Help me up," I yelped. The unmitigated boor! As he pulled me to my feet I began to giggle helplessly.

"Are you hurt?" he managed finally.

"No. I don't think so."

"You say that you arrived only recently?"

I nodded.

"Then I feel obligated to show you the sights. I shall be at Wynds at precisely ten o'clock tomorrow morning, mounted on Satin. Alert the stable to prepare the nag you rode up on this evening." Digging into a vest pocket, he extracted a watch at which he glanced, frowning. "Damn! I am already overdue. Mrs. Tufty's seventh is expected. And, I am told, that little woman is never late!" I watched as he swung into the saddle with easy grace and galloped off into the night.

"Officious lout!" I muttered, laughing. I turned then to thank Ian; he was gone.

My solitary supper served before a warming fire was enlivened with what seemed now an almost ritualistic visit by the conniving Miss Sharp, who, well-named, proffered an endless storehouse of clever manipulations and maneuverings. My overwhelming drowsiness then was induced not by any lack of imaginative pursuits on the part of my mischievous literary companion, or by a waning interest on mine; it was simply a natural extension to hours in the saddle, buffeted by a winter's capricious wind. Undressing, my thoughts traveled lazily over the events of the day: the ride out with Ian, restless discontent; and later, the bombastic interview with the redoubtable Dr. Briggs. I giggled to myself: the man was incredible! I crawled between the smooth sheets, grateful for Annie's thoughtful contribution of a hot brick, and closed my eyes almost warily, in both anticipation and dread.

I should not have been troubled: I did not have the dream that night.

Chapter 19

Dr. Briggs was pointedly pacing as I came upon him in the courtyard the morning following. He had one eye cocked skyward and another at Ian, who was making the final adjustments to the stirrups that dangled limply from Smoke's saddle. I threw them each a cheery greeting, although Ian, seeming in a sullen humor, merely touched his cap politely and in perfunctory response. He was silent as he helped me mount, then disappeared abruptly through the arched passway leading to the stables.

"Now, then," announced Dr. Briggs almost at once in a manner as jaunty as the variegated feather jabbed in his tweed cap. "I have concluded that our first port of call should be the coast at Wynds—a masterful sight, that—from there a trot to the village for a look round; finally, a visit to the Wayside Inn for a spot of luncheon."

"Sounds delightful," I agreed instantly.

"Wayside Inn," he mused. "Devil of a name for the place! All inns have to be at the side of some way or other!"

The sea put on a fine show of color and rhythm, and the white-winged gulls, not to be outdone, dipped and soared in a frenzy of their own, snared, then released, by the eddies of a keening wind. . . .

The doctor avoided the moor, and we traced the main road to the village, passing as we did so the listing hut and the man leaning on the handle of his weathered scythe, staring with his owl's eyes . . .

Leisurely we poked around the village, dismounting now and again to enter a shop. Martin's provided particular fascination: There seemed to be no end to the variety of merchandise offered by that place of business and its enterprising proprietor, who remained in fawning evidence at all times. Miss Fannie's, as the fabric shop was named, proved less interesting, and I was disappointed to find my original assessment entirely correct: The goods there were of serviceable and sturdy quality, only harsh to the touch and incurably drab to the eye—and, judging from Miss Fannie's own dowdy aspect, she believed in what she sold. . . .

The inn offered an establishment dedicated to the cultivation of a quaint atmosphere rather than an outstanding cuisine. The food, while plain, nonetheless seemed wholesome enough, and I found myself eating with almost as much gusto as the good doctor, who frankly relished it. "May not win a contest," he admitted freely, smacking his lips, "but damned reviving those times you're forced to get by with little or no sleep."

"You mean, last night?"

He nodded.

"The baby!" I remembered. "Was it on time and what did it turn out to be?"

"Yes . . . A boy . . . stillborn."

"Oh, dear."

"Not to fret," he advised blandly. "Mrs. Tufty isn't. Actually relieved there's not still another mouth to feed. Besides," he sighed heavily, "there will be a replacement along next year, about this same time. I hear that the little lady is as regular as the seasons."

"Why don't—" I began, and blushed.

"Ignorance, my dear. Simple, straightforward ignorance. You can hardly expect more . . ." He leaned across the table. "Look, you've seen the people cringing about the village here? Laborers. Poor scum hired out to work the farmers' fields. And a meaner crowd you'll not encounter. Poor damned fools!" He shook his head sadly. "Their young are a brutish lot: drunken, lying. Foulmouthed louts . . . And the girls fare no better—a degenerate bunch. All of 'em muck about, mouthing like a pack of aborigines. By the time they reach middle life half of them wish they were dead; the other half are too stupified to know enough to care."

"Sounds like Bethnal Green," I murmured. "Why can't something be done?"

He shrugged. "It's the system. Starts at the top."

I looked at the doctor with questioning eyes.

"The squire. In this case, Sir Robert."

"Sir Robert treats the people badly?" I asked, shocked.

"I think not consciously. But like every squire before him, he avoids all possible contact with them. The theory being, I suppose, if he doesn't see pain, it can't touch him. No," Dr. Briggs said, "the squire deals directly with the farmers—and a less sympathetic breed does not walk, I am afraid . . . Even flick the whip, I hear."

I flamed, "Do you mean to say that Sir Robert does not know, or care, that the laborers are being maltreated by the farmers?"

"Who knows? Perhaps he does. I suspect, more likely, that if the farmer is prompt in his rents and pays proper tribute, Sir Robert simply goes about enjoying his own life and pursuing his own interests."

"This is barbarous!" I cried hotly.

"No doubt about it," the doctor agreed. "A pure caste system down the line. . . . The squire rules a veritable dominion, you know. His holdings contain vast tracts of land—even whole villages and everything in them. The arable land and the farms he leases to the tenants (the farmers), who in turn pay rent for their use and hand over a tidy obligation, besides, to their landlord. The farms themselves can be fairly sizable—so extensive that they cannot be operated by one man or one family. The farmers then hire laborers to do the actual work for them. Standing over their drudges with whips and sticks, the farmers exploit unmercifully, prodding them into early graves. . . . The laborers, ignorant, defeated, accept their role in this established order of things, dying sooner or later from overwork and an exhausted spirit."

"Aren't the laborers provided any schooling?"

"Oh, there's a schoolhouse," Dr. Briggs sneered, "and a schoolmaster, Lineas Stafford—an incorrigible tosspot, drowning in his own miseries."

"It is no wonder that Ian can't wait to leave," I thought aloud.

"The stable hand?" the doctor asked. "Godspeed to him, I say!"

"Do you know of a farmer named Wade?"

"Cyrus Wade?" he nodded. "Often wondered why someone hadn't slipped a knife in him years ago."

"Doctor!"

"Forgive me, Miss Knowlton. I have grown callous since I have been here. M'dear," he advised suddenly, "don't be too hard on Sir Robert. No squire is anxious to relinquish his birthright, after all, and I can't say I blame him." His bushy eyebrows rose in an expression of confounded irony. "No. Don't judge him too harshly. The laborers don't. In fact they have a kind of long-standing reverence for the gentry, which I find amazing, myself. They think that people who make money from 'trade'—for example—don't know how to behave. That they're vulgar, low class." He shook his head. "They stand in tremendous awe of Sir Robert. Even love him."

On the way back to Wynds, Dr. Briggs announced in his inimitable preemptive manner that he would come by on Sunday morning at precisely ten thirty in order to escort me to church. "I shall bring the trap, Miss Knowlton, so that you may dress appropriately."

"But—"

"You do attend religious services, Miss Knowlton?" he inquired superciliously.

"Doesn't everyone?" I countered coldly.

"In that case, since you are no stranger to the hallowed hall, it would behoove you to take advantage of the opportunity offered here by Drewsby's village temple, the Anglican Church, presided over by the Reverend Archibald J. Smythe."

"Really!"

"Not that I find you in need of immediate salvation, Miss Knowlton." It seemed to me that the doctor was being deliberately patronizing. "However, the Reverend and his good wife, Abigail, are a couple offering congeniality and shelter to all who are new and friendless here."

"You presume too much, Doctor," I bristled.

"Perhaps so," he conceded coolly. "Nevertheless, they attended me nicely when I arrived in Drewsby last year; I thought they might serve you much in the same way."

I had the grace to blush.

"And they have a daughter, Caroline—about your age—who might provide you with some suitable female companionship."

"I do have a position of employment, Doctor," I said with some asperity.

"Now, that," he chuckled broadly, "does not seem to be inclusively time-consuming, does it?"

A sharp chill was needling the air, and gray clouds folded over the horizon. A few tentative snowflakes fluttered downward; one, I noticed, lighted at a rakish angle on Dr. Briggs's jutting feather before continuing its earthbound flight. "Looks like we may be in for it," he remarked, "we should get a move on. I'd challenge you to a race, but with that sidesaddle nonsense you women affect, there would be no contest." I noticed—with a grudging respect—that Dr. Briggs sat a horse exceedingly well; his form was almost as effortless as that of Ian, whose lithe body seemed to mold itself to his mount's as the most natural thing in the world.

"Doctor," I said, "you have lived in Drewsby only a year?"

"Subtract a month and a handful of days and you'd be right." He laughed, "Took over the practice for the aged Dr. Mondale. Peppery old grouch. Miserable. Was sent here to assist him, actually. Slippery devil was so relieved to be delivered of his responsibilities, he shut his eyes for good—and mostly in spite, I have no doubt—a week after my arrival. No," he confessed, "I originate from that sinkhole Liverpool."

"Then you haven't known Lady Frances for long."

"No."

"Was she—er—like this—when you first met her?"

"Hmm." He took a careful moment to respond. "I would not say that her frail aspect was as aggravated then as it is at present." He rubbed his chin in concentration. "No," he decided. "No. But mealy. Even then, mealy . . . Don't like my women mealy," he declared. . . .

I headed straight for the stable yard so that Smoke might be attended promptly. "Oh, dear, I hope this snowfall does not mean that we must forgo our ride tomorrow." I mentioned my concerns to Ian as he helped me dismount.

"Naw." His smile was confident and I watched as a web of fine lines crinkled his blue eyes. "Naw. This be a saltin' s'all, miss. Ain't to fret none . . ."

Almost immediately after Annie had removed my supper tray, Miss Sharp and I went our separate ways; my eyes drooped as if drugged, from all the air and exercise. Before climbing up into the bed, however, I parted the window drapes and scanned the night sky: A moon was drifting lazily between thinning clouds; the snow had stopped altogether. I smiled: Ian and I would have that ride tomorrow. . . .

"Elizabeth . . . Elizabeth . . ." I sat up, immediately awake. "Elizabeth . . . Elizabeth . . ." My eyes flew to the corner of the room. It was there: the golden path. "Elizabeth . . . Elizabeth . . ."

I must confess to a disgraceful eagerness, which propelled me down the curving stairs before I hesitated for a moment at the landing. As before, the door stood ajar. And, as before, I nudged it open: They were there. He was smiling, one hand encircling her tiny waist, the other loosely winding a wayward lock of her lustrous hair around a square tanned forefinger. "Like spun gold . . ." His voice was a caress . . . Languidly she slid her arms up to his head and drew it down to meet her own. They kissed, long and deeply. "Come . . ." he whispered finally. "Do you think I should?" her laugh was throaty, seductive . . . "Yes. I think you should," he breathed. She moved parted lips against his. Again they kissed. "Come . . ." he murmured. Clinging thus, they withdrew . . . Slowly the light faded . . . I was alone. . . .

Wound spring-tight, curled in the bed's wrinkled sheets, I trembled, burned with shame: shame for what I had seen; shame for the wanton longings released within me . . . I slept at last, fitfully, my dreams invaded by wild imaginings; my body assailed by strange, fierce sensations . . .

Chapter 20

Sunday morning, at precisely ten thirty, the loud arrival of
Dr. Briggs was heralded: The wheels of his trap ground
harshly against the grit on the cobblestones, and his lusty
voice boomed imperiously its orders to the horse to halt at
the main entrance. Moments later the peace of the courtyard was totally shattered by the din of the great bronze
knocker as it was slapped roughly against the nailed door,
accompanied by Dr. Briggs's ringing, authoritative tones as
he requested—demanded—Miss Knowlton's immediate attendance. A youthful footman was frankly cowed by the
doctor's preposterous performance but managed to mumble
something barely coherent and raced off for aid and comfort from Auntie Maude, who, fortunately, lurked near the
inglenook. It was with luck that she was amused rather
than affronted by the doctor's exhibition and somehow
summoned me through a relay of messages delivered by
one servant to then another. The procedure was not as long
as my telling implies; to Dr. Briggs the delay must have
seemed interminable. By the time I glided down the broad
stairs to join him, his facial expression managed to communicate eloquently an uncharitable assessment of my appearance; displeasure at my tardiness; and unflattering evalua-
tion of my general character. Adjusting his frock coat with
some ceremony, he extended his arm with stiff reluctance
and announced ungraciously, "If you feel that you are
ready at last, Miss Knowlton, we may proceed."

Certainly far from the luxurious vehicle provided by the
establishment at Wynds, the trap was nonetheless comfortable—even cozy, if somewhat threadbare. Pulled from the
material near the interior door handles, a few longish
strands of fraying material hung loosely. "Don't trouble
them," Dr. Briggs warned curtly, "else there will be a hole
as big as a woman's mouth."

I ignored the obvious barb and inquired conversationally,
"How long before we reach the church?"

"We shall, of course, be late."

"A fine sunny day," I observed, choosing to ignore his
sour mood.

"It was."

"One might think it spring," I babbled.

"Hardly that."

Suddenly the horse stumbled, throwing me against the
door of the trap. Dr. Briggs moved quickly; in no time I
was drawn back to safety and settled firmly on the seat.
The brief struggle, however, caused my bonnet to slip side-
ways and dangle drunkenly over one eye. The passing look
of concern occupying his hazel eyes was replaced immediately by one of boisterous high humor. I giggled. We were
friends again. . . .

All eyes of Drewsby were fastened on me as I entered
the tiny church that morning. I wished then that my meager wardrobe had been more liberally equipped, fresher anyway. Dr. Briggs, sensing my fading composure, held my
arm in a companionable grip so firm as to be almost vise-
like. While his support was well-intentioned, he came close
in fact to stopping my circulation altogether.

The pews were short in length and ungenerously spaced.
Dr. Briggs selected one at random, ushered me in politely,
and entered the enclosure with considerable difficulty before he himself could sit, knees bunched impossibly against
the back of the seat ahead. I looked around. Subtle lines of
demarcation effectively separated the assembly: Those
members garbed with taste and at some expense (if not
always with creditable style) congregated pointedly together; others neatly threadbare sought their own modest
kind; the rest, avowed slovens, gravitated toward the rear
of the nave where, dispirited, they slouched, evincing little
or no interest in the general proceedings. Even from the
back of the church I could feel their quiet hostility; it was
almost a physical force.

I had gathered sufficient knowledge of the social opera-
tion in Drewsby to apportion the congregation into implied
categories: the affluent farmer; the penurious laborer, not

as yet entirely demoralized; the latter's immediate colleague, irreversibly destroyed.

It was difficult if not impossible to feign an attitude of
disinterest, abjuring all normal curiosity in the scene
spreading before my eyes; I was, in fact, openly staring,
when my vision fastened directly on the squat figure of a
man strutting ostentatiously up the center aisle. An air of
flaunted self-importance, accentuated by an exaggerated
mode of dress, identified his classification easily as that of
farmer, newly successful. Porcine, his body supported a
fleshy, glabrous head hosting a flabby face that seemed
oddly continuous, scored only and dramatically by a
straight bar of shiny black eyebrows. Small hands clutching
a hat (correctly formal and somber) were fitted with
stubby fingers; feet, similarly structured, seemed inade-
quate to their heroic load. With a forced smile Dr. Briggs
acknowledged the man's elaborate greeting, which was distracted by an attentive eye moving over my person. I was
compelled to restrain myself until the man had passed before daring to nudge my companion and ask the stranger's
identity.

"Wade," supplied Dr. Briggs.

I watched with amusement as Mr. Wade struggled to
settle himself in the stingy space allotted in the pew, further hindered by the magnitude of his wife, who shared the
limited enclosure as well as his attitude of self-
satisfaction. . . .

The church proper was simple in architecture, modest of
fittings—effective, actually, in its severity. The honey-
colored stone of the nave was relieved only by stained-glass
windows, which were of a rough, almost primitive, flavor,
and the carvings gracing the altar and chancel were intermittent and chaste, offering an elemental beauty of their
own. The seat cushions, as well as those provided for kneeling, were more elegant: a royal crimson velvet. For an uncomfortable moment I was mindful of my dream. . . .

Suddenly a hemorrhage of raw notes from an organ
sadly out of tune bled me of my reverie and I glanced
about, confident that this outburst signaled the entrance of
our vicar. Black robes flapping, arms threshing, hands al-

most pawing the empty air, in strode the desiccated figure of the Reverend Archibald J. Smythe. Stopping directly before the altar—his mien earnest, scholarly, his scrawny shoulders rounded, head leonine—the Reverend massaged his predatory nose with a thoughtful, scabrous finger and stared down at his congregation as if to grip them in the magnetic thralldom of deepest religiosity—an astounding feat, actually: Rather than peering out from the theatrical hollows of the ascetic, the Reverend's eyes instead bulged incongruously.

I suppressed a giggle.

"What is it, Miss Knowlton?" whispered Dr. Briggs.

"His eyes are very like those of—a Pekingese dog . . ."

Dr. Briggs remained silent for a moment, then leaned closer. "Overactive thyroid."

An exquisite sense of timing served the Reverend well: it was not long before his intense gaze had thoroughly raked the room and he had cleared his throat with significant emphasis, that he permitted his surprisingly deep and sonorous voice to ring throughout the hall. "My children," he began softly, almost hesitantly, "my children, I see your dear faces upturned before me." He smiled, revealing protuberant, severely mottled teeth. "Looking at me—looking TO me—for solace, for comfort—much as the innocent sheep looks at his shepherd—looks TO his shepherd for solace, for comfort. "Ah!" he stopped. "Innocent. Innocent." He paused again, as if musing, then lifted luminous eyes: Their expression proclaimed a great burdensome sorrow. "Innocent . . . Aye . . . The innocent sheep . . . But, I ask now. Here. Today. Are these my innocent children?" His thin lips twisted wryly, mingling threads of pain and suffering with those of bitter irony. "Are these my innocent children?" He gestured toward the congregation with a vague motion of his hand before he leaned across the altar, stabbing at the air, wounding it with a fiercely pointing finger. "Are these my innocent children? Ask yourselves . . . Ask one another . . . Ask—the Almighty God . . . Are these HIS innocent children?" Then, whispering the words, he asked, "Are YOU innocent children?"

Abruptly he clasped his hands behind his back and

paced for a few frenzied moments, back and forth, behind the altar. I felt a ripple of uncomfortable response in the congregation.

Much as a buzzard who stops in midflight, so did the Reverend: Head high, hands outstretched, wattle quivering, he faced his congregation squarely, bravely. "I ask you," he said quietly, "my children . . . Should you be looking to me for guidance, for comfort, for solace? Should you, as sheep, be seeking guidance, comfort, solace from your shepherd? Or rather"—his voice grew shrill—"should you not be begging for redemption from your God? Pleading for forgiveness from your Host? On your hands and knees this very moment, praying for salvation from your Savior?" He raised his arms high in supplication. "I suggest to you that you are NOT innocent—but wicked!" He leered. "Evil! Sinners!" He thundered, "EACH AND EVERY ONE!"

At the last dreadful pronouncement the congregation shifted uneasily. Little nervous coughs erupted.

The Reverend sagged against the altar pitifully. He extracted from underneath his robes a very large, not entirely clean, handkerchief with which he proceeded to mop his troubled brow and wipe his streaming eyes.

I could not help myself: I tittered.

"For God's sake, Miss Knowlton," hissed Dr. Briggs, "what is it now?"

"The late, lamented," I choked.

The doctor sat stiffly silent for a full moment before he jiggled my arm. "I indicated that he might be thyroidal, not terminally ill. . . ."

Still far from fully recovered, the Reverend made heroic attempts to straighten his rounded shoulders, to lift his head high, hold it erect, weighted though it was with the impossible sorrows of sin, suffering as he did from the transgressions of his wayward, wanton flock. His dedication unflaggingly courageous, the Reverend began again, voice muted now, hoarse with righteous fatigue. "Brethren . . . Attend me . . . We approach the tender season of the year. Ah, you may say"—his smile was unsightly, all-knowing—"but Reverend Smythe, it is now winter; the air is harsh; the ground is stiff and will not yield . . . yet you

can speak of the tender season!" He nodded. "True! True!
But, my flock, the tenderness in our lives should not be
searched for in winter's snowy fields; made the quest of
winter's bitter winds; awaited in winter's stormy
skies. . . . The tenderness, rather, should be sought within
our hearts, our spirits . . . where there is never winter!"
Again he smiled, baring aggressive, discolored teeth. "Ah,
yes, my brethren, the tenderness in our lives lies within us.
Shall it lie fallow, as the winter fields, or shall we cultivate
it, extend it freely, lovingly, gladly, to those we serve right
here on earth? Alas, my brethren," he paused, seeking emphasis, "I find that I am some distressed. Worried . . ."
His voice trembled. "Afraid . . . Why?" His protruding
gaze swept his congregation. "I ask humbly: do we now
extend true tenderness and love to our God on high, Whom
we serve and Who cares for us? Do we now extend true
tenderness and love to our masters here on earth, whom we
serve and who care for us? Do we?" His voice fell. "I suggest to you, my brethren, that we do not!" His accusation
was soft, deadly.

The congregation was frankly disquieted now.

"That Babe, Whose birth we shall honor—within days
now—knew and understood His place in this earthly world.
Ah, yes! 'But,' you say, 'He was the Son of God.' . . .
True . . ." Grinning in yellowed irony, the Reverend's delivery became soft, caressing. "In Heaven, He was the Son
of God. But," he continued in silky tones, "on this earth,
was He the son of a king? No! Was He the son of a duke?
No! The son of an earl? No! A lord? No! No, my brethren,
He was naught but the lowly son of a lowly carpenter!" His
voice crescendoed, "And He knew it! And He understood
it! And He accepted it! And what is more, my brethren,"
he exploded, "WITHOUT QUESTION!" Reverend
Smythe sought to punctuate his remarks. "Jesus knew it!
Understood it! Accepted it! WITHOUT QUESTION!"

Noisily the crowd shuffled its feet.

"If Jesus, Son of God, knew of his lowly origin, understood it, and accepted it WITHOUT QUESTION, why,
then, cannot lowly man accept his own lowly origin?" The
Reverend's gaze was fiery, angry now: incredulous. "Is it
conceivable that man feels himself superior to the Son of

God? Considers that he can stand taller than the Son of God? . . . How is it, may I humbly ask, that you here before me can presume to a plane higher than that of the Son of your own God?" His furious fist flailed the altar. "I say unto you that you cannot!"

The congregation writhed.

Once again Reverend Smythe produced the handkerchief and, with a dramatic flourish and a practiced hand, moved it over his troubled brow. "Ladies and gentlemen," he reflected soberly, "the Son of God recognized the Supreme Rightness of the Established Order. He knew it. Understood it! Accepted it! WITHOUT QUESTION. My brethren," he boomed, "so, then, should you. EACH AND EVERY ONE!"

I could feel a flush of anger flood my face; I glanced quickly over the congregation to see if Ian might be in attendance.

"The Son of God represents the ultimate sacrifice: beautiful; generous; selfless. Why this blood offering? Simply a gesture? Empty? Theatrical? NO! My brethren, no! The Son of God was loaned to us on earth to show us that, although pained, broken, reviled, man can remain true to a holy order . . . serving his master on earth as well as in heaven. . . ." The Reverend shook his head sadly. "And how do we repay this gift? By what means do we indicate our appreciation?" He closed sorrowful eyes. "By embracing our God in heaven and our master here on earth? By unswerving loyalty and devotion in the face of pain and sorrow? No!" he sobbed. "No!" An enraged hand struck the altar. "For naught was the Son of God conceived? For naught did He live? For naught did He die?" Reverend Smythe's shaggy head bowed in mortal shame. He wept. "Perhaps so. For we sin. We sin! We rail, foolishly, stubbornly, vainly. Struggle against our place in the natural order of things. That natural order which is supreme. My children: To know one's God in heaven and to know one's master here on earth is the only way—the righteous way. . . ." He lifted tear-filled eyes and whispered harshly, "Forgive us, oh God, for we have lost our direction . . . stepped off our path." Sinking elaborately to his knees, the Reverend addressed his congregation: "Let us pray . . ."

As if one body the assembly knelt, all except Dr. Briggs. So cramped was he in the meager space allotted him in the pew that he was unable to lower his knees beyond the angle of the seat ahead or, for that matter, once committed, remove them, thus remaining semi-impaled between the two. I could hear some agonized scuffling, punctuated by a few muttered epithets, each pithier than the last. Out of the corner of my eye I was able to evaluate the distress in his perspiring face and the quivering helplessness of his imprisoned legs. I all but collapsed in hilarity, causing the good doctor's language to worsen appreciably.

The Reverend Smythe, unaware of the immediate predicament of one of his parishioners, chose to drone on in a rather too-lengthy diatribe against his dissolute flock, which, accustomed to the assault, submitted quietly. Dr. Briggs's dilemma was neither all-suffering nor silent. "My God's!" abounded at the altar, only to be outnumbered close by in the pew. The vicar, oblivious to all except the mellifluous sounds of his own voice, continued on— praying for forgiveness . . . castigating sin . . . pleading for salvation . . . begging redemption . . .

I confess to enormous relief when the Reverend at last prepared an energetic rush through the gates of Heaven, flinging himself into the arms of his eagerly awaiting Maker: readying the perfect curtain line. Loath to conclude, however, the Reverend delivered a parting thrust: Piercing the air with an accusatory forefinger, he threatened his flock with the ultimate in punishment by the age-old and dire pronouncement: " 'The wages of sin is death!' " Exultant, having condemned his flock to eternal damnation, he lifted his head, guiltless, triumphant; bowed almost imperceptibly; and turned to withdraw through the chancel. His departure was slow, befitting a spiritually cleansed, emotionally exhausted man. Saintly, but spent. His black robes trailed limply somber in his wake.

On signal the organ blatted a few discordant notes in strident proclamation that the service was thus terminated and that the congregation, thoroughly chastised and forever destroyed, might retire. Amen.

Once extricated, Dr. Briggs was returned to bruised good humor and, seizing my elbow, for both guidance and support, escorted me down the aisle to the outer lobby, where the Reverend was holding forth, watching his flock parade sheepishly before him. He smirked and fawned as his parishioners, one by one, in gloomy procession passed in review. None escaped the vigorous Pastoral Handshake. None evaded the Whispered, Individualized Admonition. And to this the relentless Dr. Briggs unmercifully propelled me . . .

Stationed at a discreet distance from him and slightly to his rear stood two women, whom I learned to be the Reverends' wife, Abigail, and daughter, Caroline. Abigail, because she was a woman of astonishing girth, might have inspired unflattering commentary—even cruel barbs; her very round, pleasant face with its determinedly benign expression made such ridicule inappropriate, perhaps impossible.

Alas, through Caroline the Reverend favored the world with a replica of himself, nearly identical: The girl's pale eyes protruded uncomfortably and, while still in the blush of girlhood, she slouched unbecomingly. She was spared, fortunately, her father's dental irregularities: her teeth, while large and generally forbidding, were quite white. Her sallow complexion pinked as she caught sight of Dr. Briggs striding down the aisle, and her eyes narrowed when she spied me on his arm.

In our ensuing introduction Dr. Briggs informed the Reverend of my recent arrival and advised him of my situation at Wynds. The Reverend evinced considerable interest in the latter and insisted that it would be indeed both his pleasure and privilege and (of course) equally that of his wife and daughter to acquaint me with those of his parishioners whom he considered appropriate (he gave the word a subtle emphasis), and he expressed an eagerness to make me conversant with any and all customs peculiar to the area. "My wife, Abigail"—he nodded in her direction, issuing a tacit command that she honored obediently by waddling closer and smiling without restraint—"and my daughter, Caroline . . ." Conveying less obeisance, Caroline nonetheless followed reluctant suit, reddening as she

neared Dr. Briggs and, from under staunchly lowered lids
(a feat, honestly), cast oblique glances at me.

Dr. Briggs bowed ceremonially at both ladies and with
enthusiasm pumped the hands of first one and then the
other, at the same time slyly managing to commit me to
afternoon tea on Tuesday at the parsonage, three thirty
sharp. Promising that he would conduct me to the affair
personally, he thus assured the vicar that I would be both
present and on time.

Opposing emotions warred with each other on the plain
face of Miss Caroline: It seemed to my untrained eye that
she was at once delighted for an opportunity to make hopeful inroads on a possible suitor and fearful, even a little
despairing, at unexpected competition for his interest.

Dr. Briggs remained unaware of any underlying nuances
as he continued to collaborate with the vicar, blithely ar-
ranging the upcoming event. Social graces, long ingrained,
precluded even gracious refusal; and so, completely infuri-
ated with his cavalier performance, I was stony as I allowed the doctor to usher me from the church to the awaiting trap and sat woodenly while he climbed aboard, adjusted
the reins, and urged the horse forward.

Adding to my mounting irritation was the fact that the
despicable Dr. Briggs was immensely pleased with himself.
His lips puckered in a faint little whistle as he guided the
trap along the bumpy road. Determined to repay him for
his domineering tactics, I resolved not to communicate another word to him on the journey back to Wynds. Too, his
whistling was proving more than simply annoying: The
doctor obviously had a tin ear, and the notes constituting
his doubtful repertoire ran a dismally close second in disso-
nance to those of the organ we had suffered only moments
before.

We passed, once again, the listing house; the man with
the owl's eyes was there, staring. . . . Instinctively and
without conscious thought I moved closer to the doctor,
who responded by patting my hand in an awkward but affectionate spirit of camaraderie and increasing the volume
of his painful music-making.

Suddenly, my resolve quite forgotten, I asked, "Doctor?"
"Yes, m'dear?"

"However do you suppose Mrs. Smythe contrives to sit in one of those pews?"

Dr. Briggs's hoot was stentorian. I am sure that it must have resounded clearly through the Sabbath quiet of the countryside, lingering in the form of short, sporadic chuckles of delicious remembrance all the way to the manor, where he deposited me with the observation: "Miss Knowlton, you are magnificent!"

Chapter 21

Unable to conceal her eagerness, Auntie Maude awaited my return to Wynds, demanding promptly, "Well, Elizabeth, how was it?"

Since this was the Sabbath and the day designated to visit Auntie Maude's personal quarters, I suggested that she must wait until I had removed my only reasonably respectable outfit, so as not to wear it out altogether. I promised that I would join her forthwith, as soon as I had done so. I had to chuckle at her disappointment at the delay, but indicated the wisdom of caring for a scanty wardrobe as the only precaution prudent for one in my impecunious state. Sighing, Auntie Maude relented. "I shall wait for you in the inglenook. Only, dear," she implored, "try not to tarry!"

As Auntie Maude and I undertook our protracted tour of the kitchen wing and environs, I characterized in colorful detail the antics and person of our Reverend, and gave a rather full description of the family of his bosom. My aunt enjoyed my portrayal of the sermon, punctuated as it was by the ardent flailing of arms and useless clawing at the empty air, vis-à-vis Reverend Smythe's colorful performance. Miss Caroline and her rotund maternal parent earned a delicious grin; Mr. Wade commanded an illicit titter; Auntie Maude became totally undone, however, when I recounted Dr. Briggs's distressing inability to disengage himself from an awkward position during the Pastoral Prayer. Only the general lassitude that often follows moments of abandoned mirth, and the abrupt realization that a posture of dignity is mandatory in the exalted position of housekeeper in an establishment of this éclat, curbed my aunt's hilarity . . .

The servants' wing bore eloquent testimony to the thorough luxury extended to the rest of the household. Although my own home on Leicester Square had held an elegant head high, it could have in no way approached the wealth attendant upon Wynds. No area of service was overlooked or relegated to an attitude of insignificance, it seemed, and the quarters designed for each specific activity were generous and well appointed.

Everything pertaining to the kitchen—scullery, pantry, dairy, et al—was spotless; no neglected pool of soapy water offended the stone flooring of the washhouse; and the drying room, furnished with pullout racks (a convenience hitherto unknown to me), remained remarkably free from lingering lint or dust balls. The special laundry room reserved for the folding of clothes held no slighted tenants. Truly this was a complete and ordered establishment.

A timid peek into Judd's personal domain was braved only during that gentleman's convenient absence. His pantry and plate-scullery were, as one might easily expect, immaculate, as was his monastic bedroom adjoining. The plate safe alone held my interest: large and forbidding. "I have not that key here," Auntie Maude confessed, pointing to her own bulging key ring.

My aunt decided to forgo a visit to the lower servants' quarters, which housed the bakery, brewery, and the private rooms assigned to the individual members of the lesser staff. "It might appear as though you were prying," she confided. "Besides, it is almost the hour for dining: I must be punctual at all times—set a proper example." She winked. "The Accepted Wynds Method, you know . . ."

Casual mention of the stone cellars, which were situated at the base of the great tower, intrigued me; I meant to explore there as soon as I found it feasible . . .

Signaling a servingmaid to ready our meal, Auntie Maude headed for the housekeeper's apartments, where she opened the storeroom and china closet, juxtaposed, and stopped briefly at the stillroom. "Cakes!" I exclaimed. "My word! I have never seen so many cakes in my life!"

"Christmas," Auntie Maude reminded me. "Remember, dear, Christmas is but a few days away."

I had, indeed, forgotten.

"And there are, it seems, always great festivities at the house during the Yuletide season."

"Oh?" my eyes brightened.

"Sir Robert entertains his people, for one."

"What people?"

"Why—the people in the—er—village—I guess . . ." Her voice trailed away.

"The entire village?"

"I don't exactly know, dear." Auntie Maude was vague. This was something I should learn from Ian tomorrow.

Auntie Maude's bed and sitting arrangements, while pleasant enough, were austere and functional only: plainly the quarters of a servant. I did not enjoy the meal in these surroundings, although it was served agreeably and consisted of essentially the same menu as I might have been offered in my own apartments, and presented the added inducement of my relative's welcome congeniality. I felt a keen sense of guilt: I resided at Wynds in a state of luxury with, thus far, no duties assigned, and was free to avail myself of the not inconsiderable amenities provided here; Auntie Maude was a mere servant, executing a position of some authority, undeniably. But a servant nonetheless . . .

It was with a feeling of disloyal relief that I managed to escape into my rooms to finish out the remainder of the day. I longed to seek the stables, prevail upon Ian to saddle Smoke, preparatory to a bracing gallop across the bleak and cleansing moor: I knew, however, that riding on the Sabbath for pleasure alone was quite without sanction. Instead I settled myself before the hearth, steadfastly ignoring the enticing invitation of Miss Becky Sharp to lose myself in her vagaries and determined that since Christmas was almost upon us, I had best do something about it.

I rummaged through my trunk, searching for possible ideas that I could translate into appropriate gifts for Auntie Maude, Ian, Dr. Briggs, and Annie. My rewards, however, were modest indeed: little scraps of material left over from my days at Miller's sufficient to fashion a colorful pin cushion for Auntie Maude; a couple of ribbons suited to Annie's wild crop of hair; and, finally, a few stray pieces of linen, reasonable in size and probably adequate to design a handkerchief each for Ian and the doctor. My skill with the needle never enviable, I eyed the dreadful little instrument with an emotion akin to real loathing and experienced the inevitable recollections that brought back my days "in the trade" and evoked the unavoidable comparison between such labor in these elegant chambers and slaving in the stark workroom or the shop. I wondered then for the hundredth time how fared Ada and Molly and asked myself (a little wistfully, even so) what they might be doing now. Sunday: I was certain that they could be found strolling arm in arm through the squalid streets of London, reveling in their evanescent freedom.

Christmas at Wynds . . . How my life in the past two years had seesawed—from euphoria to cheerless drudgery—rising again to touch this pinnacle—a style of life far transcending any sumptuosness I might have dared contemplate—even in fantasy . . .

Sir Robert . . . It was evident that my destiny lay in his hands. My future here at Wynds depended solely upon his charity; my employment on his approval. Would he return from his business dealings in time for the holidays? Auntie Maude had implied as much: Surely a festive occasion— and one arranged for the pleasure of his people—would hardly be complete, or even appropriate, without the attendance of the master. Would he return only to excuse me from my duties here and terminate my connection with this establishment altogether?

I was afraid. . . . What if Sir Robert were to regard my ministrations to his wife as nonessential, after all? Could Lady Frances, indicating her strange objections to my presence, persuade her husband that my services were not merely superfluous but actually harmful? And after dutiful consideration could Sir Robert then determine that I was no longer welcome in his home? What should I do then? Where could I go?

I must guard against complacency. Certainly these were princely environs. Once again I was pursuing the frivolities of a lazy, pampered daughter of society. An artificial situation at best: I was here on sufferance alone—not as a close member of a wealthy family and thus automatically entitled to its privileges. No matter how I might rail against the idea, I was no more than a poor relation—and a distant one, at that. I had no recourse. Held no claims. Helpless, I remained a captive of the nugatory whim of another in the disposition of my fate.

Profound concentration and dire thoughts caused me to prick my finger rather seriously, and I decided then and there to abandon all worthwhile deeds and cross over to a more kindred inclination: Miss Becky Sharp.

Annie brought a light supper tray, and after the meal and a thorough bath, I was more than ready to climb between the sheets. I fell asleep, praying that the good weather would hold so that I might roam the countryside on Smoke tomorrow. . . .

"Elizabeth . . . Elizabeth . . ." Swiftly alert, my eyes slid to the corner of the room, searching for the path: Its gleam beckoned . . . "Elizabeth . . . Elizabeth . . ."

No sound, this time, came from the room. Were they not there? Almost savage in my disappointment, I pushed roughly at the half-open door: The man and woman stood locked in crushing embrace, his square, tanned hand lost, at first, in the lush tangle of her golden hair before it wandered slowly, caressingly down her face, her neck, pushing now at her gown, slipping it from her shoulders. Farther. Farther still. Until one snowy breast was bared. A delicate tracery of blue veins traveled lightly over the intimate tones of her skin . . .

With a sinuous motion she twisted free . . . "Beautiful . . ." His voice was husky. His handsome face flushed . . . "Beautiful . . ." Amber eyes heavy with desire, she reached for him; smooth, slender arms drew his head downward so that his parted lips first brushed hers as they moved on, on, hungrily seeking her naked breast . . .

The light dimmed. Faded. And was gone . . .

Chapter 22

I awoke to a sun that was already high in the sky, and to disturbing sensations of promise yet unfulfilled. I stretched, rose, and moved almost hypnotically to the mirrors. Languid amber eyes gazed back at me, and lips spread in a slow, sleepy smile . . . Involuntarily my hands shifted the nightdress so that my breasts were exposed: Their network of faint blue lines was there, traversing its gentle path across a firm white expanse. I moved suggestively.

At Annie's cheerful tap on the door I plucked at my gown to hurry it into proper position before bidding the maid enter. My voice was breathless . . .

Ian awaited me; his efforts to mask a high anticipation with a nonchalant air were unsuccessful. . . . I flashed him a breezy smile that unaccountably caused him to flush deeply.

My laugh was soft as I allowed him to hand me into the saddle and inquired where we were headed for the day. He shuffled in unaccustomed discomfiture. "I think us'd go for the moor. If that be your wish, miss," he amended quickly. The moor! Raw, cruel, rocky earth spreading baldly under a broad bruised sky! "Perfect!" I agreed without hesitation.

We raced to the moor, reveling in our youth, the vigor of our mounts, and the exciting, bracing winds that whipped our cheeks and stung our fingers. We reined briefly to rest the horses, at which time I asked Ian to explain the forthcoming social event at Wynds. "Does this Christmas party involve the entire village?"

"Most likely," he said. "Ain't jest at Christmas Eve, nowise," Ian added, "there'd be another sech in the summer, too. Lotsa food—beer, almost spillin' all over . . ." His vinca-blue eyes bazed off into the distance. "Us workin' people, now, us don't get near spittin' way of the house. Nowise . . . Us gets ours out under a mark—whatcha call it—"

"Marquee?"

"That be it," he nodded. "It be some freeze there in the winter, but us drinks us mighty damn warm, let me say!" His eyes narrowed. "Them farmers gets to eat in the hall— wassailin' a fare-thee-well . . . All fancy-like . . . Us"— he grinned—"us has more fun, leastwise. Drunker'n hell, most likely!" He chuckled. "And the special guests—la te da! All dressed, frippered-like, them, and eats in the dinin' room!" He slapped his thigh. "Them dumb farmers thinks them so good—them don't hardly get near the dinin' room—them don't get close to them fancy guests! Nowise! Them jest stays in the hall—don't dare to go nor farther! Sir Robert and his lady—them's the ony ones what sits with them farmers! And it ain't 'cause them craves it, nei- ther. Sir Robert gets paid the tribute then. What the hell," Ian shrugged elaborately, "us'd sit with the Devil hisself— or even with that bastard Wade, to get a share of them shillin's!"

"But Sir Robert isn't here."

"He will be. Ain't missed yet."

"What of Lady Frances? She has not even stirred from her rooms since I have been here at Wynds."

"She will"—it was a positive statement—"the Squire's ladies don't miss 'em. Leastwise, never has."

"Christmas Eve . . . That's in three days."

"Seems so."

"I haven't seen much in the way of preparation," I ob- served.

"Oh, they be lots—you jest ain't been where it be goin' on, s'all . . . You wait," he promised, "the great hall be full of diddles soon . . . I seen it onct," he confided, "When I had to clean up, after. . . . Musta looked nice," he added wistfully.

"Let's race!" I proposed suddenly. "To that tree over there—"

"What tree?"

"Silly—there is only one tree in sight!" At a touch of my whip Smoke responded.

Even with a late start Ian easily outrode me and was

waiting at the tree, grinning in evident satisfaction. "Aw, that'd be baby's play, miss!"

Reining up, I laughed softly.

He reddened. Turning his face from me then, his eyes made a show of searching the darkening sky. "We'd best move on now," he murmured.

Standing at his usual post before the listing house, the man fastened his owl stare obliquely on us as we passed by. . . . Ian urged his mount forward and slapped at Smoke's rump with the full palm of his hand. His face was a mask: unreadable.

Reaching the stable yard, Ian helped me dismount. "If we ain't snow tomorrow afternoon, we can get to them woods there and pick us some Christmas holly," he suggested.

"Tomorrow afternoon?" I was disappointed. "I am expected at the vicar's for tea then."

"When be that?"

"Dr. Briggs is coming for me at three o'clock," I said. "We must simply go in the morning instead."

Ian turned from me quickly. "I be busy then." He disappeared into the stable. . . .

Chapter 23

Dr. Briggs was more than prompt for our appointment: To be precise, he was almost fifteen minutes early. It was fortunate, then, for the peace of the household that I was prepared for his arrival. The hint of snow in the air was a perfect reminder of the season, and the doctor's festive mood reflected the approaching holiday. His conversation was of a lively nature, and a jovial smile warmed his hazel eyes.

"Perhaps we shall not be obliged to stay long," I ventured hopefully.

"Stay long?"

"At the Reverend's."

"You mean—er—ditch it?"

"I suppose we can't, altogether. But there is no reason to prolong the agony unduly, either, now is there?"

"Er—no. I suppose not."

I smiled.

"What, then?" he asked.

I stretched lazily. "Oh, I don't know. . . . We could—see the sights . . . visit the inn . . ." My eyes slid drowsily toward his. "You decide . . ."

The doctor blushed.

As we pulled up before the manse gate I could detect frantic flutterings behind the curtained windows. "We must be aeons early," I warned.

Dr. Briggs extracted his watch from a vest pocket and grinned sheepishly. "Some," he admitted.

"They are evidently not ready for us," I concluded. "We daren't appear on their doorstep as yet."

"Er—I suppose not—"

"And we certainly cannot remain—stationed out here, either," I giggled.

"Er—no—naturally not," he agreed. "Ah! We could ride about for a bit—"

"Too obvious."

"Stay down the lane a ways?"

"Worse."

"I know!" Suddenly he jumped from the trap. "I shall give a tour around the cemetery!"

"The cemetery?"

"Confoundedly interesting place, my dear!"

"I'm sure."

"Come, come, Miss Knowlton," commanded the doctor, by now his momentary state of indecision fully dispelled. "We are simply wasting precious time!" As he handed me down from the trap I flashed him a blinding smile inviting him to lead the way. Faint color spread over his face.

Although the burial ground was modest in size, I am sure that, if required, each weathered stone might well attest to a nearly limitless sequence of passions and events lived by those who had walked these lands before. "You see, m'dear, an entire history is written here," declared Dr. Briggs. "Look . . . look at the interments in 1732, for example. Must have been a particularly virulent plague of some kind. . . . Came damned close to wiping out a whole family, it seems . . . Emily Armstrong, age forty-one, February third; Nathaniel Armstrong, age sixteen, February sixth; Beatrice Armstrong, age eleven, February tenth . . . All died within days of each other. . . ."

"Why!" I said, "this one is only a baby—Alice Baker, age three . . . and another—Theodore Durant, age two years, four months and five days, beloved son of Charles and Mary . . . Charity Durant—'Light of her Mother's Life for but thirteen days' . . . How tragic!"

"How do you like this vigorous old stud—Amos Robert Cartwright—buried three women and was still chasin' 'em around until the ripe old age of ninety-two . . ." Dr. Briggs chuckled, "I say, mark this old girl: Matilda Whitman White Stuart Ditmar Dole . . . She must have lowered her share!"

I wandered over to the mausoleum rising in imposing magnificence above all the rest. "I presume that this monument is reserved for the Wyndhams."

"Absolutely! Handsome piece, what?"

"I suppose," I shrugged. "A bit overpowering for my taste."

"And designed to be just that, I am sure." Dr. Briggs strolled over to the tomb and inspected it more carefully. "See, Miss Knowlton, even the very letterings are far more intricate and elaborate than anything else you'll find here."

I moved closer and began to read the engraved lineage: "Sir William . . . Lady Isabelle . . . Sir George . . . Sir Mark . . . Lady Margaret, beloved wife to Sir Robert Wyndham . . ." I paused. "Died March 10 in the year of our Lord 1857 . . ." I looked up. "Who in the world is that?"

"Let me have a look . . . Lady Margaret . . . 1857 . . . Mmm."

"Who could she be?"

"Sir Robert's wife, evidently . . ."

"Lady Frances is his wife."

"Well then—his first wife."

"Did he have a first wife?"

"Judging by what I see here, he must have done." Puzzled, Dr. Briggs massaged his chin. "First I have heard of her, though, I will admit."

Eighteen fifty-seven . . . Four years ago . . . "Could that be Sir Robert's mother?" I asked.

"Possibly. There is no birth date recorded. . . . Strange." Dr. Briggs frowned. "I wonder . . ."

"What?"

"Nothing, m'dear. Nothing." He drew his watch from his pocket. "It is safe now, I believe, to descend on our host. Miss Knowlton, may I have your arm?"

"Of course," I said absently.

The little honey-colored vicarage had a charming, cozy flavor, further enhanced by the aroma of freshly baked bread, greeting us immediately as we were received by Reverend Smythe, who liberally bestowed on us his hospitable, if unsavory, smile. "Please, please," he entreated, "make yourselves comfortable in the library . . . with Caroline." He eyed Dr. Briggs conspiratorially. "Meanwhile, I shall inform dear Abigail that you have arrived. . . ."

Arrayed in rather forced finery, Miss Caroline was ar-

ranged, as prettily as nature would permit, before an inviting hearth fire.

"Ah! Miss Caroline!" boomed Dr. Briggs. "You will remember our Miss Knowlton, I trust!"

"Of course," she murmured, nodding stiffly; a deep red
stain of embarrassment fanned upward from her neck to
her uneven hairline. She was gowned in an unfortunate
clash of dark maroon velvet and yellowed antique lace, her
costume merely heightening the sallow tones that naturally
plagued her complexion and mirrored the savage flush now
discoloring her saturnine features.

"Well now! Ha! Ha!" continued Dr. Briggs, more than a
shade too heartily. "And how is our charming Miss Caroline this fine December afternoon? Ha! Ha!"

I looked at him aghast.

Miss Caroline's flush deepened.

"Feels like snow," the doctor ventured, fiercely cheery.
"Best beware," he cautioned, waggling a finger playfully.
"Christmas is just around the corner!" His observation was
totally redundant, I thought: The house was almost surfeited already with greenery and Christmas decorations.
The awkward moment was eased, and none too soon, by
the welcome appearance of Mrs. Smythe, who like a plump
projectile burst from the kitchen, her husband lost in her
ample wake as he tottered under a tray piled mountain-
high with our tea.

"Allow me!" Dr. Briggs offered gallantly. "I shall make
a place here on the table." After much shifting from here
to there of items on the table, so as to accommodate the
broad circumference of the tray and its enormous burden
by both Mrs. Smythe and the too helpful Dr. Briggs, along
with an accompanying prolonged debate as to what might
prove the ultimate location convenient to all subscribers,
the problem was solved at last and the tray deposited. And
with not a moment to spare: Toward the end of the lengthy
disputation the rather scrawny arms of the heroic Reverend
Smythe began to quiver dangerously under their prodigious
load, and the already vibrating tea cups commenced to
clatter, loudly responsive to their jeopardy.

The amount of foodstuffs proffered was staggering and
its variety unexcelled. "Ah, Miss Knowlton!" urged Mrs.

Smythe, all smiles. "Pray have a slice of my prune bread. Do! I took it out of the oven only minutes ago!"

"Yes, indeed, Miss Knowlton!" echoes the doctor. "Mrs. Smythe's prune bread is plum delicious!" He jabbed delightedly at his thigh to punctuate the dreadful pun, almost upsetting in the process the pitcher of milk near his elbow.

Miss Caroline laughed in prompt appreciation, trilling her voice daintily.

"And, Dr. Briggs, I didn't forget you!" Mrs. Smythe gushed. "I baked your very favorite! Apricot turnover!" She paused a moment to emphasize her declaration. "It is scalding hot! Mind you don't burn yourself!"

"Dear lady, you are entirely too kind!" Dr. Briggs smacked his lips in anticipation.

"Caroline!" scolded her mother. "You have hardly touched your plate. You are not ill, dear?"

"If Caroline is indisposed," the Reverend interjected with some triumph, "she has picked the right company!" Grinning, he winked significantly at the doctor, who had the grace to shift uneasily in his chair.

"More tea?" asked my hostess.

"Why, er—no, thank you," I refused, adding graciously, "but everything was certainly delicious!"

"Doctor?" Mrs. Smythe suggested, "may I not cut you a slice of my own special chocolate cake?"

"Never can refuse it!" vowed Dr. Briggs.

Despite Dr. Briggs's exhibition of a healthy, manly appetite, Mrs. Smythe managed to consume a disproportionate amount of the generous fare, while Miss Caroline merely picked (sheer nerves, I suspected, as well as affecting the pose of the delicate female, scrupulously devoid of all bodily functions) and the Reverend himself ate little. I could not help but wonder if his dental irregularities might not have curtailed his desire for food. When the first edge of hunger had been blunted, Dr. Briggs eased back in his chair. "You have outdone yourself, Mrs. Smythe! Once again!"

That good lady adroitly wedged a large portion of buttered scone between her teeth before simpering prettily, "Oh, pshaw, Dr. Briggs! You flatter an old woman!"

"Not at all, madam," protested the courtly doctor.

This tiresome banter might have continued, dominating the remainder of our visit. had I not innocently effected an abrupt end to it by inquiring, "Reverend Smythe, was Sir Robert married before?"

Momentarily confounded. the Reverend sat an uncomfortable moment before recovering. then he looked me straight in the eye and answered levelly, "Yes."

"The Lady Margaret—buried next door?"

He hesitated for a fraction of a second. "Yes."

"What did she die of?" I asked.

The Reverend spread nervous hands; obviously he found the subject unwelcome. "Ah, let me see . . . Some internal ailment, I believe." His response was vague.

"Did they have children?" I pursued.

"Ah, no."

I was joined in the interrogation by Dr. Briggs. "What was the final diagnosis, do you know?" he asked, now wholly the professional.

"I—I really have no idea," the Reverend hedged.

"Pregnancy, perhaps?" projected Dr. Briggs.

Miss Caroline gasped. Cheeks vividly saffron, she hurried a dainty lace handkerchief over her eyes as if to shield them.

"Doctor!" The Reverend stiffened. "Need I remind you, sir, that there are ladies present!"

Dr. Briggs reddened. "Er—no offense—er, sorry, old chap—"

"Are you looking forward to the celebration at Wynds this Christmas Eve, Miss Knowlton?" interrupted Mrs. Smythe, valiantly seeking to maneuver the conversation into a safer channel.

"Yes," I responded politely, "I am sure it will prove a new experience."

"Oh, my—indeed so! You will find all of the festivities tremendously exciting!" my hostess gurgled. She turned then to Miss Caroline in a desperate effort to draw the girl into the discussion. "Tell Miss Knowlton, dear . . ."

Miss Caroline was visibly suffering, but good manners demanded that she respond civilly. She contributed a sketchy outline, depicting the descent upon Wynds every Yule by the townspeople, there to be wined and dined completely through the courtesy and at the expense of the squire. Hers was an unelectric delivery, differing from Ian's passionate and bitter recitation by still another fundamental element: vantage point. Miss Caroline terminated her measured discourse with the remark, "Of course, Mama, Papa, and I miss a good deal of the rougher observances; we are seated in the dining hall. . . ."

"Personally," the vicar added, "I have always thought it supremely magnanimous on the part of the squire. A princely gesture, if you will. The household goes to considerable trouble to decorate the hall and even provides suitable cover for the laborers' activities outside. I'll say this"— he leaned forward in his chair— "I would not care to have my home invaded by that seditious rabble twice yearly. No, sir!" His bulging eyes narrowed. "Sir Robert takes a healthy chance!"

"My, yes!" agreed Mrs. Smythe unequivocally. "A truly ugly group!" She looked toward her daughter: Miss Caroline shuddered delicately.

"Come, come, old man," countered Dr. Briggs mildly, "surely those poor souls are not the demons you represent 'em . . ."

"Sir," challenged the Reverend, warming to his subject. "Sir, you have lived in Drewsby but a year. I contend that you cannot—in such a short time—be wholly aware of the profligacy, the degeneracy—the lack of moral fiber that characterizes the laborer in our village!"

"They are a disgrace!" echoed his wife.

"These are not human beings—they are far worse, sir, than the basest animals!" The Reverend rose and began to pace up and down the room. "They sin. . . . Do they try to atone for their transgressions? Do they show repentance for the error of their ways? I ask you, sir, do they indicate remorse? No!" He gestured wildly. "The door to my church is open all day—every day—for private prayer. . . . Do they take advantage of the opportunity to cleanse their souls? No! Do they bend their sinful knees to their Savior? No! Never!"

Dr. Briggs's smile was slow. "Perhaps they are occupied at work in the fields all day." His eyebrow quirked. "Every day—"

"Bah! You are too easy! No! They offend God's will! Question their place in the established scheme of things! Court insurrection!"

"They are but poor suffering illiterates," defended Dr. Briggs without passion. "Rather to be pitied than damned so."

"Ah!" Now jubilant, the Reverend pounced. "You have pronounced the very word: illiterate! I-L-L-I-T-E-R-A-T-E!" Victorious, he smiled, "These creatures: unlettered, un-educated—never availing themselves of the fine oppor-tunities for learning offered in our village, uncultured, they have the unmitigated gall to rail against the supreme sys-tem!" He waved an angry fist under the doctor's nose. "They should be grateful! Not complaining! Loyal, not mu-tinous!"

"Grateful?" asked Dr. Briggs, incredulous. "For what, pray?"

The Reverend expressed sincere surprise. "Why, does not society in fact provide them with their very suste-nance?"

"Archibald speaks the undiluted truth!" Mrs. Smythe, with unexpected heat, underscored her husband's words. "I have, as the vicar's wife, been obliged to visit these—people—in their very homes. I have attempted to advise them—to exhort them to God's will—I have read the Bible to the sick and the aged—I have implored the wayward mothers to bring their children for baptism, for worship—I have endeavored to counsel thrift, to show them how to save what monies they have—and to what end?" She snorted effectively. "They do naught but frequent that dreadful public house and, and—drink!" She all but whis-pered the last, noisome word. "Caroline can bear witness, for has she not, many times, accompanied me on my visits of mercy?"

The girl nodded her head vigorously.

This disagreeable dialogue promised to be of interminable duration; the wanton, resisting laborer, it seemed, providing the solitary target for the Reverend's social conscience. About to rise, readying direct departure, I was aided un-expectedly by Dr. Briggs, who studied his pocket watch pointedly, muttering something inane about his presence being required elsewhere.

Mrs. Smythe conveyed her considerable disappointment by crying, "But, Doctor! We have not had our 'sing'!"

"Quite so," he admitted with regret. "However, good lady, it is growing dark. . . ."

"Oh, please! Just one tiny carol!" Mrs. Smythe dimpled. "It is, after all, getting on toward Christmas!"

"Well, then," he relented, "just one." He grinned at me in sheepish apology.

"Caroline, dear," her mother directed happily, "you do the honors, love. . . ."

Miss Caroline rose obediently and made for the walnut upright stationed in the corner of the room, seated herself at the bench (careful, the while, to arrange her skirts in full becoming folds), and waited for the doctor to join her at the piano. She lifted long lashes, fastened her eyes in a dewy gaze on his face, before requesting archly, "And what is your pleasure, sir?"

"I find that I am most partial to 'Good King Wenceslaus,' " Dr. Briggs confided. "Would you happen to be familiar with that one?"

"Why, of course, Doctor!" Miss Caroline treated the company to her trilling laugh.

Prowess at the pianoforte was evidently Miss Caroline's social stronghold: Her fingers moved over the keys with surprising strength and authority. Body swaying sensually back and forth on the bench, one rich chord after another was struck, perfectly orchestrated, firmly executed. The prelude devised for the simple carol proved a miracle of intricacy and was extended to a singularly ambitious length; scarcely a note on the keyboard went unrewarded, while Dr. Briggs stood patiently, waiting for the introduction to subside sufficiently so as to accommodate his entrance. Frequently, when it appeared that Miss Caroline might be winding down for the purposes of accompaniment alone, the doctor cleared his throat self-consciously, opened his mouth in anticipation, only to be buried under still another avalanche of polyphony.

Monuments of parental pride, the Reverend and Mrs.

Smythe, beaming in smug satisfaction, nodded their approval first at Miss Caroline and then at each other.

Meanwhile Dr. Briggs remained impaled.

Incredibly I managed to suppress a state of almost helpless mirth.

At last Miss Caroline's initial fervor seemed to mitigate and her delivery to soften: She slipped into a simple one-line rendition of the lead melody, deliberately stressing the note upon which Dr. Briggs should commence his vocalizing. He stood benumbed. Miss Caroline, a trifle more forcefully, reemphasized his entry. Dr. Briggs remained unresponsive. Another effort, one even more pronounced, proved equally unsuccessful. Finally, finding no tactful alternative, Miss Caroline blinked her lashes with unmistakable meaning and unequivocally smote the appropriate key. Dr. Briggs colored and began to sing. A bass-baritone, the doctor's voice enjoyed a mellow timbre, pleasing resonance, and a volume that was nicely modulated; he was, however, completely lacking in tonal fidelity, and any relation that his personal interpretation might bear to the tune at hand was fortuitous at best. Even more trying: An elusive sense of rhythm rendered even elementary piano support frankly hazardous.

Too, it was unfortunate that both Miss Caroline and Dr. Briggs sought to prolong the concert by discharging every verse, however obscure. The performers enjoyed themselves thoroughly, and I must credit their efforts with the fact that Dr. Briggs had committed each phrase to unhesitating memory and that Miss Caroline exhibited faultless patience and remarkable adaptability throughout. . . .

We escaped at last into the refreshing chill of early evening, to a sky darkened almost completely, and to a smattering of pale stars already in modest raiment. "Heavens! What a relief!" I sighed frankly as Dr. Briggs handed me into the trap and covered my knees with a heavy woolen rug.

"Mrs. Smythe is a damned fine cook," he contended.

"Perhaps so," I allowed. "However, I feared we might be doomed to a recapitulation of Sunday's sermon!"

"He does rant on a bit," the doctor admitted.

We rode on in a companionable silence, broken only by

the steady clack of the horses' hooves as they struck the rocky path. Nearing once again the listing house, now merely a bizarre silhouette drawn against the dusky sky, I could but barely discern the bent figure of a man moving clumsily across the uneven, sterile ground toward the solitary candle, lone beacon, casting its feeble light through a shadowed window. At the sound of the vehicle passing, the figure turned slowly: Even in the thickening gloom I felt those staring owl's eyes . . .

Chapter 24

To my surprise Wynds was ablaze with light and alive with activity; the din echoed throughout the courtyard. "What in the world!" I exclaimed.

"Quite a show," conceded Dr. Briggs as he reined to a full stop. "Perhaps the master has returned."

"Sir Robert?"

"No. I rather think Saint Nicholas," he teased.

In my haste and excitement I stumbled as I stepped from the trap, falling against Dr. Briggs. My laugh was low, easy. He held me close for a moment before asking hoarsely, "Are you all right?" From under lowered lashes I could sense a new intensity in his eyes. . . .

Judd was holding court in the great hall, officiously supervising the frantic efforts of a battery of servants, men and women alike. Auntie Maude stood by, nervously awaiting instructions, her round little body poised in readiness; actually, she seemed simply confused. Fragrant boughs of holly and enormous ornamented wreaths, worked of fresh-cut greenery and delicate glass decorations, were being hefted into place by a brigade of housemaids, passing them relay-fashion to footmen straddling high-reaching ladders, Colorful festoons of bright ribbons and variegated paper chains hung suspended from the walls and were strung along three great banquet tables set in a gothic U-shaped design, leaving a spacious open area in the center.

Under Judd's watchful eye it was not easy to take Auntie Maude aside. I stood for some awed moments in total absorption as the stunning production was enacted before me, until I was free to ask Auntie Maude what in heaven's name transpired here and if all this commotion heralded Sir Robert's long-awaited arrival. "No, dear," Auntie Maude whispered, "I have heard nothing of the master's return. All this—" she indicated the industry around her—

"is for the Christmas festivities involving the townspeople. . . ."

Suddenly I was mindful of Ian's wistful confession: "I seen it onct . . . when I had to clean up, after. . . . Musta looked nice . . ."

In between directives the glowering Judd put an end to our conversation: "Best run along, dear." Auntie Maude gave me an anxious nudge. "I daren't spare a moment from this. Although," she confided miserably, "I haven't the slightest idea what to do!" I patted her hand affectionately and sought my own quarters, realizing, albeit grudgingly, that it was probably in my favor that I had been obliged to endure Mrs. Smythe's culinary excesses, for when might a meal be anticipated on this busiest of nights?

Several hours, in fact, passed before a frazzled Annie, bearing a simple supper tray, tapped lightly at my door; my mood was such that it took conscious effort on my part to greet her civilly. Even then I was sure that in no way was the girl culpable—or lax in her duty toward me; with Judd issuing an endless succession of commands, a mere housemaid had no recourse other than slavish obedience. The thought occurred to me then that the butler's attitude toward one even in my own position was cavalier. I felt a tardy compassion for one in a truly subordinate capacity. Still, I was dismally uncomfortable. My room was tomb-cold; no fire had been lighted; worse, none had been laid. I had spent the time hunched in my cloak, pacing the length of my apartment, annoyance mounting. Affixed, the target of my present woes: Judd . . . In effect that petty tyrant had condemned me to this frozen cell by tacit intimidation. What possible harm in my remaining in the hall to observe the preparations in progress there? What conceivable injury could I have perpetrated on that little scene? Were I mistress here I certainly would not countenance a despot on my staff. . . . What was the matter with Lady Frances? . . . Why did she not exercise her position as mistress of the house . . . use her power? . . . Why did she extend dictatorial authority to a mere servant in her employ? . . .

Annie was immediately contrite. "Oh, miss, I am that

sorry! But Mr. Judd—he has kept us all hoppin'!" She grinned sheepishly. "That he has!"

I nodded.

"It still be not finished, and all. The chairs must be set around still and the tables laid . . . an' all." She was breathless.

"Has Sir Robert returned?" I asked, watching the girl shovel ashes into a blackened pot, preparatory to laying fresh wood.

"Ah, no. Not as yet," she said. "But he'll be here in time for the big do—I can tell ye that!"

"Will Lady Frances attend the affair?" I made my question casual.

"To be sure," Annie replied, wide-eyed. "The lady has got to show."

"Annie," I began carefully, "I never realized that Sir Robert had been married before . . ."

Annie did not answer; she simply continued to attend to the fire, employing the bellows to blow it alive.

"She was a Lady Margaret?" I pursued.

"Miss." Annie avoided my eyes. "I can't hardly talk about the master, now can I?"

"Very well," I said coldly. "You may be excused."

Deeply chilled, the room did not dispel its uncomfortable damp for some time. Quite without appetite I sampled each offering on the tray, finding nothing to suit my finical fancy. I abandoned the whole procedure quickly and deposited the receptacle, as was, outside my door, so as to preclude further contact with Annie this evening. Sanctimonious little snob!

Feeling grimy and ill-used, I craved a hot bath; naturally such a nicety on this night would be unavailable; nor would I ask Annie for anything more! Splashing standing cold water over my face and hands did little to lift my spirits or sweeten my humor, nor did the drear ministrations firm my resolve to stitch the pincushion and handkerchiefs—a prudent pursuit, since Christmas was a mere two days away. Almost defiantly I settled in the big bed, wrapped myself cozily in the quilted coverlet, and prepared to invade Mr. Thackeray's more entertaining world. Or so I had hoped; even his magical words could not weave their spell this night.

I blew out the candle and retreated further into the bed-clothes, only to find that sleep quite eluded me. The noise born of the excitement downstairs reached my ears, inspiring sensations of both irritation and envy. How I longed to be a part of that activity—if only as an observer!

Twisting and turning, angry, anguished, I grew restless, teased by obscure feelings of unease . . . taunted by desires that I could neither identify nor explain. . . . If only I could sleep!

My dream . . . would I have my dream . . . would the whispering start . . . Elizabeth . . . Elizabeth . . .

I sat up, cocked my head, and listened. . . . Nothing . . . My eyes flew to the corner of the room, seeking the golden path . . . Nothing . . .

Oh, please, let me have the dream . . .

I lay stiffly prone and willed my eyes to close. . . . Sleep. Perhaps if I could sleep—really sleep—the whispering would commence; the path would appear and I would see—them . . .

Did I hear the call? Was that not it? The whispering . . . Elizabeth . . . Elizabeth . . .

Oh, why does not that infernal din downstairs cease! What if the unearthly commotion was keeping the whispering at bay . . . stemming the path . . . frightening—them—so that they dare not appear . . . Oh, God . . .

I must sleep . .

Tears, spawned of all three—rage, frustration, and disappointment—spilled down my cheeks. I pressed my face deep into the pillow and sobbed without restraint.

I must have slept finally. If there was a whispering, I did not hear it . . .

Chapter 25

It was late the next morning when Annie tapped timidly at my door, bearing the breakfast tray. Irritable and exhausted, I answered her strained greeting with a cool nod, which indicated both acknowledgment and dismissal. After I drank a small quantity of the tea, I examined the sky and was perversely relieved that gray clouds hung heavy and low, meeting my surly mood. I dressed quickly, determined to visit the stables to arrange for a ride through the moors both to expurgate my disagreeable disposition and to gather information from Ian, since Annie would not oblige. Impossible chit!

Ian was not there.

"Him be in the woods, miss," one of the stable hands informed me.

"When do you expect his return?" I asked.

The boy shook his head doubtfully. "Him be gone for the day, miss."

"The day?"

"Him be helpin' with the Yule log, seems so."

"Very well, then," I said, concealing my sharp disappointment. "If you will be so good as to saddle Smoke for me."

"I dunno, miss." The boy scratched his head. "Me not sure about them."

"You are not sure about what?" I asked with surprise.

"Mr. Hartley nor Ian sez if you can take out a horse, miss." His eyes fell to the ground. "And they ain't here, leastwise . . ."

"No trouble, my good lad," I smiled winningly. "It will be all right."

"I dunno, miss," he hesitated.

"You will please saddle Smoke, my man. At once. If not"—I was brazen—"Sir Robert himself will be so informed. . . ."

The moors were as bold as I that day, and Smoke responded accordingly. We galloped wildly across the rocky expanse, one with the earth and sky, ignoring the mocking bursts of ocean wind. Tearing off my bonnet, I allowed my hair to fly free—letting it flutter like a frenzied, golden fan behind my head. . . . We trampled gorse and heather . . . Startled foolish grouse . . . Chased frightened hare into the copse . . .

The evening star was riding in the sky when I returned to the stables. Ian, it seemed, still had not returned. The stableboy eyed Smoke with dismay. "Him be lathered some fierce, miss," he observed, his tone reproving.

"I am sure that you will take good care of him," I said carelessly.

"Ian . . . Ian don't like no horse to come home that way."

"Ian isn't here, you said," I smiled.

"No, miss."

"Then he need never know," I said smoothly. "Good night—and thank you," I called brightly over my retreating shoulder. . . .

After a thorough bath and change I ate lustily from the supper tray and even managed to weave the final stitches into my meager store of Christmas offerings. A few chapters of Mr. Thackeray were enough to cause my eyes to droop impossibly. I blew out the candle and snuggled close in the warm bedclothes. Sleep claimed me immediately.

"Elizabeth . . . Elizabeth . . ." I jerked awake. . . . "Elizabeth . . ." My eyes sped to the corner of the room. It beckoned: the golden path . . .

Muffled murmurings came from behind the door. I pushed it open. . . . They were there, reclining on a white brocade couch, her head a golden cloud against his shoulder. . . . His lips embraced the smooth skin of her neck, her arms. . . . "Love . . . Sweet . . ." he whispered. . . . Her laugh, silky, rippled. . . . Square, tanned hands rent her velvet bodice; freed her creamy breasts. . . . Quivering suddenly, she lay back, trembling in invitation. . . .

His body covered hers . . .

The light diminished . . . paled still more . . . and was gone. . . .

A stray sunbeam escaping the heavy shield of drapes that guarded the window prodded me gently awake. . . . Soft and warm, my breasts swelled against the nagging confines of my nightdress. I pushed aside the offending material and lay naked across the broad expanse of the bed. . . . My hands traced languidly the contours of silken flesh . . . undulating . . . vibrant . . .

I smiled. . . .

Rising, I went to the dressing nook and stood before the bank of mirrors. . . . Slowly lifting my arms high, I watched the flow of golden hair spill across my shoulders down to my breasts; chuckled in triumph as pinkly erect nipples parted the shimmering strands. . . .

A timid knock at the door startled me: Annie. Drat the girl!

"I am occupied," I called quickly.

"Your breakfast tray, miss . . ."

"Leave it!" I ordered sharply.

The door handle moved almost imperceptibly.

"I said, leave it!" I shrilled.

Through the thick oak of the door Annie's reluctance could be felt as a tangible force; finally I heard the protesting clink of the dishes as she set the tray down. And her sigh: clearly audible . . .

Let her think what she likes, I thought. . . . Bloody snoop . . . It was some moments before I was able to cover myself enough to retrieve the tray; the food by this time was tepid. Unpleasantly so. No matter: Ian was what I sought. Ian: and the stables . . .

His mood was sullen, almost contemptuous, when I approached the stables that morning. . . . His eyes, cloudy, barely acknowledged my cheery greeting. "Good morning," I hailed, "how long before Smoke will be saddled and ready?"

"Dunno, miss," was the peevish rejoinder. "Him be all the way tired. Seems so."

"Nonsense!" I laughed. "Surely Smoke has had more than ample time to recover his strength since our ride yesterday!"

"Him be on the way to bein' lame," Ian protested.

"Lame?" I countered. "Ridiculous!" There was an edge to my voice. "Come along, Ian. Don't be tiresome!"

He was obdurate. "Me can let you have Prince, maybe . . ."

"Ian," I said, "I am used to Smoke . . ."

He shook his head.

I moved close to him. My hand lingered on his arm. "I trust Smoke . . ." I moved closer. "I trust you . . ."

He reddened. "I dunno, miss . . ."

"Ian," I purred. His eyes shifted uneasily from mine; his upper lip glistened with perspiration. Gently squeezing his arm, I whispered, "I shall be here, waiting. . . . Pray do not tarry . . ."

I led the way straight for the moors, letting Smoke have his head, delighting in the savage tug of his muscles, in the long pull of his stride. Recklessly I tore my hair free and rejoiced as the impish winds wantonly scoured its glossy strands. . . .

Exhilarated by the ice-blue sky and frosty air, I urged my mount forward, digging my heels into his broad, fleshy barrel, shouting wild exhortations in his ear. Soon, despite my frantic pressing, the horse began to fade, stepping now with uneven gait. Ian immediately overtook me then, grasping Smoke's bridle and slowing him, gentling him the while. "How dare you touch my horse's reins!" I demanded.

"Him be lame, some, miss," Ian explained as he dismounted to examine Smoke's injured leg.

"It is probably nothing more serious than a stone caught in his shoe," I remarked indifferently.

"No, miss"—Ian stood firm—"him be lame."

"Help me dismount," I ordered.

As Ian held me I could feel his strength, his maleness, smell the pungent odor of the stables. Through half-closed lids my eyes lazily searched his face, saw desire there. . . . "Us let Smoke rest some—then us best turn back." His voice was husky.

I moved suggestively in his embrace. "No," I protested softly.

Cheeks florid, expression strained, Ian swallowed with difficulty. "Us must, miss. You ride Prince."

"What will you do?"

"Walk," he managed.

"Ian," I asked as we began the slow journey back to Wynds, "did you know the Lady Margaret, Sir Robert's first wife?"

"I seen her sometimes," he admitted.

"What was she like?"

"Her be beautiful," he replied.

"Why—how did she die?"

He shrugged. "Something in the stummack, leastwise, I heard."

"Did she ride frequently?"

"Not so much nor you, miss." His face flamed.

It was at Ian's insistence that we traveled the main road. "It be not so many bumps, miss," he explained. "Smoke'll find it some easier."

We passed the listing house. . . . He was there: mouth slack, hooded owl's eyes staring obliquely out from the furrowed, sallow face . . . horned hands resting dully on the scythe . . .

Bloody old fool . . . Why on earth does he simply stand there, day after day? . . . "Ian," I said, "who is that man?"

A muscle leapt in Ian's set jaw.

"Ian," I persisted. "That man . . . Who is he?"

After a long moment Ian sighed deeply: "Me da . . ."

Chapter 26

Behind us a sudden hawking cry and the crunch of whirring wheels rent the silence of the countryside. The ugly moment passed. Flailing his whip and shouting, Dr. Briggs reined up in a flurry of excitement. "Ah, m'dear," he called. "I was on my way to Wynds to fetch you!" His gaze took in Smoke and then Ian. "Well, lad. What's amiss?"

"Him be lame, sir," Ian answered.

"Devil of a shame, old boy," the doctor said, as much to the horse as to the youth. "Help if I had a look?"

Ian shook his head.

"Miss Knowlton, I had a mind to escort you to the village for a festive libation this afternoon, since I have been given a few hours to myself—and since, more particularly, this happens to be Christmas Eve—and one should always engage in cheerful pursuits on such an occasion."

"How lovely." I smiled.

"But as you seem to be otherwise engaged," the doctor continued doubtfully.

"Not at all," I assured him. I turned to Ian, "Help me dismount . . ."

Turning the trap adroitly, Dr. Briggs watched the forlorn figure of Ian as it trudged slowly homeward, the two horses in tow. "Feel a bit guilty—for that," the doctor confessed. "Poor lad! He'll be on the road for some time with that lame horse . . ."

"Better he than I," I dismissed Ian's plight easily. "After all, that is what he is engaged to do."

"The horse appears in poor condition."

"Let's forget about the tiresome old nag." I snuggled deep in the warmth of the woolen robe. "Tell me, where are we going?"

The doctor looked surprised. "Why, the inn. Naturally."

"Why—naturally?"

"There is no other respectable public establishment in Drewsby, that's why—naturally."

"Must we be respectable?"

"Come, come, Miss Knowlton," the doctor scolded mildly, "you don't really mean that—"

My chuckle was low, throaty. "Try me . . ."

Dr. Briggs flushed.

"What about the pub . . . The Rooster, or whatever?"

"The Golden Cock?"

I nodded.

"Ladies do not frequent pubs," he said definitively.

"What a fat lot of bloody nonsense!" I sputtered.

Dr. Briggs laughed aloud. "Miss Knowlton! For shame!"

I nestled closer. "Please . . . Can't we go to the Golden Cock?"

"I suppose you would be safe enough with me . . ." He hesitated.

"I know I should," I agreed, pretending to feel the muscle of his forearm. . . I allowed my hand to remain there. . . .

The Golden Cock was filled well beyond the outer limits of its modest capacity that Christmas Eve, and the dregs of the village were fully represented: a dismal clientele already well established in the extremes of insobriety: some frankly staggering, others still good-naturedly tipsy. The place reeked of unbathed bodies, damp wool, and the sharp, distinctive odor of spirits. . . .

Each table was taken; every stool occupied. "We shall be obliged to stand," muttered the doctor. "Although there doesn't appear to be much space left over for that, either."

"I don't mind," I laughed amicably. "I believe I shall have a beer, Doctor."

Eyebrows elevated slightly, my escort gave the signal for two beers and waited while the frazzled maid completed our order. We toasted the health of each other companionably, but in virtual silence; The din in the room was of such intensity that normal conversation was rendered impossible. A drunken patron, losing his already unsteady footing, caused me to fall sharply against Dr. Briggs. "Watch it, lad," the doctor cautioned lightly.

"Mind your own bloody arse," the man jeered.

"Now, see here," Dr. Briggs warned.

"See what?" the man scoffed. "Up 'er skirts, eh?"

"Why, I should—" Dr. Briggs bristled.

"Why don't yer, Guvner?" the man hiccoughed. "Bloody frighted—that's the ticket . . ."

Face grim, Dr. Briggs commandeered my elbow. "Come, Miss Knowlton, let's go—"

"Ruddy milktit!" the man bellowed after us. "Bloody pixie!"

Our retreat from the pub at that precise moment was fortuitous: We discovered the doctor's horse, tethered innocently at curbside, suffering base mistreatment cruelly administered by a band of rough urchins, rudely clothed and of incorrigible speech. Heaving rocks and shrilling ugly abuse, the gang of ruffians seemed to delight in their helpless target's plaintive nickers. Dr. Briggs was murderous: Snatching the whip from inside the trap, he brandished it wildly before the surly faces of the miscreants. "Bastards . . . Goddamned bastards!" he roared. "Get the hell away from here before I use this!"

Frightened, the boys scurried away. Like rats.

After a cursory and reassuring examination had revealed that the animal exhibited more fright than real injury, Dr. Briggs took some moments to calm the frantic beast as well as to mollify his own dangerous rage. As he handed me into the trap, finally, I heard him mutter, "If I weren't a physician and hadn't seen what the whip can do, I'd have used the thing—straight across their ruddy faces!"

Even through the heavy insulation of the woolen robe I could feel Dr. Briggs tremble with remembered anger. I snuggled close and placed a soothing hand on his arm. "Put it behind you, Doctor," I advised. "It is Christmas Eve, after all. . . . Time for good cheer . . ."

Smiling down at me, he patted my hand. "You are right. Of course. I shall reform," he promised.

Soon we came upon the listing house. . . . He was there . . . motionless. Hooded owl's eyes staring . . . I remembered the pain in Ian's face, the anguish in his blue eyes, the tremulous sigh, as he delivered those dreadful words: "Me da . . ."

I shivered . . .

Dr. Briggs regarded me with instant concern. "Cold?" he asked solicitously.

I shook my head; nonetheless I moved closer.

Twilight had already claimed the sky as we pulled into Wynd's cobbled courtyard. The marquee purposed to shelter the laborers had been erected: Blazing lanterns suspended from its topmost beams swayed in dizzy invitation. "Oh, my!" I exclaimed in delight. "This is truly exciting!" My eyes danced in anticipation as I waited for the doctor to hand me from the trap. Holding me close in his arms, he murmured, "Merry Christmas, Miss Knowlton . . . Elizabeth . . ." He bent to kiss me: My lips parted under his and I could feel his desire mounting. . . . Released at last, I smiled provocatively up at him. . . . I escaped then into the hall, only to find a nearly frenzied Auntie Maude awaiting me at the door. "Elizabeth! Child! Where on earth have you been!" she cried. "Sir Robert has returned!"

I regarded her coolly.

"And," she whispered, "when he asked for an audience with his wife's new companion, no one could find you!" Her gray eyes were wild with concern.

"Well, Aunt, I am back now," I said, my tone airy.

"You must be careful, Elizabeth!" she hissed. "We must not offend the master!"

"Dear heaven," I asked, suddenly impatient with all this, "how have I offended him?"

"You should be avilable when he requests your presence," she insisted.

"Nonsense! I can hardly predict his own whereabouts, now, can I?"

"Elizabeth . . ."

"I must dress. Aunt, pray—let me pass."

Annie was busily mending the fire when I entered my rooms. "I presume that there will be sufficient hot water for a decent bath this evening" was my only greeting.

Color tinged her face. "Aye, miss. Right away, miss."

"And Annie—" I stayed her departure. "I trust that the towels will be fresh also?"

She curtsied. "Yes, miss . . ."

Stretching my limbs luxuriously in the soapy water, I watched in fascination as tiny bubbles, buoyant, translucent, collided with my silken, thrusting breasts. . . . My thoughts whirled in fanciful expectation: It had been years since I had attended a party of any kind. How I looked forward to the festivities of this night. . . . A tapping at the door invaded my reverie. "Yes?" I called, irritated.

"Sir Robert has asked everyone to be in the great hall by eight of the clock, miss," Annie said, "to greet the guests."

"What time is it now?" I inquired lazily.

"It be a quarter 'til, miss."

. . . Smoothing the amber-colored silk of the sole garment in my limited wardrobe even remotely festal, I reflected that the gown—designed by one of London's more distinguished couturiers and fastidiously cut from the finest material—had withstood its age well and was still becoming, despite the fact that my figure had matured considerably since the original fitting and that my breasts now swelled against their confinement. . . . I pinned my hair, piling it high, allowing a few golden curls to escape and drape themselves carelessly over one shoulder. . . .

I was ready.

Moving slowly down the broad staircase, I found the great hall a beehive of activity: Footmen and maids scurried to and fro, burdened with heavy trays, steaming dishes or platters hoisting huge joints of meat . . . Scraping against a background of hurrying feet and muffled voices, the faint sounds of a violin tuning . . . I paused midway in my descent to savor fully the panorama unfolding beneath me. . . .

In the doorway to the inglenook, his back toward me, lounged a tall, slim figure, elegant in formal attire. His hair was richly black and his bearing suggested a leisurely feral grace.

He turned slowly. . . . Our eyes locked. . . .

It was he: the man in my dream . . .

Coming forward, his stride easy, fluid, eyes dusky and intense under their mocking brows, he approached the stairs. He held out his hand. . . . The silk of my gown whispered its excitement as I made unhurried progress to the bottom step. . . . I placed my hand in his warm outstretched one. . . . He brought it to his lips, they were firm, cool. . . . "Miss Knowlton?" he murmured.

I nodded.

"I am Robert Wyndham. . . ."

Chapter 27

A brief but emphatic knocking instantly mechanized Judd, who had until that moment been officiating in the hall, issuing a constant barrage of instructions to his scurrying staff; with alacrity he repaired to the door.

"Our guests, it seems," observed Sir Robert wryly, "have arrived."

Imperfectly masking an air of condescension, Judd ushered into the hall first the swinish Mr. Wade, then his equally corpulent wife, followed in turn by a squat young man flourishing an unappetizing complexion. "Sir Robert," Judd announced, stiffly formal, "Mr.—ah—Wade . . ."

As expected, Mr. Wade was obsequious in the presence of his squire. "Sir Robert!" he fawned, rubbing fat fingers together. "Merry Christmas, sir!"

"Mr. Wade," acknowledged Sir Robert.

"Fine evening, sir! Fine!" Mr. Wade exclaimed, "thought for a while we might have snow! Ha! Ha!"

Sir Robert smiled wanly.

"Hard on the people, but good for the crops, I always say," Mr. Wade decreed. "A little snow in proper season is just what Dr. Nature ordered."

Sir Robert nodded absently.

Mr. Wade's buried eyes slid over me expectantly. "Ah— Miss—er, ah—" he petitioned pointedly.

Sir Robert stood in polite silence.

"Ah, Miss—er, ah—please to meet my son, Michael!" Proudly Mr. Wade pushed the pustular youth forward. "Ha! Ha! Perhaps you young people will have a chance to get acquainted over supper! Ha! Ha!"

Sir Robert turned to me. "Would you be so kind as to attend my wife. . . . I am sure Mr. Wade will excuse you. . . ."

Relieved to escape the servile Mr. Wade and his improbable suggestions, I went in dutiful search of Lady Frances, who was (I subsequently discovered) huddled miserably before a fire blazing in the inglenook. Ignoring her cringing aspect, obviously aggravated by my appearance, I greeted her with studied graciousness. "Lady Frances! Here you are! Is there something I might fetch for you?"

She shook her head violently.

"Your guests are beginning to assemble," I informed her. "I think, perhaps, you should make an effort to receive them."

She shrank deeper into the chair.

I eyed her with overt distaste. . . . Bloody fool . . . Plainly the woman was deranged. . . . What sense in trying to humor a lunatic. . . . A consummate waste of time and energy . . .

I sank onto a waiting bench and stared bleakly into the fire, listening with a growing resentment as voices raised in noisy conversation and roisterous laughter, emanating from the great hall, signaled that other guests were streaming in: their numbers great; their mood cheerful . . . While I was relegated here, sequestered with this unresponsive ninny. . . .

I looked fully at Lady Frances: noted the dreary pinched face; the scrawny frame; hair, wispy and lusterless . . . much like a molting hen . . . I observed with angry irony that her emerald gown was elegantly styled and fashioned from the most delicate of fabrics; served thus, it was as a shimmering rag covering a broom. . . .

Judd entered the alcove and stood before his mistress. "Madam," he began, his manner deferential, "the master would wish you to assume your position with him at the head table."

Blanching, Lady Frances pressed deeper into the recesses of the chair. . . .

"If you please, madam—"

She began to tremble.

Ever the imperturbable servant, Judd yielded; bowing formally, he withdrew.

Incredible . . .

It was not long before Sir Robert himself sauntered into the room. Deliberately casual, he approached his wife. "My dear," he said quietly. "Your guests await you."

"No—" she breathed.

"Come, Frances." He held out his hand. "Your appearance is required. Even briefly."

She recoiled from his touch.

"Frances, my dear," he cajoled, "for a short time only. Please, my dear." Taking her pincer-like hands in his, he gently drew her from the chair, murmuring soft exhortations, gentle encouragement. Threading her lifeless arm companionably through his, he smiled down at the wretched creature. "Now perhaps you can be persuaded to eat a little something—" Politely he included me. "Miss Knowlton, would you care to join us?" With difficulty and supported entirely by her husband, Lady Frances dragged unwilling, flaccid limbs forward. . . .

. . . Bloody gawk . . . Vapid as a somnambulist . . . What on earth ails the woman? . . . If I were on Sir Robert's arm, I should certainly not proceed thus: fleshless, wooden puppet . . .

The great hall had burgeoned into a crush of people of all ages; even small children, obviously on their best behavior, could be found amongst the company. I followed Sir Robert and the lagging Lady Frances to the main table. There he sat her carefully, directing Judd to attend her plate forthwith, before handing me into the chair adjacent and taking his own place as host.

It can hardly be said that the conversation was sparkling or the company stimulating: These were, after all, farmers—hardworking, God-fearing, some claiming substantial means. Diverting, they were not. Sir Robert conducted himself brilliantly: Interested and courteous throughout, he orchestrated the assembly with an attentive smile here, a nod there. Wedged in between the cowering Lady Frances—who merely stared fixedly at her plate except at those moments when Sir Robert leaned close, urging her to taste even a small portion—and an old whale of a man (who proved as noisily ravenous as Lady Frances was silently without appetite, and severely hard of hearing as well) I found my immediate dinner partners discouraging entertainment indeed.

Directly across the table the unwholesome Michael

Wade eyed me acquisitively: Intended to be inviting, his soulful glances were easily interpreted as suggestive leers. To his left a young woman tried valiantly and without success to engage him in prolonged conversation; avidly tracking my attention, he was less than carelessly polite, so much so that her eyes flashed angrily at me from time to time. Had she been dressed with more aplomb and less bombazine and her hair not tortured into frizzled curls, hers might have been a mild beauty, certainly deserving of a swain more appealing than Michael Wade. . . . Wade . . . Ah—Ian's bitter pronouncement suddenly surfaced: "If my name was Wade 'stead of Childer, I'd be ridin' some higher nor this. . . . Him's got the best farm hereabouts—well as to go runnin' to Sir Robert on every other thing. . . ."

So, that was it: the girl's parents doubtless sought to establish a profitable alliance with the wealthiest farmer in the district, their daughter to become the sacrifice on fortune's altar. . . . Bloody nonsense . . . More the fool, she . . .

To his right sat another of Drewsby's eligibles: a buxom little thing with a nice smile and dreamy blue eyes. Upon receipt of regular signals flashed by her frantic mother, sitting farther down the line, the girl made an occasional halfhearted overture in Michael's direction. Her real target of interest was Sir Robert: Her gaze seldom left his face. . . .

Mr. Wade paraded in conspicuous evidence at all times, making a serious effort to publish his position as headman in the district (under Sir Robert, of course). His mien before the squire was sycophantic; his mien before his peers, frankly superior.

Mrs. Wade managed to submerge her own feeling of self-satisfaction beneath modest airs that might have been assumed in deference to her host. More likely the woman was captured by the feast spread before her, food being Mrs. Wade's raison d'être, as evidenced clearly by both the enormity of her physical person and her gluttonous performance. Eating without conversation and determinedly daintily (the little finger gracefully crooked always; the

napkin scrupulously employed), she contrived adroitly to
deplete three successive platters, each piled higher than the
last. . . .

Sitting without the pleasure of, or the distraction provided by, capable dinner companions, I was able to assess
the general group unobtrusively and at my leisure, an opportunity not usually granted at social functions. I recognized names made familiar by Ian: Schneider; Ditman; Os-
born; Whitfield; Cawley; Baily . . . and took particular
interest in at last identifying Mr. Hartley, the stable master, although I confess that I was somewhat surprised at his
attendance. Hartley, a born lackey, sought whenever possible to attract Sir Robert's attention on any spurious pretext,
offering a kind of sick subservience made all the more offensive by the fact that he was a man of middle years,
extreme height, and powerful build. I recalled then the
words of the disgruntled stable hand: "Hartley wants Sir
Robert to look at he's some kind of big. Save the master a
few coppers . . . it don't matter us works like hell. . . ."
Glancing at Sir Robert, I observed with admiration that his
manner, even while contemplating these fabricated advances, remained unfailingly gracious.

The group ate and drank lustily; joints of meat, picked
to the bone, were replaced on an almost continual basis,
and the wassail and mum bowls were replenished, of necessity, even more faithfully. Trays bearing mince pies and
plum puddings, spitting their blue flames, drew shouts of
applause from the gathering at large, and the eyes of the
children grew enormous in their small faces. Thus, as the
food supply remained abundant and the spiced ale and rum
flowed generously, tongues were loosened, spirits crested,
and hearts were lifted in jubilation. Instinctively realizing
that drink had eased the reins of absolute discipline, and
restive from a too lengthy confinement, the children began
to revert to their more normal rowdy state. Sir Robert rose
and hastily announced that the time for games had arrived,
indicating that the quieter pursuits of backgammon and
draughts might be adjourned to the inglenook; blindman's
buff could be played in the hall proper. And he solicited
suggestions for an amateur theatrical "To be conducted by

our Miss Knowlton," adding blandly, "that is, if she voices no objection. . . ."

Drat that bloody Lady Frances . . . This is her obligation. . . . There she sits—in that chair, cringing, whimpering . . .

"Later," Sir Robert promised, "the band will strike up the music for dancing . . ."

Actually the impromptu drama—rough by virtue of the brevity of time allotted in which to assemble ideas and by the tender age and remarkable dearth of talent contributed by the cast—proved a small triumph. One somber lass, probably no more than six or seven, dangerously myopic and brandishing the protruding teeth often accompanying that particular affliction, insisted that we reenact the manger scene—of course, on the condition that she would be allowed to portray the Virgin Mary. The Nativity was the obvious and ideal choice. I was presented with a plethora of shepherds, innkeeps—even donkeys; I lacked only the Christ child and feared that I might be forced to assume the part myself. My rescuer came in the rotund body of a lad with an infectious giggle, a speech impediment taking the form of an exaggerated lisp, and a fistful of incredibly dirty fingernails. Whispering confidentially in my ear, "Mith, I got a awful thummach ache," he lay prone without a fuss and the show began. . . .

Blindman's buff, one of my own favorite childhood party pastimes, can become rough and disorderly, particularly if little boys are active participants and their parents comfortably tipsy, so much so that momentarily the conduct of their offspring assumes little or no real importance. Fistfights can ensue, a host of bawdy words exchanged, before the skirmish can be forcibly discharged and the players restricted from further immediate engagement. . . . It was during such a hiatus that I was appalled to observe Michael Wade as he grabbed the blindfold, whipped it across his scabietic face, and headed in my direction.

Bloody fool . . . I won't have that disgusting toad touching me. . . .

I stood, repelled to the point of paralysis. . . . He came nearer, his hands weaving before him, searching out their quarry: my person. . . . I could taste the saliva souring in my mouth. . . . Pudgy hands extended, he drew nearer still. Sir Robert, moving quickly, stepped in front of me. Michael then, offering up the customary shrill cry of conquest, threw wide his flabby arms, winding them indecently around his prey. Crowing in victory and clutching his prize with one covetous hand, he peeled off the bandage with the other. "M-my God, s-sir," he stammered. "I— I thought—"

"Yes," said Sir Robert dryly, "I know what you thought."

The subsequent and awkward hush of embarrassment was lifted by Sir Robert, who nodded significantly at Judd and announced that the troupe of musicians would be in readiness shortly and that dancing should soon commence. At a sign from the butler a division of footmen materialized, and there followed the scraping of chairs and tables, shifted so as to enlarge the dance floor. Faces flushed from both spirits and expectation, the group milled about excitedly, waiting to glimpse the musicians as they filed through the hall and took their prescribed places just before the inglenook. The band was modest, consisting of one trumpet, two violins, and a single percussion instrument. At a signal from the leader the spirited notes of a jig were unleashed, ringing from the walls, setting alive the feet of the guests. Most, save those whom the punch bowl had rendered almost insensible, bobbed and hopped with unexpected vigor, their energetic footwork swishing skirts and flinging hair.

Eager to join in the frivolity, the portly Mr. Wade optimistically steered his wife into the midst of the dancers and found his movements curtailed by the generosity of his own middle region, surpassed still by that of his partner (her measurements further extended by dangerously oscillating breasts). His short arms were able to reach only partway to her general waist area. Both were puffing like steam kettles: The smile on her face was determined; the sweat on his brow, prodigal. Warily I looked around for the other Wade, the hoggish Michael, and was gratified to see that his attentive dinner partner had contrived to snare him for the dance. . . . Sir Robert had returned to the table to join his wife, making vain attempts to coax her out onto the floor.

Suddenly a hand jiggled my arm. Looking up, I met the triumphant smile of Dr. Briggs. "Miss Knowlton!" he beamed, "I have escaped!"

"Escaped," I echoed, "from what?"

"From my prison in the dining hall!" he announced gleefully. "Squeezed in between Miss Caroline," he confided, "and Mr. Lineas Stafford, our fuddled schoolmaster. I suspect," Dr. Briggs reflected, "that he must be frankly sleeping by now. . . ."

"I did not fare much better," I laughed. "Lady Frances and a deaf old gentleman with the most appalling table manners!" I made a face, "And still less tempting—directly opposite, the warty Michael Wade!"

"Come," the doctor invited, "let's remedy our plight by taking a turn on the floor."

Unaccustomed to the jerky rhythms of a jig, I made many missteps, falling forward onto Dr. Briggs or colliding awkwardly with another bouncing couple. When the dance ended, I leaned weakly against my partner. "That was rather fun!"

The doctor's arm immediately encircled my waist. "Rather!" he agreed roundly.

Sir Robert was threading his way through the crowd. Nodding to Dr. Briggs in greeting, his glance returned to the head table. "Doctor, perhaps you might be so good as to have a look at my wife."

"Oh?"

"Yes. She seems to be feeling particularly poorly at the moment."

"What seems to be the trouble?" Instantly Dr. Briggs's manner became professional.

Sir Robert's face clouded. "I encouraged her to join me in a dance," he said, "which seemed to trigger a bout of severe trembling."

"Has this happened before?"

"She often exhibits unease," Sir Robert admitted, "but this attack seems more aggravated than usual. Perhaps," he added, "you might wish to examine her without intrusion."

"Of course."

"Her personal maid, Sarah, is in attendance now and will assist you in escorting Lady Frances upstairs. . . ."

I watched Dr. Briggs draw Lady Frances gently to her feet and, supporting her weight in his arms, all but carry her up the stairs. Her face contorted with worry, Sarah trailed after.

Sir Robert's shadowed eyes gazed down at me. "Would you join me in a dance, Miss Knowlton?" he asked.

"Certainly."

"What is your pleasure?"

"A waltz?"

Sir Robert motioned briefly to the orchestra, and immediately the lyrical cadence of a waltz graced the hall.

He took my hand; I melted against him.

As the last cadenza faded Sir Robert murmured, "Your gown matches perfectly the color of your eyes. . . ."

Further conversation was deferred: Dr. Briggs was at that moment crossing the floor, seeking audience with Sir Robert. "Lady Frances is resting comfortably now," he reported.

"I am gratified to hear that," answered Sir Robert.

"I have prescribed a mild dose of laudanum," the doctor declared, "not without considerable reluctance, you understand, in view of her condition."

"I see."

"One runs a moderate risk introducing any drug in cases of pregnancy," Dr. Briggs continued, frowning, "particularly a narcotic. However, Lady Frances's emotional state was such that I feared continuance of hysteria held an even greater peril."

"Thank you, Doctor."

"She should be kept as tranquil as possible for the next few days," the doctor advised. "No taxing duties, no untoward excitement—difficult at Christmas, to be sure. Nonetheless, any additional stressful situations could prove dangerous at this time."

"You may rely on my utmost discretion, Doctor," Sir Robert assured him.

Dr. Briggs nodded. "I must remind you that I am proceeding in the dark, even at that."

"I am afraid I don't entirely understand—"

"Without a determination as to the cause of her

anxiety," the doctor explained, "she cannot begin to be properly treated."

Sir Robert sighed, "I have no idea . . ."

"Phobias are immensely complex: tricky to diagnose and even more difficult to dispel." The doctor smiled and added by way of encouragement, "You may have every confidence that I shall utilize all available scientific intelligence to try and alleviate her symptoms at least and by so doing hasten her eventual return to more normal living."

Sir Robert bowed formally. "I shall be forever in your debt, Doctor."

"And who knows"—Dr. Briggs regarded the squire kindly—"perhaps your wife will regain perfect emotional health simply upon the birth of the child."

"Let us pray that is the case." Sir Robert's eyes were grave.

Dr. Briggs turned to me. "Miss Knowlton, may I have the honor of the next dance?"

"I beg your pardon, Doctor," Sir Robert interposed. "I had presumed that you were on your way just now to rejoin the other—er—more august company—in the dining hall—"

"Why, ah—"

"You see, Doctor," Sir Robert smiled ruefully, "since I am obliged on this occasion to forgo the pleasure of my more, ah, select guests, I was rather hoping that you might agree to act, say, in loco parentis in a sense. . . ." He shrugged, "Just a thought, of course . . ."

"Be glad to. Perhaps Miss Knowlton would care to accompany me—"

"Ah!" sighed Sir Robert. "Forgive me, Doctor, but that, I fear, is impossible. Miss Knowlton is a member of my staff and, as such, is expected to discharge certain duties peculiar to this particular festivity. . . ."

Dr. Briggs reddened. "But—"

"Any other time, of course, I am sure that Miss Knowlton will be delighted to join you."

An expression of angry resentment flicked across Dr. Briggs's flushed face. He bowed stiffly first to me, "Miss Knowlton," and then to his host, "Sir Robert," turned, and headed for the dining hall. He did not look back.

At a directive from the squire the music began again. Sir Robert extended his hand to me. "I believe this is a waltz, Miss Knowlton. . . ."

I could have stayed in his arms forever; the music halted abruptly, however, as the grandfather clock, sentinel of the vestibule, thundered the hour of midnight. "Merry Christmas, Miss Knowlton," murmured Sir Robert.

There followed a general confusion: The children, suddenly recouping flagging energies, bounded in delirious anticipation; parents, some maneuvering unsteadily, struggled to ready their unruly offspring for the journey homeward in the brisk air of a winter's night. The yawning musicians rose and stretched, returned instruments to their cases, and withdrew as unobtrusively as they had appeared hours earlier. Mr. Wade stood pointedly aloof from the departing guests; florid face slick with perspiration, he gripped a bulging portfolio in his damp fingers. His small, glittering eyes remained fastened on his squire.

Sir Robert guided me to the broad staircase. "The hour has arrived, I fear, when I must attend to the business of the evening . . . and when you, Miss Knowlton, should retire." Bowing lightly, he bade me a formal good night. Midway in my ascent up the stairs I turned: Under brows raised as if in salute, his eyes—dark, intense—consumed mine. . . .

Reaching the upper hallway, I became aware of the din emanating from the courtyard: The steady roar of voices, stabbed first by a sudden bawdy shout, then by a burst of ribald laughter, drew me to the window. By the wild flames wavering erratically from torches held against an empty sky I could discern easily the stingy shelter of the marquee, which spilled its contents: weaving women, stumbling men pummeling each other, caught up in boisterous drunken play. A lone figure, standing away from the rest, stared fixedly at the house; tall, statue-still, legs spread slightly apart, he seemed oddly familiar: Ian, I knew at once. Something in his stance, disquieting, even menacing, stayed my hand as it lifted to tap the pane in greeting. . . .

Annie had left a stout fire burning, I realized immediately when I opened the door to my room; the flame-light flickered like sensual little tongues probing the walls beyond, and I was enfolded in a blanket of heavy, almost tropical, warmth. I lighted the candle standing ready on the wardrobe and looked dreamily into the wall of mirrors; from a face delicately flushed, a pair of amber eyes returned my languid gaze; soft, full lips parted in a lazy smile. Slowly, deliberately, I loosened my gown and watched as it slithered unheeded from my naked shoulders and hips to lie discarded on the floor. My hair, already seeking to escape its bonds, I unpinned, and reveled as the wonderful release of shining gold veiled my firm, rich breasts.

I was . . . beautiful . . .

Once in bed, I was restless. . . . I could feel, still, the gentle pressure of Sir Robert's arms as they embraced me in the dance; sense his demanding nearness. . . . I was scorched by his searing gaze; my face, bruised by the intensity in his dark eyes . . . Uneasy, stirred, I fled one side of the bed to seek comfort from the other. . . .

Then I heard it. . . . Soft. Insistent . . . The whispering . . . Elizabeth . . . Elizabeth . . .

I rose eagerly and followed the golden path. . . .

Chapter 28

Christmas morning dawned bright and cheerful; I stretched contentedly and watched in absent absorption as a sliver of golden sunlight speared its way into the room. Annie's timid tapping at the door elicited from me an agreeable response, and the girl entered, bearing a breakfast tray piled high with all manner of festive fare, embellished, besides, with a sprig or two of fresh holly.

"Good morning." I wriggled under the sheets. "Merry Christmas!"

"The same to you, miss," the girl curtsied, " 'tis a fair day, and all . . ."

"Open the drapes," I ordered, "so that I might see the blue of the sky."

Annie complied readily. "See, miss," she observed, "beautiful, it is!"

"Annie," I suggested, "if you were to reach into the top drawer of the bureau, you might find there a small token from me."

The girl flushed in surprised delight.

I laughed. "It is hardly monumental, mind. A simple Christmas remembrance, nothing more . . ."

Annie was enthralled. Nothing would do but that she must adorn her fuzzy locks with one wide crimson ribbon and, at the same time, a narrower green one. "Christmas colors, you know," she preened, then reddened in embarrassment.

"Very becoming," I murmured.

"Thank you, miss!" I feared, for a dreadful moment, that in her rapture she might seek to kiss my hand. Bobbing one curtsy after another, she backed out of the room, clutching the precious little packet. Suddenly she gasped. "Oh, I near forgot. . . . The master asks that you come to the great hall directly after the meal. For the opening of the gifts," she said. "Thank you."

The master . . . Sir Robert . . . I smiled sleepily . . . A merry Christmas it is. . . .

Halted by the hubbub rising from the hall, I stopped midway in my descent down the broad staircase: below, the household staff milled about in noisy anticipation, barely able to conceal a restless excitement not unlike that exhibited by small children. The debris from the festivities of the evening previous had been cleared away, leaving the ornaments and greenery in lonely attestation to the joyous season.

Holding forth in the midst of frankly envious housemaids, Annie, newly beribboned, flaunted her finery and was awarded the appropriate "ah's" and "oh's" attendant upon such treasures. The disdainful Judd, pointedly positioned at some little distance from the group at large (removing himself from contamination, as it were), stood, folded arms stiff in disapproval. Auntie Maude wandered, awkward and uncertain, until she spied me; a bright smile broadened her round face.

When I reached the foot of the stairs, I could see into the inglenook, which was crammed ceiling-high with bundles of all sizes and shapes.

"Merry Christmas, dear," Auntie Maude embraced me warmly.

"My word!" I exclaimed, looking around.

"It is the tradition here at Wynds," Auntie Maude explained, "for the squire and his lady to dole out the seasonal tribute to the household in the great hall on Christmas morning." Glancing in his direction, she added, "Mr. Judd has informed me that it is a most formal occasion indeed."

"One scarcely senses a feeling of solemnity," I observed dryly.

"The servants are excited, of course." Auntie Maude's reproval was implicit. "You should well understand, dear," she reminded me.

A sudden reverent hush blanketed the hall: Sir Robert, a drawn Lady Frances clinging weakly to his arm, slowly, laboriously descended the stairs. But a death mask, the lady's face bore a sickly pallor that was pathetically reemphasized by sparse hair that hung limp and lusterless. Colored a vivid carmine, her gown betrayed even at a distance its exquisite texture of finest silk and fluidity of design; it hung from her spectral frame as would a bloody shroud. . . .

Fool . . . to appear thus before this gathering . . .

Before a husband such as Sir Robert . . .

Judd was galvanized into immediate action: Snapping authoritative fingers, he signaled a pair of footmen to set a chair in readiness for his troubled mistress. She sank into it gratefully.

Sir Robert's dark eyes swept over the crowd, rested on me briefly, and moved on. With a gracious bow he addressed the gathering. "I extend to each of you hearty greetings on this merry occasion."

The crowd responded with respectful murmurings.

"Wynds has been well served this year, and for your attendance and fidelity the Lady Frances and I are truly indebted. Is that not so, my dear?" he prompted his wife, who recoiled deep within the chair. "As a measure of our esteem," Sir Robert continued, "your mistress has selected a few mementos for services rendered." He nodded at Judd. "If you please . . ."

Judd retired into the inglenook and, aided by several waiting houseboys, brought out the items one by one, presenting first those gifts designated for the servants of meanest rank. Most of the articles were practical in nature—mainly wearing apparel: footwear for the men and supplies of serviceable materials for the women. A frivolous bag, containing sweets for the women and tobacco for the men, was attached to each package, drawing, of course, the greatest burst of delight from the recipient. It was a gay affair, really. Sir Robert was charming; his warm smile suggested a sincere pleasure in sharing this experience with his people. All efforts, however, to coax Lady Frances into the celebration resulted in her further withdrawal . . . What a bloody bore . . .

Auntie Maude unwrapped a bolt of black silk and a bundle of skeins sufficient to fashion a warm cloak—along with a generous supply of exotic teas. Judd, in turn, almost flushed with rapture as he unveiled his own treasures: a pair of highly polished boots with a bottle of delicate French wine tucked playfully inside one toe.

All eyes were now on me. I was the last served, demonstrating the superiority of my position. As my fingers dug at the ribboned knot of the large package, I wondered what it might contain. I must confess to a bubbling inner excitement; it had been years since I had received a gift of any substance, and one from a household of this ilk held particular promise. After dismissing a small packet of sugar-coated drops, I gazed on the offering beneath: a bolt of cloth—bombazine of only average quality and, further, of an insupportable hue—earth brown . . . I dropped the cloth from my hands; it slid carelessly to the floor. Looking up, I saw that Sir Robert's angry dark glance was fastened upon me. "My dear," he turned to his wife, "there has been an error, I believe."

Lady Frances murmured something unintelligible.

"My dear," Sir Robert repeated, "there is a mistake here, I am confident."

She cringed.

"Did you not supervise the selection of the gifts?" he asked. "Personally?"

"Y-yes." It was barely a whisper.

"How, then, did this oversight occur?"

"I—"

Sir Robert leaned closer. "What did you say, my dear?"

"I—"

"I am waiting, my dear," Sir Robert said softly.

"I—"

"My dear," Sir Robert reasoned patiently, "I am sure there is a simple explanation."

Claimed by violent spasms, Lady Frances began to tremble uncontrollably.

The squire sighed. "Sarah," he alerted his wife's personal maid, "would you escort your mistress to her rooms. I fear that she is unwell."

Sarah bobbed a curtsy. "Of course, sir. Right away, sir."

I watched their slow procession up the staircase; leaning against the young girl for support, Lady Frances pulled one uncertain leg after the other, struggling to maintain her very balance. . . . Lunatic behavior, surely . . .

Smiling sadly, Sir Robert offered his regrets to the company of servants. "Lady Frances is feeling poorly," he apologized. "But she joins me in wishing you most heartily an agreeable holiday. . . ."

Gaiety momentarily dampened, the crowd dispersed then, and one by one gathered up each precious parcel and headed for the servants' quarters, where the high spirits of festivity would rise again.

Abandoning the brown bombazine and packet of cloying sweets to a fate deserved—half-unwrapped and desolate on the floor—I moved to retire to my own room. "Miss Knowlton," Sir Robert stayed my departure, "if I might have audience with you in my study for a moment."

After seating me carefully, he walked in back of a massive walnut desk and removed from its position on the wall a painting, behind which a safe was concealed. Twisting the tiny dial expertly, Sir Robert extracted a small, square box that was covered in ancient purple velvet and placed it in my hand. He closed the safe, twirled the dial, restored the painting, and motioned me to open the box, teasing, "I assure you, Miss Knowlton, this is not brown bombazine."

Indeed, it was not.

Reclining on its bed of puffed white satin lay an exquisite amber drop, suspended from a delicately ornamented gold chain. "If I may?" Sir Robert moved behind my chair, drew the necklace from its nest, and arranged it around my neck; in so doing his hands rested lightly on my shoulders. The contact, however brief, seemed to scorch my very skin, penetrating even the heavy material of my morning gown. He stood before me now, dark eyes imprisoning my own gaze in their shadowed depths. "Ah!" he applauded. "Infinitely more suitable!"

Low in my throat I chuckled.

"Pray, excuse my wife's mistake in judgment. I am sure no mischief was intended. It is simply that she is taxed beyond her strength just now." He smiled. "I know that your understanding will prevail."

"Of course," I assured him. "Do not concern yourself . . . And I thank you for this." I fingered the amber stone.

He nodded. "A family heirloom. Still, it might have been

recently fashioned. Expressly for you," he mused. "Perhaps it was, at that."

I was puzzled.

"We do share a common lineage—albeit distant—"

His words were interrupted by a timid tapping at the door: Sarah. "Beg pardon, Sir Robert," the girl curtsied, "but the mistress sent me to tell you that her be too ill to prepare for church, betimes."

"The service is not scheduled for some hours yet," Sir Robert protested.

The girl blushed.

"Lady Frances will not have recovered by then, girl?"

"No, sir. She says not."

Sir Robert sighed. "Very well, Sarah. You may go."

"Thank you, sir."

"Miss Knowlton." Sir Robert swung around suddenly. "Might you be kind enough to grant me the honor of your presence at the Anglican Church this afternoon for the traditional Yuletide service—a prescribed adjunct to last evening's protracted affair and one at which Wynds must be properly represented."

My eyebrows rose. "The Reverend Smythe?"

He laughed. "The Reverend Smythe."

Chapter 29

I wrapped my cloak snugly around me against the bitter wind that cracked its cruel whip across the dirt footpath leading to the stables. The well-trodden earth had frozen unevenly, and I could feel its sharp ridges cut the thin soles of my shoes. The stables seemed unnaturally hushed as I approached. Absent was the usual bawdy exchange between the lusty grooms; only the muffled thump of a restless hoof as it moved gently in its stall or the soft nickering from a velvet mouth broke the somber silence.

"Ian," I called. My voice fell oddly heavy on my ears. "Ian! Merry Christmas!" The wind tugged savagely at my cloak, easily piercing the worn, rubbed nap. "Ian!" I stamped my foot. Drat the churl! "Ian!"

Sluggishly and as if weighted with great reluctance, stepped young Peter, newest of the hands, from behind the stable door. His face, still unbearded, was severely mottled and his eyes, bearing harsh testimony of recent tears, nervously avoided my own. Respectfully touching his stained cap with grubby fingers, Peter asked dully, "Yes, miss?"

"I want Ian," I said curtly.

The boy shook his head.

"Do, for the Lord's sake, speak," I snapped, perplexed at his almost witless demeanor.

Peter snuffled. "Him be gone."

"Gone!" I repeated. "Gone where?"

Uneasily the boy ran a frayed sleeve across his face.

"God, but you are mulish today!" Irritation mounting, I glared at his blotchy face.

The boy sniffed.

"Where has Ian gone?" I asked impatiently.

He shrugged. "Dunno, miss."

"What do you mean—you don't know?" I demanded crossly.

"Him not here no more, s'all."

"I understood that Ian was the head lackey," I retorted.

"Him was. Seems so . . ."

"What is all this?"

"Him gone. Not here no more."

"And why not?"

Peter shifted uncomfortably. "Mr. Hartley give him the sack, seems like."

"You mean, Mr. Hartley dismissed Ian?" I was incredulous.

He shrugged. "Seems so."

"Oh!" I took an angry step toward him. "You are infuriating! Why did Mr. Hartley give Ian the sack?"

" 'Cause of—" Peter's voice thickened.

"Because of what?" I asked sharply.

"S-Smoke—"

"Smoke?"

The boy's lower lip trembled. "Seems so . . ."

"What of Smoke?"

"H-him be gone, t-too."

"Smoke—gone? Oh, I see. Ian took Smoke with him," I reasoned.

"N-no."

"Then where has Smoke gone?" My voice rose in exasperation.

"H-him d-dead," Peter choked.

"Dead!"

"Shot," he whispered hoarsely.

"Shot?"

"Mr. Hartley. Him done do it."

"Dear God! Why?"

"Smoke bad lame, seems like."

"Mr. Hartley shot Smoke because he was lame?" I snorted. "Ridiculous!"

The boy sniffed.

"Obviously, you have been misinformed," I smiled. "A lame horse can certainly recover."

The boy shrugged.

"Well?"

"Not Smoke, miss. Not him. Him too far gone." A shudder passed through the boy's small frame.

"This is preposterous!"

"Anythin' else you be wantin', miss?" Miserably, Peter turned to go.

"I brought Ian a Christmas gift," I stopped him.

"Ian not here," the boy muttered.

The lad was maddening! "I am aware of that fact by now, after all!" I snapped.

Peter shuffled restless feet. "I got me chores, miss."

"Will you be so good as to give this gift to Ian?"

"No, miss," the boy sighed. "Me won't be seein' he, most like."

"Well, then, keep the bloody thing for yourself!" Angrily I flung the gaily wrapped box at his manure-caked boots. Drawing my cloak close, I added nastily, "For God's sake, tend to that filthy nose of yours! Use the handkerchief instead of your sleeve—you are positively disgusting!"

Chapter 30

The crease of concern, marring the broad and otherwise unclouded expanse of her face, was instantly eradicated by the equally broad and loving smile Auntie Maude trained on me as I returned from the stables and headed promptly for the cozy chimney corner offering the welcome of its lighted hearth.

"I am frozen!" I declared, my teeth chattering.

Auntie Maude hovered around me. "Where on earth have you been, dear?"

"Out."

"It is almost time for our own special Christmas feast," she reminded me. "And," she added, obviously disappointed, "I was so hoping we could have some real time alone together, beforehand . . ."

"Well, I am here now."

"Let me take your cloak, dear. I'll hang it on a peg for you."

"Don't bother." My refusal was less than gracious. "I must go upstairs anyway and fetch your gift, after all."

"Oh, Elizabeth!" Auntie Maude flushed with childlike pleasure. "You shouldn't have!"

"It's not much," I told her truthfully . . . .

Auntie Maude's dreary quarters were fiercely festooned with nearly every kind of beribboned greenery available in this harsh land of scrub and heather. Sprays of bedraggled holly were draped strategically here and there: Vibrant red berries, peeking through their nest of brittle leaves, extended a fragile air of gaiety. Around a miniature Christmas tree, cleverly fashioned of pine sprigs and stationed atop a scarred oak chest, were spread a few brightly wrapped packages.

The atmosphere of determined cheer was pitiful.

"Well, Elizabeth, dear, here you are!" Auntie Maude was in high spirits. "We can have a nice little visit before

Millie brings in our tray." She patted a frayed cushion on an upholstered settee in invitation. "Here, love, sit here. You will find it more comfortable." Gingerly Auntie Maude lowered herself onto the stern edge of a straight chair. "There, now," she beamed, "how is that, dear?"

"Fine," I answered politely.

"Not quite like old times," Auntie Maude sighed, "but at least we are together."

I nodded absently.

"I have a few little things for you," she crooned. "Why not open one of them now?"

"All right," I consented dully.

Tenderly Auntie Maude extracted an oblong parcel from beneath a straggly branch of the makeshift tree. "Rather cunning, don't you think, dear?" she asked, viewing her contrivance with a diffident show of pride. "How I miss our old ornaments from Leicester Square. . . . But," she scolded herself promptly, "We mustn't dwell, now, must we?"

"No," I agreed.

Handing me her first selection, Auntie Maude waited in a state of naked anticipation for me to open it. Her smile was beatific as I tugged at the flimsy paper and drew out a knitted, tasseled scarf. "Very nice," I said automatically, trying to conceal my distaste as I eyed the drab gray of the wool.

"Do try it on, dear!" she urged gaily. "It should keep you snug and warm on those rides you insist on taking!"

The yarn was coarse and plucked at my skin as, at her insistence, I wound it around my neck. Despite its dun color and harsh texture, I had to admit that the scarf was certainly thick and promised stout defense against the cold and penetrating winds of the moor. "Thank you, Auntie Maude," I said dutifully.

Her eyes were radiant, and I could see that her gaze was drawn compulsively and regularly to the small parcel resting in my lap: my Christmas remembrance to her. "Why not have a look at yours?" I suggested.

"Oh, no! I couldn't!" she refused happily. "I shall save that treat for the very last, if you don't mind, dear!"

"As you wish," I shrugged.

"Would you prefer to open the remainder of your gifts now—or wait until after Millie has brought our feast?" Auntie Maude's brow wrinkled with the delicious conflict. "If we open everything now, the surprise will end too quickly! Oh, my!" she giggled, "I am really in a quandary!" Abruptly she resumed her perch on the stiff chair. "Perhaps we should wait, after all, and have our visit now. . . ." Her eyes flew to the little tree. "Then again, maybe we should simply continue on with our gift-giving and visit after dinner. . . . Dear me, I cannot seem to make up my mind!" She sprang eagerly from the chair to consult the tree, lovingly fingering a scrubby branch; immediately a tiny shower of needles sprayed the top of the ancient chest.

Sudden activity in the hall put an end to Auntie Maude's delectable dilemma: Millie, all but buried beneath a tray laden with our Christmas meal, was struggling with the door while still contriving to keep the container upright. Small of stature, the girl was almost bent double under the weight of her burden, and her expressive eyes desperately sought an ultimate destination for it. "Oh, Millie!" Auntie Maude glowed, "that looks scrumptious indeed!"

"Miss—ah—Treadway—" the girl gasped.

"Set the tray here, Millie—" Auntie Maude indicated the bed as the only surface eligible to receive such a vessel, since the chest was preoccupied with the Christmas tree. "A trifle awkward," Auntie Maude confessed ruefully, "but we won't mind that, will we, dear?" She turned to me.

"Will there be anythin' else, ma'am?" asked the breathless girl.

"No. Thank you, Millie," Auntie Maude answered after careful consideration. "I am sure we have everything we need—"

Millie curtsied and prepared to leave.

"Millie—"

"Yes, ma'am?"

"A Merry Christmas, child."

Millie flushed. "And the same to you, ma'am, I'm sure," she smiled.

The meal was interminable. Auntie Maude resolved to cover my plate with monumental portions of this and that until my physical discomfort grew to the point of actual nausea. I noted with some dismay that since Auntie Maude's departure from Leicester Square and our former life together, her mien at table had seriously deteriorated. She had developed the noisome habit of licking her fat fingers after partaking of a particularly tasty morsel, and smacking her lips in what was loud appreciation. I found that sharing her board had become a disagreeable experience. A disproportionate period of time passed, it seemed, before her hunger was finally appeased. What had happened to that ladylike restraint—that studied poise affected by the dainty maid reared in delicate circumstance—readied for a coveted position in society? Although it did occur to me (in fairness) that my aunt's drop in station naturally occasioned lesser associates and entailed a certain amount of drudgery besides (possibly contributing to what was, I thought, an appetite to excess), I found the spectacle degrading and longed for that moment of escape to my own room or, better still, to the outdoors and its bracing wintry air. Auntie Maude, however, was determined that "our feast"—as she would have it—should last indefinitely. At last, drained of all patience, as well as uncomfortably surfeited, I rose abruptly and announced that I must soon leave for the village and suggested that we had best not dawdle further in completing our ceremonial exchange of presents.

Auntie Maude could not mask her disappointment. "Y-you must go to the village?"

"To church."

"Oh—lovely, dear." Her response was vague, but her face brightened as she added with a wink, "In the company of the good doctor, perhaps?"

"No. Sir Robert."

"I see," Auntie Maude nodded in instant approval, "to help with Lady Frances . . ."

"No. She will not be accompanying us."

Auntie Maude's eyebrows flew upward.

"She is unwell."

"But, dear—" Auntie Maude swallowed. "Why you?"

"It is Sir Robert's request."

"But, dear. I don't believe I quite understand."

"I really do not think it necessary that you should," I snapped.

To conceal the tears of hurt that welled up in her eyes, Auntie Maude turned quickly toward the tree and its as yet untouched yield. "Dear," she said softly, "there are two more gifts for you. . . ."

"Very well." I resumed my seat and waited.

Auntie Maude drew the smallest of the remaining packages and placed it almost shyly in my hand. "Here. A little frivolous, perhaps, but I hope you will enjoy it."

Although the cloying scent, easily escaping its wrappings, betrayed the contents of the parcel, I simulated eagerness and tore at the paper as if in anticipation: a sachet—as I had predicted. The effort considerable, I smiled my appreciation while managing to keep the noxious little packet as fair a distance from my nostrils as decently possible. "And—the best for last!" Auntie Maude purred, draping the final and largest bundle across my lap. "On this joyous day, Elizabeth, given with all my love . . ." Nesting in its web of tissue lay a' nightdress of unrelieved white flannel, itself coarsely woven and almost boxlike in its design (sleeves wide and long and neckline rising high enough to strangle). The pristine collar and cuffs each bore an edging of simple embroidery: it, too, was white. "Do you like it, dear?" Auntie Maude hovered anxiously.

"Fine," I managed.

"Do you think it will fit?"

The bloody thing would hang on a rhinoceros. "Fine," I repeated.

"Perhaps I could have used a lighter fabric," Auntie Maude reconsidered thoughtfully, "but the flannel seemed so warm and—well—practical. Don't you think?"

I nodded politely.

"Nothing like good flannel in the winter," she observed while her eyes, tantalized, strayed once again to rest on the gift awaiting her. "I do believe I shall open it now," she breathed. "Oh, I am excited!" Her ardent gaze all but devoured the rude pincushion as she held it this way and that in order to examine it thoroughly from every angle. "Precious! Simply precious! And sewn so beautifully!"

"I am glad you like it," I said perfunctorily.

"Like it!" Auntie Maude exclaimed. "Why, this must be the very nicest present I have ever received!" Her eyes were tender. "And made by my dearest Elizabeth's loving hands!" Tears of delight bright in her eyes, she embraced me warmly. "Thank you, dear, thank you!"

I moved. "I must be on my way."

"Oh!" Auntie Maude's face, clouding momentarily, made a forced recovery. "Yes. Yes, of course," she smiled bravely. "It was a lovely Christmas, wasn't it, Elizabeth?"

I nodded and turned to go.

"Wait, Elizabeth." Auntie Maude stayed my departure. "I have stored your material in my cupboard."

"My material?"

"The presentation from Sir Robert and Lady Frances." At my frozen expression, she continued, "I had planned to help you fashion a dress for yourself, but now," she added with enormous pride, "now that I have seen your workmanship, perhaps you have no need of my assistance!" She giggled. "I remember how you used to—"

"Don't bother," I interrupted coldly.

"The cloth will work up handsomely, I think." Oblivious, Auntie Maude droned on, "With a little clever design—a stitch here and a tuck there—and you do handle brown so well, with your unusual coloring—"

"I don't want it."

"If you haven't as yet developed enough confidence to tackle an entire dress all by yourself—" Auntie Maude's eyes searched mine.

"I don't want it," I repeated.

"Come, dear," she clucked. "Your wardrobe does need refurbishing—"

"Not by brown bombazine it doesn't."

"Bombazine is serviceable—and until you are in a position to acquire something more stylish." She was dogged.

And so was I. "Enough, Aunt. Keep the stuff for yourself."

"Oh, I couldn't!" Auntie Maude was shocked. "Why, that would be impertinent! Sir Robert and Lady Frances gave the goods to you . . . to refuse their gift would constitute bad manners, as well as imply ingratitude!"

I shrugged.

"Dear, we must be careful!" Auntie Maude lowered her voice. "We must abide by the rules—no matter how—"

"I will not accept that material. And that is final," I hissed.

"Then you have no present from the house—" Her lower lip began to tremble.

"Oh, yes, I have," I contradicted smugly.

Auntie Maude was puzzled.

I touched the delicate chain suspended from my neck. Her eyes grew round. "Is that—gold?"

"Of course."

"It looks to be v-valuable!"

"So I would presume."

"Where—where did you—"

"Sir Robert."

"Sir Robert!" she parroted dumbly.

My patience was fast evaporating. "I trust you heard me."

"Elizabeth—" she hesitated, "is it proper to receive jewelry from—ah—men—outside the family—"

"Sir Robert is not entirely outside the family," I reminded her, smiling. "At least, not outside *my* family," I emphasized cruelly.

Auntie Maude colored.

"We will speak no more of this."

"Oh, Elizabeth." Auntie Maude's pleading eyes filled. "Do be careful . . ."

"Oh, Aunt! Pray, desist!"

"Take the bombazine. I beg you!"

"Keep it for yourself, or pass it along to the serving girls. It suits their style." I opened the door.

"What about the little bag of c-candy?" Auntie Maude asked desperately.

"Pitch it about for the birds," I tossed the words carelessly over my departing shoulder . . . .

Upstairs I flung Auntie Maude's detested Christmas offerings on the bed and headed straight for the dressing nook and its bank of mirrors. "He was right," I observed complacently, "the amber does match my eyes. . . ." I twirled the graceful drop around, allowing it to catch the late sun's faded rays that softly invaded the room. The pendant slipped gently from my caressing fingers and nestled itself within the deep cleft between my breasts. I swayed dreamily, watching the chain swing back and forth, seductive captive of my lazy undulations. A tap on the door intruded on my reverie. "What is it?" My voice smarted with irritation.

"Me, miss. Annie."

"Well?"

"The doctor is downstairs, awaitin' your pleasure, miss—"

"Very well, Annie," I sighed. "You may tell Dr. Briggs that I shall be down directly."

From the top of the stairway a mere glance down to the great hall permitted an unobstructed view of the restless bulk of Jonathan Briggs as he paced back and forth, scarcely able to conceal an air of heady anticipation. Radiant light suffused his already florid face when, at last, he became aware of my imminent descent. "Miss Knowlton!" he boomed, "Merry Christmas!" Bounding halfway up the stairs to greet me, he pumped my hand boyishly and placed an awkward kiss on my cheek.

"Heavens!" I protested, laughing. "You are about to hurl me down the stairs!"

"Never!" he bragged, "I would stay your flight with one hand!"

"You are strong," I admitted, feeling the savage pull of muscle in his arm.

"Damme!" he bellowed, "if I just won't pick you up right here and now and deposit you on terra firma myself!" With that pronouncement Dr. Briggs caught me up in his arms and whisked me down to the great hall; I felt as though I were flying. "Damme, if we haven't landed directly under a sprig of my favorite flower—"

"What flower?" I giggled.

"The mistletoe!" he proclaimed.

"Sir, you are taking undeserved liberties with my innocent person!" I feigned objection by struggling mildly in his grasp.

His already firm grip tightened. "It is Christmas, after all, m'love!" he reasoned heartlessly. He bent his head, seeking my lips in an enthusiastic kiss. I could feel his body tremble. "Elizabeth," he murmured huskily. Dr. Briggs's eyes, stricken now with passion, covered my face as if still locked in the embrace. "Elizabeth . . ." The sight of a smirking servant passing at that moment through the hall returned the good doctor to his senses. He set me gently on my feet. "Ah, now," he pronounced formally, pressing a package in my hand, "may I present you with a modest token with which to commemorate the arrival of the joyous Yuletide season!"

He watched with glowing pleasure as I unwrapped his gift, which turned out to be a pair of warm leather gloves, perfect for riding. "Just what I need!" I said truthfully.

"Thought they might come in handy!" He seemed to swagger a little.

"And," I said, extending my own contribution, "for you."

Jonathan Briggs hastily tore aside the paper. "By Jove!" he exclaimed, unfurling the handkerchief. "By Jove!" Beaming, he examined the embroidery. "Damme, if these don't look like my initials. Here is the 'J'—plain as—" he stopped. " 'G'?"

"Silly! That is meant to be a 'B'!"

"By Jove!" He looked again. "A 'B'?"

"A 'B'."

He squeezed my arm, "My dear, the handkerchief is handsome! Why," he threatened, "I've a good mind to steer my clever sempstress over to that mistletoe again!"

"Ah! Dr. Briggs!" a hospitable voice called in greeting: Sir Robert was leisurely descending the stairs. "Have you come to look in on your patient this afternoon?" His smile was warm. "I am most grateful indeed!"

"Why—ah—as a matter of fact, no. I had not planned to attend Lady Frances today. Unless," Dr. Briggs added, "there is a particular need."

Sir Robert sighed, "No more than usual, I suppose."

"Nothing new or untoward has developed overnight?" Dr. Briggs asked.

Sir Robert shook his head sadly. "Things seem to be as always."

Dr. Briggs nodded gravely. "No more than can be expected."

"You are here, then, on purely social matters?" Sir Robert inquired idly.

The doctor grinned. "Ah, yes! To wish our Miss Knowlton a Merry Christmas, as a matter of fact!"

"Splendid!" Sir Robert gave his hearty commendation. Then, turning to me, he asked, "Had you not best fetch your cloak now, Miss Knowlton?"

"Cloak?" Dr. Briggs was puzzled.

"Yes. We are scheduled to attend services in the village," Sir Robert informed the doctor. "And should be leaving straightaway, Miss Knowlton," he reminded me.

"Jolly!" Dr. Briggs roundly endorsed the idea at once. "I shall be delighted to escort your little expedition. My trap is just outside—"

"I think not," Sir Robert refused the doctor's offer with polite regret. "Miss Knowlton has been gracious enough to assume my wife's obligation, in view of Lady Frances's fragile condition. . . ."

"But—"

"I fear that you do not quite understand," Sir Robert observed pleasantly. "Our appearance in the village is of a representative nature—a formal renewal of the yearly pledge of the House of Wyndham to its people," the squire explained. "An ancient tradition, I am afraid, Doctor, and one regarded as quite sacred, after all. So—" his smile was rueful—"if you will be good enough to excuse us both—"

Face swart in angry disappointment, Dr. Briggs bowed brusquely and turned to withdraw, the sharp clatter of his heavy boots resounding on the stone floor diminished finally by the abrupt slamming of the front door.

Sir Robert's dark eyes held mine. "Your cloak, Miss Knowlton?" he murmured. . . .

Chapter 31

It was clear that the Reverend Smythe, in anticipation of the tribute to be bestowed upon him in full view of his modest congregation (in the presence of the hallowed squire), had rallied his forces for the honored occasion by preparing a monumental script well in advance of his hour of glory. I shuddered perceptibly as he took the dais after the rebellious organ had rendered an abusive processional, clutching a sheaf of papers that contained, I surmised weakly, his sermon. Mrs. Smythe, overflowing her assigned pew, smiled in placid wifely approval, while daughter, Miss Caroline, visibly relieved that I did not currently usurp the arm of the coveted Dr. Briggs, relaxed somewhat, even managing to flick a wan smile in my general direction.

Although girded for this, his finest moment, the Reverend Smythe seemed oddly to have lost much of his natural vigor and further to suffer from imperfect concentration. With distracting frequency a palsied hand swept over his glistening brow, tugged at his quivering dewlap, or drew from a limp fold of his black robe a trailing length of handkerchief, not altogether clean, with which to stab savagely at droplets of moisture collecting around the corners of his unnaturally slack mouth. Certain of his words were slurred quite beyond comprehension, and his actual voice projection dwindled, at some frightening moments, to mere sibilancy. Throughout her husband's evident travail, Mrs. Smythe's round face remained tranquil; her back, rigid.

I raised questioning eyes to Sir Robert, who whispered, "The wassail bowl—"

"I s-say unto you, s-sinners, heed my words . . ." the Reverend was bleating, "h-heed my words . . ." His hands groped uncertainly for the support of the altar. "H-heed . . ." His voice ebbed feebly away.

Mrs. Smythe coughed discreetly.

With a struggle the Reverend's bobbing head wobbled to rights. "Ah . . . y-yes, heed, I s-say . . ." Unsteady fingers passed over his glazed forehead. "Y-yes . . ."

Mrs. Smythe cleared her throat loudly.

"Ah . . ." The Reverend's eyes swam. "H-heed . . . my . . ." Suddenly his fragile frame was forcibly rocked by a resounding belch.

As if shot, the rotund Mrs. Smythe leapt to her feet and began to intone—her soprano reedy but tenacious—"Adeste Fideles . . ." Thus prompted, the organ joined in. There followed some confusion: Each was in a different key and each was dogged in the determination to remain there. . . .

The Reverend grinned foolishly.

That the service had terminated abruptly did not activate those in the congregation still happily suspended in their alcoholic haze. They remained as they were, sprawled in their pews, the soft charity of oblivion smoothing work-lined brows and lifting sunken cheeks. The Virtuous, heads held ostentatiously high, sailed from the nave, borne on the grim seas of condemnation, propelled by the stern winds of True Christian Self-Righteousness. Ever gracious, Sir Robert lingered in the antechamber, to return an obsequious handshake; acknowledge a fawning leer.

Smiling fixedly, Mrs. Smythe, followed by a sullen Miss Caroline, assumed her husband's accustomed station in the vestibule. ". . . merely as a temporary stand-in, mind . . ." she hastened to assure the squire and parishioners, ". . . as . . . as the Reverend has been taken ill . . . you know, this time of year is always so precarious . . . ha, ha . . . he did not look a bit well this morning. . . . I tried to persuade him not to carry on . . . but . . . you know these men of dedication . . . ha, ha . . ."

Sir Robert nodded politely.

". . . nothing would have it but that he should don that robe and mount the pulpit . . ." She frowned. ". . . 'but, my dear,' I advised him, 'you are in no fit state to take on the rigors of the cloth—much less the challenge of a winter's wind . . .'"

"I quite understand—" interrupted Sir Robert.

". . . our devoted Caroline has been concerned about

the condition of her beloved father for some days . . . am I not right, dear?" Mrs. Smythe jabbed an emphatic elbow in her daughter's ribs.

"I quite understand," repeated Sir Robert.

". . . Archibald is never stubborn about anything—except his service to God . . ."

"Madam—"

". . . his devotion to his church and . . . of course . . ." Mrs. Smythe's smile became impish, "his . . ."

"Madam—"

". . . obligations to his loving family . . ."

"Madam—"

". . . he feels so strongly . . ."

"Madam." Sir Robert's voice grew dangerously soft. "I have said that it is quite all right. . . ."

Mrs. Smythe colored.

Their glances sourly reproachful, The Pious scorned Mrs. Smythe's elaborate declaration: "Disgraceful! Shame! Unforgivable!"

It seemed forever before Sir Robert and I were able to escape into the timid blue of a winter's dusk and the carriage that patiently awaited our convenience. The horses stamped restless hooves and the driver blew on frozen fingertips. "A stop at the local pub would not go amiss just now," Sir Robert confessed wryly as he settled the furred rug snugly over our knees. "However," he decided with regret, "I fear that such conduct on the part of the squire might be deemed somewhat less than judicious. Questionable, anyway." He laughed. "Particularly in view of our good Reverend's bravura performance this afternoon!"

The carriage rocked gently forward, and soon speeding hooves established us well on the main road toward Wynds. Earth shadows deepened in the twilight as the fading sun surrendered its sky to tiny stars appearing magically, one by one. Rapidly slipping away from the village, we passed through lands sleeping as if in death, parading winter-broadened vistas of barren fields that offered the season's bitter yield to restless cattle, or an awkward tract of spiny gorse, now and then a stand of dreary, leafless trees.

Suddenly it was there, rising in bizarre relief against the pale horizon: the listing house . . . Positioned as before, mouth slack, horned hands leaning on aged handles of a rude scythe: the man with the owl's eyes . . . Ian's "da" . . . Somehow, I could not pull my eyes away. . . .

Hazy movement in the background secured my reluctant attention. It was difficult to determine at first if the almost-silhouette represented that of a human figure, so deformed it was and bent nearly double with the weight of a heavy sack slung across its sagging shoulders. Over harsh, uneven ground the figure staggered, each sluggish, burdened step dragging ever nearer the listing house. . . .

Ian . . .

I began to shiver uncontrollably.

"Are you chilled, Miss Knowlton?" asked Sir Robert, immediately solicitous as he tucked the robe more firmly about me.

"N-no . . . Y-yes . . ."

Chapter 32

Even the hot brick that Annie had buried between the sheets could not lessen the vague feelings of unease that made restful sleep elude me that night. The bed itself had become a stormy sea, pitching me ruthlessly, bow to stern, in a vain struggle for repose. . . . Suffocating one moment; chilled the next . . . Anguished phantoms stirred behind my eyes:

A proud gray head bowed—wide eyes fixed, accusing . . .

. . . A horse, after all . . . Only one bloody horse . . . The stable is full of them . . .

Shambling, misshapen outline, dim-sketched against a darkening sky—eyes, downcast . . .

. . . No suckling babe, Ian . . . Act a man . . .

A gallant heart forever stilled . . .

. . . Oh, God . . .

Grotesque, shuffling specter . . .

. . . Pray, God, stop . . .

Eyes. Staring eyes . . .

. . . No . . .

Eyes: sightless . . .

. . . No, God . . .

Eyes . . . despairing . . .

. . . No . . . No . . .

Knobbed hands . . . Jaw slung . . . Eyes unblinking . . .

. . . Please . . .

Owl's eyes . . .

. . . No . . . Stop . . . Please, dear God . . . Make them stop . . .

"Elizabeth . . . Elizabeth . . ." the now familiar velvet voice coaxed. "Elizabeth . . ."

I rose quickly, eager to follow the path . . . the glorious, gilded ribbon . . . stretching the length of the cold floor . . . winding down curving narrow stairs . . . leading to that wondrous room . . .

The door stood partially open; it moved easily at my feather touch . . .

Unfurled across his chest, the fluid banner of her golden hair provided their only covering. He, lips pressed against her ear, murmured soft endearments while his hand, caressing, stroked her breasts . . . demanding, searched her satin thighs . . .

Shuddering abruptly, she jerked back as, awakened, her hips rose and fell in urgent invitation. . . .

Tethered only by its delicate chain, an amber drop rode saucily on the rich swell of a heaving breast. . . .

Spinning in a vortex of wildly intoxicating sensations, I pulled the blankets high and hugged my throbbing body. . . .

Behind closed eyes erotic images lingered, flaunting their delicious promise, to be suspended suddenly by a clumsy figure . . . distorted, stumbling . . .

. . . Hell . . . Move along, dunce . . .

Sounds evocative were corrupted by a nicker, softly plaintive . . .

. . . Goddamn . . . Have done with it, useless gelding . . .

. . . Desist, fools . . . Bloody nuisances, both . . .

Chapter 33

Winter's winds slapped sharply at the path leading to the stables; I was grateful for the scratchy warmth of the dun-colored scarf hugging my neck and the fleece-lined gloves which protected my fingertips. Overhead the sky was a clear, crackling blue and the ground beneath firmly frozen. Much as the day previous, the stable was quiet as I approached; only those gentle, hazy sounds made by bedded animals betrayed the fact that life was housed there at all. I rapped smartly at the closed door. After what seemed an unreasonable delay, the boy Peter timidly pushed the door forward a mere wedge. And much as the day before, his eyes, buried in a dirt-streaked face, were unnaturally inflamed. His nose was all but pouring.

Irritated, I snapped, "You certainly took your time!"

He blushed.

"And," I added sourly, "why on earth don't you use the handkerchief I gave you yesterday?" I looked away. "Your nose is a positive disgrace!"

His swollen gaze dropped immediately and remained there as if its deep scrutiny were congealed in the frosted ground below.

Really, the boy was utterly impossible! "Ready a mount for me," I directed. "And quickly."

The grimy face flamed. "Ah—" he murmured.

"Speak up, boy, for pity's sake!"

"Ah—"

"Never mind. Simply saddle a horse and do so immediately!"

Incredibly Peter moved to draw the stable door closed. I jerked it free, demanding, "What is this? Your manners are as deplorable as your filthy nose!"

"M-Mr. H-Hartley—" the boy stammered.

"Mr. Hartley? What of him?"

"He tole me you can't have no horse no more." Peter's crusted fist crawled across his face.

"You're lying!"

"N-no, miss, ain't so-so—" he stuttered.

"I will hear this from Mr. Hartley"—I lifted my head high—"himself!"

"Ah—m-miss, I don't want no t-trouble—"

"Well," I sneered, "you've got it! Fetch him. Now!"

Uncertain, Peter lingered.

"He is on the premises, is he not?"

The boy nodded miserably.

"Fetch him, then. This instant!"

Peter's face was stricken.

"Hurry, before I lay the crop to you!" I stormed. As he prepared to withdraw I shrilled, "And, mind, bring back that handkerchief!"

Moments later the door eased a crack and Peter's reluctant head reappeared. "H-him comin'—"

"Use the handkerchief," I ordered.

At once his glance slid to the ground.

"No impudence, pray," I warned grimly. "I repeat: use the handkerchief! Or is it," I taunted, "that you simply do not know how?"

He colored.

"I am waiting."

"D-don't got it—" he whispered.

"Have you managed to lose the thing already?" My exasperation soared.

Dumbly he shook his head.

"Well, then?"

"I—", he began. "I—I done give it away—" he swallowed.

"You have so much," I mocked, "that you can afford to give things away, willy-nilly?"

He flinched.

"I asked you a question, you fool."

"N-no," he whispered.

"Then, might I ask"—I regarded him contemptuously—"why did you dispose of the handkerchief?"

"Dint want it—" His words were almost inaudible.

Suddenly the door flew briskly open and there stood the

imposing bulk of Mr. Hartley. The man laid a hand on Peter's scraggy shoulder. "All right, lad. Back to your work, the now." The boy flashed his master a grateful smile and disappeared. Mr. Hartley nodded in my direction.

I acknowledged his presence coolly. "Your boy has informed me," I remarked, barely civil, "that it is by your personal instruction that I have been denied use of the stable."

"That be so, miss."

"I would inquire"—my eyes, scornful, rudely raked his humble person, frankly telegraphing disdain for his soiled cap and mud-caked boots—"precisely by what authority you presume to make such a determination?"

"It be me right, as master of the stables," he replied, his manner unexpectedly brazen.

"I demand an explanation."

"You done rode a horse to his grave's why—" the man accused without hesitation.

"What nonsense!" I bridled. "The animal was defective, obviously!" My smile was disagreeable. "I can hardly be to blame for an inherent weakness, now, can I?"

"Don't ken all them words, miss—" Hartley shook his head. "But, all the same"—he was obdurate—"you can't have no horse. Leastwise, not in my stable."

"*Your* stable!" I jeered. "Might I remind you, *Mr.* Hartley, that this is hardly *your* stable!"

"It be mine, aright. Long's I be master here," he asserted easily.

"Your arrogance, my man, is outrageous!"

"I be master here."

"Perhaps," my lips curled, "perhaps I shall be in a position to alter that."

The man lifted his shoulders.

"I find your insolence beyond anything in my experience!" I sputtered.

"Hartley," a voice spoke casually behind me. "What seems to be the trouble here?"

Quickly Hartley removed his cap. "No trouble, Sir Robert," he hastened to assure the squire. "No trouble, sir."

"Oh?" Sir Robert frowned. "I received the distinct impression that there was some minor difficulty between you and Miss Knowlton, here," he corrected the stable master lightly.

"Miss Knowlton, sir," Hartley explained, "she wanted a horse, s'all. And I can't give her none. Seems so."

"Oh? And why not?" Sir Robert inquired, his smile pleasant.

"She done kilt our Smoke's why, Sir Robert," Hartley said simply.

"Killed Smoke?" Sir Robert chuckled. "Come now, Hartley . . ."

"She done ride him till him be lame, bring him back and then took him out again the next day—lame nor nothin'—Anyways," Hartley sniffed, "him not get better . . ."

"Now, now, good fellow," cajoled Sir Robert, "no horse ever died merely because he became lame."

"Seems so . . . I done shot him."

"I see."

"Him not get better. I done shot him," the man repeated dully.

"You can hardly fault Miss Knowlton for this," Sir Robert reasoned. "The stable hand in charge—or even perhaps you, yourself, Hartley," he added with pointed emphasis, "should have made sure that the animal did not leave his stall if he was unfit."

Hartley nodded grimly.

"How did such an oversight occur, Hartley?" persisted Sir Robert, his tone still mild.

"Ian—" the stable master admitted with obvious difficulty. "Ian . . ."

"Ian," Sir Robert mused. "Ian. I see. The culpability, then, lies with Ian?"

Hartley's sigh was deep.

"From all indications Ian seems the one to be punished and not Miss Knowlton," Sir Robert decreed blandly. His dark eyes narrowed. "That is your responsibility, Hartley, surely."

Miserably, Hartley nodded. "Him be gone."

"Gone?"

"Seems so."

"Well, then," Sir Robert declared, smiling, "it is settled."

"Seems so," Hartley mumbled.

"Miss Knowlton had planned a ride this morning. And she will have that ride. In fact," Sir Robert announced, "I shall select her mount myself. Miss Knowlton"—he turned to me—"if I may be permitted that pleasure?"

"Of course."

It was not long before a chestnut mare, standing more than fourteen hands high, was led protesting from the stable. Ears proudly erect, her handsome head promised the spirit of a young queen; the long, fluid muscles of her legs boasted grace, speed, and unerring confidence. She was a beauty.

"Miss Knowlton," hailed Sir Robert, "will she suit?"

My unfeigned delight must have demonstrated itself clearly; Sir Robert's responding smile was boyish in its triumph. "What is her name?" I breathed.

"Damned if I know," replied Sir Robert, grinning. "Supply us, Hartley."

Hartley's jowled, peasant's face drooped with disapproval; but he pronounced the mare's name with unwavering obedience: "It be Artemis, Sir Robert."

"Artemis!" I marveled. "Artemis! The virgin huntress! Perfect!"

Sir Robert's shadowed eyes searched mine. "She is yours, Miss Knowlton, for as long as you care to use her."

Hartley shook his head sorrowfully.

"Attend me, Hartley," Sir Robert commanded sharply. "Miss Knowlton is to enjoy unqualified use of the stables." The squire's voice hardened. "Is that clear?"

"Y-yes, sir. Sir Robert, sir."

"Assist Miss Knowlton into the saddle," Sir Robert ordered. "And then have Ebon prepared for me, at once."

Hartley displayed a new deference as he lifted me into the saddle. Albeit with reluctance, I could not help but respond to the easy strength in his arm. "Thank you," I acknowledged stiffly. Hartley bowed respectfully, then withdrew to execute his master's instructions.

"Had you a specific destination planned, Miss Knowlton?" Sir Robert's inquiry was offhand.

"No. None," I replied, trying to restrain my willful mount.

"Then perhaps—if you would care to accompany me," he invited, "I am obliged to ride a portion of the bounds this morning—quasi pilgrimage, if you will. Another tiresome tradition, I am afraid." His smile was rueful.

"I should be delighted. But," I confessed, laughing, "my only hope is that Hartley does not linger overlong. . . . I cannot contain this wayward lass indefinitely. . . ."

Hartley reappeared, leading Sir Robert's panther-black stallion from the stable. "Have a care, Sir Robert," warned the stable master as he held onto the restless horse's bridle, "him be some wild today! Seems so!"

The squire laughed as Ebon stamped aristocratic hooves and boldly snorted his impatience. "Hold on there, boy." Sir Robert stroked the bobbing head. "There's a good fellow—" He swung effortlessly into the saddle.

Although spirited and fleet, Artemis could provide no contest for the long strides of the magnificent stallion, nor I compete as equestrian: Sir Robert seemed to ride as one with his mount. Looking back at last, Sir Robert reined up in realization and grinned sheepishly as I finally drew alongside him. "Forgive me, Miss Knowlton," he apologized, "I confess that I quite forgot myself." With affection he smoothed Ebon's snarled mane. "Sometimes I feel that he and I share a common bond." Sunlight had fired his dark eyes and wild winds tugged at his own ebony hair, touching something primordial, elemental, in him. . . .

We trotted together then, almost perfectly abreast, while the squire indicated an important landmark here, a point of interest there; I did not bother to divulge the fact that I had already traversed this identical route with Ian. Besides, each tour offered a different text: now the easy authority of ownership; then the sharp rebellion against being owned . . .

Poised at the crest of a hill, we peered over the tops of leafless trees down onto a level meadow, its brown grass severed raggedly by a narrow rushing brook, and still beyond to the crashing sea. "Have a look now," Sir Robert advised, "in summer one cannot see a thing!" He chuckled. "This is Wynds' only real elevation," he explained, "and in the category of mountains it is a harmless clump. But," he went on, "it bears the picturesque name of Smugglers'

Peak." He smiled. "The proper origin of the title is ambiguous; there have been so many conflicting tales of wicked smugglers—and all remaining popular legends with the villagers." His expression changed. "Are you hungry, Miss Knowlton?"

"As a matter of fact, yes," I admitted, suddenly famished.

"I wonder if the apple tree in the next meadow has anything left hanging." Sir Robert nudged Ebon's sleek barrel with the toe of his boot. "Come on, Miss Knowlton! Race you there!"

Race you there . . . I had said those same words to Ian . . .

The tree had shed its fruit; only a few withering apples swung grotesquely from bare, misshapen branches, while the rest of its harvest lay scattered on the ground in varying degrees of black decay . . . rotting.

Like Ian . . .

Almost as if willing signs of neglect, or abusive handling, Hartley's small, suspicious eyes raked Artemis upon her return to the stables. Just as pointedly he disregarded Ebon's foam-flecked flanks and tangled mane. "Give them both a good rub," Sir Robert instructed the stable master as he dismounted with careless grace. "No," he stayed Hartley's approach, "you attend the horses. I shall assist Miss Knowlton." Hands firm about my waist, Sir Robert lifted me easily from the saddle. For the moments that our bodies pressed close I was seized with a wild exhilaration. Recklessly, my eyes sought his, only to be drowned in their dusky depths. . . .

Chapter 34

Its horse tethered to a post in the main courtyard, a trap, although momentarily unattended, stood in obvious readiness. The vehicle seemed almost aggressive in its shabbiness and the pitiful harnessed beast so thin as to be virtually skeletal. Surely not Dr. Briggs: his equipage was avowedly modest, but jaunty withall, and his horse well fleshed and high-stepping. I glanced at Sir Robert. "The Reverend's wife and daughter, I presume," he murmured.

I laughed. "You mean that emaciated animal is actually called upon to move the mountain known as Mrs. Smythe?"

"A husky challenge at that," he admitted, chuckling.

We were received into the great hall by an anxious Judd, trailed in turn by a hovering Auntie Maude, in whose wake paced a distraught Sarah, wringing nervous hands. Even a blazing hearth in the cozy inglenook managed to extend at best only an uneasy hospitality to its two guests, Mrs. Smythe and Miss Caroline, as they sat apprehensive and unspeaking before its crackling warmth.

"What is amiss here?" inquired Sir Robert as he leisurely removed his riding gloves.

"Oh, sir!" Sarah's rush of words was stemmed by a scowl from the butler.

"Well?" queried Sir Robert mildly.

"It is the Lady Frances, sir—" said Judd.

"What seems to be the matter?" Sir Robert's manner remained calm.

"She will not to come downstairs," put in Sarah excitedly.

"Oh?" Sir Robert's voice sharpened.

"Yes, sir," Sarah continued, "all's I did was tell her that the time had come for her to join with Mrs. Smythe, here, and Miss Caroline. The Lady Frances"—Sarah bit down hard on her rather full lower lip—"she done said she'd die before comin' down them stairs."

Solemnly Judd concurred. "What Sarah says is true, Sir Robert."

"I see."

"Whatever should I do?" asked the girl in desperation.

"I shall see to the Lady Frances," promised Sir Robert, his jaw set. "She will be down momentarily, I assure you." Ascending the stairs two at a time, Sir Robert quickly disappeared along the upper hallway.

"Dear—" Auntie Maude sidled up to me. "Where have you been?"

"Out riding."

"With—Sir Robert?" The question may have seemed diffident; my aunt's voice was honed with the fine edge of disapproval.

I nodded.

"Dr. Briggs came by to see you." She shifted now to an air of exaggerated carelessness.

I shrugged.

"He was ever so disappointed to find that you were out." Auntie Maude's attitude grew mildly accusatory.

I made no response.

"He waited the better part of an hour for your return, before he was obliged to leave." Now she was reproachful. "Had to look in on a patient . . . I do think, dear," Auntie Maude warned, "that you might be wise to alert someone in the household of your projected whereabouts before you—ah—leave the premises. . . ."

My gaze, deadly, met her eyes.

"W-what I-I mean is," she stammered, "the—doctor—seems an awfully good catch—er—potential—well, you know, dear—a prospective—ah—who should be encouraged rather than—"

"Enough, Aunt."

"I am only thinking of your welfare," she persisted. "Dr. Briggs is obviously interested—and I merely—"

"Desist, Aunt."

"And riding out with Sir Robert"—she leaned close—"who is—married! Dear," she whispered, putting a hand on my arm, "this is hardly practical under the circumstances. I mean, Elizabeth," she swallowed, "it cannot be in your best interests—to spend—"

Angrily I wrenched free of her grasp. "Oh, for God's sake!" I hissed, and turned to go. My actual withdrawal from the hall was stayed, however, by the sight of Lady Frances as, leaning heavily on her husband's arm, she slowly descended the stairs. Puffy lids and mottled cheeks attested to prolonged weeping, further ravaging an already hopelessly haggard face. Her hands, limply suspended, appeared almost without flesh, allowing the dark tracery of veins to disfigure them irregularly and at will. A gown of pink brocaded silk hung without form or grace on a body made shapeless by emaciation, and her hair, escaping in truant wisps, fell lank and lifeless. She was moaning. Threaded through her feeble protestations were Sir Robert's softly murmured words of encouragement as they made painful progress, one careful step at a time.

. . . Useless bitch! More in need of an undertaker than a husband . . .

"No," Lady Frances whimpered, "no, Robert, please . . ."

"Yes, my dear."

"I can't, Robert," she wailed.

"Of course you can, my dear." Sir Robert was gently persuasive.

"I—can't, Robert." She began to sob weakly. "Can't . . ."

"Now, now, my dear."

"Robert—" She swayed. "No . . ."

Sir Robert's grip tightened. "I am afraid I must insist, my dear."

Below, posed as if comedic statuary, we watched the grim processional: Sarah, blanched; Auntie Maude, transfixed; Mrs. Smythe and Miss Caroline, uncomfortable, bonded to the bench in the inglenook; Judd, feet rooted; I, frozen in disbelief . . .

. . . What an incredible performance . . . The woman was ridiculous . . .

Over the crackle of the hearth fire the toneless lament droned: "No . . . No . . . I can't . . . No . . . Robert . . . Please . . . No. No. No . . ."

. . . My God, the bleating bitch . . .

As Sir Robert touched the bottom step he signaled Judd with a discreet lift of his brow. "Have Angus harness my carriage at once," he directed. "It is more suitable than that of the Reverend's."

"Yes, Sir Robert."

"Miss Knowlton," Sir Robert motioned to me, "if I might request a particular favor of you?"

"Of course," I agreed promptly.

"If you would be so kind as to accompany the ladies on their calls this afternoon—"

I was puzzled.

"It is customary," Sir Robert went on to explain, "for the mistress of Wynds to travel abroad, attended by the wife and other female relatives, if any, of the clergy—"

"In order to visit those families of the village who are in need of advice or exhortation," Mrs. Smythe sang from the inglenook. Leaping eagerly to her feet, she came to join us in the hall. "Ah, yes, Miss Knowlton," she trilled, "this is a mission embraced gladly by all ladies in our privileged stratum of society!" She sniffed elegantly. "It remains always our sacred duty—nay, our trust—to inspire those less well endowed in circumstance, or," she added priggishly, "in strength of character. . . ." Her voice climbed. "We must reunite those who have strayed . . . fallen . . . those prey to the easy evils of earthly temptation with the members of our Christian flock who have stood righteous, stalwart, against the deadly forces of Satan and his busy brothers . . . those who have remained unscathed on the battlefield of sin and degradation. . . ."

Judd returned. "The carriage awaits your pleasure, Sir Robert."

"This is God's work, Miss Knowlton! God's finest work!" It was with a solemn reverence that Mrs. Smythe bowed her head. "And, I am proud—nay, more—honored to be permitted my small share in it!" Beckoning her daughter to her side, the woman announced, her pride enormous, "Caroline can attest to the worth of this holy endeavor! Love"— she turned to the girl—"acquaint Miss Knowlton with some of the blessed rewards you have enjoyed in spreading the word of our Lord with me these many years. . . ."

"Mrs. Smythe," Sir Robert coughed, "I believe that the carriage is without."

"Caroline," the mother exhorted the girl, who blushed

hotly and allowed her embarrassed gaze to fall to the floor and remain there. "Come, sweet," Mrs. Smythe nudged her daughter with an insistent elbow, "come, dearest, describe the feelings surging upward from your heart."

Sir Robert cleared his throat, "Mrs. Smythe—"

"Caroline is too modest to reveal her prowess in this campaign," Mrs. Smythe declared, her manner now absurdly arch. "Why, only last year—was it not during this very season, in fact, dear heart, that you—"

"Robert, please . . . No . . ." Lady Frances begged.

"There was a young woman," Mrs. Smythe confided, "who had fallen into sin"—her eyes flew heavenward— "basest sin . . ." Her eyes narrowed. "Contemptible wickedness . . ."

"I can't," whined Lady Frances. "No . . ."

"A transgression of the worst kind . . the greatest magnitude," Mrs. Smythe mouthed pointedly.

Caroline flushed deeply.

"But Caroline, here, full of the true spirit of Christ—"

"Mrs. Smythe, if you please!" Sir Robert's voice rose.

"Caroline—despite her youth—regardless of her tender age—her—ah—er, inexperience—"

"Mrs. Smythe"—Sir Robert's words became a command—"the carriage is waiting. I suggest that you ladies board it immediately." It was necessary that he all but propel his wife out of the door and into the carriage. "Perhaps if you would sit beside Lady Frances, Miss Knowlton?" Sir Robert suggested.

"No! No!" Lady Frances cried out.

"Here, tuck the robe about you snugly." Sir Robert drew the fur over his wife's trembling knees. "Miss Knowlton, perhaps if you could grab one end . . ."

Lady Frances shrank from me.

"There is a robe provided for you ladies also," Sir Robert informed Miss Caroline.

"Thank you, Sir Robert." The girl pinked.

The squire bowed formally. "A pleasant afternoon, ladies." He gestured briefly to the driver; the carriage jerked, then rolled forward smoothly.

. . . Pleasant afternoon . . . in the company of that fatuous ass across the way . . . and next to this cringing arrangement of bones . . . pleasant afternoon indeed . . . If only Miss Caroline were not such a total gawk . . .

Mrs. Smythe settled back in complete contentment, fastening her gaze on Lady Frances. "What is the itinerary planned for today?" she inquired, exhibiting a new air of importance.

Lady Frances started.

"What—family—should we visit first?"

"Oh, God . . ." Lady Frances moaned.

"I am sure you have your own particular favorites!" Mrs. Smythe was most ingratiating.

Lady Frances closed her eyes.

"One or two—surely?" Mrs. Smythe's inquiry was accompanied by a fawning smile.

Lady Frances's desiccated hand fluttered, then lay still.

"You have no—ah—preference?" Mrs. Smythe indicated real surprise.

Weakly, Lady Frances swayed back and forth.

"Would you wish me to direct the driver, in that case?" Mrs. Smythe's nobility gew; she was prepared now to rise to any and all occasions.

"Do as you will," murmured Lady Frances.

Mrs. Smythe beamed. "We shall call first on Gracie Turner, then," she decided, adding significantly, "she has not been near the church of late."

Caroline blushed.

"Oh, God . . ." Lady Frances sighed.

"Caroline," her mother issued the crisp order, "pray instruct the driver to stop at the Turner house. It is only a short distance now, I believe."

"No . . ." Lady Frances's voice had faded to a mere whisper. "No . . . No . . ."

As we reined up before a ruined structure, more a dilapidated hen house than a human dwelling, I thought to myself that the driver was mistaken; surely no one lived here. Mrs. Smythe, however, briskly threw aside the fur robe and waited with delicious anticipation to alight. Old Angus pulled open the carriage door and braced himself against the onslaught of Mrs. Smythe's monumental proportions on his aged, fragile person. A reluctant Miss Caroline was next, and I followed, no less unwillingly. Lady Frances remained crouched in the carriage. Her eyes were wide with terror.

"Come, Lady Frances," invited the ebullient Mrs. Smythe.

Lady Frances retreated deeper into the recesses of the carriage.

"Lady Frances," Mrs. Smythe cajoled; a tiny frown tried to crease her fleshy brow.

"No!" Lady Frances recoiled. "No . . . no . . . no . . ."

"Perhaps I should wait with her," I said, hesitating.

My suggestion drew an immediate "No . . . no . . . no . . ." from the quailing Lady Frances.

. . . Oh, for Christ's sake! Stop that monotonous droning. No . . . No . . . No . . . Which might provide the more dismal interlude—remaining out here, nursing a blenching idiot—or being obliged to dip into the squalor of an unknown hovel? . . . Mrs. Smythe—or the Lady Frances? . . . Bloody bores, both . . .

"I really do not know what to say," Mrs. Smythe wavered. "Perhaps it might be best to leave Lady Frances alone—she seems distressed, somehow. . . ."

I shrugged.

Mrs. Smythe waddled to a door that hung awkwardly from a solitary hinge—and that, rusted. She rapped smartly. "Gracie," she called gaily, " 'tis I!"

There was no sound.

"Gracie! Gracie Turner!"

Still no response.

"Gracie! It is I!" A pause. "Mrs. Smythe!"

The door creaked open. Slowly. I frankly gaped: The spectacle of Gracie Turner was as untenable as her abode. Both proved grotesque caricatures of their assigned shapes: the careening broken shell; the bloated and distorted body. Scarely more than a child, Gracie Turner stood draped in a formless shroud of rags, filthy beyond recognition. Her hair, matted stiff with grease and scurf, straggled promiscuously across shoulders that were improbably humped. Her eyes, set deep and mired hopelessly behind a simian brow, stared as if stupified. What should have been a pliant, unblemished complexion was lichen-gray and irreparably wounded by stiffening scars, the legacy of drying pustules. Despite a wildly distended abdomen, the girl was gaunt to near absurdity.

Mrs. Smythe was oddly unabashed; she boomed, "Well, gel, where are your manners! Aren't you going to invite us in?"

Dumbly the girl stepped aside. Mrs. Smythe, seizing the opening, pushed past, motioning vigorously for us to follow . . . Expecting quarters stark and barely habitable, I was in fact wholly unprepared for the sickening conditions befouling the hut's interior. Readily discernible were fecal droppings, randomly deposited the length and breadth of the small enclosure. The resultant pervasive stench was noxious beyond all imagining.

I could define no furniture in the single room. What I presumed to be sleeping arrangements were casually supplied by nothing more sophisticated than a few handfuls of gamy straw flung haphazardly at the farthest corner. Other than a blackened iron pot, no facilities for cooking were in evidence; certainly no provisions for washing; and eating utensils consisted of one broken crock, a bent fork, and an equally missshapen spoon. A shallow excavation in the sod floor served as the fireplace; a well-charred log still smoked faintly. Before its doubtful warmth squatted a small child of indeterminate age, mercilessly thin and clad in little more than a uniform coat of grime. Grubby baby fingers explored absently a nearby mound of fresh excrement.

Involuntarily I gagged.

So intent on her good works, Mrs. Smythe seemed remarkably oblivious to her repellent surroundings, even so far as to acknowledge the child with apparent sanction. "My!" she exclaimed, "the baby has certainly grown!"

Gracie grinned, unveiling a jaw full of badly rotting teeth.

"Her name—now, don't tell me, let me guess! Victoria! After the Queen!"

"Gracie."

"No, dear," corrected Mrs. Smythe with amazing patience, "Gracie is your name!"

"Gracie."

"Dear," begged Mrs. Smythe, "pray, don't be a tease . . ."

"Her be Gracie," guffawed the girl. Her breath was fetid.

"That is not what you called the child last year." Mrs. Smythe's face drooped in disappointment.

Gracie sniggered, "I done changed it." Chuckling, she slid to the dirt floor and rocked back and forth, savoring the delirious moment.

"You have not been to services for some time now." Mrs. Smythe introduced a new subject, injecting into her voice a note of mild reproach.

Sobering, the girl shrugged.

"Now, Gracie," said Mrs. Smythe firmly, "you must never forsake your God."

Gracie giggled.

"I am thinking of the child as well."

"Her be all right," said Gracie, promptly defensive.

"Has she ever been baptized?"

Gracie lifted indifferent shoulders.

"My dear." Mrs. Smythe was properly shocked. "This is a mortal sin!"

"Her be all right," Gracie frowned.

"What if she were to fall sick, the poor child!" gasped Mrs. Smythe. "God forbid!" she added hastily, looking heavenward, "and not baptized!"

"Her ain't sick."

"She needs the protection of her Savior in the event that she does take sick."

"Her ain't sick," Gracie glowered.

"Now, now, dear, let us not become agitated." Mrs. Smythe began to retreat.

"Her all right," Gracie chanted.

"Of course she is," Mrs. Smythe soothed, "of course she is. I simply want to make sure that our little Gracie becomes acquainted with God's holy sacrament, that's all."

"Her be all right."

"Before it is too late," warned Mrs. Smythe.

"Her got me."

"I know, my dear," persisted Mrs. Smythe, "but she also needs her God."

"Me her god."

Aghast, Mrs. Smythe stepped back. "Th-that is s-sacrilege!" she sputtered.

Gracie spat.

"Gracie," said Mrs. Smythe firmly, "the child needs friends. She needs to make friends with her God."

"Her get friend," Gracie tittered, indecorously scratching at her swollen belly.

Mrs. Smythe gaped. "Gracie! You're not—" She looked away, horrified. "You are not—surely—not—"

Chortling broadly, Gracie flaunted her protruding abdomen.

For a moment Mrs. Smythe stood stupified. "Not another!" she rasped. "Surely not another!"

Gracie swiveled her hips indecently.

"Stop that at once!" screeched Mrs. Smythe.

Gracie hooted and spread apart her legs, posturing obscenely.

Miss Caroline ran shrieking from the hut.

"Who is the f-father?" Mrs. Smythe managed, her desperate gaze trying to escape Gracie's contortions, accelerating now and becoming more and more explicit.

The girl's small, buried eyes rolled from side to side.

"You—don't—know?" Mrs. Smythe's whisper was barely audible.

Gracie snickered.

"How on earth will you feed it?"

"Same as her."

"She looks half-starved," Mrs. Smythe snorted, as if noticing the child's deplorable condition for the first time.

Gracie glared. "Her all right."

"And she is surely in need of clothing," observed Mrs. Smythe practically.

"Her all right."

"The new—er—infant—will have to be clothed as well," Mrs. Smythe muttered to herself.

Abruptly the child drew herself up and, unsteady on wobbling, malformed legs, toddled toward her mother. Strange guttural sounds rumbled deep in her throat.

"No!" Brutally Gracie pushed her away. "You don't need nothin' yet."

Whimpering, the child again approached the mother.

"No!" snarled Gracie. "You get nothin' yet!"

Fiercely determined, the child fell on the mother's lap. "Shit!" shrilled Gracie. "Bloody bitch! Get off—" Grunting with wild insistence, the child clawed savagely at her mother's tattered garment. Angrily, from its nest of rags Gracie yanked a monstrous breast, crusted white with dried milk. "All right, slut," she yielded. The child's mouth pounced greedily on the riddled nipple, which was ringed by a series of oozing sores, and the moment of stunned silence was ruptured by liquid sucking sounds. In helpless fascination my eyes were held fast by the sight before me: kitten-like, ordure-filmed, the child's baby hands kneaded her mother's breast as she drank thirstily. Howling suddenly, Gracie cuffed the child, "Watch them damned teeth!"

With difficulty Mrs. Smythe regained her powers of speech. "Gracie," she swallowed, "you cannot go on living like this—"

Again Gracie rapped the child a stinging blow to the side of her head. "One more fucking bite and—"

"Gracie—" Mrs. Smythe tried again.

Gracie's feral eyes narrowed dangerously behind those projecting brows. "Fucking snoop." She bared her teeth.

Choosing to ignore Gracie's mounting hostility, Mrs. Smythe drew from her reticule a small Bible. "Now," she announced, "we shall share a few of God's words together."

"Out!" Gracie mumbled.

"I shall first read from—"

Viciously tearing the bloody nipple from her child's teeth, Gracie flung her to the ground and stood. Shoulders hunched, she moved slowly toward Mrs. Smythe. "Out!" she growled.

Mrs. Smythe was paralyzed.

"Out!" Gracie snatched the Bible from the older woman's frozen hand and hurled it across the room.

With a yelp Mrs. Smythe scurried to retrieve the book, which lay broken on the fouled floor.

"You do not mean to touch it now!" I cried.

"Miss Knowlton!" Mrs. Smythe was seized with horror. "This is the Bible!"

Miss Caroline and Lady Frances sat stiffly huddled in opposite seats in the waiting carriage. Obviously, not a word of conversation had been exchanged, and each face showed unmistakable evidence of tears.

Thoroughly shaken by her recent ordeal, Mrs. Smythe nonetheless sought valiantly to conceal her discomposure by unceasing chatter. The topics covered were unrelievedly church-related, extolling the merits of God and the Reverend, not necessarily in that order. The matter of Gracie and her digressions was scrupulously avoided, in consideration of Lady Frances and the simpering Miss Caroline, no doubt; I sensed, too, that Mrs. Smythe was using aimless conversation as a ploy here, to gird herself against the possible rigors of the next visit. At last the lady had quite pulled herself together and was attempting to decide (with Lady Frances's sanction, of course) precisely what the next stop was going to be. "I really feel that we should look in on old Tess Caldwell," Mrs. Smythe was suggesting.

"No!" Lady Frances screamed.

"But—"

"No!"

"Excuse me, Lady Frances"—Mrs. Smythe was startled—"but the poor soul has not been at all well since she left Wynds—and," she preened, "Tess does so love to hear my Bible readings—"

"God!" Lady Frances began to shudder violently.

"Are you cold?" Mrs. Smythe was instantly solicitous as she pressed the robe more tightly across the shivering woman's knees.

Lady Frances pulled away. "Don't!"

Smarting under the rebuke, Mrs. Smythe buried her nose in her little book as a means to conceal her embarrassment. "Er—Mattie Hawlins—Lady Frances—how does she suit—"

"All right," Lady Frances whispered, and retreated still deeper into her corner.

Angus pulled up before a cottage that was shabby but not derelict, showing weary traces of attempted care. The building, almost diminutive, suggested the need of a thorough whitewash, and its shutters, angled crazily at clouded windows, indicated that they should soon be replaced. A

quasi garden heralded our approach; a cultivated, if bedraggled, shrub of a species unknown to me stood as silent
sentinel at the head of the uneven stone path, and a row of
brown-dried hollyhocks listed in flagging attention before
the paint-peeled front door. Mrs. Smythe's pudgy gloved
hand sought the iron knocker, and the door swung wide
more enthusiastically than I might have expected. Mattie
Hawlins easily filled the narrow doorway. Her broad,
grooved face brightened with a sunny, toothless smile as
she recognized, after some admittedly awkward moments,
the Reverend's wife and daughter and regarded even me,
the stranger, with cordiality. "It be the Reverend's lady,
seems so," the woman said in welcome.

"And daughter, Miss Caroline—" Mrs. Smythe was, as
usual, readily expansive. "And our new friend, Miss
Knowlton, companion to the Lady Frances."

"Aye." The aged woman directed her dim focus onto my
face. She nodded. "Aye."

Of monumental girth herself, Mattie Hawlins nonetheless displayed considerable ingenuity in engineering the entry of her guest, Mrs. Smythe, easily her equal in circumference, into the tiny abode and without serious collision, at
that. Truthfully, it was with clever maneuverings that Miss
Caroline and I managed to follow: The room proved
smaller than any in my experience, and as minimally furnished. In dominant position stood a wooden table, addressed by two straight-backed chairs, each empty of any
ameliorating cushioning. A small, once painted stool
hugged the tiny hearth, which was functioning bravely with
little more than a token offering of kindling. A braided rug
lent its indefinite faded color to rude plank flooring, while
curtains, frequently bleached and much mended, doggedly
dressed the windows, muting somewhat the fogged condition of their severely wavy panes. The home was indigent
but scrubbed clean.

Seated across the table from Mrs. Smythe, Mattie Hawlins fidgeted nervously. "Dint know you was to come," she
murmured, "shoulda put on a cuppa. . . ." A thin film of
moisture beaded her upper lip.

"Well!" Mrs. Smythe beamed, establishing herself more
firmly on the stiff chair, "it is never too late! I can always

spare the time for tea to brew! Isn't that so, Caroline?" she consulted her daughter, who was clumsily straddling the stool crouching near the meager fire.

"Yes, Mama," agreed the girl obediently.

Mattie Hawlins made no move toward the crude cupboard serving the simple kitchen alcove.

"I always have time for tea!" reiterated Mrs. Smythe, hinting broadly.

Mattie Hawlins's rough hands worked aimlessly. Still she did not rise.

"Perhaps you would like Miss Caroline to assist you," Mrs. Smythe offered generously. "Dear," she addressed the girl, "we should be ever so obliged if you would consent to brew a pot for us. And Miss Knowlton," she turned to me, "perhaps you might be good enough to serve. . . . It is gratifying to have a bit of help now and again," she confessed to her hostess.

An expression of pure pain stabbed the old woman's hazy eyes. Slowly she licked her lips. "Ain't no tea," she whispered faintly.

"Oh!" Mrs. Smythe's instant disappointment was admirably concealed by a hasty dive into her reticule that yielded the Bible, rent now, rapidly discoloring and reminiscently malodorous. "Then we shall have a treat of quite another nature, sustenance promising infinitely greater satisfaction: food for the soul—the blessed word of God!"

"Aye." The awful moment of embarrassment past, the old woman eased back in her chair, a shy smile returning to her round face.

"I think perhaps that we might find a lesson from Isaiah comforting on this winter's day," suggested Mrs. Smythe in fullest glory. "Mattie?"

The old woman nodded. "Aye."

"Splendid!" Sifting through the pages, Mrs. Smythe's expert fingers easily uncovered the desired passages. Clearing her throat with some degree of ceremony, she began: " 'Therefore I will shake the heavens and the earth shall remove out of her place, in the wrath of the LORD of hosts, and in the day of his fierce anger . . .' " Inexorably the monotonous voice droned on, varying in modulation only in deference to an occasional stirring verse.

Blurred sunlight, invading the veiled windows, settled upon the aged Mattie Hawlins, wrapping her in its soft warmth. Her filmed eyes, fixed dutifully on the face of her guest, began to droop slowly, snap open, only to sink again.

" 'Every one that is found shall be thrust through; and every one that is joined unto them shall fall by the sword . . .' "

Mattie Hawlins's eyes were frankly closed now.

" '. . . their children also shall be dashed to pieces before their eyes; their houses shall be spoiled, and their wives ravished . . .' "

Jaw sagging, the old woman sank deeper in her chair.

" '. . . their bows also shall dash the young men to pieces; and they shall have no pity on the fruit of the womb; their eye shall not spare children . . .' "

Mattie Hawlins's slack bulk was unrestrainedly rocked now by stertorous breathing that matched in even rhythm Mrs. Smythe's measured chanting:

" '. . . but wild beasts of the desert shall lie there; and their houses shall be full of doleful creatures; and owls shall dwell there, and satyrs shall dance there . . . And the wild beasts of the islands shall cry in their desolate houses . . .' "

The fire was rapidly diminishing, and a dreary chill began to permeate the room. Only the snoozing Miss Hawlins, swathed in the sun's fading rays, and Mrs. Smythe, enveloped in her own enthusiasms, could have failed to record the drop in the temperature. Miss Caroline shifted the stool closer to the dwindling fire; I stood, openly shivering.

" '. . . and dragons in their pleasant palaces; and her time is near to come, and her days shall not be prolonged . . .' "

We were delivered, at long last and only moments before the fire's smoldering remains relinquished their final spark, by Mattie Hawlins herself. She expelled a single, explosive belch of such magnitude that it diverted Mrs. Smythe from her mission at hand, but was not, however, of force sufficient to awaken the old woman. . . .

Lady Frances, too, was dozing when we reboarded the carriage. She jerked awake immediately; even sleep to this woman seemed a snatched and uneasy conquest.

"It was lovely to look in on old Mattie Hawlins," gushed Mrs. Smythe as the carriage rolled smoothly forward. "She does enjoy our little visits so—don't you agree, Caroline?"

"Yes, Mama."

"The poor soul derives such inspiration from my Bible readings!" Mrs. Smythe leaned back, well satisfied. "Eh, Caroline?"

"Yes, Mama."

"Mattie has failed considerably since the passing of her brother, William, last year," Mrs. Smythe observed. She shook her head sadly. "To reach advanced age and remain a maiden . . . to wander through the trails and trials of life not experiencing the magic of a companionship provided through a blessed union sanctioned by God's holy church . . . A pity . . . tragic omission . . . Approaching life's weakened years without the comfort of children who might ease one over the high hurdles of nearing infirmity . . . A sorrowful plight." Mrs. Smythe, with abrupt candor, trained meaningful eyes on her daughter, "Let Mattie Hawlins serve as a lesson. Caroline, love!" She waggled a gloved forefinger under Miss Caroline's generous nose, "No woman is complete without her mate!" A knowing smile curved her lips. "Eve was fashioned from Adam's rib, after all. . . ."

"Where is the next stop?" interrupted Miss Caroline in a desperate attempt to redirect the conversation.

"Let me see." Busily Mrs. Smythe consulted her small black notebook. "Cyrus Soames," she murmured. "We must not fail him. He suffers so."

"Must we, Mama?"

"For shame!" Mrs. Smythe chided her daughter. "The man is bedridden and thus deprived of the Lord's devotions! Yes," she was determined, "Cyrus Soames it is!"

Although betraying the signs of long neglect that presage imminent decay, the Soames dwelling escaped the advertised aura of total dereliction flaunted by Gracie Turner's disreputable lodgings. There remained no residue of attempted beautification, vis-à-vis the efforts of old Mattie Hawlins; still, the place indicated a stab at inhabitation anyway, as evidenced by the steady wisp of gray smoke rising from a jaunty chimney pipe—a hopeful sign, surely.

At Mrs. Smythe's insistent knocking the latch lifted and the door budged slightly. "Etta Soames, is it?" Mrs. Smythe peered with interest.

"Aye."

"Ah—er—may I—er, we—come in?"

"Why for?"

"Well, ah—to see—the man of the house—" In the face of obvious resistance Mrs. Smythe frequently introduced a note of playful gaiety.

"Him sick."

"I know," Mrs. Smythe clucked her sympathy. "Your husband's indisposition is precisely why I—er, we—have come!"

"Him abed."

"Not to trouble, Etta," Mrs. Smythe hastened to reassure the woman. "Your Cyrus will not be obliged to stir a teeny muscle for us!" Her plump, tenacious fingers joggled the door. "Come now, my dear. Do let us enter. Please," she wheedled.

It was with a grudging defeat that the doorway was cleared enough to let us pass, permitting then a thorough examination of our reluctant hostess. Uncommonly tall, Etta Soames's heavily boned yet spare structure was supported by enormous, clumsy feet. Viewed, her lean face proved as cheerless as her flat voice. A stiff knot of dull brown hair drawn high atop her head gave the illusion of awesome stature. Set wide apart, her eyes were a clear gray, possibly limpid once; now they seemed simply without color. An apron of coarse muslin protected a drab skirt woven of a rough wool that was faded and bore the wounds of repeated darning. Her serviceable boots were badly scuffed but clean.

The distressing sounds of a racking cough assailed us as we crossed the threshold.

"Him be bad today," offered Etta Soames tonelessly.

"He requires succor from a power greater than either of us!" declared Mrs. Smythe solemnly. Holding up her reticule, she brightened, "And that help resides right here!" Her voice rang with consummate pride.

The Soames ménage was reminiscent of that Mattie Hawlins and as marginally furnished. A pair of stools, roughly hewn, squatted awkwardly before a primitive clay fireplace. In the farthest corner of the room a sturdy wooden table, its unadorned surface scrubbed bone-white, was flanked by a trio of correspondingly plain chairs. No curtains softened the eyes of the staring windows and the wide floorboards, scour-bleached, were bare of any covering. Rude, open shelving functioned dually as a modest workspace for cooking and a facility for utensil storage; this was randomly occupied by an occasional cracked pottery piece, a blackened iron skillet, and one or two wooden stirring spoons.

Pervasive over all: the sweet, sickish smell of approaching death.

"He is in his quarters?" Mrs. Smythe inclined her head toward a recessed area concealed by the flimsy remnants of sheeting material.

"Aye."

The cloth screening was helpless against the rich, productive coughing that continued seemingly without interruption. Although the screen spared the sight itself of the spasms, the horror of the imagined agony remained.

"Would you be so kind as to announce us?" Mrs. Smythe asked.

The woman sighed deeply. Pulling aside the curtain, she disappeared. "It be her," I heard the muffled announcement.

"Who?" A groan struggled out of a thickened throat.

"The Reverend's lady."

"What the hell her want?" the voice strangled.

"To see you."

"What the hell for?"

"Dunno. Same's last time, I guess."

"Christ!" The effort of speech triggered a still more vigorous bout of coughing.

Etta Soames reappeared. "You go, I think."

"But—"

"Him sick."

"Ah, my dear Etta—a few moments in the company of our divine Savior could be the very tonic your husband needs to—"

"You go."

"Perhaps," Mrs. Smythe posed conspiratorially, "suppose I were to stand here. Right here. And read the gospel through the curtains—"

"Him sick."

"The curtains would remain closed, of course. I would read God's holy scripture through the closed curtains." Mrs. Smythe knelt humbly. "I long to bring the suffering one closer to his Maker!"

Lifting apathetic shoulders, Etta Soames capitulated.

Elated by even this token victory, Mrs. Smythe swept through the Bible, determined to select the ideal passage. "Let me see," she murmured to herself. "No, I think not . . . stimulating, but not entirely appropriate . . . what about . . . no . . . Ah!" she crowed, "I have the perfect— Cryrus Soames!" she squealed. "Can you hear me?" Without waiting for his response, however difficult, she began to read, her voice at highest pitch: " '. . . yet he shall perish forever like his own dung; they which have seen him shall say, Where is he? His bones are full of the sin of his youth, which shall lie down with him in the dust . . . yet his meat in his bowels is turned, it is the gall of asps within him . . .' Mr. Soames, can you still hear me?" Ignoring the troubled, garbled reply, Mrs. Smythe continued, " '. . . when he is about to fill his belly, God shall cast the fury of His wrath upon him, and shall rain it upon him while he is eating . . .' Mr. Soames, attend the sheer poetry of this prose!" Triumphant, Mrs. Smythe's strident voice smote the small room. " '. . . the increase of his house shall depart, and his goods shall fly away in the day of his wrath . . .' Mr. Soames? Mr. Soames . . . Mr. Soames . . ."

It was no use: however stentorian, Mrs. Smythe's bawl could not prevail over Cyrus Soames's still noisier catarrh. . . .

Once in the carriage Mrs. Smythe sank back gratefully on its leather seat, both exhausted and frankly subdued. Angus had exhorted the horses and the wheels had lurched forward, taking us some little distance before Mrs. Smythe seemed able wholly to reconstruct her severely curtailed powers of speech. I wondered idly if her vocal chords might not have suffered permanent impairment, subjected as they had been to the impossible task of carrying the solace of the holy gospel to the unresponsive ears of the consumptive Cyrus Soames. But her recovery was effected readily and her throat free of all outward signs of injury. "How rewarding!" she sighed finally, "to be privileged to bring comfort to one beset by the weaknesses of the soul and of the flesh! To aid one in his hour of misery and travail . . ." Mrs. Smythe's smile was beatific. "I am fulfilled!" Bowing her head in deep humility, she announced, "Now that I have shown Cyrus Soames the blessed path to the golden portals, I can do no less for another similarly beleaguered. . . ." Her tireless fingers flipped the worn pages of her little leather book. "Now, let me see . . . who . . ."

. . . Oh, God . . . the bloody windbag will blow on forever . . .

"Amos Childer!" Mrs. Smythe ventured thoughtfully.

. . . Childer . . . Ian? Oh, God . . . no . . . no . . .

"Not the Childer place, Mama," Miss Caroline voiced immediate objection. "We are not welcome there."

"Not welcome there? Not welcome there?" Mrs. Smythe bridled. "The word of God is welcome everywhere!"

"Not there—"

"The sacred message of our Savior—"

"He threw a pitchfork. Last time the old man threw a pitchfork—"

"Scythe . . ." Mrs. Smythe corrected absently.

"Whatever—it nearly hit you in the—"

"Never mind!" Mrs. Smythe colored. "I will admit that Amos Childer is quite an impossible fellow. But," she muttered, "I mean to investigate that establishment one of these days. . . ."

. . . Gracie was right: fucking snoop . . .

"Well, then," Mrs. Smythe changed course, "Edward Parks and his crippled wife . . ."

"It is growing late, Mrs. Smythe," I interceded suddenly.

"Late? What is late when we, as Christian women, His appointed ambassadors, are sent to spread abroad the word of our Lord and Creator!"

"There will be other opportunities, Mrs. Smythe," I reminded her firmly.

"Miss Knowlton." Mrs. Smythe drew herself up. "You overstep your bounds, I fear . . ."

"My bounds?"

"Your bounds," Mrs. Smythe repeated tartly.

"And what, pray, Mrs. Smythe," my voice was stony, "are my 'bounds'?"

"You are merely the companion to Lady Frances," she observed with some disdain.

"Precisely." My smile was deadly. "Precisely."

Mrs. Smythe blushed.

"And," my tone was flat, "as the companion to Lady Frances, it is my considered opinion that my charge has endured enough at your hands for one afternoon."

"Really!"

"Yes," I echoed, beginning to enjoy myself, "really!" Tapping on the roof of the carriage, I instructed the driver to return to Wynds at once.

Mrs. Smythe's broad pink face was perspiring dangerously. "Miss Knowlton, I must warn you that I feel obliged to report your questionable conduct to—"

"To whom, Mrs. Smythe?" I inquired, unperturbed.

"To Sir Robert!"

"Please do."

"And," Mrs. Smythe added smugly, "the very moment we reach the manor!"

"Mrs. Smythe"—I leaned forward—"If you fail to make such an accounting, then I certainly shall. You may rely on it."

Her face flamed.

Lady Frances moaned feebly.

"I do not know when I have—" sputtered Mrs. Smythe, now irate.

"Mama, please . . ." urged Miss Caroline.

"Caroline, pray do not interfere!" her mother snapped.

Whimpering softly, Lady Frances retreated farther into the dark corner.

"The working class is becoming intolerable!" Mrs. Smythe grumbled.

The sharp brilliance of the evening star penetrated the fragile blue of the twilight sky just as we prepared to pass

the Childer homestead. . . . The old man stood, a motionless silhouette, resting horned hands on the worn wood of
the ancient scythe—jaw flagged and vacant eyes unblinking . . . Owl's eyes . . .

Inside the carriage I could feel the porcine body of Mrs.
Smythe shift; hear Miss Caroline's involuntary gasp . . .
. . . Amos: ferocious custodian . . . good for you.
Keep it up . . .

Exposed for many hours to winter's chill, Angus easily
whipped the matched pair to a frenzied pace, and it was
not long before the lights of Wynds winked their welcome
in the distance. I, too, would be delighted to put an end to
this dreary excursion. . . . What a bloody bore . . .
What dismal companions . . .

The journey home, not surprisingly, was an uncomfortable one: A guarded silence prevailed. No doubt Mrs.
Smythe was marshaling her testimony, readying herself for
its presentation before Sir Robert; Miss Caroline, I was
sure, sat dreading in advance the scene about to be enacted; Lady Frances, of course, crouched warily in the far
corner.

Sarah, who must have been watching for signs of our
return, came running from the house even before Angus
reined up, followed by a troop of servants, including an
officious Judd and anxious Auntie Maude. Judd rudely
swept past the attending footman in order to open the door
of the carriage personally. He helped Lady Frances alight as
if she were precious cargo; the Smythes and myself were
left to fend for ourselves. This would never do. "Young
man," I crooked a preemptive finger at the footman. "Assistance. And at once!"

Auntie Maude's eyes bulged.

I intercepted Mrs. Smythe and Miss Caroline, who were
heading for their trap still hitched to the iron post. The
woman flinched. "You seem to have confused your direction,
madam. I understood you to have pressing business with
Sir Robert," I reminded her. "Surely," I observed, "the
squire is not now sitting in your trap eagerly awaiting your
return. . . ."

"I—er—" She flushed.

"Yes? Mrs. Smythe?" I prompted, my voice sugary.

"I-I have d-decided to overlook our—slight—ah—difference of opinion, this afternoon," she stammered.

"Oh?"

"Y-yes. Perhaps I was a trifle h-hasty, my dear," the woman's mouth curved in a sickly smile.

"Really?"

"Y-yes. I-I would prefer to disregard our opposing—er viewpoint . . ."

"I rather thought you might," I grinned.

"After all, we were embarked on a holy mission . . ."

"Oh, absolutely."

"As a true Christian, I must force myself to forget and to forgive the transgressions of others—particularly when the sinner is thoughtless—Er—" she amended hastily, "because of youth . . . Ah—" She hesitated.

"Yes, Mrs. Smythe?"

"Well—since I am prepared to ah, er—show considerable generosity—"

"Go on, pray—"

"There will—be no need for you—to, ah—"

"Report the matter myself?" I supplied sweetly.

"Well . . ."

"Well, what, Mrs. Smythe?"

"You—you know what I mean," she finished lamely.

"Ah, yes, Mrs. Smythe," I said softly. "I know exactly what you mean . . ."

Chapter 35

Auntie Maude trailed my steps closely as I strode angrily into the house. "Elizabeth!" she hissed, her nervous hand plucking at my sleeve.

"Pray, do not detain me, Aunt," I pulled away. "Where is Annie?"

"Annie? Er—I really couldn't say . . ."

"I want her fetched this instant!"

"What on earth is the matter, child?" Auntie Maude tugged at my arm.

I flung her hand aside. "The matter?" I rasped. "The matter? What on earth could be the matter?" My arms flailed. "After suffering an unbelievably degrading afternoon in the company of the most irrepressible bores of my experience—you show the incredible stupidity to ask me what is the matter!"

Her eyes filled. "But dear . . ."

"Pray, Aunt, fetch Annie."

"Dear—"

"I require the services of Annie," I explained through clenched teeth, "so that I might indulge myself in a thorough bath." I peered into her white face. "A bath. B-a-t-h! Is that too difficult to comprehend, Aunt? A bath? And, why might I require such a thorough bath?"

Mutely, Auntie Maude shook her head.

"I shall be happy to divulge the information, Aunt." My voice was sharp with sarcasm. "Because, Aunt, I have been all but rolled about in a dung heap!"

"Elizabeth!" Auntie Maude shrieked. "Your language, dear! Please!"

"My language!" I hooted. "My language!"

"Oh, my!" Auntie Maude's worried eyes searched the now deserted hall. "Elizabeth," she ventured, "perhaps you are—unwell? Let me take you upstairs and help you to bed."

"Oh, God!" I retorted, exasperation complete. "All I requested was a routine bath and you drone on as if I had contracted some fatal disease! Aunt, you bore me!"

Auntie Maude's lower lip began to tremble. "All right, Elizabeth, I shall see if I can locate Annie."

"Do that," I nodded irritably. "And inform the slut that the water must be piping hot, else she can damned well fetch some more!"

Auntie Maude's devastated face crumpled altogether. "Very well, dear," she agreed quickly, "very well." Her step heavy, she disappeared in the direction of the kitchen.

I raced up the stairs. "Damn her abominable hide!" I muttered as I crossed over the threshold of my nearly frigid room. "No fire! That slattern has left the hearth unattended, and it will be hours before the place can be even reasonably habitable!" In a fit of rage I threw myself upon the settee and pulled my cloak tightly about me. "Bloody bitch!"

A timid tapping on the door announced the maid, who, stung by my glowering expression, attempted an immediate series of halting excuses. "Ah—Miss Elizabeth—"

"Never mind your makeshift evasions!" I spat. "Just what do you mean by permitting the fire to extinguish entirely?"

"Why—" The girl's face flamed.

"What were you doing that was of such magnitude that you neglected the fire in my grate?"

"Ah—miss—"

"Come, come, wench, have you not retained the normal use of your tongue—or are you capable of no more than these useless mutterings?"

Working feverishly, Annie piled log upon log on the hearth. "It should be ablaze soon, miss—"

"I certainly hope so, for your sake," I warned. "I want a bath. The water must be hot and plentiful!" My narrowed eyes never left her frightened face. "You understand my meaning?"

"Yes, miss!" Annie's tense figure bobbed in a series of frantic curtsies. "Yes, miss! Right away, miss!" The girl's flushed face was slick with perspiration by the time she had lugged the last bucketful of water to my room. "There, miss," she declared breathlessly, splashing its contents in the awaiting tub, "this be all it'll hold, I vow!"

"I presume that the water is hot," I said, venturing an exploratory finger into the steaming vessel.

"Hotter than the gates of hell," she pledged. "Will ye be wantin' aught else?"

I shook my head. . . . Soaking luxuriously, I lazily watched the iridescent soap bubbles skim over the surface of the water, collide, disappear, and then multiply as if by magic. This was indeed delicious. . . . Totally alien to the activities of the afternoon . . . How had the day, begun so auspiciously, deteriorated! First a glorious ride with Sir Robert, then mired soon thereafter in the absurd company of that meddling zealot, Mrs. Smythe, and her dullard offspring. Only to sink to the ultimate depths amongst the witless recipients of their religiosity . . . Lots of damned nonsense . . . Idiots to open their doors to that sanctimonious busybody and her silent toady in the first place . . . Amos Childer had the right idea: chuck the scythe at them . . . I giggled . . . Or Gracie. Incredible, depraved rascal: gyrate indecently and run one off; toss the Good Book into the bog and rid yourself of the other . . .

Nor do I mean to slight her ladyship: molting in the carriage like some sick hawk in the mew . . .

It was with a reluctance that I stepped out of the tub at last and enfolded myself in a fluffy towel. Lounging full length before the fire to bask in its warmth from every angle, I was claimed by a delectable sense of euphoria. Nor was it lessened by a tapping at my door. " 'Tis I, miss. Annie."

"What is it?" I yawned.

"I've brought your supper tray, miss."

"My supper tray!" I sat up. "I am to have supper here?"

"I cannot hold on to the tray much longer, please, miss—" the girl whined.

"Then bring it in, dolt," I snapped.

Balancing the tray with difficulty as she opened and closed the door, Annie approached me. "Shall I set it on the chest, miss?"

"What is the meaning of this?" I demanded, ignoring her question.

"I do not ken your words, miss."

"Why am I to have the meal in my room?"

The girl stood mute.

"By whose instruction am I to have supper in my room?" I repeated.

The girl shrugged, "Cook, miss. Her told me to ready up the young miss's tray and bring it up." She tried a wan smile. "It be Yorkshire pudding tonight . . ."

"I presumed that I was to dine with the family."

"I don't get told them things." The girl shifted her weight. "Shall I set it down, miss?"

"Dump it in the privy for all of me," I muttered sourly, "I mean to get to the bottom of this . . . Send Miss Treadway to me. Straightaway!"

She shook her head. "Her be busy in the cake room, the now, miss."

I took a menacing step toward the girl. "How dare you!"

Annie's eyes widened.

"Do you or do you not understand a simple request?"

Her terrified gaze fell to the floor.

"You were told to send Miss Treadway to my room. See to it! At once."

"Y-yes, yes, miss!" Annie scurried from the room.

Angrily I paced the floor. . . . A tray in my room . . . I was again to be relegated to my quarters. . . . Sentenced to isolation like a recalcitrant child or the family fright. . . . I'll wager that Auntie Maude contrived this little piece of strategy: "Let me help you to bed, dear. . . . You are unwell, dear. . . . dear . . ."

What a tiresome old fool, she: "Do this, do that, Elizabeth . . . Don't do this . . . Don't do that . . . Elizabeth. No. No. No . . ."

The door opened a crack: Auntie Maude poked her head in the room.

"My God! Can't you knock!" I rasped.

"Dear, it is only I," Auntie Maude said meekly.

"You knock at my door. Always! Understand?"

Auntie Maude blinked, but ventured a timid smile. "Annie said that you wished to see me . . ."

"I want to know why you arranged to have me eat my meal in this room."

She seemed puzzled. "But—"

"I am tired of your constant interference in my life."

"Elizabeth, dear, I—" Her eyes welled with tears.

"I am perfectly well and will not be treated as a puling invalid, whatever your intentions in the matter, Aunt!"

"But, Elizabeth—I had nothing to—"

"You can take this bloody tray and all of the rotten food piled on it back downstairs—and eat it yourself!"

"Elizabeth—"

"I shall, of course, join Sir Robert and any gentry visiting in the dinning hall."

"Elizabeth, darling, listen to me!" Auntie Maude cried. "Sir Robert is not eating in the hall this evening."

I stopped short. "How do you know that?"

"I heard Judd change the dining arrangements with Cook this very afternoon."

"Sir Robert is not here?" I said slowly.

"No, dear." She moved toward me, as if to take my hand. "You are overwrought, child. You will make yourself ill if—"

I pushed her away. "Oh, stop!" I screamed, "stop this ceaseless fretting over me!"

"What is the matter, darling?" Auntie Maude was herself distraught.

"Go! Go away!" I shrilled. "And take that miserable tray with you! Take it back to the kitchen where you and it belong!" I flung myself on the bed. "Get out! Do you hear me! Get out! Get out! Get out!"

I could feel her steps falter as they crossed the room, hear the stifled sob and the subtle clacking of dishes as Auntie Maude staggered under the heavily laden tray. The door opened and closed and she was gone.

Facedown, I lay on the bed, allowing my anger to subside into piqued bewilderment. . . . Sir Robert . . . Why the abrupt change in the dinner plans? . . . How could he expose me to an afternoon of squalor and penury so casually and then, as recompense, consign me to virtual solitary confinement? . . .

If this was not a plot, then, devised by Auntie Maude, anxious meddler . . . could it have been a clever design of Lady Frances . . .

. . . Lady Frances . . . I spat . . . That cringing ninny. No more capable of clever schemes than the school-room dunce . . .

. . . No . . . This must be Sir Robert's work. . . . Where was he? . . . And why would he not dine in the hall tonight? . . .

I rose from the bed and began to pace the room. I was restless. Discontent. Churned by waves of hidden hunger. The fire was diminishing perceptibly, taking with it its vague warmth; my body, under the plush toweling, commenced to shiver.

I should summon that silly chit, Annie, to tend the fire. Lazy slattern . . . Why bother . . . There was nothing to do here in my rooms . . . Nothing to sit up for . . . I had seen Miss Becky Sharp through her last entanglement some weeks ago. What girlish pap did Mr. Thackeray pen, after all! Perhaps a spicier book awaited me on the library shelves. Before I could undertake such a search I would be obliged to dress. Why bother? I was too agitated to read . . .

Perhaps if I went to bed the dream would appear . . .

. . . Damn your eyes, Annie, you useless sloven, it is cold in here . . .

I viewed with almost tangible distaste the shapeless bulk of the flannel nightdress, Auntie Maude's Christmas offering, still folded on the chest. Avowedly fashioned more for warmth than for style, the gown carried utility to extremes; since by this time I was frankly shaking, reluctantly I drew it on.

Repose, that fickle demon, eluded me. Determinedly I clamped my eyes closed and waited, trying to empty my mind first of the taunting image of a slut and her vermi-nous offspring, then the gaunt specter administering to no more a husband but a rheumy cough . . .

Did I hear my name? Elizabeth? Eagerly I sat up. My eyes flew open. . . . Was there a light? Did it flood the path? Did it coax? Beckon? Pour its golden stream down the spiral staircase to the wondrous room?

. . . . No. There was nothing . . . Nothing. The room remained deep in shadow. No. There was nothing . . .

I fell back. Again I squeezed my eyes shut, as if to woo sleep, but praying for the return of the dream . . .

The dream . . .

Miserable, I tossed from one side of the rumpled bed to seek vain solace from the other. . . . Where was the dream? Why did it not appear? Why? Why?

Wretched, I thrashed . . .

. . . Knotted hands . . . Clouded eyes . . . Ragged stumps of teeth paraded in a mocking grin. . . . A meadow, brown in winter sleep . . . Apples lying formless at the base of a leafless tree . . . The lunatic stare of fear . . . A black mane tossing . . . A distant sea . . . An ancient scythe . . . Dark, insistent eyes . . .

Sir Robert . . .

God . . . Where was the bloody dream . . .

Sir Robert . . .

I threw back the covers and rose in a state of near hysteria. I began to pace the length of the room . . . Despite the flannel shroud I could feel the penetrating chill of the night air. . . . Where was the dream . . .

In fury I strode . . . The dream . . .

A sudden flash stayed me. The light? Would the path appear now? The path . . . draping its golden ribbon . . . leading to the dream? I waited.

There! There it was again! A light, flickering through my window . . . Quickly I knelt at the sill. . . . There! Again! Almost rhythmical in its track! Back and forth. Swinging, back and forth . . .

The tower. Was it coming from the tower?

In faint outline the tower burst against the dark night sky. Framed high within its stone bulk a light was swaying. To and fro . . . Hypnotically . . . Facing the sea . . .

I stared.

The tower . . .

Chapter 36

Auntie Maude's softly insistent "Elizabeth. Elizabeth," roused me. "Dear," she asked in concern, "are you ill?"

"No." I stretched.

"It is already well past noon."

"So?"

"It is late to be still abed, dear."

I turned my face away from her anxious one.

"Dear," she persisted, "are you certain that you are not ill?"

"Of course," I muttered crossly.

"Then why do you lie here hours into the afternoon?"

"Oh, God, Aunt! Pray, desist!" I was fretful, unrested. I had kept a vigil at the window long after the light had vanished abruptly from the tower, crouching by the sill, willing the return of its wavering gleam much as I had yearned for a glimpse into the dream. Toward dawn, exhausted and thoroughly chilled, I had crawled between badly wrinkled sheets only to shiver for hours before drifting finally, to sleep.

"Dear," Auntie Maude suggested, "perhaps it might be wise to ask Dr. Briggs to have a look at you—"

"No!"

"I am positive he would not mind! In fact," she smirked conspiratorially, "I might just venture to say that the young man in question would be more than pleased to attend you . . ."

. . . You simpering old fool . . . "Stop that ridiculous prattle, Aunt," I sneered. "I shall get up in good time."

"Let me help you dress," Auntie Maude offered eagerly.

"I am scarcely an infant."

"We all need a bit of babying now and again—" She tugged playfully at the covers.

"Stop that at once!" I commanded, yanking the blankets forcibly from her grasp.

"But—" Auntie Maude's face crumpled.

"I suggest that you leave me now."

"But—"

"I have not the slightest intention of stirring one toe from this bed until the fire is blazing properly in that grate and my breakfast fetched!"

"Annie! I shall summon Annie! Right away, then, dear! Right away!" Auntie Maude's face brightened at the prospect of her little errand.

"Annie!" I spat. "Lazy slut!"

"Elizabeth!" Shocked, Auntie Maude's hand flew to her mouth.

"Sputter all you like, Aunt," I invited nastily. "She is a lazy slut, for all your aimless protestations!"

"Very well, dear, if you say so," my aunt hastened to agree, her attitude promptly conciliatory.

"Leave me," I ordered her abruptly.

"Er—" she ventured timidly, "shall I alert your little maid?"

I shrugged. "As you wish." I snuggled deeper into the bedclothes. "On your way out," I said with pointed emphasis.

She colored. "Yes, dear. Of course." She hesitated before the door.

"Out!" I repeated . . . Old fool. Fawning old fool. What a bloody bore. Skulks around like a whipped dog . . .

Then, I remembered: the light in the tower . . . Could it have been starlight? It swayed, back and forth. Does starlight sway? Merely reflection, perhaps . . . Glass. Are tower windows fitted with glass?

Quickly I leapt out of bed. Kneeling at the window, I squinted against brilliant sunshine and scanned the horizon. The tower stood, its golden stone boldly thrusting. At its upper reach a primitive fenestral slit stared: vacant, eyeless. It was without glass . . .

A light knocking produced Annie, who nudged the door hesitantly, her arms heavily laden with firewood. "I come to make up the fire, miss," she curtsied, moving awkwardly under her burden.

"And about time."

"Beggin' yer pardon, miss, but—" she murmured, busily laying a bed of kindling.

"Spare me your contrived excuses!" I interrupted sourly, "and address the task at hand. It is freezing in here."

"Yes, miss." She blew hard on the struggling flames. "It'll be no time afore you be toasty warm."

"Mentioning toast," I said tartly, "when am I to expect my breakfast?"

"Breakfast?" she looked blank.

"Need I remind you that I have not as yet been served a solitary morsel of food this day—and it is nearly two in the afternoon!"

The girl flushed. "I thought—"

"It is not within your province to think, my girl," I interrupted disagreeably, "simply to obey."

"Aye, miss—" she blinked.

"And now—you have your orders."

"Aye, miss."

The tower . . . Who was in the tower? What hand held that waving lantern—for lantern it must have been . . . Who had business in those eerie heights at so deep an hour? I must find out . . .

Where was the access—the stairway leading up to the window that fixed its empty gaze on the fields below, toward the sea beyond? . . .

I would learn these things . . .

. . . Drat that bloody wench! She has had more than enough time to prepare a feast for the Royal Family . . .

At last I heard vague movement at the door. "Praise Allah!" Bowing, I greeted the girl, my mood stiff with sarcasm, "I was on the point of expiration!"

"Shall I set the tray here, miss?" Annie asked shyly.

I nodded. "Hot, at least." I noted with approval the wisps of steam escaping from the covered dishes.

"Aye, miss," the girl was encouraged, "everything be lovely." She twisted her hands self-consciously. "Will that be all, miss?"

"Annie," I said slowly, "have you ever been up in the tower?"

"The tower?"

"Wynds tower."

"Oh, no, miss!" Her eyes were wide.

"Would you know where the staircase is located?"

"Staircase?"

"Yes. Staircase."

The girl frowned in concentration. "It be behind a door, most like . . ."

. . . The bloody dunce . . . "Yes, Annie," I said, striving for patience. "Do you know where the door is?"

"I be not sure, miss." Annie became strangely evasive.

"Very well." My tone was cold as I dismissed her. "You may go."

I had finished dressing and moved to fasten my cloak snugly about my shoulders when I was stayed by a timid commotion at the door. "Who is it?" I asked crossly.

"Er—Auntie Maude—" Her voice was whisper-thin.

"Oh, all right." Opening the door, I viewed my aunt ungraciously. "Well?"

She eyed my cloak and observed shyly, "Oh, dear, you are planning to go out?"

"What is it, Aunt?"

"May—er, we—er, I—sit down?" Her request was almost servile.

"I hope that your business here will not prove of a tiresome length," I remarked bluntly. "I have planned an outing."

"Oh," she assumed a chatty manner, "where are you bound?"

I ignored the question. "What, if anything, have you come prepared to say, Aunt. My time is limited."

"I was going to suggest," my aunt struggled with the words, "that if you feel that you are not—er—comfortable with—with—"

"With what?" I prompted.

"With—er—Annie as your personal—er, ah—attendant—"

"Maid, you mean," I supplied smoothly.

"Well—yes. Maid." Auntie Maude flushed. "I was going to recommend that a—substitute perhaps—you know—might prove welcome. . . ."

"Very well"—glibly I passed off her proposition— "assign another girl to take her place." I yawned. "The entire matter is of little import to me, after all."

"You don't—quite—understand—dear—"

"No," I admitted coolly, "I confess that I do not."

"There is no—er—girl here, at this time, to take on the responsibility—er, who has the training—to be a—ah, lady's maid—"

"Then"—I regarded her with open exasperation—"why do you dazzle me with the prospect if the scheme is not feasible in the first place?"

"But dear—" Auntie Maude swallowed. "I was thinking of, er—Molly—or Ada."

"What about them?"

"I thought it might be nice to contact them."

"Whatever for?"

"One—or both—might serve."

"Ridiculous!" I snorted. "They are both in London."

"But Elizabeth, dear—" Auntie Maude asserted, "they could arrive within a fortnight! I am certain that I could find positions for both of them here at Wynds."

"The idea is preposterous!"

"No, dear, not at all." Doggedly she shook her head. "I could post a letter this very day."

"Do not trouble yourself."

Auntie Maude's face brightened. "It would be no trouble at all," she vowed. "You need the company of young women of your own age—and Molly, Ada, and you were so close—"

"All this is nonsense!"

"And since you do not find Annie—"

"Do as you like," I snapped. "I cannot be concerned with such trifles." Swirling my cloak carelessly about me, I flounced from the room, leaving Auntie Maude captive of the tedium of her own dialogue. . . .

Chapter 37

The boy Peter was oiling a saddle when I approached the stable. "Prepare Artemis for me," I ordered crisply.

His eyes remained stubbornly fastened on the gleaming leather.

"Did you not hear, boy?" I demanded. "Prepare Artemis for riding. At once!"

"Her not go with you, seems so," he murmured.

"What!" I cried. "And why not?"

"Him tell me not let you have no horse. Seems so."

"Him! Who?"

"Mr. Hartley," the boy said softly.

"Mr. Hartley!" I exclaimed. "This is a question which has already been resolved! How dare Hartley countermand his master's authority!"

"Him boss."

"Sir Robert is the boss," I corrected smugly.

Peter's slim shoulders lifted.

"You are infuriating!" I shrilled. "I command **you to** saddle Artemis for my use and without further delay! Do you understand, boy?"

"Me can't do nothin'—seems so—" the boy maintained.

"Well, I certainly can!" I promised grimly. "I shall report this matter and your rudeness at once to Sir Robert!"

"Him not here—"

"It won't take long to fetch him."

The boy shook his head. "Him be gone away."

I stopped. "Gone! Gone where?"

"I be not know them things," the boy confessed. "But him be gone. Seems so."

"When did he go?"

"Sunup."

"When will he return?"

The boy shrugged.

"When will he return?" I repeated frantically.

"Me not know them things," he reiterated.

"Where is Hartley?" I demanded suddenly.

"Him in the stalls."

"Fetch him. At once."

"Him busy." The boy's refusal came with no hesitation.

"At once! Do you hear me!" I screamed. "At once!"

"What is all the fuss, lad," a calm voice inquired almost lazily: The bulk of the stable master easily filled the doorway.

"Where is Sir Robert?" I asked without preamble.

"That, miss, is the squire's matter, not mine."

"The boy, here, says he left at dawn."

The man nodded.

"Very well," I sighed in defeat.

"That be all, miss?" Hartley asked with a lift to his brow.

"No. Ready Artemis for my immediate use."

"Yes, miss." The man inclined his head toward Peter, "Saddle Artemis, lad."

The boy raised objecting eyes to his master. "Mr. Hartley, sir, you—"

"Do as I bid, lad," the man directed Peter sadly. "As I bid . . ."

The sky was clear and the air benign, but the expected pleasure of the day had vanished, much as early mists flee before the bright meridian. . . . Sir Robert, gone . . . Gone where? . . . And when would he return? . . .

Recklessly I urged the chestnut mare to her greatest speed; slapped smartly; struck cruelly; pressing forward . . . ever forward . . . My cloak, whipped, flying at my back, I was the wild-eyed goddess of the Hunt . . . fleet . . . borne on the very winds . . . tormented . . . savage . . . I could feel my mount tire, her step falter. . . . All right, mere mortal, I consoled her: we shall rest atop the hill. . . .

Smugglers' Peak: the villagers' name for Wynds' only point of real elevation . . . I gazed over stark spiny trees, past tawny fields sliced by a swollen stream rushing to meet the roiled sea beyond . . .

Carried aloft in little swirling eddies, a gull struggled for release, another floated on a cushion of wind, still another dipped suddenly, falling below the horizon . . . down to the churning sea . . .

Smugglers' Peak: Wynds' pinnacle . . . Except for the tower, perhaps? Could one glimpse the sea from the upper reaches of the tower?

Chapter 38

"Ah! There she is!" Dr. Briggs sprang from his roost before the fire in the inglenook and seized both my hands, pumping them roundly.

Auntie Maude, clinging to a remote corner of the alcove, ventured a sheepish smile. . . . So, she did send for him, after all.

Jonathan Briggs viewed me with cocked head and a narrowed, clinical expression. "There is a bloom to her cheek, Miss Treadway!" he announced gaily. "As well as," he grinned, "fire in her eye!"

I swung my smoldering gaze toward my aunt. "Meddler!" I snarled.

"Here, here," Dr. Briggs calmly intervened, "what is all this?"

"Damned busybody," I muttered.

"Come now, dear girl, can it be considered interference to suggest that a physician look in on his favorite patient?"

"I am not your patient," I reminded him coldly.

"A mere formality," he chuckled.

"The dreary creature cowering upstairs," I sneered, "is the one you should be favoring with your attentions, not me."

"All in good time, m'dear—" The doctor, with supreme good nature, ignored my ill-humored protestations. "I shall address that lady's chronic disabilities after I have identified your more acute one—"

"My acute what?" I demanded, angry now.

"That, m'dear, is something I have not as yet determined." With a grip of steel he reached out and caught my wrist. "Mmm," he murmured, "a trifle rapid, but nothing to be alarmed about." He extracted a wooden depressor from his bag. "Stick out your tongue," he ordered.

"Gladly!"

Jonathan Briggs roared with laughter. "Miss Knowlton, I devoutly pray that you are never really ill!" He shook his head. "I doubt that I could cope with you as a bona fide patient!"

"She is really all right, then?" Auntie Maude was visibly relieved.

"Recalcitrant and perverse," he judged, "but not physically indisposed. Not at all." He chortled. "I prescribe a good spanking over my knee—"

"You just try!" I warned, not in the least amused.

"Although perhaps a quick turn in the trap to bank the fires might prove better medicine," he declared. "How about it, Miss Knowlton?"

"I have spent the afternoon in the saddle," I declined rudely.

"I am not asking you to contend with the saddle," the doctor explained, undefeated. "Rather a jaunt—with you inside the trap, wrapped nose-high in a warm robe."

"Elizabeth—" Auntie Maude was abruptly silenced by Dr. Briggs's quick signal.

"Let's go," he urged, all but shoving me out the door, "while there is still light. . . ."

True to his pledge Dr. Briggs wound me in a woolen cocoon before urging his horse forward. We proceeded at a leisurely pace for some time before he attempted conversation. Even so, his initial sallies were only conventional overtures, trivial in nature: Was I warm enough . . . Had I noticed that the days were beginning to lengthen appreciably . . . Not many months and we'll be complaining about the excessive heat . . . At last he asked, his question abrupt, "Why did Miss Treadway consider it necessary to summon me to Wynds this afternoon?"

I scowled. "I think she has the vapors."

"Correction, my dear," he contradicted quietly, "she thinks that you are off-course."

"Auntie Maude is a crashing bore," I muttered.

"She loves you very much."

I sighed. "I know. Sometimes I wish she didn't."

"I gather," he observed thoughtfully, "that at one time you two were very close."

"I suppose."

"Why has the relationship changed?" His manner was carefully casual.

"I have grown up and she has simply grown old." My reply was testy. "If you continue this line of interrogation, Doctor, I shall ask you to return me to Wynds."

"Miss Treadway is only concerned about your welfare."

I sat up. "I meant precisely what I said, Doctor! Turn this carriage around," I ordered sharply.

"Now, now, my dear," he tried to pacify me. "I shall forbear. . . . What shall we discuss? Perhaps, instead of mere conversation," he chuckled, "you might rather prefer a modest choral offering . . ."

"Choral offering?" I could not help but smile.

"I always come prepared—"

My peevish mood lifted; I began to giggle. "Help! Save your serenade for the appreciative Miss Caroline!"

"Miss Knowlton"—With mock severity the doctor clucked his tongue—"Can I believe that you are being uncharitable?"

"Or," I teased, "you might try out your charms on the seductive Gracie Turner—"

"Gracie Turner?" he asked in surprise. "How in the world do you know that name?"

"I not only know her name—but I have been in her house."

"God Almighty! When?"

"Yesterday."

"What in heaven's name for?"

"Acting as official emissary for Her Royal Highness, who was, as usual, too infirm to discharge her function as the squire's lady."

"That," he admitted, "I do not entirely comprehend."

"It seems that Lady Frances is expected to call on members of the parish periodically—"

He nodded.

"Goodwill—or as Mrs. Smythe would say—God's will—"

"You did not wander into that sty alone?" The doctor was horrified.

"No. I was properly chaperoned by the righteous Mrs. Smythe and the stalwart Miss Caroline, who," I laughed, "was forced to run out all in a dainty heap because Gracie chose to cavort obscenely. . . ."

"Jesus," Dr. Briggs whispered to himself.

"A unique performer, at that," I reflected, grinning. "Gracie even managed to exorcise the obdurate Mrs. Smythe neatly besides."

"Remarkable," the doctor agreed absently.

"She's pregnant again," I informed him casually.

His eyebrows rose. "Probably drop it in the field like a goat."

"And she still nurses little Gracie. Is she," I asked suddenly, "retarded?"

"Which one?"

"Both, I guess."

"Possibly. There is little hope for the survival of either, in any case, I'm afraid." It was a grim prognosis. "Just a matter of time." He turned to me, narrowing sober eyes. "I do not want you to set foot in that place again."

"What—"

"Ever." His voice was flat. . . .

It was dark by the time we pulled up at Wynds. Auntie Maude had arranged a small intimate dinner for the doctor and myself, to be served before the fire in the inglenook. Afraid that her quarry might well escape before she had a chance fully to impale him, Auntie Maude had kept a breathless watch at the window, waiting for our return. Dr. Briggs was, of course, delighted at the invitation and so, as a matter of fact, was I: I did not look forward to another solitary dinner in my room.

Our conversation was rollicking while we saluted an epic procession of wine bottles; and so, before the doctor took his leave, we were both more than moderately tipsy. I am sure that intoxication (alcoholic, that is) was hardly Auntie Maude's intent, but she had withdrawn with unaccustomed tact to her quarters in the servants' wing and remained blissfully unaware of our excesses.

As might have been anticipated, Dr. Briggs grew frankly amorous; I confess that I did nothing dramatic to discourage his ardent, if awkward, campaign.

It was the ornamented clock, sentinel of the hall, that chimed a final and decisive end to our besotted merrymaking. The yawning—even a discreet cough or two hazarded by the disgruntled staff assignees—indicating that the time was late for our innocent game and please God to let them clear away the debris and retire after a long and arduous day—did nothing to effect the cessation of our activities. No: It was the clock, loudly marking the day's passing, that gave the impetus to Dr. Briggs, a clumsy victim of insobriety, to right himself with a degree of accuracy sufficient (and barely so) to head for the front door. "G'night, m'dear," he declared, drawing me manfully to his breast. His mouth, greedy but imprecise, sought mine. "G'night, m'dear," he repeated; his lips, aimed in the direction of my own, again achieved no notable success.

Unsteadily the doctor lurched against the door, displacing as he did so a sudden burst of icy air, which persuaded him at last to complete his intended exodus. "G'night, m'dear," he said once more. Outside, his drunken ebullience echoed in the empty courtyard. Giggling helplessly, I leaned against the wall for support before daring the uncertainties of the hall stairs. Tittering foolishly, I climbed, viewing the enormity of each step, one by one, with pithy commentary. Wrapped in this deliciously sodden state, I reached the safety of my rooms, remarkably without injury.

Tossing individual articles carelessly about the room, I managed to strip myself of all offending clothing. Once in the dressing nook, I stared gloomily in the mirrors. "What the hell good are you?" I whispered to the gleaming body reflected there. "What bloody use . . ."

I belched loudly then, which restored my high good humor.

Spread in sober readiness across my bed: the flannel nightdress. "Ho, ho, you abhorrence!" I sneered, pitching it gleefully to the floor. "Not tonight, you scratchy sack!"

I slipped my naked body between sheets still warm from the efforts of a heated brick deposited there earlier. "Good ole Annie, filthy slut!" I hiccoughed, "must have felt the fear of God in her at long last. . . ." My head on the pillow swam in hazy circles. Delectable. I stretched in languorous luxury and drifted off to sleep, savoring the drugged euphoria. . . .

Elizabeth . . . Elizabeth . . . I sat up. It was there:
the path . . . Beguiling. Wooing . . . Eagerly I rose and
ran down the curved staircase. . . . The door stood
closed. Tightly closed. Gently I tried the handle: It did not
move. I uttered a little cry of dismay: No! It cannot be so!
Again, my timid fingers touched the knob: nothing. I
pushed. In fear, at first, then boldly. The door opened . . .

But she was alone! Alone! Sitting alone! Her slender fingers twisted a lock of amber-colored hair. Beautiful: but
alone. She was alone. . . . Where was he? Oh, God,
where was he? I was frantic, cheated. . . . Where was he?

I tasted the warm salt of tears on my face. . . . Oh,
God, where was he . . .

The heavy drapes shifted and he appeared . . . his eyes
dark, shadowed under mocking brows. Standing before her,
he drew her to her feet and pressed her close against him,
parting her eager lips with his own. White arms wound
around him; rocking hips caressed him in slow, deliberate
rhythm. His hands, insistent, moved restlessly over her,
tugged at the bodice of the crimson gown that slithered
over rounded breasts, past sinuous thighs, and lay unheeded, finally, on the floor. With a low chuckle she loosened his robe and it, too, slipped to his feet, forgotten.

Slowly he lowered her to the couch. She lay back, shimmering loins trembling, spreading. . . . He positioned
himself and mounted her, fitting his body deep in hers.
Locked, he rode. Thrusting, driving . . . Hard . . .
Fast . . . Faster . . . faster, faster, faster, faster.

The light faded . . .

Chapter 39

The next weeks were spent, the elements permitting, racing Artemis through the winter-starched countryside. We clattered over shale, pounded deserted sands, picked our way through ice-laced moor grass, to stand atop Smugglers' Peak in silent homage to the panoramic majesty of sea and sky. . . .

Below us the petulant, uneasy sea sounded its complaint; above, trees, barren still, waved dingy fingers as if to court the empty sky. The days were lengthening preceptibly. The sun, riding higher now, pledged a new warmth to the stricken earth; a richer color to the sea.

The sight was breathtaking; could this same scene be viewed from the tower? . . .

The tower . . . Somehow I must investigate the tower. Somehow I must find access to its upper reaches. I must know: Do its slitted eyes squint against the sun? . . .

The light . . . Although I had not seen it again, the flicker of that swaying lantern lingered perfectly in my memory. . . . In whose hand was it held? . . . And why? . . .

The tower offered no visible approach from without, protected as it was by an impenetrable stone wall by land, and its face to the sea impossible to scale. An entrance, then, must be located within the house proper. But where? . . .

Although fully aware that I had no friends amongst the stable hands, I made individual inquiries, starting with the lowly Peter, who was busily sweeping out a stall when I neared, determined to be pleasant. "Good morning!" My cheery greeting elicited a look of comic surprise. "Another fine day!" I babbled.

The boy blushed.

"Perhaps a harbinger of spring . . ."

He stared.

"Won't be long now—" I chattered.

Peter shifted uneasy feet.

"I say"—I tried to thread my way into my intended topic casually—"have you ever been in the tower?"

His eyes widened.

"You were raised in Drewsby," I said, more in declaration than as a question.

He nodded.

"Come now, Peter," I cajoled. "In your games as a child you must have sneaked into the tower—somehow—and explored." I smiled conspiratorially. "I know I would have done. . . ."

He shook his head.

"Not even once?" I wheedled.

"No, miss," he whispered.

"A clever lad like you?" I was frankly arch.

"No, miss," he vowed.

"Once, surely," I coaxed.

"Never," he rasped.

"You wouldn't tell me if you had, you snide bastard!" I muttered. "Saddle Artemis," I ordered, tired of the game, "I propose to waste no more time on the likes of you. . . ."

Hartley, queried at still another fruitless session, proved equally obdurate: "No, miss." His reply was civil enough. "Ain't never had no call for such. . . . Seems so . . ."

"Surely in your younger—er—freer days," I persisted.

He hesitated.

"A strong, adventuresome fellow!" I flattered the man outrageously.

He simply stared . . .

Thomas Pipenbrink, a cocky youth and recent addition to the manege, was plainly uninterested: "Best be axin' some else" was his airy advice. . . .

The staff serving Wynds was staggering in both number and variety, yet I felt without recourse in their domain: Annie, when questioned about the tower, had exhibited a primary fear that, although characteristic of her breed, lacked apparent cause; Judd was, of course, unapproachable; Auntie Maude occupied a post of some stature but was too newly employed to have garnered confidences. Cook was glimpsed on but one occasion, and then so filmed with flour and batter that I would be hard put to recognize her a second time; the footmen were as blurred faces in the crowd; Angus, aged and failing, was sure to be held in the rhapsodic thralldom of nostalgia; the army of maids and lackeys scurried as fickle creatures, uniformly attired and not readily identifiable. . . .

No. Not from these would be torn the answer to the riddle of the tower . . .

Dr. Briggs, normally a rich font of miscellaneous data, proved surprisingly uninformed on the subject of the tower. "Ah, m'dear. There it stands," he said. "I know that and nothing more." He mused for a moment. "A light, you say? Wavering? Can't imagine. Unless," he threw me an amused sidelong glance, "you recorded the phenomenon the evening we imbibed too freely. . . ."

Sir Robert . . . He would know . . . I would ask Sir Robert when he returned. . . .

When he returned . . . When would that be? He had been gone for six days; it seemed more like six eternities. . . .

I was restless, aflame, cooled only by a frantic chase over desolate, wasted lands; quenched only by a path of gold . . .

Midway into the second week of Sir Robert's absence, the weather, which had proved blissfully benign, changed abruptly. Gone were the steady suns and tempering breezes. A dismal shroud now enveloped Wynds. For four days the heavens, gray and glowering, spat a skyful of rain, sleet, and sporadic snow onto the earth below, their hapless victim.

By day I stared grimly through misted windows at the sodden, brooding garden; paced the dreary prison of my room; savagely I stormed the great hall, my stride rapid and frenzied. I was beside myself. Wild. Trapped. Desperate for relief. Waiting for a sun that would not shine . . .

By night I twisted, caught in the snare of rumpled sheets, willing release: the dream . . . a glimpse into heaven . . . the call that did not come . . .

Auntie Maude continued to eye me anxiously, but without comment. Early one wretched afternoon she found me huddled in the inglenook and broke her self-imposed silence. "Dear," she approached me shyly. "May I help?"

I looked at her as if she were a stranger.

"Is there something I may get for you?"

I did not answer.

"Perhaps a book? I know how dearly you love to read."

"Nothing," I said curtly.

"Sir Robert's library is handsomely equipped," she ventured, naïvely encouraged by my spoken response.

I turned my head away.

"I know!" She clapped her hands. "I could arrange to have tea served us in my room!"

I kept my face averted.

"Perhaps Cook would agree to bake some of her lovely bread—"

I shook my head.

"Smothered in creamy butter! And," she exclaimed, "I am sure I saw one jar of rose hip jelly left in the pantry—"

"Shut up!" I shrilled, leaping to my feet. "Can't you ever shut up!"

"Dear—" Auntie Maude's voice quavered.

"Leave me alone! Do you hear me? Leave me alone!" Without looking back I ran up the stairs. Trembling with anger, I slammed the door to my room. . . . Why can't she let me alone. . . . Why must she pester, pester, pester. . . . Helpless with rage I flung myself on the bed and with balled fists began to brutalize the pillow. . . . Nag . . . Nag . . . Nag . . . The flogging intensified. . . . Nag . . . Nag . . . Suddenly drained, I collapsed and surrendered myself to involuntary sobbing.

I must have fallen into an exhausted sleep. I awoke some time later to the sound of a voice calling my name softly. The dream . . . I sat up expectantly: Dr. Briggs was standing at my bedside. "Oh," I murmured, disappointed.

"Hardly a gracious greeting," he remarked with undaunted good humor.

"What do you want?"

"I was in the neighborhood, so I thought I'd stop by." He was deliberately casual.

"Damned liar," I muttered.

"Well, m'dear," he observed brightly, "you certainly look much the worse for wear."

"Thank you," I replied stiffly.

"Your eyes are so puffed they resemble currants inhumed in a cake," he chuckled.

"We are a positive fountain of flattery today, aren't we—"

He consulted his watch. "It is not quite three thirty. When was your last meal?" he asked conversationally.

I shrugged. "This morning . . . last night . . . I don't remember."

"You are going to take some nourishment now." This was a command.

"Oh, go away," I said listlessly.

Dr. Briggs cupped my chin in his hand. "Listen, my girl, I am not nearly so easily intimidated as your poor Auntie Maude."

"She is a bloody bore."

He chose to ignore my acerbic remark and went on, instead, to inform me that I was descending, on his arm—and forthwith—to the inglenook for a high tea in the Old Tradition. "And," he added, his voice climbing to shaky falsetto, "I shall even pour!"

"You utter ass," I giggled.

He pulled me to my feet. "For God's sake, straighten your dress and wash that blotchy face," he ordered. "I can't stand my women messy."

"I am hardly your woman," I reminded him coldly.

"Not yet, perhaps."

"If you wish me to conduct all these personal ablutions," I declared with hauteur, "you might at least have the grace to vacate the immediate premises and allow me to proceed in privacy—"

"And have you lock the door in my face? Not on your life!"

"You are uncouth!"

"Perhaps so. There is water on the stand."

"How do you know?"

"I looked."

"Another damned snoop!" I snorted. I poked a tentative finger in the awaiting basin; I drew it quickly away.

"Now what is the matter?"

"The water is freezing."

"Good for you. Refreshing."

"I refuse to bathe in freezing water."

"Your refusal has been taken under consideration. Now, get busy. Before I conduct your 'ablutions' for you."

"You wouldn't dare!"

He laughed. "Try me."

Halfway down the stairs I caught a fleeting glimpse of Auntie Maude as she scurried guiltily down the great hall, quickly disappearing in the direction of the kitchen. "There goes your fellow conspirator," I observed disagreeably.

Dr. Briggs's expression remained guileless. Unperturbed, he guided me into the inglenook. "Pray be seated!" He awarded me a courtly bow before exclaiming in unfeigned delight, "This is indeed a sumptuous spread!"

"Pure gluttony," I decreed sourly.

"Well, m'dear," the doctor waited, "I like my tea with three sugars and a dash of hot milk."

"I understood that you were to pour."

"Bless my soul . . . I was, at that!" Prancing in circles, he minced about the room, then alighted and reached for the teapot, fingers crooked daintily.

"You look deformed."

Dr. Briggs quirked an offended eyebrow. "You're thimply enviouth," he lisped.

I laughed, "Give me that before you spill tea all over both of us."

Without obvious persuasion Dr. Briggs managed to transfer monumental portions of food onto my plate; and although unaware, I was ravenous. Too, I was compelled to confess: Cook had gone to uncommon lengths in the preparation of our feast. The variety attending the pastry tray alone was unrivaled in my experience. Ingenious concoctions in cunning shapes abounded—each with a crust uniformly feather-light. The loaf of fresh-baked bread was indeed "lovely": fluffy white inside, heartened by a dark, crunchy crust. And, as promised, a glass of wild rose-hip jelly, smooth and subtly sweet. The tea was hot and strong and plentiful. I patted my lips with the damask napkin and sighed.

"Feeling more yourself?" asked Dr. Briggs.

I nodded.

"Now, m'dear, suppose you tell me what is wrong."

"Nothing."

"Oh?" He leaned back. "It is my understanding that you were in a state of considerable agitation earlier today."

I dismissed the idea with a wave of my hand. "That is only Auntie Maude."

"She is very worried about you."

My shoulders rose in indifference. "Auntie Maude expects me to be pliant and syrupy at all times—as if I were still in the nursery—"

"Knowing you so well—she is naturally sensitive to your moods."

"She doesn't know me at all," I contradicted flatly. I stood. "If you will excuse me—"

"Where are you going?" He rose, surprised.

"There are a few pressing matters requiring my attention."

His face drooped in disappointment. "I say," he suggested then, "if the rain subsides tomorrow, I should like to squire you about the village . . ."

"If the rain subsides tomorrow, I shall be on the trail with Artemis—"

"There is time in the day for both, surely," he frowned.

"We'll see."

"Dammit, Elizabeth—" Dr. Briggs pulled me to him roughly. "I love you." His lips trembled on mine in a long kiss. "I love you," he breathed, his hazel eyes warm, caressing. Deeply tender, he kissed me again and again until I managed to free myself from his grasp. "Enough," I laughed gently.

"Tomorrow," he whispered. "Say it: tomorrow . . ."

"All right," I promised, "tomorrow."

Chapter 40

It was sometime after midnight that the rain finally stopped, and by dawn a watery sun weakly pierced the solid cover of clouds. The ground was soggy underfoot, and the still-dripping trees sprayed me with brief showers as I made my eager way to the stables.

Peter eyed me with disapproval, "Best to wait, miss."

"Wait for what?"

"It be wet and icy still. Best wait until it dry some, seems so."

"Saddle my horse this minute," I ordered.

The boy hesitated. "Mr. Hartley, miss—him say—"

"Do spare me Mr. Hartley—"

"Him say there be puddles and ice. And for horses—"

"I am waiting, Peter," I advised him stonily.

Sighing deeply, he disappeared into the stable and returned moments later with the chestnut mare, giddy at the prospect of an outing after four long days of confinement. "Ah!" I gloated, reveling in her bobbing head and prancing feet.

The moors were sodden, mired. I found the subtle danger in their hidden pockets exhilarating. "Faster, Artemis!" I urged, "faster . . ." Shallow puddles, thinly glazed with ice, studded open fields, and their brown tufts of frosted grass crinkled under Artemis's driving hooves. The little meadow stream, now a stolid silver band, lay silent, unmoving; but the sea, fierce in anger, writhed against the hectoring sun, jouncing gulls on its choppy waves.

We rode for hours. Wild. Free. Lighter than the very air we breathed. It was only the promise extracted by Dr. Briggs the day before that persuaded me to turn my mount in the direction of Wynds. "But," I pledged as I stroked the mare's sleek neck, "there will be tomorrow . . ."

As easily predicted, Dr. Briggs was already pacing the

length of the great hall, impatiently awaiting my return—
as he had been for some time, he hastened to inform me.
"Only two hours late," he announced, pointedly referring
to his watch.

My smile was sheepish.

He melted at once. "Perfectly all right." His warm hazel
eyes ran appreciatively over me. "You look wonderful!" he
declared, "absolutely wonderful!"

"Ready to go?" I asked.

He bowed gallantly. "At your service . . ."

Dr. Briggs wasted no time in bundling us companionably
sung in the woolen carriage robe. Pure joy radiated from
his face. "Worth the wait," he beamed, "well worth the
wait . . ." The cobbled streets of Drewsby were slick and
shone wetly in the fickle sunlight. The carriage swerved
several times, jerking me against the doctor, which delighted him no end. "All right, m'dear?" he grinned, drawing me closer still. . . .

Only a handful of villagers ventured abroad that day and
these mostly children, skipping over puddles or roguishly
defying their murky depths. Pale faces alight with the dev-
iltry born of pent-up energies, they gestured lewdly as we
passed, giggling afterward behind grubby hands.

"Good to see the little beggars laugh once in a while!"
Dr. Briggs was indulgent. "God knows there is little
enough mirth in their lives."

A sudden sea breeze, whipped sharp by a frenzied sea,
swiped at the trap, causing it to sway dangerously. The
horse stumbled. "Easy, Hector," crooned his master. "S'all
right, boy. Easy now . . ." Frowning, Dr. Briggs turned to
me. "More ugly weather abroad," he predicted gloomily.
"Best be heading back."

Amos Childer stood, silent sentry, before the listing
house. Mouth slack and eyes staring, he leaned against the
scythe. Moving slowly across the darkening sky, a silhouette, bent low under its heavy, lifeless burden: Ian . . .

I turned my eyes away . . .

As we swung into the courtyard lights flared, drapes
fluttered, and the front door swung open in immediate welcome. Auntie Maude, watching Dr. Briggs hand me down

from the trap, flapped about, her round face glowing with approval. "My!" she exclaimed, color high, "did you two have a pleasant outing?"

"Indeed!" nodded the doctor, "although it is beginning to blow up a bit—"

"Come in! Come in!" invited Auntie Maude. "I know that Elizabeth would be delighted, Doctor, to have you join her in a little informal supper—" Carefully, she avoided my eyes.

"Well—" Dr. Briggs threw me a doubtful glance.

"I simply won't take no for an answer!" gushed Auntie Maude, pronouncing the mawkish, if empty, threat of hospitality.

"Put like that, Miss Treadway, I can hardly refuse. . . ." Grinning broadly, he took my elbow and guided me into the house.

Auntie Maude's "little informal supper" proved even more elaborate than the extravagant tea conducted the afternoon before, served as it was in the formal dining hall with full appointments and the inevitable parade of attentive waiters and helpers. It was unfortunate that we were seated at opposite ends of the table, making conversation difficult, hampered further by a ubiquitous audience, sizable if discreet. To shout at such distances can tend to render one hoarse as well as self-conscious; Dr. Briggs became both.

By the advent of dessert, a light confection, Dr. Briggs's ability to communicate had all but disappeared. His naturally ruddy complexion had darkened to a rich carmine, signaling both strain and acute embarrassment. "Well, m'dear," he croaked.

"Yes?" I prompted, my own voice softly husky.

"M'dear—"

"Yes?" I found myself whispering in a kind of reflexive sympathy.

His discomposure now complete, Dr. Briggs rose suddenly, aimed a clumsy peck somewhere in the vicinity of my left ear, and fled from the room. I heard the front door slam loudly behind him.

Auntie Maude, lurking in the inglenook in an effort to

remain unobtrusive without missing any consequence of
her carefully engineered tête-à-tête, ran out into the hall as
soon as she determined the doctor's speedy departure. Her
face was white. "Elizabeth!" she cried, "was that Dr.
Briggs?"

"What was left of him," I giggled.

"But—" she protested, "it is still so early—"

"Evidently he did not find it so. . . ."

Alone in my room I could feel the odd, restless yearning
build inside me. I began to pace, vaguely at first, then with
mounting impatience . . .

Auntie Maude tapped lightly at the door. "Dear—" she
called.

"What is it?"

"It is still early—why don't we sit and have a little
visit—the way we used to—" She tested the handle.

I locked the door. "No, Aunt. I am rather tired."

"I have brought a pot of tea and some of Cook's special—"

"No."

"But it is the same marvelous feather-light confection
you were served for dinner—"

"I said no, Aunt."

"Darling"—Auntie Maude tried the handle again—"I do
miss our little talks—"

"Not tonight."

"But, Elizabeth," Auntie Maude coaxed. "Please. We
never seem to talk anymore."

Angry, I unlocked the door. I stared with loathing at the
old woman holding a tray piled high to absurdity. "If you
do not remove that sniveling whine of yours from my ears
and that abominable tray from my sight, I promise you I
shall scream loud enough to bring the rafters down around
your grizzled head!"

"Elizabeth!" she gasped, slow tears welling in her eyes.

I slammed the door. And locked it.

Neither an energetic blaze crackling in the grate nor the
hot brick shoved between the sheets could still my trembling limbs, or quell my torment. . . . I must have the
dream. . . . The call. Where was the call. Why didn't it
come. . . .

A light, then, in the tower? No. Not even that. Only a dark and brooding sky . . .

Eleven days. It had been eleven days since Sir Robert had gone away. . . . When would he return. . . .

Oh, God, when. . . .

Chapter 41

The next weeks settled into a predictable pattern: Clear skies saw morning rides, afternoon excursions in Dr. Briggs's trap (these frequently expanded into the dinner hour and sometimes beyond, abetted by the indefatigable Auntie Maude); stormy days brought imprisonment and the desperate pacing; nights, fair or foul, were spent in anguished longing.

One fine morning Dr. Briggs altered the established routine and joined me on horseback, confessing. "Satin, here, could use a bit of a go-round. And," he grinned, "more's the point—and the pity: I'm tied up in the surgery all afternoon—" Jonathan Briggs was a superb horseman, astride a powerful stallion with an easy gait. Seeing that the chestnut mare was quickly outstripped, he shortened his mount's stride and we jogged along comfortably abreast.

The sharp lap of wintry gusts was swiftly tempered by the sun's soft warmth, which was gradually drawing the ice and snow from the sleeping earth. Although only January, could this be a subtle precursor of spring?

Seen from atop Smugglers' Peak, spiny trees clawed at the sky, and the meadow brook, now freed, was fevered in its rush to the foaming sea, as if to make up for time lost. "Quite a vista," the doctor admitted, reining up. "Most impressive."

High overhead, wings dazzling the sky, a gull feinted, thrust, and parried before finally piercing the heaving waters below. With envy I watched the glorious performance.

"You are as wild as the sea," Dr. Briggs murmured. "Elizabeth . . ." He reached for my hand. "Elizabeth . . ."

The surf thundered in my ears.

He sighed, "I can never give you all this—" His eyes traced the broad sweep of the valley. "But marry me and what I have will be yours—yours—as this, my darling, can never be—"

As this can never be. . . . I glared at him. Jerking my hand free, I spun my horse, jabbed my heels hard, and raced toward Wynds. . . .

Unaccountably the manor had assumed a sudden festive air. The household staff whirled in a mad flurry of activity, heightened by quickened steps and snatches of excited conversation. In the midst of the melee fluttered Auntie Maude. She seemed more confused than committed. "What on earth is going on?" I confronted her as she flitted about in the great hall.

"Er—Founders' Day, dear," she replied uncertainly.

"Founders' Day! What in the world is that?"

"A day commemorated in—er—Australia, I believe."

"Australia!" I yelped. "But Auntie Maude, this is England!"

"I know that, dear." Auntie Maude flashed me a sheepish smile.

"Why are we in England celebrating an Australian holiday?"

"Well, dear, it seems that one of Wynds' most venerated ancestors, Henry, I think—or Harlow—Hiram . . . Herbert . . ."

"Go on," I urged.

"I am almost positive it begins with an 'H' . . ."

"Auntie Maude!"

"Henry—or Harlow—was involved directly in the founding of Australia . . ." Her voice trailed away.

"How?"

"How? Well, er—he—ah—by aiding a certain Captain Phelps—no, that's not right—Phillip—in sailing his convict ships to Australia in 1788—or was it '89? . . ."

"Convict ships?"

"Yes, dear," Auntie Maude nodded. "I believe, as a matter of fact, that there were eleven of them—"

"I have never heard of such a thing."

"Nor had I, dear," my aunt confessed. "But"—she spread her hands helplessly—"the celebration is held always the first Monday after January twenty-fifth. And that is the day after tomorrow—"

"The day after tomorrow—"

"Yes, dear." Auntie Maude glanced fearfully about before confiding, "I fear that Mr. Judd has not allotted sufficient time to prepare for the banquet."

"There is to be a banquet?"

"Er—yes—"

"For whom?"

"Let me see, now—Dr. Briggs, of course." Her silly smirk was readily interpreted. "The vicar and family, the schoolmaster"—she moved closer—"that is, if he is not—" She made a face. "You know—" Her brows met. "And the Wades; the Cawleys; Schneiders; Ditmans; Osborns; Bailys . . . oh, dear, I am sure I have left some out—"

"A trivial oversight," I muttered sourly.

". . . and some influential squires from neighboring villages."

"Sound like a bloody bore." My tone was snide.

"Of course, Lady Frances will host—"

I hooted.

Auntie Maude blinked. "She will be obliged—since Sir Robert is not here."

"Sir Robert will not be back?" My heart sank.

"No one has heard from him," she whispered, "not a word!"

Not a word . . . Sir Robert absent for nearly a month and no word . . . Had something happened to delay him? . . . Was he lying somewhere injured? . . . Dead? . . . I gave a little cry of dismay. . . .

". . . and so, dear," Auntie Maude was saying, now in normal decibels, "naturally, it is possible that you will be called on to preside."

"Preside!"

"Yes, dear. Assume the duties of hostess—since Lady Frances continues to be—er, indisposed—much of the time."

"I have no intention of presiding over that tiresome banquet, Aunt," I told her flatly, "and that is final!"

"Dear! Don't say that!" she hissed, glancing surreptitiously over a nervous shoulder, "someone may hear and report to Lady Frances."

"So—if they do?"

"Elizabeth!" Auntie Maude's voice sharpened with fear, "you are merely employed here, remember that!" She spoke rapidly. "You have been engaged to perform certain duties—"

"Desist, Aunt." I curled my lip.

"Your duties are concerned with Lady Frances—and when your mistress has obligations that she is unable to fulfill—for whatever reason—it is your job to—"

"I will not stay to listen to—"

"You will!" Auntie Maude gripped my arm roughly. "You will do nothing to endanger your fine position here, Elizabeth! Nothing! Do you understand?"

"Let me alone, old woman, do you hear!" I jerked my hand free. "Let me alone . . . Or," I gibed, "I'll see about your own 'fine position'. . ." I waited until her face had drained of all color before I flashed her a raffish smile and turned to mount the stairs in measured, triumphant strides.

Chapter 42

The next two days rendered Annie as sparing of her considerations as she had been during the period of the Christmas preparations: The hearth was not faithfully tended; trays were skimpy and improperly equipped (a fork missing—a butter knife sent to carve a joint—a spoon that could have been cleaner); bath water proved not only tepid but ungenerous in supply, as well; sheets had not been fully smoothed, nor pillows plumped; a grayish film attested to haphazard dusting; and the hot brick in the bed was now only a dim memory.

By good fortune (for us both) the weather held. . . .

Early mornings found Artemis and myself sprinting over hoary fields, sucked in spongy bogs, wading through icy streams, and while the mare grazed on thin brown tufts of waving grass I filled my eyes anew with the wondrous meld of earth and sea and sky. . . .

Founders' Day itself dawned clear and mild, and it was not until twilight threatened that I returned Artemis to the stables. We had ridden long and hard, and the mare was drenched. Peter was busily hanging up a saddle when I made my approach. "Give her a good rubdown right away," I ordered, dismounting.

He flicked a glance of disapproval at the lathered mare before replying, "Aye, soon's I be through with Ebon, here—"

"Ebon?" My heart raced. "Sir Robert is back?"

"Aye."

"When? When did he come?"

"Just now, seems so."

He was back . . . Sir Robert was back . . . I sang the glorious chant. . . . Sir Robert was back . . . I hurried into the house and almost collided with an anxious Auntie Maude in the great hall. "Where on earth have you been, child?" she cried, her face ashen with worry. "I have been

beside myself!" Her pale lips trembled. "You must make
preparations for the banquet. The first guests are due to
arrive shortly."

"Where is Annie?"

"Annie? I-I don't know. . . . Elizabeth—" She took my
arm to draw me to the stairs. "Elizabeth, dear—go and
change your clothes."

I shook myself free. "I need a bath. Send Annie to tend
me immediately."

"Elizabeth—"

"Aunt—note, I said 'immediately'—longer than that
and I box the young chit's rosy ears!"

Within minutes a breathless Annie appeared, staggering
under an enormous container filled to overflowing with
steaming water. A batch of fresh toweling stuffed under
each arm, still she managed to extract from the pocket of
her wilting apron a new cake of scented soap. "I thought ye
might be enjoyin' this—" she simpered.

"The water had better be hot—"

"Aye, miss. Aye." Her curtsy was deep. "Pipin' to
scald!"

"Leave me now."

"Aye, miss." She hesitated. "Shall I be puttin' out a
gown for the party?" she asked.

"I said, leave me."

. . . A gown for the party . . . what gown . . . I had
no bloody gown for the party . . .

Wrapped in a fluffy, sweet-smelling towel, I felt my anger soar. . . . What luscious silk would be draped over
that wretched gawk this evening. . . . Lady Frances, that
cringing stick . . . Perhaps shimmering satin, filmy gauze,
hanging shapeless as on a scarecrow . . .

Almost senseless I ran to the armoire. I jerked it open,
yanked my garments one by listless one, from their hangers
and flung them to the floor. . . . Gown for the party
. . . Ferociously I trampled, snagging the tired fibers with
my savage naked feet . . . Gown for the party . . . Fists
balled, I began to pound the wardrobe itself. . . . Gown
for Sir Robert . . . My fury raged. Again and again I
struck at the captive wooden surface. Harder. Faster. Hys-

terically. Suddenly I heard a soft cracking sound. . . .
Break, lifeless bastard, I screamed in malicious
triumph. . . . Break . . . Break . . . One entire side of
the wardrobe was pulling away. . . . Break, I gloated
. . . Wider and wider it yawned . . .

The wardrobe was not broken: A panel had merely become disengaged; it swung loosely on dull brass hinges.

I gaped: The panel was bursting, rainbow-filled. I
played eager fingers over its contents, spilling brilliant silks
and shiny satins at my feet. I stopped, suddenly paralyzed:
At a little distance, swaying gently on its gilded hanger—a
gown. Of rich velvet and deeply crimson . . . the gown in
my dream . . . her gown . . .

Almost fearful, I reached into the panel and drew the
gown forward. It seemed alive in my trembling hands. Fire
burned hot in my cheeks, and my heart thundered as I
slipped the supple cloth over my shoulders and felt it caress
my hips as the heavy skirt slid with surprising ease to the
floor and hung there in graceful folds.

I turned to face the bank of mirrors in the dressing
nook: The gown molded perfectly to the contours of my
body, its crimson served as dramatic contrast to the purity
of my slender arms and the faultless swell of my breasts as
they rode high and white above the deep bodice. I saw hair
that glittered in a glossy cloud as it floated over smooth,
bare shoulders, amber eyes that stared, soft and dreamy,
and a mouth curved in a slow, seductive smile.

I saw her: the woman in the dream . . .

I was glorious. . . .

Auntie Maude was banging furiously at the door. "Elizabeth! Hurry, child!" she cried, "the guests have already
been seated in the dining hall." Her voice climbed in desperation. "Elizabeth, dearest! The meal has started!" She
jiggled the handle. "Elizabeth, I am coming in!" The door
flew open. "Oh, there you are!" she began in relief, then
stopped still. She stood rigid, eyes wild with fright. "What
do you have on?" she gasped.

I turned, smiling, to face her fully.

She seemed to sway. "What do you have on?" Her voice
was a thin whisper.

"Pray, do not detain me, Aunt," I said. "I am late enough as it is."

"Elizabeth"—Auntie Maude garnered strength—"you cannot go downstairs in that—"

"Out of my way, Aunt."

"No, Elizabeth!" She blocked my path. "I cannot permit you to be seen like this!"

"You can't permit me!" I laughed.

"It—it is indecent!"

"Out of my way," I warned.

"Elizabeth—"

Roughly I pushed her from me. She staggered a little, and I could hear her helpless weeping as I descended the stairs, followed by the soft slap of red velvet on each downward step. . . .

Bowing, Judd stood aside to let me pass into the dining hall before announcing me formally: "Sir Robert, Miss Knowlton."

All heads turned; conversation ceased. Sir Robert rose immediately. "Miss Knowlton," he murmured in acknowledgment, his dark eyes on my face. "If you would permit Judd to assist you—" He indicated a chair. "And Judd, fill Miss Knowlton's glass."

A sudden commotion shattered the silence at the table. Lady Frances seemed to crumple; she let out a feeble cry before toppling from her chair onto the floor. "She has fainted!" Mrs. Smythe screamed. "Lady Frances has fainted!"

Dr. Briggs leapt to his patient's side and began his preliminary examination. "Someone fetch my bag," he ordered brusquely. "It is in the trap." At Judd's signal a boy hastened on the errand. "Has she had too much wine, perhaps?" the doctor asked Sir Robert, who shook his head, saying, "She has touched nothing of the meal."

Fingers clamped on her bony wrist, the doctor frowned. "The pulse is only moderately erratic, but she remains unconscious. . . ." He stood. "Have the boy remove my satchel to her room." He scooped the stricken woman in his arms and carried her from the hall.

Sir Robert turned to address his guests. "Pray resume your seats," he suggested. "Lady Frances could not be in better hands, after all." His expression was grave. "I trust that she will revive shortly."

Chairs scraped and tentative conversation began as the company complied. Sir Robert directed the butler to refill empty goblets before commencing the next course. Again I took my seat at the right of Lineas Stafford, village schoolmaster, who, having already spun his alcoholic web, had not troubled to rise at all during the fracas but had reclined instead, happily bemused. By now his eyes were glazed, speech slurred, and his hand, reaching regularly to drain his glass, seemed perilously unsteady.

To my left was seated a squire from Shelbourne, a neighboring village situated slightly north of Drewsby. Sir Noel Outbridge, by name, approached his sixty-odd years with a florid complexion, a full head of smoke-gray hair, and an eye that dived inside my bosom whenever the watchful stare of his wife was otherwise diverted. His conversation, a tedious monologue of Rugby and the Hunt, was distracted only by a truant foray into my décolletage.

Positioned in the chair directly opposite, Miss Caroline assiduously averted her gaze from my person, although now and again her eyes slid across the table, lighted on my bodice, and flew away, singed. An ugly flush then captured her rather plain face, zigzagging a path from her neck to her hairline.

Mrs. Smythe openly clucked her disapproval, casting pointed glances at her husband, who shook his head in righteous disbelief before bowing it in sorrowful meditation.

Still another neighboring squire, the aged Sir Basil Croftmore, traveling from the western village of Courtney, contributed little to the group at large, other than to bolt his food with noisy enthusiasm and eject gas in still louder appreciation directly after accomplishing the awesome mechanics of actually swallowing it.

Mrs. Wade fixed her small, dour eyes, buried under their shelves of flesh, at some point just above the wainscoting. Her stout husband followed her gaze, except during those illicit moments when his attention strayed (unobserved, of course) in the direction of my bustline.

At last Dr. Briggs returned to the dining hall, where he exchanged serious words in private with Sir Robert, who listened thoughtfully. "Thank you, Doctor," the squire said when the consultation had concluded. "Pray, be seated. I shall have Judd prepare a fresh plate for you."

Dr. Briggs's hot, bewildered eyes never left my face. He tasted no food but rather snapped angry fingers at Judd with repeated orders to refill his glass. . . .

I myself ate little: too aware of my own febrile cheeks, my thudding heart; of breasts that rose up from crimson velvet; of eyes, dark-shadowed under mocking brows as they met mine . . .

In accordance with established tradition Sir Robert lifted his glass, proposing a series of toasts, hailing the historical contribution of his revered ancestor, as well as offering polite acknowledgment to Founders' Day itself. By the time the ceremonial adjuncts to the festivities had begun, many of those attending were in a near stupor. Miss Caroline, eyes hazy, had slipped a trifle in her chair. And, with his wife's powers of concentration considerably dimmed, Sir Noel felt free to fasten an open, unblinking stare on my bosom, attended closely by an equally intense study conducted by Mr. Wade, who managed adroitly to escape his wife's weakened vigil for increasingly longer periods. The Reverend Smythe, employing even cleverer means, masked his own consuming interest with a head cocked to a discreet but profitable angle while still bowed as if in solemn prayer. Dr. Briggs's complexion took on a dangerous ruddy color, and his eyes remained riveted, now drunkenly, on my face.

Mrs. Smythe sat piously sober, alone in this but for Sir Basil, who, aided by a silver toothpick, deftly explored a back molar, with heady results. . . .

At last Sir Robert dismissed the gathering, and the guests, promptly obedient (if reeling), rose and prepared to depart. All except Dr. Briggs, who remained in his chair. The amenities over, I headed for the stairs and had reached the landing when the doctor, moving carefully, crossed the hall toward me. Green flecks now savage sparks in his hazel eyes, he demanded: "What are you . . . My God, what are you . . ." He swayed. "Elizabeth . . ."

"Dr. Briggs," Sir Robert intervened smoothly, "your room is readied and your horse has been stabled."

The doctor swung around. "Er—what's that?" He seemed confused.

"As you requested earlier in the evening," Sir Robert smiled, "to attend Lady Frances—"

Dr. Briggs raised a trembling hand over his eyes. "Oh . . . Yes . . ."

"If you would accompany me," Sir Robert suggested, "I shall settle you in myself."

"Er—yes . . . of course . . ." Slowly, Dr. Briggs followed Sir Robert up the broad staircase. His step was heavy. . . .

Annie had straightened the room. She had retrieved my clothes from discard and had hung them neatly in the wardrobe. The hidden panel she had left ajar, and it was evident that she had examined its contents thoroughly. . . . Let her . . . Bloody snoop . . .

Standing before the wall of mirrors, I unfastened the crimson dress and let it tumble carelessly to the floor. Yellow candlelight flickered over the flawless white of my body, naked now but for an escaping curl that nudged one breast below. . . . My amber eyes were feverish and my cheeks aflame . . .

I tossed the hot brick from my bed. No need of that: I was on fire. . . . I stretched sinuously down the length of the silken sheets. . . . My hair spilled in a golden pool on the pillow. . . .

The door opened. Footsteps started slowly toward the bed. Nearer. Nearer. ". . . Elizabeth . . ."

I gave a low chuckle and opened my arms to my lover. . . .

Chapter 43

He stayed with me all night. Toward dawn he leaned over, kissed me lightly, and rose to leave. "No," I protested, "it is still early."

He smiled. "The sun is almost up."

"Who cares?" I pulled him down beside me and snuggled close. "Who cares . . ."

He laughed. "Insatiable little minx."

I giggled softly.

His hand stroked my breast. "What will you do today, minx?"

I lifted my shoulders. "I don't know. Ride, probably . . ." I wound my arms around his neck. "Will you come with me?"

"I think not . . . I have things to do—"

"What things?" I pouted.

He shook his head in mock reproof. "We men must slave to give you women all the things you—"

"All I want is—this—" Trembling, I drew him over me. We moved together in perfect rhythm . . .

Afterward, as he dressed, my eyes devoured his long, lean lines, reveled in his easy grace. . . .

Later I stood before the mirrors in the dressing nook and traced the rich contours of my own body . . . soft, filled. Overnight, I had ripened. . . .

I had time now to investigate at leisure the wardrobe's hidden treasures. They were indeed exquisite: silk, flimsy as a cobweb; luminous satins; mellow velvets . . . colors—jewel-bright . . . I laughed: no brown bombazine here . . .

A riding habit! Amongst these gems was there a riding habit? My fingers took immediate inventory, resting finally on heavy faille, peacock blue. . . . I stepped into the narrow skirt; it followed the line of my hips flawlessly. The short fitted waistcoat fastened with a series of tiny fabric-covered buttons . . . What a bloody nuisance . . . A jaunty hat was angled by a billowing plume of a lighter hue. I preened, delighting in the perfect fit and the color that complemented my amber eyes and golden hair. . . .

I was dazzling. . . .

It was with open amusement that I observed Hartley's struggle to mask his stunned surprise at my improved costume. "Miss," he bowed, extending more courtesy than was his wont, "would ye be lookin' to have Artemis saddled?"

I nodded, taking a child's pleasure in the simultaneously bobbing plume. "Immediately, if you will."

"Certainly, miss. I'll see to her myself. Right away!" The man hustled off, returning shortly with the chestnut mare. I prepared to mount. Today Hartley rushed gallantly to my side. "Permit me, miss." He bowed again and hoisted me, suddenly precious cargo, into the saddle. He raised his hat in salute and watched me clatter out of the stable yard and on toward the moor.

The saucy plume, our feathers, Artemis, and I seemed to fly: across meadows; over streams; through the thorny heath—to soar, finally, to the crest of Smugglers' Peak. I slid from the mare's back and, while she grazed, tramped over the pebbled earth. Dark, empty clouds taunted the sky, and sly gusts of wind tossed the sea, which hurled back its protest.

Suddenly I heard the thunder of hoofbeats. I swung around, exultant. He was there. His flying hair blacker than the sky. . . . His horse an ebony streak daring the horizon.

He lifted me high in his arms and our lips clung as if forever. . . .

"You came," I breathed.

"I could not stay away."

"Love me. Now."

We sank to the harsh ground; wild as the day itself, our bodies heaved under the tempestuous sky.

Chapter 44

An uneasy Auntie Maude approached me shyly as I crossed the great hall and headed for the landing. "E-Elizabeth—"

I halted. "Yes, Aunt?"

"The—er—riding habit—" Her eyes shifted away from mine.

"Yes, Aunt?"

"W-where—where did you get it, dear?" Moisture filmed her upper lip.

"That is hardly a concern of yours, after all, Aunt."

She swallowed. "But, dear. It is—so—well, extravagant—"

"And indecent?" I jabbed.

She flushed.

"Aunt, if you have nothing more pertinent to say or can select a subject no more valuable with which to claim my time, I shall run on to my room and freshen up."

"Dr. Briggs was here," she said quickly.

"Yes," I reminded her, "I believe he stayed the night."

"I mean," she cleared her throat, "he was looking for you—after breakfast." Her face was strained. "He waited until well after two this afternoon—the doctor, that is," she finished lamely.

"That is all?"

"Well," she twisted her hands. "Yes, I—"

"Then if you will excuse me, I have other more pressing matters to attend to."

Auntie Maude's lips quivered. "Elizabeth—"

"What now?"

Her sigh was tremulous. "Nothing, dear. Nothing at all . . ."

After a languorous soak in the tub, courtesy of Annie, who eyed me quizzically now, I chose green satin for the dinner hour. A treat, surely, to dip my hands into this end-

less cask of treasures and emerge with a different costume
for each day of—weeks, probably. What a rascal: the
wardrobe! Defying my eyes! Concealing its bounty! Thinking back, I can recall my initial surprise and chagrin that
this enormous piece of furniture offered only niggardly
storage capacity, scarcely in line with its size, which was
truly massive. My own garments numbering so few and in
such a sorry condition, I had dismissed the notion of
crowding as not really applicable or of much concern.
Scamp; for shame!

The satin gown slithered like a cool snake over my
thighs and hips and proved even lower in the bodice than
had the crimson velvet. Nipped tight, it clung to flatter
my tiny waist; bold, its color heightened the translucent
tones of my skin. . . .

Sir Robert, already seated at the table in the dining hall,
rose immediately when I made my entrance. His eyebrows
lifted in silent appreciation. "Judd," he directed, "you may
seat Miss Knowlton."

The butler guided me to the farthest end of the table.

"What is this?" Sir Robert asked sharply.

"Miss Knowlton's customary place, Sir Robert," Judd explained.

"Wynds now retains a flock of carrier pigeons?" the
squire inquired dryly.

"Er—Sir Robert?" Judd blinked in his confusion.

"Set Miss Knowlton's place here." Sir Robert indicated a
seat close to his.

"Yes, Sir Robert."

"And Judd," Sir Robert added, "this wine is sour. Fetch
another bottle from the cellar. After," he reminded, "you
have taken proper care of Miss Knowlton. . . ."

I asked my host impishly, "Lady Frances declines our
company this evening?"

"She is feeling—ah—poorly."

I sighed. "A pity!"

"Yes. Indeed."

"Has she recovered from last evening's, er—indisposition?"

"Not entirely, I think."

I sighed again. "A pity."

"Oh, yes. Indeed."

"Tragic—so young and so—"

He nodded gravely. "I know."

"Do you suppose I might have another spot of wine?" I asked demurely.

"Of course." Sir Robert inclined his head. "Judd, refill Miss Knowlton's glass. And mine."

"Yes, Sir Robert."

"Tell me, Miss Knowlton"—Sir Robert regarded me over his goblet—"how did you amuse yourself today?"

"Let me see." I looked at him through lowered lashes. "I went riding—"

"You enjoy that, then?"

"Oh, yes, very much." I smiled.

"You will have dessert, Miss Knowlton?" inquired Judd.

"Yes, I believe I shall. Yes. Thank you." I was charming.

The butler bowed. "Very good, miss. And you, Sir Robert? Will you join Miss Knowlton?"

"I shall join Miss Knowlton," Sir Robert agreed, his manner serious.

"Would you have a preference for coffee, or tea, Miss Knowlton?" asked Judd politely.

"Coffee, thank you."

"Sir Robert, coffee, or tea?"

"I shall have coffee, also."

"Very good, Sir Robert."

"Tell me, Miss Knowlton." Sir Robert sipped his wine slowly. "How do you usually spend your evenings here at Wynds?"

"Reading, as a rule . . . I am afraid," I admitted with an adorable smile, "that I have taken the liberty of borrowing from your personal library—"

"Splendid!" Sir Robert's approval was instantaneous. "Any time!"

I dropped maidenly eyes. "Thank you."

"Do you ever play chess, Miss Knowlton?"

"Chess?" I cried. "Chess! My gracious, no! I fear that I have never been fortunate enough to possess the strong concentration required to engage in a game of such consummate skill!" My confession was becomingly modest.

"Whist, perhaps?"

"Mercy! I cannot record that accomplishment, either!"
My smile was shy and appropriately rueful.

"A pity!" It was Sir Robert's turn to shake his head in
disappointment.

"I think I actually prefer sports—to games," I conceded
diffidently.

"Sports?"

"Yes."

"Sports," he mused. "Like—riding?"

"Yes," I dimpled, "like—riding . . ."

It was only moments after we had parted in the dining
hall, he ostensibly for his study, I for my room, that he
came to my bed. I was crazed with desire. My hips thrust
high in urgent response, as he rode me again and again
throughout the night. As darkness lifted from the sky I
stirred in his embrace. "You were wrong, you know—"

"Wrong. About what?"

"It was Aphrodite. Not Ceres."

He laughed. "What on earth are you talking about?"

"The frieze . . . The Wyndham crest carved on the
goddess's breast . . . She was Aphrodite and not
Ceres. . . ."

"Upon my word!" He tongued my nipple. "Ever grateful
that you set me straight!"

I wriggled deliciously. "You're welcome."

"Do I err on Saint Paul as well?"

"Saint Paul?"

"Saint Paul."

I giggled. "I don't know, I'm sure . . ."

"I do." He moved over me. "Permit me to demonstrate . . ."

Chapter 45

Dr. Briggs called the following afternoon. Auntie Maude dashed up to my room to tell me of his arrival. "Dear," she called excitedly through the door, "Dr. Briggs awaits you in the inglenook!"

"I am undressing, Aunt," I replied.

"He seems very anxious to see you." Her voice strengthened, "Very anxious—"

"Inform the doctor that I will be happy to see him another time—"

There was a pause. "May I—er—come in?"

"I have said that I am undressing, Aunt."

"Yes, dear," she faltered, "but, dear, this is very important!"

"I am too tired to see anyone," I told her curtly. Surely Dr. Briggs, of all people, should comprehend fatigue . . ."

"Dear—"

"No!"

"Elizabeth, please—"

"Get away from my door this instant!" I shrilled, "or I shall have you dismissed from this place within the hour!" Firmly I turned the key in the lock. "Is that clear?"

Auntie Maude's footsteps were heavy as they moved slowly down the hall. . . .

Chapter 46

It was not long before the novelty of the armoire's finery began to fade. I wanted new gowns: these were not, after all—fashioned for my taste, alone; they fell in essence (handsome or not) into the category of hand-me-downs. I yearned for a change. By now I loathed the riding habit. Its brilliant color had begun to pall, and I found the tiny cloth buttons an annoyance far exceeding any normal requisite. . . . Besides, I was set on jodhpurs. . . .

. . . This I informed Robert, when I burst into his study one morning directly after two strategically located buttons had popped from the waistcoat, never to be found again. "This bloody thing!" I fumed, "I am sick unto death of it!"

"What is the matter?" he laughed, drawing me to him.

"I want new clothes," I sulked.

"Then, by all means, order them!"

"Anything I want?"

"Of course. Get ten of everything, if you like."

I threw my arms around his neck and hugged him close. "I am going to buy some jodhpurs! First thing!"

"What are jodhpurs?"

"Riding pants."

"Pants!" he exclaimed.

"Pants. So that I can ride astride," I declared. "No more prissy sidesaddle for me!"

"You little devil!" he chuckled. "But jodhpurs are entirely out of the question."

I protested loudly. "Why?"

"Because," he said, lowering me to the leather couch, "then I would not be able to do this. . . ."

Chapter 47

My world exploded: Each hour ignited the next. My eager body had become the arena in which passion rode: day and night—inflamed atop a windswept hill; fired beside a swollen, rushing stream; bursting within the dark temple of tangled sheets . . .

I was as Robert had said: insatiable . . .

One night I waited: Robert did not come. I was beside myself. What had happened? What had I done? . . . In desperation I reconstructed the events of the day. My thoughts flew to Smugglers' Peak where, entwined, again and again desire had flowed. . . . Remembered clinging apricot silk and a low murmur, "You are enchanting . . ." Saw dark eyes, ardent . . . full of promise . . .

What, then? Why did he not come?

Hours passed. I shivered: The fire, too, had fled. Where was he? Why didn't he come? . . .

I thrashed now in the bed where before I had rocked, delirious in love's play . . . My body cold where it had burned. Stiff where it had been soft, yielding. Empty where it had been filled . . .

Restless, I began to pace the room; an icy fever mounted with each successive step. . . . He must come. . . . Oh, God, make him come. . . .

I halted before the window. Was it? Yes . . . A light in the tower. In quick excitement I knelt: There was a light in the tower! Hypnotized, I watched its yellow flame sway back and forth, back and forth . . .

I stayed, held by the magnet of that uneasy glow, until it, too, disappeared. I was alone now, except for an aged, misshapen moon that traversed the sky without warmth or beauty.

Robert did not come. . . .

Sunrise found me high on Smugglers' Peak, waiting,

straining for the sounds of driving hooves; for the sight of a black mane flung against a stormy sky. . . . Aching for demanding lips to sear my own . . .

Sick with longing, I fell retching to the ground. . . .

Still Robert did not come. . . .

In angry bewilderment I urged Artemis forward. Whipped her to her wildest speed. Ruthless, I slapped. Cruelly I jabbed . . .

Hartley evinced some surprise at the violence with which I rode into the stable yard. He helped me dismount at once and murmured that he himself would take care of the mare. He refrained to add that the animal was lathered and exhausted, even dangerously. I asked him, "Has Sir Robert ridden out today as yet?"

"Oh, yes, miss."

"When was that?"

"Before dawn, miss."

"Before dawn?"

"Yes, miss," the stable master nodded.

"When will he return?"

"I got no way of knowin' that, miss." The man shook his head. "Sir Robert did not say. But," he added, "the squire was carryin' a satchel . . ."

A satchel! My heart sank. A satchel: Robert had gone away. . . . Oh, God. Robert had gone away. . . .

The days directly after Robert's sudden departure, it rained. A squally, beating storm assailed the manor, shattering windows in its spite. Threshing gales emptied turgid clouds. Branches were ripped from twisting trees, and winter's fragile grass lay spent and sodden.

Half-crazed with longing, I welcomed the tempest's rage, shared its wrath, reveled in its destruction. . . . I did not stir from my room, I stayed, rather, at my post by the window, delighting in the agony of hanging limbs, the pain of torn branches. Rain slapping at the window was as my own tears. The wind: my fury . . .

Annie, treading warily, tended the fire and carried trays, their cautious fare supervised by Auntie Maude, I was sure. Her own touches were in evidence: special pastries and sweet puddings; precious stacks of bread and butter along with exotic jellies and sturdier jams; the cunning dishes on which all were served so selected to tempt even the smallest appetite. Every few hours Auntie Maude tapped on the door, inquiring in a worried voice as to the state of my health as well as to that of the tray. "Are you finished, dear?"

"No."

"Is there anything else you might wish, Elizabeth?"

"No."

"Perhaps sticky buns, instead of the bread—"

"No."

"Darling . . . may I come in?"

"No."

"More tea, perhaps . . ." she added, "although milk is more nourishing . . ."

"Leave me alone, Aunt."

"I have a bit of chocolate left over from Christmas—"

"Go away!"

I hugged the window, watching the primordial struggle until the last vestige of light was drained from the troubled sky. The world, without, lay in darkness, unrelieved by moon, star, or pierced by a light in the tower. Nothing . . .

My world, within, lay in darkness. No glow guided my footsteps to the golden room. . . . No path gleamed to show the way. . . . Nothing . . .

Robert . . . Oh, God, Robert . . . Where did you go? Why didn't you tell me that you were going? . . .

Come back, my love . . . come back . . .

Early in the afternoon of the fourth day of Robert's absence, the ragged sky began to mend. Auntie Maude was at my door, trying the handle, begging entrance.

"I told you, Aunt, no!" I shrilled.

"Dr. Briggs is here, dear—"

"I don't want to see him."

"I really think you should, Elizabeth."

"I have said no!"

"Elizabeth, dear—you are not at all yourself—"

Bloody bitch . . . Not at all myself . . . I'll show her how myself I am . . . I raced for the door and flung it wide. There beside Auntie Maude stood Dr. Briggs, bag in hand. "Hello, Elizabeth," he said quietly.

"What do you want?"

"I came to see you." His eyes recorded my disordered appearance, my frenzy. "As a physician," he added softly.

"You might have saved yourself the trouble, Dr. Briggs," I snapped. "I am perfectly well, as you can see for yourself. Now, if you will excuse me—"

"No. I'm afraid I will not." He wedged his boot securely in the door. "I am coming in."

I shrugged. "What the hell. Suit yourself." I bowed low. "Welcome to ménage-à-Knowlton, in all its splendor—"

"May I sit down?"

"Oh, please do!" I said. "And may I offer you tea, sherry—or a jot of port? How about whiskey? You men do love your whiskey!" My voice was rich with sarcasm. "Or would you prefer a magnum of champagne to celebrate the auspicious occasion: Dr. Briggs in my room!" I leered. "In my *bedroom*!"

"It is excessively hot in here," he observed, looking about.

I chuckled lewdly. "You don't know how hot!"

"Would you leave us?" the doctor asked Auntie Maude.

"Er—I—"

"Please."

"Very well, Doctor."

I chortled. "Should I be afraid—alone like this, Dr. Briggs? Should I fall cringing under the bed like some quaking virgin—or"—I undulated my hips seductively— "should I—"

"Stop that!" He slapped my face, hard.

I began to cry. Convulsive sobs tore my body. Dr. Briggs gathered me into his arms and held me close. "Cry, darling, cry." Awkwardly he stroked my hair. "Cry. Let it all out. . . ." When the spasm subsided, he handed me a handkerchief. "Blow," he instructed.

I laughed shakily, "I have soiled your shirt, I think."

"It exists for no nobler purpose," he smiled. "Feeling better?"

I nodded.

"Tell you what. My trap is outside and Hector is spoiling for a run. . . ." His eyes, anxious, probed mine.

I hesitated.

He squeezed my hand. "Doctor's orders . . ."

* * *

Thick smoke escaping from a poorly tended hearth mingled uneasily with the miasma wafting from the crowd of
poorly tended creatures constituting the pub's clientele. It
was difficult, actually, to determine where individual bodies began and then left off: The throng was wall-solid.
"Shall we simply leave?" frowned the doctor.

"Not yet."

"In any case," he advised, taking a firm grip on my
arm, "stay close to me."

Sipping warm ale from a glass that was none too clean, I
viewed dissolute faces and listened to inarticulate, guttural
speech. Made up mostly of vowels, specific words were unintelligible; oblique glances, boisterous laughter, and ges-
tures, explicitly suggestive, betrayed their foul content.
Looking about, I wondered idly which of these feral youths
might, in visiting Gracie, have fathered the existing child
and the one still unborn. I wondered, too, if Gracie herself
knew. . . .

Outside, the twilight sky was sharp and clear; as yet, the
evening star its solitary occupant. Dr. Briggs handed me
into the trap, spread the robe over my knees, and climbed
in beside me. "Different kind of experience, at any rate,"
he maintained. "Sometimes beneficial to see the starved
side of life—" He flicked a meaningful glance in my direction before urging Hector forward. The trap proceeded at a
comfortable unhurried speed. I leaned back and closed my
eyes; I had not known, until that moment, how tired I really
was.

"Not sleeping well?" the doctor inquired lightly.

"The storm," I replied vaguely.

"Take heart," he encouraged, "no hint of weather tonight! You should be able to make a fine night of it!"

A fine night of it! A night in torment. A night thrashing
in an empty bed . . . A night without Robert . . . Oh,
God . . . I squeezed my eyelids tightly together. . . .

"You know, it might be a good idea," Dr. Briggs introduced the matter casually, "for you to drop into my surgery some afternoon soon."

"What for?" I stiffened in suspicion.

"Oh." His manner was offhand. "For a routine—ah—examination . . ."

I straightened. "No."

"Your Aunt feels that you are unwell—"

"To hell with my aunt!" I spat.

"I myself confess that I suspect you may be working up to a little something," he admitted, then mitigated his disclosure with an indifferent wave of his hand. "Probably nothing more startling than a simple anemia . . ."

"I am not ill."

"Then why don't we make a real determination of that!" Now he was jolly. "What say!"

"I have said no!" Deliberately, I closed my eyes again. "I will hear no more about it!"

He sighed.

We rode for some time in heavy silence. I could feel the intensity of Dr. Briggs's anxious gaze on my face. . . . If only it had been the demanding gaze of dark eyes shadowed under mocking brows. . . . Oh, God, Robert . . . Where are you? . . . Tears escaping from my lids slipped down my cheeks.

The trap jerked to a sudden stop. Dr. Briggs's hand pressed mine. The gesture was compelling: I opened my eyes. "Elizabeth," he murmured. "Look at me." His arm slid across my shoulders. "Elizabeth . . . what is wrong?"

"Nothing." I tried to pull away.

He drew me closer. "I know something is very wrong. Tell me . . ."

I squirmed in his embrace.

"Elizabeth, my darling . . . marry me and I shall make you safe." He bent his head; his lips sought mine. "I love you," he whispered, "love you . . . love you . . ."

Savagely, I tore myself free. "Don't you touch me!" I screamed. "Don't you dare touch me!"

"Elizabeth!"

"Don't you lay a bloody hand on me!" I shrieked. "Take me home!"

"I—only—"

"Take me home!"

Dr. Briggs's sigh was tremulous as he lifted the reins. The wheels rolled forward, beginning the last lap of our journey, which was to continue without further attempt at conversation. I had moved on the seat as far away from him as possible and, head averted, deliberately fixed my eyes on the rapidly darkening countryside. The horse maintained a consistent, accelerated pace, and it was not long before the listing house and the gaunt figure of Amos Childer, its catatonic guardian, came into focus. . . . Humped in the doorway, a solitary flickering light its frame, a shadow wavered: Ian . . .

It was evident that Auntie Maude had been training a watchful eye on the courtyard: The door was flung open immediately as Hector's first hoofbeats sounded on the cobblestones. Her expectant face tightened with real fear when she glimpsed the grim set of Dr. Briggs's jaw and the anguish clear in his eyes. She paled. "Doctor?"

He shook his head.

"Dear heaven!" she rasped, "What are we to do?"

"I don't know." His voice was thick. "Before God, I do not know. . . ."

Chapter 48

"Elizabeth . . . Elizabeth . . ." I sat up: "Robert? My love, have you returned?"

It was there; its steady gleam summoned me: the path . . . I followed quickly and soon stood before the door to the golden room. Eagerly I nudged it open.

They lay together on the couch: her hair a dazzling tangle tumbling carelessly to the floor. His tanned hand gently explored her willing thighs. . . . "Rid of her . . ." he was whispering, ". . . rid of her . . ." She stirred in his arms. "How . . . my love, how . . ." He smiled. "Find a way . . ." His lips parted hers. "Find a way . . ."

The light faded. . . .

Once in bed, I was wild; throbbing with passion . . . Robert . . . I wanted Robert . . . I craved his lips on mine . . . his hands to search my own trembling parts . . .

". . . Rid of her . . ." What did that mean? ". . . Rid of her . . ." Who? ". . . Find a way . . ."

Robert . . . My body, starved, cried out its desire: Robert . . .

Chapter 49

Auntie Maude's worried, wounded eyes trailed me everywhere about the house. I was spared her silent suffering only behind the securely locked door of my room, or when I galloped, untrammeled, over rocky meadows, seeking the savage heights of Smugglers' Peak, wooing its harsh winds to cool my mounting frenzy. . . . Robert . . .

One afternoon, upon my return from the moors, Auntie Maude advanced toward me with a timid smile, a letter held in her hand. "Elizabeth,"—a tentative gleam of excitement sparked her eyes—"dear! I have a news!"

"Oh?"

"Guess what?"

"I could not possibly."

"I have here a letter from—Ada!" She made the intelligence a delectation. "Ada!" She pressed the envelope into my hand. "Go on, read it, dear!"

I pushed it away. "I really do not care to, Aunt."

"But, dear,"—bravely, Auntie Maude submerged her disappointment—"this is a letter from Ada! Your Ada!"

"So you said."

"It was addressed to me, but I know that it is really intended for you!" She laid an affectionate hand on mine. "Let's sit down over a cup of tea and read it together. . . ."

I peeled away her clutching fingers. "I have said, Aunt, that I am not interested."

Pretending not to hear, Auntie Maude tenaciously continued her suit. "Darling, Molly has married!" She flashed a proud smile. "And Ada has changed positions! Both girls are—"

"If you will excuse me, Aunt." I started for the stairs.

"I have their new addresses right here—" She tried to block my way.

"Aunt," I said coldly, "pray, allow me to pass. . . ."

* * *

Cold . . . Cold: Would I ever be warm again? I shivered; an irritable fire spitting in the grate; a thick cover of warm wool; the heavy flannel nightdress—none could drive the chill from my limbs. . . . Cold . . .

At my instruction Annie had laid the fire shortly before retiring to her room. "It had best last the night," I warned.

"Yes, miss." She curtsied. "It should—and more. Seems so . . ."

"If not," I promised grimly, "you will find yourself back here to tend it!"

"Yes, miss—"

"In the middle of the night, if need be—"

"Yes, miss. Oh!" she gasped. "I near forgot. Miss Treadway give me this letter. She says it be for you—"

A letter? From Robert? "Let me have it!" Greedily I snatched at her hand: It was only Ada's letter. Angrily I flung it to the floor.

"M-miss?"

"Toss it in the fire."

"Er—yes, miss." The girl paused. "Anythin' else, miss?"

"No."

. . . Anythin' else . . . Anythin' else . . . Oh, God: Robert . . .

I dozed then, and only fitfully, waking to a frigid room and to find the fire all but extinguished. In a fury I jerked myself to a sitting position. . . . Bitch . . . I shall call the chit now. . . . Scream down the whole bloody house, if necessary . . . The door opened. . . . There's the slut now. Serves her right; can't even build a simple fire . . . I lay back. Footsteps approached the bed. . . . "Elizabeth . . ."

It became a night of ecstasy. An intoxication of teasing lips, compelling hands. Shuddering, I yielded. Once mounted, he plunged deep. Deeper. Locked in lust, I cried aloud, senseless in my delirium . . . Unquenched, unquenchable, I begged, "Again . . . Again . . ." My hips swayed; trembling, my velvet thighs spread wide in invitation. "Again," I groaned. "Again . . . Oh, God, again . . ."

"Minx," he murmured as he drove himself hard within me.

Even as dawn's pale sun probed the corners of the room, passion was not spent. "I love you," I whispered, stretching my limbs against him, enticing his lean, male strength.

"Delectable minx." His mouth was on my breast.

I sighed. "You were gone so long . . . I died a little . . ."

"Hush . . ."

"Never leave me like that again," I pleaded, "I cannot live without you . . ."

"Shh . . . I am here now . . ."

"Where were you for so long?"

"Hush. It is over." He silenced my lips with his.

My arms wound around him. Our bodies joined, and once again I was consumed. . . .

Chapter 50

One midmorning I was aroused by a flurry of activity in the courtyard. I yawned sleepily. Warm and full, I stretched . . . Robert . . . I smiled: Robert . . .

"Miss!" Annie, breathless with excitement, was pounding at my door.

"What is it?" I said crossly.

"The van—"

"What van?"

"What's bringin' your goods—"

"My goods?"

"Cloths," she said. "Leastwise, seems like they be yours, named for you, an' all!"

I leapt from my bed and knelt at the window. Annie was right: A van had stationed itself before the manor and was discharging its cargo of shimmering silks, smooth velvets and satins, more dazzling still than jewels. . . . A gnome of a woman was carefully handed down from the vehicle. From bespectacled eyes she stared up at the golden stones of the manor, which seemed to dance like little sparklers in the sun, straightened her sagging shoulders, and disappeared finally into the great hall. The sempstress!

Quickly I slipped into my undergarments and waited. It was not long before Miss Martha Webster had assumed her post directly by the large window to my room (thus utilizing the strongest available light) and was, with needle and thread, busily employed. The daughter, poor but proud, of an impecunious schoolmaster, long deceased, Miss Webster, herself now elderly, was severely myopic, incorrigibly stooped, and a born gossip. I removed myself from her presence with dispatch as soon as she had measured and cut and pinned, leaving her with enough work for a galley of slaves and the truant company of Annie, impatient to exchange delicious tidbits.

When I had returned from riding and was passing

through the great hall, Auntie Maude, cheeks unnaturally bright, intercepted me. "Who is this Miss Webster?" she asked without preamble.

"I should think the nature of her occupation obvious."

Auntie Maude's flush deepened. "Who engaged her?"

"I did."

"You did!" she gasped.

"Of course," I said airily.

"And that costly material—who ordered that?"

"I did."

"Elizabeth," she said sternly, "you have no money for such things—"

"Who needs money?" I quipped, leaving her open-mouthed as I sailed up the stairs to another fitting. . . .

Miss Webster, it developed, was both remarkably industrious and efficient. A master of her trade, she applied the needle with fluidity and surprising grace and with a speed approaching that of a machine. She was also morally righteous and tediously chaste. Her dealings with me were unrelievedly formal and not without a certain undertone of disapproval. Still, she could not conceal entirely a consuming curiosity as to my personal affairs, and I detected a titillating twinge of envy in her dreadful imaginings. I chuckled: She was dried up, but not buried, after all. . . .

She was scheduled to remain at Wynds until the completion of her assignment. A bedroom in the servants' wing had been set aside for her use, and she was invited to take her meals in the kitchen in their company; although, whenever possible, Annie managed to bring a tray to the room on the flimsy pretext that Miss Webster preferred not to take unnecessary time from her work.

Toiling well into the night—at the window as long as light prevailed, later, surrounded by a battery of candles—Miss Webster was making heroic strides toward accomplishing her monumental task in an incredibly short space of time. Robert, however, was wild. "Doesn't that woman ever tire?" he growled, coming late to my bed. "Do you know the hour?"

I snuggled close and sighed. "I know. I thought she would never leave—"

"Should have thrown her out and told her to take her

trappings with her. It's a wonder that I could find you at
all in this jungle—"

"Lost?" I giggled, fitting myself to his loins. "I'll be delighted to show you the way—"

He laughed. "Minx . . ."

Miss Webster had no sooner boarded the van, taking her
"trappings" with her and leaving behind a repository filled
with brilliant creations, than I was off to Smugglers' Peak,
aflame in my new finery: a velvet riding habit, the color
of fire. Robert was waiting for me as I streaked up the
precipice. He dismounted immediately, lifted me out of the
saddle, and fastened his lips on mine.

"Like my outfit?" I asked, posturing this way and that.

"Glorious," he breathed.

I moved toward him. "Sure?"

He smiled. "Positive."

"Well, then"—I slipped my arms around his neck—
"why not show your appreciation properly . . ."

"Minx . . ."

Chapter 51

Hartley was unharnessing Dr. Briggs's trap when Robert and I clattered onto the cobbles of the stable yard. Robert's dark eyes narrowed. "Hell," he muttered.

"What is it?" I asked, alarmed.

"My wife," he said grimly.

The tense hush surrounding a morbid event befalling any establishment had settled on Wynds, infecting the household staff with a general attitude of unease, causing it to perform simple, routine duties with an urgency that suggested the activities were neither routine nor simple. There was much stifled whispering and wild eye-communication; Judd's comportment became sterner than usual, as were his directives. His expression, normally dour, now was actually glowering. He approached as Robert strode through the great hall. "Sir Robert," the butler bowed in apology, "I fear the Lady Frances has taken a bad turn."

"I see."

"The doctor is with her now—"

Robert nodded gravely.

"He has requested audience with you as soon as it is convenient, sir."

"Of course." Robert mounted the stairs.

The butler bowed again solemnly and withdrew, not before flashing Auntie Maude a mildly reproving look as she hastened toward me, wringing anxious hands. "Dear," she hissed, "the Lady Frances is very ill—"

I shrugged. "One can hardly find that unusual—"

"Elizabeth!" she gasped. "Dr. Briggs is concerned about—pneumonia!"

"If it isn't one thing, it's another," I replied callously.

Applying monstrous control, Auntie Maude struggled to conceal her dismay by altering the course of the conversation. "Er—Dr. Briggs is here, Elizabeth," she said. "You will no doubt be seeing him. So—"

"So?"

"Do try to be—er—polite to him, dear," she pleaded, "he is in—"

"If you will excuse me, Aunt," I interrupted, "I am due for a bath."

"But dear, you can hardly expect Annie to be—er—attentive today!"

"And why not?"

"With Lady Frances's condition—it is quite impossible—"

"I think not."

"Elizabeth . . ." Auntie Maude's eyes, sick with worry, trailed my progress up the stairs. . . .

In my new gown of clinging lemon-yellow silk I joined Robert and Dr. Briggs, already in the dining hall. Both men rose immediately, and, as like any other woman who knows her beauty, I basked in the shining looks of admiration that ignited their eyes. Dr. Briggs's naturally ruddy face reddened perceptibly as his gaze traveled over the supple grace of my naked arms and rested unwillingly on the dramatic surge of my breasts, rising high above the low bodice. "Doctor." My smile was brilliant.

Blushing hotly, he bowed.

"Judd," Robert directed the butler, "seat Miss Knowlton."

"Yes, Sir Robert."

"May I inquire, Sir Robert," I asked quietly, "how does Lady Frances fare this evening?"

"I think perhaps that this gentleman"—his smile poignant, Robert inclined his head toward Dr. Briggs—"would be in a far better position to answer your question than I."

"There has been no significant change." The doctor issued his sober judgment.

"Auntie Maude said something about—" I paused. "Pneumonia?"

Dr. Briggs drew together thoughtful brows. "I am sorry to say that we cannot rule out that possibility—"

Sir Robert sighed heavily.

"Can nothing be done?" I asked in earnest concern.

The doctor spread his hands in the conventional gesture of helplessness. "The usual supportive treatment indicated in cases of this kind . . . and . . . duration." He shook his head. "Lady Frances has been seriously weakened by the pregnancy and, coupled with her nervous, run-down condition . . ." His voice faded. "That," he mused softly, "I still find puzzling."

"But she will be all right?" A worried frown creased my brow.

"I fervently hope so."

"More wine, doctor?" Robert inquired hospitably.

"Yes. A spot, please."

"Miss Knowlton?"

I lowered my lashes demurely. "Thank you, Sir Robert. But, no. I believe that I have had quite enough."

"Judd," Robert summoned the butler, "refill the doctor's glass."

"Yes, Sir Robert."

"Doctor, I have alerted the staff to prepare accommodations—" Robert began.

Dr. Briggs put up a restraining hand. "I would prefer a cot in my patient's room, if that can be arranged."

Robert's dark brows rose. "Oh, really?"

The doctor nodded. "I do not wish to alarm you unduly, Sir Robert, but I expect the crisis sometime tonight. I want to be in close attendance when it comes."

"Very good of you," Robert murmured in appreciation. "Will you require additional supplies? Perhaps a servant to assist—"

"In the event that I do, I shall advise you."

"Splendid . . . Miss Knowlton," Robert addressed me, "the doctor faces a long and strenuous night. . . . Perhaps you might challenge him to a game of cribbage after dining—by way of relaxation."

Dr. Briggs colored.

"I do confess to being a trifle tired, Sir Robert." My sigh was rueful.

"Well, then," Sir Robert offered generously, "perhaps the doctor will join me in a brandy; unless, of course"—innocently he regarded Dr. Briggs—"you two"—his discreet glance embraced us both—"might care simply to visit; before you feel you must look in on your patient, that is, Doctor." Robert's eyes swung back fully to remain on Dr. Briggs's crimson face.

I yawned prettily behind my hand. "If you will forgive me, Doctor . . . Sir Robert—I feel quite fatigued. With your kind permission, both, I should like to retire."

"I do hope that you are not courting the onset of indisposition, yourself, Miss Knowlton!" Robert was instantly solicitous.

"No," I hastened to assure him, "I am perfectly well."

"Perhaps it might be prudent for the doctor to prescribe a little something for you," Robert suggested. "If only a mild tonic—"

Color flooded Dr. Briggs's face.

"Thank you, Sir Robert." I declined politely. "I need nothing more than a good night's sleep." I rose. "If you gentlemen will excuse me?"

Perpetual activity and a general tension continued throughout the night. Behind my closed door I could feel, more than hear, the hurrying feet—sense, rather than know, their destination . . . nor could I decipher excited whisperings and sharp commands above an occasional metallic clink or the light ringing of glass. Suddenly I was drawn back in time to Leicester Square and my father's last illness. . . .

But, this was Wynds—not Leicester Square . . . Not my father, but Lady Frances: Robert's wife . . . An absurd, cringing wraith. Robert's wife. Grotesque. Useless in her misery . . . Robert's wife.

My father died. Why not, then, Robert's wife?

Indeed, why not Robert's wife . . .

Die, Lady Frances. Die . . .

Despite, or perhaps because of, the steady parade marching past my door, I managed to fall asleep at last, not stirring until I felt Robert slip into bed beside me and begin kissing me awake. I melted against him. "How did you manage—"

"I won't say there weren't obstacles—"

I giggled. "Cribbage?"

He laughed.

"Perhaps I need a tonic, at that," I murmured.

"Think so? I shall be happy to prescribe one. . . ."

Chapter 52

Although still maternally advising and pathetically all-suffering, Auntie Maude now began to view me with open suspicion. She became censorian. Directive. Worst of all: meddlesome. The next morning she knocked on my door and announced preemptively that breakfast awaited me in the dining hall. Incredulous, I rolled over, muttering, "Go away! I shall rise in good time—"

"Elizabeth," my aunt declared firmly, "I am coming in!" Standing beside my bed, she viewed with fresh dismay the disordered bedclothes and the nightdress lying casually discarded on the floor; her eyes bore still more shock and pain when she realized too that I was completely naked. "You must come down to breakfast," she managed.

"Good God," I yawned, "whatever for?"

"Lady Frances is ill—"

"Oh," I smirked, "then she is planning to be at table too?"

"Your flippancy is in the poorest taste!" she rasped. "The woman may be dying, for all we know!"

. . . Dying . . . The woman may be dying . . . Die, Lady Frances . . . Die . . .

"I have promised Dr. Briggs that you will join him in fifteen minutes."

"What right had you to do that?" I was outraged.

"He is a guest in this house, Elizabeth." Auntie Maude's soft mouth drew a stern line. "And you are companion to its mistress. You have an obligation." She leaned closer. "You are only in a position of employment here, you know."

"As," I reminded her coldly, "are you. "Pray," I warned, "do not overstep either your authority or your privileges."

Deep color suffused her face.

"Now, leave me," I ordered, "so that I may dress."

She was waiting for me in the hallway. I regarded her

with real aversion. "Have you no duties to perform other than to spy on me?"

"Elizabeth!" Swift, disapproving eyes traveled over my flame-colored riding habit. "Surely you do not intend to wear such an outfit this morning?"

"And why not?"

"Lady Frances—"

"She is dead? The house is in mourning?"

"Er—no—"

"Desist, Aunt," I hissed, "desist . . ."

Dr. Briggs was standing at the sideboard, raising the lid of a chafing dish, when I stepped into the dining hall. I noticed immediately that his eyes were pink-rimmed with fatigue and the hand holding his plate shook a little. I sent him a brilliant smile. "Good morning!" I said breezily, "and how is your patient this morning?"

His own smile was tentative. "On the mend, I hope. The fever broke early this morning. But," he admitted a lingering concern, "there is a long way to go before she is well."

. . . On the mend . . . on the mend . . . Lady Frances, why didn't you die? . . .

"She does not have pneumonia, then?"

He sighed, "Just a hair this side, fortunately! Come," he suggested, "permit me to serve you. Now, Miss Knowlton, kidneys, sausage, eggs, or ham—or perhaps a spot of each?"

I laughed. "Good heavens, no! Just some bread and jam, I think—"

"Well," he chuckled, "I have no intentions of behaving modestly this morning! I confess that I am ravenous!"

I was sipping my second cup of tea when Robert appeared; he, too, was dressed in riding clothes. He acknowledged us both with a brief, courteous nod and motioned to Judd to prepare his plate before he joined us at the table. "Ah, Doctor," he smiled, "I hope that the kitchen has treated you well?"

"Perfectly!" The doctor leaned back in his chair. "Superlative cuisine!"

"Splendid!" Robert beamed in approval. He directed his attention toward me. "And you, Miss Knowlton? Has your appetite been satisfied?"

I lowered my eyes shyly. "For the moment . . ."

"What are your plans for today, Doctor?" Sir Robert inquired, "where they concern my wife, naturally."

"As I informed you earlier, Sir Robert, I have administered mild sedation, so that Lady Frances is resting comfortably," Dr. Briggs explained. "I must return to my surgery for a while this afternoon," he added almost in apology, "to treat my other patients."

"Of course." Robert nodded sympathetically. "You intend to spend the night again?"

"Definitely!" Dr. Briggs passed a weary hand over his eyes. "It is her mental attitude which is of a great concern—as much so as her physical state, I am afraid." He shook his head. "Your wife's will to live is not nearly as strong as I might wish it—"

. . . Will to live . . . Die, Lady Frances . . .

Robert's eyes were grave. "Then she is not out of danger yet?"

"By no means, Sir Robert. By no means."

"I wonder, Doctor," Robert said slowly, "if you will have need of me for a few hours?"

"Well—"

"There are certain pressing estate matters I should like to resolve," Robert owned with some reluctance. "My previous extended absence has allowed my business affairs to slip drastically."

"Perfectly all right," the doctor assured the squire. "Go right ahead."

"Thank you. And—Miss Knowlton—can she be of service to you in the nursing of your patient?"

Dr. Briggs reddened. "No. No." He seemed flustered. "Lady Frances's Sarah is sufficient . . ."

"In that case, Miss Knowlton," Robert asked me idly, "what is to be your itinerary this morning?"

My reply was vague. "Oh, I thought perhaps I might ride. . . . It seems a fine day," I added.

"Then, if you can spare me, Doctor, and if you will excuse me, Miss Knowlton"—Robert rose and bowed politely—"I must get to work. . . ."

Dark strings of clouds warped the sun, and keen gusts vexed the spitting sea and whipped my flaming skirts as I raced up the heights of Smugglers' Peak to meet my lover. He was there, straining against the sky, ready to seize me from my horse, eager to fasten his lips on mine. "Come to me, pressing business," he exulted, lifting me high and claiming my mouth with his.

Intoxicated, I clung to him. I was wild with desire.

As he lowered me to the ground he whispered, "Miss Knowlton, has your appetite really been satisfied?"

"Never," I trembled, "never . . . never . . ."

By afternoon the household's almost demented air of industry had diminished perceptibly, promising a rapid return to normal routine. Dr. Briggs had departed for his surgery; that move, too, suggested an easing of concern. He was to reappear in time for the evening meal and to spend the night—more, it seemed now, in the attitude of a guest rather than as a physician attending a deathwatch.

Auntie Maude continued to lurk in the hall, intent on her own private vigil; keeping a sharp accounting of my whereabouts and activities . . .

The dining hour stretched interminably that night. Dr. Briggs, under considerably less strain, seemed disposed to idle conversation, and Robert, although oddly distracted, remained the considerate host, permitting the doctor to linger over the meal for what I considered to be an inordinate length of time. A generous supply of light claret flowed; Judd, on instruction from Robert, punctiliously kept the glasses filled. Dr. Briggs imbibed freely, although not to excess; Robert, sparingly; I, however, emptied my glass with regularity as my deep restlessness mounted. Consumed, I wished an end to this aimless chatter; craved the moment when I could run to my room—my bed—and into the arms of my lover . . .

But Robert did not come. Why? I was beside myself. The "obstacles" had been removed: The house was quiet, the hall free; no longer did the harried procession pass my door. The way was clear. Unless . . . Unless: Auntie Maude . . . had that busybody managed to station herself outside my room? . . . Self-appointed guardian: meddlesome bitch! Enraged, I leapt from my bed, strode to the door, and flung it wide: The hall was empty. Oh, God,

where was he. . . . My body ached. . . . I was on
fire. . . . Robert, come to me . . .

I stormed. I wept. Frenzied, I paced. . . . Robert . . .

Suddenly my attention was caught at the window. A
light . . . There was a light in the tower. It swayed back
and forth, a yellow gleam flickering uneasily. Shivering, I
knelt and stared in helpless fascination until, abruptly, the
nervous flame was swallowed up in darkness.

Still, Robert did not come. . . . Not before dawn began
to brighten the sky did I, weakened by exhaustion, manage
to drift off into a sleep that was without rest. . . . Robert,
Robert . . . Oh, God, Robert . . .

Auntie Maude ambushed me as, dressed for riding, I
hurried through the great hall. "Where are you going,
dear?" she asked unnecessarily, trying to stay my departure.

I did not bother to reply.

"Elizabeth," Auntie Maude followed, "where are you
going, dear?"

"To hell, Aunt!" I spat. "Where else?"

Stoically she ignored my outburst. "Dr. Briggs is waiting
for you in the dining hall."

"That is unfortunate," I sneered, "as I have no intention
of joining him there—or anywhere. And that," I flung the
words at her, "is final!"

Auntie Maude reached to take my hand. "Darling,
please," she entreated, her eyes welling with tears.

I wrenched my hand free. "Desist, Aunt . . ."

Hartley was busy tidying the stable yard. "Has Sir Robert taken his horse?" I demanded abruptly.

Hartley was surprised but answered promptly, "Yes,
miss."

"When?"

"Before dawn, miss."

"Did he say when he would return?"

Hartley shook his head, "No, miss." He put up the
shovel. "Would ye be wantin' the mare?"

My throat was filled; I could not speak. I merely nodded
my assent.

I was almost hysterical as I spurred Artemis to Smug-

glers' Peak. . . . Oh, God, let him be there. . . . Let him
be waiting for me: exultant; arms outstretched. lips eager
on mine. . . . Let him ease me to the ground; lock me in
ecstasy . . . ride me to fulfillment . . .

Clouds, thick and black, stormed in from the sea: a tribute befitting my own thick, black despair. He was gone; I
was lost . . . Robert . . .

A lonely gull dared the wind; another braved the
waves. . . . But apart. As Robert and I: apart . . .

Chapter 53

For the duration of Dr. Briggs's stay at Wynds, Auntie Maude was determined, and palpably so, that the doctor and I bolster our flagging courtship. Choosing to ignore my flagrant uninterest, she contrived little intimate teas, meetings (spuriously impromptu), and worked tirelessly to insure my presence in the dining hall at mealtime. Each affair was embarrassingly anxious, and all were arranged in a frenzied race against time: Robert was away.

Early mornings found Auntie Maude invading my room, to insist that I join the doctor for breakfast; early mornings found me raining on her such a spate of vituperation as to prompt her ultimate and tearful retreat. Tearful or not, she was indefatigable. Her attack was standard: "Elizabeth, Dr. Briggs is a guest in this house—"

"Perhaps so," I conceded tartly, "but I did not invite him."

"Nevertheless you have certain responsibilities here—"

"Not to him, I haven't."

"Darling, you will lose him—" she cautioned.

I shrugged.

Panic mounted: "Darling, a man will not stay interested forever without some encouragement."

"I don't want him interested."

"He is a fine man."

My laugh was snide. "You encourage him, then—"

"He will be good to you—"

I soon wearied of the game. "I have said, Aunt, that I do not want him."

"You may not think so now"—Auntie Maude was frankly pleading—"but—"

"Christ, Aunt!"

"Elizabeth!"

"Aunt, leave me alone!"

"I only want what's best for you—"

"Then, get out—"

"Dear—"

"Out!" I shrilled. "You bloody old fool, get out!"

Jonathan Briggs was no less desirous of establishing an alliance, but sensibly moved with wary restraint, no longer underestimating my volatility. The expression in his eyes ranged from loving but bewildered—to hurt and shy . . . "I see that you are dressed for riding this morning," he observed as I wandered into the dining hall.

"Yes."

"Fine day for it."

"Yes."

"I gave Lady Frances her examination some time ago," he remarked, "and I am free now for several hours."

"Then you can return early to your surgery."

He blushed. "I have scheduled hours there for the afternoon—" He coughed. "I was thinking more of—riding out a bit—"

"That is, of course, up to you."

"If you wouldn't object, I should like very much to join you—on the trail—"

"I really prefer to ride alone."

"I was hoping—"

"I think not. I'm sorry."

He sighed. "Another time?"

"Perhaps . . ."

Never were my outings on the moor, however prolonged, of sufficient length to escape a tête-à-tête in the inglenook, a patient stratagem inspired by Auntie Maude, who first skewered the doctor, then managed to waylay me. The scene was almost routine: A fire crackled, a hearty feast lay waiting—and so did Dr. Briggs . . . "Come in, m'dear! Come in!" he called. "These buns are a positive miracle of creation!" he declared, happily taking a generous bite and smacking his lips.

I turned my head away.

"Have one."

"I am not hungry."

"Well—ah—" he began cautiously, "my trap is still hitched out front, and there is yet enough light . . ." Summoning added spirit, he asked, "What say! How about it?"

"I think not."

"Er—perhaps tomorrow?"

"Perhaps."

Always Auntie Maude counteracted my instructions to Annie as to the location of my evening meal. I wanted a tray in my room; Auntie Maude wanted me in the dining hall, in the company, of course, of Dr. Briggs. "I will have it here!" I lay across my bed, stubbornly refusing.

Auntie Maude proved equally obdurate. "He must not be allowed to eat alone!"

"Nonsense!"

"It is such a small courtesy!" she maintained.

"You handle the amenities, then—"

"I will not take no for an answer!"

Auntie Maude was victorious, but only because I permitted it: It was of little importance to me, really, where I ate. Without Robert, nectar was straw, and the companionship of the gods a mere penance. . . .

"It is still early in the evening," the doctor commented, consulting his pocket watch. "I should enjoy a lively game of whist! What say?"

"I am afraid not."

"I know! Perhaps a couple of rounds of checkers. Now, there's a dandy—"

"No."

"Backgammon is a corking good game—"

"No, Doctor. I do not play games."

He sighed. "A dash more wine, then?"

"No. Thank you."

"Conversation, then." His hazel eyes were wistful. "I have missed—"

"If you will forgive me, Doctor, I am really rather tired. I think I shall say good night . . ."

Once freed, I ran to my room, spared the tedium of his devotion and the wearisome prodding of Auntie Maude only when I huddled in my bed, wrapped in the memory of my lover's arms, feeling his lips on mine. . . .

At last Lady Frances recovered to such a degree that the doctor was able to relinquish his post at her bedside; barring those occasions engineered by Auntie Maude, he relinquished his regular place at the dining table as well. For the first week of her convalescence his visits to his patient continued on a daily basis; soon she improved so rapidly that his services were required only for a sudden flareup or a suspected relapse. I was free, then, to resume my own routine: Except for those frantic hours spent racing through the countryside, I seldom left my room, my refuge, and never for meals. There, consumed by longing, I raged and paced and sobbed. . . . Robert . . . Robert . . .

Chapter 54

"Elizabeth . . . Elizabeth . . ." Swiftly I traced the rib-bon of yellow light down the narrow stairs to the gold room. The door was closed. There was muffled sound. . . . I tried the knob: It moved. . . . They were there, entwined, his tanned hands kneading her full white breasts. He was murmuring: ". . . in the way . . . rid of her . . ." Softly she caressed his cheek: ". . . how, my love, how? . . ." His hands strayed to her thighs: "rid of her . . . now . . ." She gave a little cry of dismay. His dark eyes were insistent: ". . . yes, my darling . . . now . . ." His hand stroked, explored: ". . . now . . ." Quivering, she drew him close, a slow smile curved her moist lips: ". . . yes, now . . ."

". . . rid of her . . ." teased my waking hours; ". . . now . . ." flailed my every thought—seared the frozen ground, whipped the frenzied sea, became the iron spur stabbing Artemis's tender flesh . . .

". . . how, my love, how . . ." filled my eyes, drowned my ears, tormented my very soul . . .

"Elizabeth . . . Elizabeth . . ." The path shimmered; beckoned . . . The door to the gold room was closed; gent-ly I turned the handle. They were there. Her hair spilled across his chest; his brown hand twisted a wayward lock. ". . . have you done it . . ." he asked softly in her ear. She shook her head, ". . . not yet . . ." "No?" He seemed surprised. ". . . not yet . . ." He rose abruptly: ". . . Then, I cannot stay . . ." She cried in protest: ". . . love, you must not go . . ." He smiled sadly. ". . . I must . . . I cannot stay . . ." The curtains parted and he was gone. She uttered a little plaintive shriek, swayed suddenly, and slipped to the floor where she lay still in a pool of golden hair. . . .

The light faded . . .

". . . I cannot stay . . . cannot stay . . ." No . . . No . . . ". . . cannot stay . . ." Oh, God, no . . . no . . .

"Elizabeth . . . Elizabeth . . ." The path, shining, pulled me to the gold room. The door stood open. She was there. Lying on the floor: sobbing; her body contorted; shuddering; alone.

She was alone . . .

The light faded.

Tears flooded my cheeks. Sobs rent my own throat . . . No . . . No . . . God, no! Come back . . . come back . . .

". . . rid of her . . . now . . . cannot stay . . . cannot stay . . ."

Robert . . .

Chapter 55

On the moor a solitary flower bloomed, and the quickened greening of a spiny bush, encouraged by a subtle softening of the air, hinted that although winter was far from over, spring was certainly on its way. Pockets of frozen earth began to yield under Artemis's feet, gulls dipped and soared as if compelled, and the driving sea hurled itself at the rocks in a frenzy of anticipation.

But what of spring, without Robert . . .

What of anything, without Robert . . .

Artemis's thick coat was sudsy with froth when I returned her to the stable, and I found myself perspiring uncomfortably under my heavy woolen habit. The mare seemed relieved, glad of a chance to rest; and I, as well, looked forward to refreshment, a bath, and a needed change of clothes.

Drowsing, I lingered in the tub. Finally I abandoned the now chill water, toweled myself listlessly, and gazed with disinterest out of the window. My idle glance caught and froze. On a bench in the enclosed garden, in the full path of the sun, huddled Lady Frances. Even from this distance her pallor was spectral, her body skeletal, and her mien, as ever, cringing. And hovering over her mistress: the solicitous, faithful Sarah. I watched, fascinated. Lady Frances's head wobbled in continuous wary little half-turns, and I could see, rather than hear, Sarah's responding reassurances. Suddenly Sarah rose and held out her hands. Lady Frances shook her head. Sarah's hands remained outstretched in pretty invitation. Lady Frances seemed to hesitate. Encouraged, Sarah gently lifted her mistress to her feet. Lady Frances swayed uncertainly for a moment, then stood weakly. At Sarah's coaxing gesture, Lady Frances wavered. Sarah urged. She placed a supportive arm around her mistress's waist, and together they began to walk slowly, falteringly in the direction of the wall of stone. Toward the wooden door that opened to the sea. The sea . . .

Quickly I sought a gown—any gown—drew it impatiently over my head, and cursed the row of buttons and my fingers fumbling to fasten them. . . . I condemned its endless flight as I raced down the staircase to the great hall, and there berated the polished tile as my footsteps clattered, noisy in their haste. Once in the garden, I slowed my pace to simulate the casual stroll of one seeking the balmy air of an afternoon in almost-spring. Lady Frances, using Sarah as her staff, was within feet of the gate. Still affecting a careless pose, I livened my steps so that the distance between us narrowed easily. "Good afternoon, Lady Frances," I called pleasantly.

She started, momentarily falling against her maid.

"Miss—" Sarah nodded a polite greeting.

"Lovely day," I remarked, looking up at the sky.

"Aye," agreed the girl, a little out of breath with her recent exertion, "seems so—"

"Here," I offered, "your hands are occupied—allow me to get the door, at least—"

Lady Frances shrank in terror.

"Much obliged, miss," the girl smiled gratefully.

I touched the latch, and the gate, slapped sharply by the force of the wind, swung crazily back and forth and immediately out of my hand. "Oh dear!" I gasped. "I can't seem to hold it!"

Lady Frances clung to Sarah.

"We must not let it close after us!" I warned.

"Mercy no!" exclaimed Sarah.

"Perhaps," I suggested to the maid, "if you could manage to get a firm grasp on the door—and then hook it—"

"But what am I to do with—" she jerked her head meaningfully toward her mistress.

"I shall hang onto her while you attend to the door."

"No!" Lady Frances shrieked.

"Easy, now," the girl soothed, "easy, now, Lady Frances. Just you go over to Miss Knowlton, now—"

"No, no!" Lady Frances cried.

"It'll only be for a moment," Sarah promised, "and I'll

be right here. Right here. All the time. Come," she wheedled, "there's a good girl—"

Lady Frances began to sob helplessly.

"Do you have tight grab of her, the now?" asked Sarah,
loosening her own grasp.

"Yes," I assured her, wrapping my arm firmly around
Lady Frances's waist. "Hurry, Sarah, see to the door—"

Standing on the lip of the precipice, my eyes devoured
the sheer drop, traveled over jutting rocks, dove straight
into the jaws of the brutal, foaming sea. The roar of the
surf thundered in my ears: ". . . rid of her . . . rid of
her . . ."

A guarded glance at Sarah, grappling with the gate, confirmed that her attention was wholly occupied. I gripped
Lady Frances cruelly, and with all my strength thrust her
toward the fine edge of the cliff. She struggled briefly. I
shoved again, even more forcefully, and watched her pitch
forward, claw feebly at the empty air, and then disappear.
Her one thin scream was swallowed up instantly by the
greedy swelling waves that slapped the shore below. . . .
Quickly I hurled myself to the ground in a last heroic attempt to save my charge. Sobbing in a frenzy of frustration
and grief, my nails dug at the shaggy path torn, unaware,
by Lady Frances as she fell . . .

"Holy Mother of God!" shrieked Sarah. "What is it!"

"Lady Frances—" My voice was strangled.

"Where is she?" Sarah's eyes were wild. "Where is the
Lady Frances?"

"She—she—she is—"

Sarah shook me roughly. "Where is she?"

"Sh-she has f-fallen—" I stammered.

"Fallen!" Sarah rasped. "Where?"

I could not speak; I merely indicated with my eyes.

Sarah sank to her knees. "Mother Mary," she whispered,
crossing herself.

"I tried—" I sobbed, "I tried . . ."

"Mother Mary," chanted Sarah, "Mother Mary . . ."

"She was so weak," I moaned, "so weak—"

Sarah cradled her head in her arms. "Mother Mary . . ."

"I tried . . ."

Sarah rocked back and forth. "Mother Mary . . ."

I began to retch, bruising my tear-streaked face on the harsh, barren ground. "I tried . . . as God is my judge, I tried . . ."

Absently, Sarah patted my heaving shoulders. "Of course you did, miss. Of course you did. Hush the now," she crooned, "hush . . ."

"Sarah," I wailed, "I tried . . . I tried . . ."

"Come, miss." She pulled me to my feet. "We'll go back to the house."

I leaned on her heavily. "Sarah, help me—"

"We'll go back to the house—"

"We can't—we can't leave her!" I beseeched, tears flooding my cheeks, "we can't leave her—here!"

Sarah's own eyes filled. "Poor lamb . . . poor sad little lamb . . . we must . . ."

"No . . . no . . ."

"We must . . . come, the now, come—"

Sustained by Sarah, I stumbled through the garden, weeping pitifully, "God help me, I tried . . ."

The household was plunged into immediate turmoil. Judd, thin-lipped and dour, rose to authority, organizing without delay a rescue party—men, surefooted and fearless, recruited from amongst the outside laborers, adding a few stocky young houseboys as well. Hauling ropes and a tarpaulin and wearing sturdy boots, the band tramped with a grim determination through the sunlit garden to the stone bastion, disappearing then behind its wooden gate, which creaked back and forth, restless on its rusted hinges. . . .

Whimpering softly, I clung desperately to Sarah, as we stood at the opposite end of the garden. A frantic Auntie Maude rushed to press me against her ample bosom. "Come, darling," she entreated, "come. We'll go up to your room—"

"No!" I cried, "no! Not until she—until they—find her—"

"But Elizabeth, that may take hours," Auntie Maude reasoned. "You are exhausted."

"Please, Auntie Maude," I implored, "let me wait here until they find her—"

"Love, they may never find her—" The statement only

begun was stopped short by my sudden paroxysm of hysteria. Auntie Maude kissed my bruised cheek. "All right, darling, all right . . ."

The sun's rays were deeply slanted and the air had cooled before the sorrowful cortege, bearing its grisly burden, marched solemnly through the garden and into the great hall. The Reverend Smythe had already arrived preparatory to receiving Lady Frances's remains, wrapped carefully now in the tarpaulin, and transporting them in his awaiting hearse. (The Reverend, it seemed, served as mortician in addition to his ministerial responsibilities.)

Reverend Smythe was in his element: He conducted the transfer of Lady Frances's body with a subtle relish and, I was forced to admit, flair. The vehicle provided was suitably elaborate, blindingly shiny and pulled by a blooded, perfectly matched team. He sidled up to Judd, promising, "I shall bring her back this evening—unless—she is—you know—" His eyes rolled in an explicit grimace.

"Yes, sir," nodded the butler.

"In some cases—you know—"

"I understand, sir." Judd stood stiffly.

"I gather the—her—ah, she—was pinned against the rocks—"

"Yes, sir."

"Battered severely—"

"Yes, sir."

"Dr. Briggs has been notified?"

"I believe so. Yes, sir."

"Good. Good . . . And I should like at some appropriate time—and that reasonably soon—to confer with Sir Robert about burial."

"Er—Sir Robert is—er, not here . . ."

"But he will return shortly." The Reverend was positive.

Judd shifted uncomfortably. "I—I would hope so, sir."

"When is his arrival scheduled?"

Judd was evasive. "Ah—"

"You—there is no schedule?"

"Ah—"

"You have not learned as yet the time of his arrival?"

"Er—no, sir."

"Extraordinary!"

"Sir Robert is away, sir—"

"But being contacted, surely—"

Judd hedged, "Er—no, sir."

"No?"

"We—we have not been apprised of his—er—where-abouts."

"Incredible!" The Reverend removed his spectacles and wiped them with a dingy handkerchief. "You realize, my good fellow," he swallowed hard, "that this puts me in rather an awkward position."

"Yes, sir."

"You understand—I cannot keep the woman—er—going—indefinitely!" He mopped his brow.

"Yes, sir."

"There are natural limitations—"

"Yes, sir."

"Even in winter—" The Reverend's small eyes hurriedly swept the room. . . . "No fires!" he hissed suddenly. "There are to be no fires in the hall—or near it—for the—er—duration!" He pushed an insistent, protuberant nose in Judd's face. "You follow?"

"Er—yes, sir."

"Not a solitary fire!"

"No, sir."

"Remarkable!" Perplexed, the Reverend was still shaking his head as he departed. "I have never found myself in a similar situation before. . . . Unheard of! Simply unheard of!"

"I am taking you to your room, darling," Auntie Maude decided. Exhausted now, I permitted her to drag me step by listless step up the broad staircase. "Here we are, dear," she sang, steering me immediately over to the bed. "Let's discard those soiled clothes and put on something fresh." She went to the wardrobe and managed stoically to ignore the flimsy creations hanging there. "Here," she caroled, holding up the flannel nightdress, "I think this will feel comfortable."

Benumbed, I slumped on the edge of the bed and allowed her to strip me of my clothing and slip the nightgown over my head. Tenderly she bathed my hands and clucked over the scratches on my face. "Come now, dear, in you go!" She pulled down the covers. "There!" Lovingly she tucked the blankets up to my chin. "Better?" She beamed. "I'll sit with you for a while—" I nodded bravely. "Dr. Briggs is coming by as soon as he has looked at—er—as soon as he can get away." Her smile was blissful as she gazed down at me. "What shall we talk about, love?" My eyes filled. "All right," she comforted, "I'll do all the talking. You just lie still and try not to think about anything."

It was dark before Dr. Briggs made his visit to my room. "Elizabeth," he murmured, his eyes troubled. "Resting quietly?"

I nodded.

"Were you hurt when you fell?" His face was deeply pained.

"No. I'm all right—" I closed my eyes. "It was Lady—"

"I know, darling, I know—" He took my hand in his. "The scratches on your face—"

"They don't hurt."

"Sure?"

I swallowed. "Sure." My voice was hoarse.

"Can you eat a little something?"

I turned my face away.

"Perhaps later," he said.

"Perhaps later," I croaked.

"I have something here to make you more comfortable." He reached into his satchel and drew out a little packet of powders.

"What is—"

"Something to make you relaxed—maybe even a little drowsy."

"I don't—" I squeezed my eyes shut.

"All right. I'll leave it here, in case you change your mind . . ."

I nodded.

"I am staying the night—so if you have any fears, or need me for anything, I'll be close by—"

I smiled bravely.

He leaned over and kissed me gently. "I love you," he whispered, "remember that: I love you . . ."

The door closed quietly. I leapt from the bed, flung wide

the window, and knelt, driving my eyes toward the wooden gate that swung, a restless captive, on its hinges. I could see little: Even the tower rose only in uncertain outline against an inky sky, itself relieved by but a dusting of pale stars. My ears strained: There it was—that faint, grating saw as the door whined in complaint against the prankish wind. Beyond: the ragged rocks. Below: the seething, exultant sea . . .

. . . seething, exultant: as was I . . .

In joyous abandon I leaned back and let the bubbles of delicious secret laughter rise: ". . . I tried," I mocked. ". . . I tried . . ." A magnificent touch . . . "I know, miss, I know . . ." How poignant! Jubilant, I rocked back and forth. ". . . she was weak, so weak . . ." I gurgled. Perfect. Inspired! ". . . can you eat a little something?" ". . . perhaps later . . ." What sensitivity! ". . . perhaps later . . ." I hooted. I was ravenous!

Fools, all. Bloody, stupid fools . . .

". . . rid of her . . ." was all that mattered.

". . . now . . .": It was done.

It was done. . . . I crawled back between the sheets and tried to bury my excitement under the covers: Any moment might bring Auntie Maude through that door to choke me with her cloying devotion, or Dr. Briggs to smother me beneath his fawning spaniel's gaze. And, while euphoric, I was really exhausted: To prolong a posture of tearful grief before an audience, however gullible, was no mean accomplishment. My eyes were hot and dry. I giggled: no wonder . . . God, I was hungry! But to request a tray would hardly be consistent with an anguished state. . . .

No. I must sleep and garner the strength needed to sustain me through tomorrow's performance. . . .

"Elizabeth . . . Elizabeth . . ." I jerked awake. The path shimmered. I was afraid. "Elizabeth . . . Elizabeth . . ." Dared I follow? What would I find? Would she be alone again? . . . "Elizabeth . . ." I had to know. I ran down the curving stairs and stood trembling before the closed door of the gold room. There was no sound. Oh, God. Was she alone? . . . Gingerly I reached for the knob:

The door swung slowly. A shaft of soft light played over the couch on which they lay, coupled. He moved deep within her. . . . Her eyes were glazed with desire . . . lips parted . . . cheeks softly fired, their glow flawed only by faint scratches . . .

The light faded.

Chapter 56

Since, in triumph so many months ago, I had fed my only black dress into the fire, marking an end forever to Miller's and the dress trade, I had no garment to wear befitting this, a house of mourning. Auntie Maude firmly contended that, in view of my recent distressing experience and now weakened condition, I could—and quite properly so—be excused from receiving guests. "Oh, no, Auntie Maude!" I protested. "It is my place to do so, and besides"—my eyes filled—"I want to—"

"Very well, love," Auntie Maude cooed.

Her expression clouded as, later, she held out a gown, one that had been in Lady Frances's own wardrobe. She handed it to me uncertainly. "If you would rather not—" She hesitated.

"Oh, Auntie Maude—" My lips trembled. "I would consider it an honor."

Eyes brimming over with affection, Auntie Maude gathered me in her arms and crooned, "There, there . . ."

The gown was of an exquisite crushed velvet, soft, as if new, and because it proved a hair snug, it followed the contours of my figure explicitly. I allowed my hair to fall loose over my shoulders and spill its rich gold to my waist. I was stunning.

Shyly, Auntie Maude hoped that I was well enough to join Dr. Briggs at breakfast in the dining hall. "Perhaps," I replied wanly, "although I am not sure I could eat anything."

Beaming, she urged, "You must try, dear. To keep up your strength, you know . . . for the next few days," she added tactfully.

I nodded sadly.

Dr. Briggs was already seated in the dining hall when I made my entrance. He jumped from his chair. "Elizabeth." His anxious eyes searched my face. "Are you all right?"

"Yes, "I murmured. "I—think so."

"Here, m'dear," he directed me to a chair. "What will you have? I shall be delighted to serve you myself, if you will grant me the pleasure—" He tried to put a merry twinkle in his eyes.

I shrugged. "Anything . . . Really, I don't feel up to much."

"How about some shirred eggs, for a start?"

"I guess so." I allowed the dish to sit for some time before prodding the food with a listless fork.

"Do eat a little something—" Dr. Briggs implored.

I sighed tremulously.

At that precise moment the rain-specked hearse was rolling smoothly over the slick cobbles of the courtyard, making its solemn approach, escorting the beloved mistress of Wynds home for the last time. Judd whispered something to Dr. Briggs, bowed, and withdrew. "M'dear," the doctor said softly in my ear, "the Reverend has arrived. My services are needed briefly."

I rose at once.

"No . . . No," he said, "you sit here and try to eat something." He disappeared.

I glanced around: The dining hall was quite empty. I raced to the sideboard and sampled some of this and more of that, cramming as much food into my mouth as I could swallow safely, repeating the process until I was at last satisfied. Quickly I resumed my place at the table and picked up my fork, and was again poking dispiritedly at the mass of eggs when the doctor returned. My lack of appetite did not escape his worried eyes. "Have some tea, then," he compromised.

"All right," I agreed dully.

By midmorning the Reverend Smythe had formally established the body of Lady Frances in its interim resting place, prominently in the great hall, where, according to tradition, it was to lie in state prior to final interment, and that, properly, in the family mausoleum. The question remained, of course: When could the date of the burial itself be announced and suitable arrangements made for the funeral to precede it. No word had been received as yet from Robert, nor had anyone been successful in contacting him.

The Reverend's professional dilemma was palpably upsetting, and he maintained perpetual watch in the great hall, nervously dispatching his enlisted lieutenant, Mrs. Smythe, to conduct regular sorties to all fireplaces located in its immediate vicinity as well. The weather had cooperated (cold, with a dismal rain), so that the temperature in the hall accommodated the deceased but proved disagreeable to anyone forced to stand and receive the villagers and neighboring gentry as they arrived to pay their respects (actually abbreviating those visits considerably).

Whatever the Reverend Smythe's ineptitudes as a man of the cloth, he more than counterbalanced in his genius as a mortician. He was an artist. Lady Frances's cheeks had been cleverly rounded, and her pallor, deadly in life, now assumed the pinkish glow of health, in death. Wisely, he had concealed her bird's hands under a frilly, lacy cuff inconsistent with the tailored gown utilized, indicating that it had been joined to the sleeve, and hurriedly. Her hair, wispy and sparse, seemed now amazingly abundant; only under meticulous examination could it be detected that all of the back hair had been forced forward to achieve the added fullness. It was, then, with understandable pride that the Reverend's eyes stole frequent glances at his creation and justified the secret smile of accomplishment that played about his lips.

After my swoon upon first glimpsing the coffin and viewing Lady Frances as she lay still on the pristine white satin, Dr. Briggs and Auntie Maude closed ranks: whenever possible, he remained at my elbow while I received the visiting mourners; whenever possible, she hovered in the great hall, her anxious, loving eyes trained on my face.

Ready to scream and wild to break free, I wondered often how long I could successfully maintain this sorrowful posture of the tragically bereft. . . .

Lady Frances reposed in the great hall—her ornamented bier flanked by stout candles standing tall in their massive candelabra—for four days. The thin stream of the lamenting, the courteous, the curious, even those traditionally indebted to the squire, dwindled dramatically; because of the extended period afforded the viewing, we were simply running out of people. I was beside myself; no less so, the

Reverend. He made it a practice frequently to draw Dr. Briggs aside for a prolonged and serious conference; after a while, both men began to appear increasingly concerned.

On the afternoon of the fourth day, as the last handful of callers was straggling in to offer appropriate condolence, those vague murmurings designed to comfort the bereaved, the reverential hush was broken by a sudden commotion. I looked up from the wrinkled face of a stooped crone, dowager to a neighboring estate, and saw him: Robert.

His strides long, his footsteps slapping the polished tile, black cape flying wildly behind him, Robert approached his wife's coffin. The visitors moved aside tactfully but remained transfixed. Thin-lipped, his face grim, Robert stood staring, then sank to his knees beside the body. Head bowed, he did not move for some time. At last he rose, placed a hand tenderly along his wife's cold cheek, and, sighing deeply, turned and abruptly began to ascend the stairs.

The Reverend, Judd, and Dr. Briggs exchanged frantic glances. "Sir Robert—" Judd ventured.

Robert moved on.

"Sir—Sir Robert—" croaked the Reverend.

Robert did not respond.

"Sir Robert!" Dr. Briggs hastened after the squire, stopping him midflight. The doctor's communication was terse. Sir Robert shrugged. "Do as you must." His voice was husky; his face, a mask of grief.

Robert had withdrawn; the visitors then grouped quietly and whispered their individual plans for imminent departure. Those servants lingering in the hall hung silent and uncertain. To fire the household machinery Judd directed first one and then another until the bustle of systematic industry was once again set in motion. The Reverend gestured importantly to Dr. Briggs, who joined him in rapid discussion, and it was not many minutes before the coffin was closed and the body of Lady Frances readied for transfer to the hearse and from there to the mortuary.

Reverend Smythe ran the tired handkerchief over his face. "I am relieved to have the matter resolved at last," I heard him confess to the doctor. "I will admit to grave concerns there for a while—"

"The funeral will be held tomorrow, then?"

"And not a moment too soon!" The Reverend shook his head. "I must set about now, preparing the eulogy. Although the devil of it is, old chap," he hissed, "I haven't the foggiest what to say; I never really knew the lady—"

Dr. Briggs had agreed to stay at the house that night in the event that his professional services might be required, and I joined him at a solemn meal served in the dining hall.

In vain I prayed for Robert to appear.

Robert . . .

He had not even acknowledged my presence. Blindly he had hastened to his wife's side: his face tragic, destroyed; the hand that touched her lifeless cheek, trembling.

Robert . . .

He spared no look for me. He had eyes for none but the Lady Frances.

Robert . . .

No word. No gesture. No glance. Nothing for me at all. Oh, God, Robert . . .

My eyes brimmed and I rose abruptly. "Forgive me, Doctor, but I should like to retire now—"

"Good night, m'dear," Dr. Briggs smiled fondly. "I shall see you in the morning."

Tears blurred my sight, making my step unsteady on the stairs. The upper hall was still. Where was Robert? . . . In his room? In her room, remembering? I stifled a sob and stumbled weakly against my door. . . . Oh, God. I fell on the bed and wept. Robert . . . Robert . . .

Slipping into my room to say good night, Auntie Maude found my eyelids swollen and my pillow damp with tears. She cradled me in her arms, rocking me back and forth. "There, there, dear. Everything is going to be all right, you'll see," she tried to comfort me. "Lady Frances is with God now. . . ." When she had quieted me sufficiently, she tenderly sponged my hands and face and, wrapping me in the flannel nightdress, settled me under the straightened covers. "Good night, darling. Try and sleep . . . Remember, I am here if you need me . . . Try and sleep . . ."

Try and sleep . . . Robert . . .

But I did sleep, finally: the restless sleep attending desperate anguish. I thrashed, haunted by the grave set of Robert's mouth, the suffering in his dark eyes, his head bent low before the bier . . . his hand caressing that passive cheek . . . Oh, God . . . Robert . . .

"Elizabeth." I sat up; my eyes automatically sought the path . . .

His lips found mine. Hot, he tongued me. I was on fire. . . . I pulled my mouth from his to murmur, "Take me, Robert . . . Take me . . ." I moved under him. "Hurry," I begged. His loins throbbed as he entered; I cried aloud in the exquisite agony of passion.

Once the first spasms of rapture had subsided, I nestled close to my lover. "I thought you would not come—"

"Have I ever stayed away?"

"This time was different—"

"Hush—" His lips moved over my breast.

"Robert . . . you are free now—"

The nipple stood erect; gently, he imprisoned it with his teeth.

"Robert," I breathed.

His hands stroked the soft flesh of my belly. Quivering, I spread my legs wide. "Robert, love me—"

I could feel him hard against me.

"Robert," I cried, "love me—now—"

"Minx . . ."

"Now!"

Passion soared to new heights. Again and again he penetrated, filled me. Crazed, I writhed beneath him. "More, Robert . . . more . . ."

He laughed. "Insatiable minx . . ."

Again and again he swelled within me, thrusting deeper, faster, until dawn had retreated before the full sun of daylight. He stirred beside me.

"Don't go," I pleaded.

"I must."

"Once more." I molded my hips to his.

He chuckled, "It is late—"

I moved against him in suggestive rhythm.

His lips sought mine, "Minx . . ."

* * *

Eyes closed, I stretched my body, newly loved, the length of the bed, wriggling in remembered ecstasy. The door opened. I smiled. "Robert?"

"It is not Robert." The familiar voice was flat. I opened my eyes: Auntie Maude stood by my bed, looking down at me. "Cover yourself!" she hissed.

Saucily I raised my arms above my head. "Why should I?" I laughed. "Robert likes me this way."

"I saw Sir Robert leaving your room just now!"

I grinned.

"What was he doing here?"

I giggled, "Come now, Aunt . . ."

"You're a wanton hussy!"

I yawned. "And you're a bloody bore."

"His wife is not yet lying in her grave!" she sputtered.

I smirked.

"I have never . . . never . . . never in my whole life! Never!"—she was incoherent—"never have I known such behavior! Such disgraceful conduct! Never . . . never . . ."

I rolled over. "Close the door on your way out."

"Why! Why, you are shameless!" she rasped. "Shameless!"

"I said, on your way out."

"This house is a—brothel!"

I sat up. "If you do not approve of the arrangement here, Aunt," I said coldly, "then I suggest that you seek a position more to your taste—elsewhere—"

She flinched as if she had been slapped. She did not speak. Suddenly all color drained from her face.

"Out!" I muttered, turning over. "Get out . . ."

Chapter 57

"And . . . I say unto you: The reward in life is death . . . My people, fear not the stern, the cold . . . the empty, the bleak . . . Only in death can we reside with the Lord. . . . Only as the last faint breath is spirited away can we fly to Paradise, where the rose buds in the snow . . . the lilac on the thorn . . . where the apple blossom flowers in the straw. . . ." The Reverend's scrawny arms flailed; his harsh voice chafed the air. "Death is our haven . . . our release . . . our final sanctuary . . ." His leonine head drooped suddenly, to rise again slowly in full majesty. "As God offered up Canaan to Abraham, so does God offer up to each and all his supreme cloister: death. And so," he whispered, "has He offered up, this day, perpetual asylum to His Own beloved daughter, Frances . . ."

A respectful hush fell over the congregation. Heads craned, seeking a furtive glance at Robert, the bereaved, whose eyes were dark with grief, whose mouth was set in sorrow. Satisfied, their attention returned to the Reverend.

"Frances . . ." The Reverend paused. "Ah . . . Frances . . ."

A muscle knotted in Robert's jaw.

"Ah, Frances: so young, so beloved. One can ask: Why? Why? Why this young and beloved woman? Why was she taken from us prematurely? Yanked from tender arms too soon. Why?"

Robert's tormented hands clenched in his lap.

"But—" The Reverend Smythe leaned forward abruptly; cruelly, his eyes stabbed his flock. "Premature? Too soon? How, my people, do we know this? How, my people, *can* we know this . . . Premature . . . Too soon? Perhaps, yes, so it seems to us . . . But is the taking of our beloved Frances premature, too soon, in our Lord God's scheme of things—in his DIVINE PLAN?"

His smile was cunning. "I wonder . . ."

For a full minute the Reverend paced the dais in dramatic silence. His body then stiffened, turned, and with a fierce, jabbing motion he leveled a crooked forefinger at his congregation. "Frances was swept from life swiftly, irrevocably, despite the struggle of another to pull her back to earthly safety. Why? Why was mortal strength unequal to the task? Why did the rescue fail?" His eyes narrowed. "Why? I shall tell you why . . . Because, my people, the death of our Frances was—planned!"

. . . Oh, God . . . My heart thrummed wildly.

"Planned!" The Reverend's voice crescendoed, "I said, my people—PLANNED!"

Saliva flooded my mouth.

He raised his fist: the standard. "Planned, my people, by our Lord God, Who offered up ultimate retreat to His beloved daughter Frances—and, my people," he smiled in triumph, "she accepted it! None, not the arm of Hercules himself, could have stayed her flight to the gaping maw of the sea . . . held her from her rocky perch!" Exultant, the Reverend's eyes rolled upward. "No!" he bellowed, "only God! Sovereign over all!"

Limp with relief, I slumped back against the seat.

"Ah." The Reverend's expression softened; his voice grew hushed. "The little flame guttered . . . innocent, unlit in the world's dark ways . . ." He bowed his head. "Rejoice, my lamb," he whispered, "sorrow not, for ye have reached, betimes, the abode of the righteous . . . entered God's perfect shelter, untouched by the storms and winds of man's imperfect life . . ."

Sarah was frankly sobbing now.

Able to relax again, I allowed my eyes to stray about the nave, which was crowded to capacity and even beyond. The congregation, made up of villagers, tenants (farmers and their laborers), members of the household staff, and neighboring gentry, responded accordingly to the service. To the villagers and tenants this was, quite obviously, an event. The demise of anyone in the squire's immediate family constituted an important occasion, to be honored with proper deference, to be sure, but one that fired the imagination and set curiosity aflame. This was unfortunate: since their rank was such that none was assigned a seat with a favorable view, little moments of human interest often went unrecorded. To the gentry the funeral implied simply a gesture of respect paid to a like fellow and a time of dignified presence, not requiring the optimum vantage point offered by the front pews they ironically occupied. To acknowledge their close personal association with the deceased, the members of the household staff enjoyed an unaccustomed position of privilege, situated as they were just behind the gentry, treating them to frequent and audible bouts of sniveling.

The passing of the young, once beautiful bride of Wynds was a tragedy made still more poignant by the snuffing out in her womb of the Reverend's euphemistic "little flame": the unborn child, heir to Wynds. This double sorrow became the Reverend's tour de force, and at first he held his audience in complete thralldom. To give the Reverend his due, he had at his command an amazing variety of sly, shadowy expressions, each designed to mitigate, even thoroughly disguise, the indelicate state of pregnancy and its titillating implications. Public interest in the subject, however, after protracted exposure, understandably waned: The congregation became frankly restive, and the Reverend's subtle indirections were lost in the sounds of shuffling feet and the involuntary fits of coughing.

Only surreptitious glances cast at the squire, sent discreetly to measure his state of grief, or at the gentry in envious appraisal of their attire, sustained the villagers and tenants through the ordeal of the Reverend's eulogy, seeming by now interminable. Rapid eye movements betrayed the newer impatience of the gentry as they began to shift about uneasily. I had been moved to the desperation of counting heads. Only Robert retained the stoical posture of the suffering, the bereaved.

The keening of the organ, interpreted as the welcome conclusion to the Reverend's oration, lifted spirits, and we were invited to rise and join in triumphant song, thus exhorting Lady Frances on her last journey. A spate of thunderous chords heralded the ceremonial removal of the body; the four pallbearers stood at stiff attention then, moving as one, knelt, and, hefting the coffin onto their shoulders, began the solemn procession down the aisle, out the door, and to the cemetery in the churchyard adjacent.

Robert stood. Dark eyes grimly staring, he marched behind his wife's remains as they were carried slowly to her grave.

A heavy mist had moved in quietly from the sea, spreading its fragile layer of moisture and softening the stark bulk of the mausoleum that stood, mouth agape, in readiness. The ground had become spongy underfoot, dampening my skirts and heightening the already penetrating chill of death and winter.

The Reverend's graveside stand was aborted early, the mist having gradually given way to a moderate but persistent rain. Although it was clear that the adverse weather conditions worked no hardship on Our Vicar, the signs and hisses from his wife (and they increasingly explicit as she watched the magnificent plume on her ceremonial black hat first wilt, then snap altogether) brought him to a final, if reluctant, halt. The crowd dispersed: The gentry into their awaiting carriages; the farmers into less elaborate traps; and the laborers to walk, hunched against the rain, back to their hovels. The household staff was whisked away immediately in vehicles supplied by the manor, hastened that they might aid in the last-minute preparations for the formal funeral feast. Robert, hair now soaked with rain, knelt before the tomb, a solitary figure.

Dr. Briggs was at my elbow. "Come on back to Wynds with me—"

"But—" I inclined my head toward Sir Robert.

"Let him be alone with his grief," the doctor said gently.

The squire's guests had congregated in the dining hall before a sumptuous buffet. Conversation was lively, if appropriately subdued, as they transferred to their plates a jot of this and a daub of that from the infinite variety of culinary delights, uttering appreciative noises in recognition of the chef's genius.

Rain spread in solid sheets down the windowpanes, and

playful gusts began to fret the trees: still, no Robert. "Where could he be?" I asked Dr. Briggs.

"The man has just lost his wife, m'dear," he reminded me softly.

"I know." My eyes filled.

"Sir Robert seems to have a great reservoir of strength." The doctor shook his head sadly. "Sorrow as deep as his could destroy a weaker man . . ."

Suddenly my ears detected a disturbance outside in the courtyard. I could hear then the front door burst open, slam closed, and the slap of boots as they struck slick tile: Robert. His dark eyes glassy, Robert stood at the threshold of the dining hall, now hushed; absently he allowed Judd to draw the sopping cloak from his shoulders, then bowed formally to his guests. "My friends," he announced quietly, "I thank you for your presence here today in my behalf. I hope that you will stay as long as you like, but," his voice broke, "forgive me if I cannot join you." He bowed again, turned, and withdrew.

"Poor bastard," muttered Dr. Briggs. . . .

"It's about time!" I snapped later as Annie carried the bath water to my room. "Where have you been, slut? It's after eight!"

"It be a busy day today, miss—the funeral and all—" she whined.

"Don't imagine that it has been a jolly picnic for me, either!" I retorted nastily.

"No, miss."

"Well, don't just stand there! Fill the tub!"

"Yes, miss."

"And it had best be hot—"

"To scald a cat," she replied listlessly.

"You are certainly a disagreeable bitch this evening!" I remarked. "And that long face! Whatever is ailing you now?"

"Nothin', miss." Her lower lip trembled.

"If you go on mooning about like this, I shall instruct Miss Treadway to replace you with someone who is more cheerful."

Annie burst into tears.

"What in the world!" I exclaimed, thoroughly exasperated.

"That be it—" the girl blubbered.

"What—your replacement!" I laughed sourly. "Surely, chit, you are not so enamored of me as all that!"

"It be M-Miss Treadway—"

"What about her?"

"Her be g-gone," Annie stammered.

"Gone?" I repeated. "Where?"

Annie's eyes filled. "No one knows, miss—"

"What rubbish are you saying?"

"Her packed up everythin' and went off—just like that—this morning!"

"Where did she say—"

"She dint, miss," the girl whispered.

"She didn't say where she was going?"

A tear rolled down Annie's cheek. "No, miss." Her soft mouth quivered. "And her a nice lady—nicest one we ever—"

"Well, fill the tub and run along," I rapped impatiently, "and take your tears with you! I have seen enough tears these past days to last a lifetime. . . ." I eased into the warm water and let the soap bubbles float in little rainbow spheres over my breasts. I chuckled. . . . So, the old girl finally had had enough. . . . And a relief . . . A bloody, blessed relief . . .

The door opened. "Get out of here, Annie, I am in the bath—"

"So I see." Robert dipped his hands in the water and slid them over my body. I shivered in delight. "How long do you plan to stay in there?"

"I'll get out now—"

He smiled, wrapped me in a towel, and led me over to the bed. "You smell good enough to eat," he murmured, running his lips over my still damp legs and thighs; they opened in anticipation. "Hurry," I begged, "hurry . . ." As he possessed me he whispered, "I have been waiting for this all day. . . ."

Chapter 58

It was mid-April now, and spring had come to Wynds: Tender buds opened against a shimmering sky; the sea lay still, a docile, iridescent pool; breezes fanned my cheek, soft in their caress; the world was as a Paradise for lovers. From dawn to dawn Robert and I ate, played, and slept, wrapped in each other's arms. We mated eagerly, our flesh united as one: Throbbing, he swelled within me; crazed with desire, I surrendered. Insatiable. Unquenchable. Again. Again. Again . . .

"Robert," I murmured, snuggling against him, "we really should get married. . . ."

"I am in mourning, minx."

"I know. But Frances died on February seventeenth," I said, "that is two months—"

"Mourning lasts a year." His hand slid up my inner thigh.

"Not that long, surely."

His hand probed, demanding, delicious.

My hips swayed. "Robert," I breathed, "what if I should become pregnant . . ."

He laughed as he swung over me. "And what makes you think that could happen . . ."

Chapter 59

May passed into June: The countryside was frankly volup-
tuous now, plumed with thick grass feathers, ornamented
by blowsy trees, yielding bouquets of blossoms everywhere.
All was promising, abundant. Inviting . . .

As was I: My breasts were sweet and rich, my hips
tempting. I was eager to surrender . . . But, what use
. . . Why . . . ? Robert was away. This was the second
week of his absence, and I was inconsolable. Insane, I
raged and wept . . . Drove Artemis ruthlessly. Through
lush meadows, over tranquil streams, resting only atop
Smugglers' Peak, its panorama now merely leaves and sky,
the view of the sea but a memory.

Despite outrageous rebuffs and undisguised uninterest
on my part, Dr. Briggs remained the patient and attentive
suitor. I did nothing to conceal my indifference; my attitude, in fact, was barely civil. Still, he was not deterred.
And now, with Robert gone, he seemed to accelerate his
petition, plying me with daily invitations: to squire me in
his trap; to dine at the inn; or simply to ride abroad with
him through the flowering fields. Generally I refused. This
day I consented ungraciously: "All right, come along if you
must. . . ."

We had ridden most of the morning, stopping occasionally at a sluggish stream to freshen the horses, and were
now atop Smugglers' Peak, dismounted so that they might
graze. The sun had been hot and the air oppressively still.
Suddenly, leafy heads began to bob and shake, buffeted by
a sharp gust that swept up from the direction of the sea.
Louder and louder it whined, menacing the rocks below
with whipping waves. A roiling mass of dark clouds bil-
lowed thickly about the sun before swallowing it entirely.
The horses nickered and stomped, their manes flying.

"Looks as though we might be in for a spot of weather."
Dr. Briggs cast a worried look skyward.

"Exciting!" I cried, reveling in the strength of the wind as it tossed my hair and lashed my skirts.

"We should be heading back——"

Giddy, I raised my arms high in supplication.

Dr. Briggs moved toward me. "You're beautiful, Elizabeth."

"Storm!" I dared the sky.

"Elizabeth, darling . . ."

Then I heard them: the sounds. The thundering sounds . . . Exultant, I began to laugh. Tears splashed down my cheeks. I hugged my body close and rocked back and forth . . . Nearer. Nearer they came . . . Black against the blackened sky, hair and mane mingling, more frenzied than the clouds . . . "Robert!" I screamed. He reined sharply, leapt from his horse, and swept me into his arms. Our lips drowned in the desperate kiss. . . .

I did not know when Jonathan Briggs rode off. Nor did I care. . . .

That night, nestled in his arms, I stirred against him. "Robert, I love you so."

He kissed me gently.

"I cannot bear it when you leave me——"

"I am here with you now, minx."

"I know. But I want you with me always. If we were married, we could always be together." I cuddled closer. "I want to belong to you—truly—in every way——"

"All right, minx," he relented, "name the day."

I sat up. "Do you mean it?" I squealed.

He smiled. "I mean it."

"Well, then—tomorrow!"

He laughed. "The banns must be read first——"

"When that's done, then."

"I shall see to it personally."

"Right away?"

"Right away."

"Oh, Robert! I am so excited!" I cried. "I love you so——"

He drew me down. "Show me . . . minx . . ."

Part III

Chapter 60

We were married on the sixth day of July. The ceremony, conducted in the tiny vestry, was private, attended only by the principals and their witnesses. A squire from a neighboring village was enlisted to give me away, as none other than Dr. Briggs in Drewsby was appropriate to the assignment. "I really think you might have asked the doctor," Robert had remarked. . . . I had giggled, "Hardly . . ."

Miss Caroline was my maid of honor, not through choice, but because she alone in my limited acquaintance was remotely suitable and because Robert felt her presence to be mitigating under the circumstances. "What circumstances?" I had pouted. . . . "Minx," Robert had explained. "Remember, I am still in mourning."

The Reverend and Mrs. Smythe could conceal neither their surprise at nor a conspicuous disapproval of the marriage: that Robert, a widower of mere months, should stand in the House of God, kneel at His Altar for the purpose of consummating a new union, was an act of licentiousness that was inconceivable, particularly in a man of his rank and breeding. Adding fire to their consternation was the fact that they, indebted traditionally to the squire, were all but forced to sacrifice their only child on economy's pyre by permitting her to contribute to this dissolute performance.

Nor could they wrench their eyes from my abdominal region, hoping, I knew, to detect the ultimate implication of wantonness. Miss Caroline, on the contrary, was overtly delighted: My marriage to Robert implied a happy removal of dread competition, clearing the path to Dr. Briggs's damaged heart and empty hand. She fairly glowed in her own anticipation.

My gown was of airy white lace, a hurried creation of Miss Webster's ingenious needle, and I carried a bouquet of delicate summer flowers. Unadorned but for a single white rose pinned at my ear, my hair hung loose in heavy strands over my shoulders. Robert's eyes were eloquent: I knew that I was beautiful.

My hand shook a little as Robert slipped the Wyndham marriage band on my third finger, and my lips trembled when his, tender on mine, sealed the final vows.

I was Robert's wife.

"Congratulations, Sir Robert," the Reverend bowed courteously, "and Lady Elizabeth."

I blushed; Lady Elizabeth: I had not thought of that. . . .

Robert had arranged the transfer of my belongings from my rooms to the suite traditionally occupied by the mistress of the house and recently made vacant by the death of Lady Frances. I had requested that my new quarters be redecorated, wiped clean, as it were, of all traces of their former assignee and stripped of their cloying floral treatment. Now, drapes and hangings of rich crimson velvet struck vivid contrast to a background of milk white: both provocatively symbolic of my dream.

An intimate wedding feast had been prepared and served in the elegant sitting room and was, save for the chilled champagne, totally ignored.

Robert raised his glass in salute: "Lady Elizabeth."

I giggled. "Thank you, Sir Robert."

"May I escort you to the other room?"

"Sir," I protested coyly, "you move too fast."

"Another glass of spirits, then, my lady?"

"Thank you, sir." I fluttered my lashes demurely. I was heady on wine. Intoxicated with desire. "Perhaps . . ."

"Perhaps, what, Lady Elizabeth?" Robert murmured, sweeping me up in his arms.

"Perhaps . . . you had best hurry . . ."

This was joy. I was drenched with love. Robert's love burst within me, filled me, lifted me to new heights of ecstasy. Never had I been so happy. "Robert, I love you . . ."

He slipped a ruby ring on my finger. "How beautiful!" I breathed. My eyes filled suddenly. "I have nothing to give you, Robert. Nothing but myself."

His eyes smiled. "That will do nicely."

For a week we did not leave the rooms. Announced by a

timid knock and a discreet cough, the serving table bearing our meals was rolled into the sitting room and once there, virtually disregarded. "Why do they bother," I tittered, listening to the servants' dutiful performance as I lay on the bed in Robert's arms. "I am hungry only for you—"

"Shh," Robert laughed, and silenced my mouth with his . . .

Glorious, this Eden: Robert's torrent of passion flooded me, rushed to mingle with the raging current of my own love. . . . We were transported . . .

Our Paradise was invaded one day by Judd, who tapped diffidently but with uncommon persistence at the door. "Sir Robert," his voice called delicately.

"What is it, Judd?"

"Mr. Wade, sir," Judd apologized. "He has been waiting in the inglenook, sir, since nine this morning—"

"What for?" Robert asked indifferently.

"To discuss plans for the Summer Festival, I believe, sir." Judd coughed. "I believe your meeting was, er—prearranged—sir—"

Robert sighed. "I forgot."

"Sir Robert, er—what shall I tell the gentleman, sir?"

"What is the time?"

"I believe it to be some minutes past—one o'clock, sir."

"Advise Mr. Wade that I shall be down directly."

"Very good, sir. Thank you, Sir Robert." The door to the hall closed softly.

I stretched languidly. "Festival?"

"Drewsby's fête champêtre," Robert drawled.

I smiled. "Sounds rather like fun!"

"It must be put off this year, I'm afraid."

"But Robert—why?" I pouted.

"I am in mourning."

We fell against each other in helpless laughter. When mirth subsided, desire climbed. . . . Not until after three o'clock did Robert give audience to his waiting tenant. . . .

Chapter 61

On the sixteenth day of our marriage, as the first faint flush of dawn began to lift night's shadows from the room, I stirred. "Robert," I whispered. Sleepily I rolled toward him to press my body close to his. "Robert?" Lazily I reached for him. "Robert, why are you so far away?" My arms stretched wide to enfold my lover. "Robert—" My grasp was empty. I was awake now, fully: Robert was not there.

"Robert, where are you?" I leapt from the bed and ran through the suite of rooms, crying, "Robert! Robert, where are you? . . ." Tears welled in my eyes. . . . He had gone. . . . Where? Throwing myself on the bed, where love had flamed, I sobbed myself into uneasy sleep, waking confused and alone.

It was midmorning before I was able to collect myself, dress, and head for the stables. "Has Sir Robert saddled Ebon?" I asked Hartley without greeting.

"Yes, miss—er—Lady Elizabeth. Before dawn, he rode off."

"Where did my husband go?"

Hartley shrugged. "I don't know, Lady Elizabeth, ma'am. He don't tell me them things. But"—the stable master hesitated—"he had his satchel—"

"I see."

"Would you be after the mare, Lady Elizabeth?"

I nodded, unable to speak.

Standing on the crest of Smugglers' Peak, listening to the muffled moan of the turgid sea below, nudging its sluggish waves toward the shore, a diamond of summer sunlight kissed my ruby ring. For a moment my eyes were blinded. "Robert," I wept, "how could you have left me behind . . ."

We rode until both Artemis and I were almost past exhaustion, then headed for the stable, where, with deference

supreme, Hartley lifted me from the saddle before returning the mare to her stall. His eyes chose to ignore the dense
layer of foam sudsing the horse's back.

Passing through on my way to the house, I found the
garden sweltering and still and the bench vacant in the
breathless July heat; the gate, unmoving.

Next to the staircase rising up from the great hall, head
cocked in the posture of the avid listener, stood a tall
woman well into her middle years; around her waist hung
the chatelaine's heavy ring of keys. She was in the attentive
company of Judd, who held her in serious conversation.
Face stern, body spare, she was a stranger. At my entrance
the butler paused and approached me, motioning the
woman to follow. "Lady Elizabeth," he asked respectfully,
"if you have a moment?"

"Yes, Judd?"

"May I present to you, madam, the new housekeeper at
Wynds"—he indicated the woman at his side—"Mrs.
Clyde."

"Lady Elizabeth," she murmured, and curtsied deeply.
I returned the fulsome gesture with a perfunctory nod.

"Mrs. Clyde comes to us with an impeccable character."
Judd seemed eager to commend his most recent acquisition. "Already she has an astonishing 'lay of the land'—"

"So soon?" I was surprised.

Mrs. Clyde seemed perplexed.

"Well, has she not just arrived?" I asked Judd.

He colored. "Er—she has—it has been over—well, two
weeks now, ma'am. . . ."

"And I came none too soon!" the woman sniffed.

"Oh?" My eyebrows rose.

"The housekeeping was in a state of shambles! The staff
totally undisciplined!" She shook her head. "Most unpro-
fessional! But," she continued briskly, "I have no intention of permitting the reins to lie slack as my predecessor
seems to have done—"

"To obviate any future indiscretion, Mrs. Clyde," I
stated flatly, "I shall inform you now: Your predecessor
happens to have been my aunt." I turned from the woman
abruptly and ascended the stairs. . . . Auntie Maude
. . . Where had she gone? . . Where was she now? . . .

Strong habit led me to the door of my old room; curiosity turned the knob. The last trace of Elizabeth Knowlton had been expunged, the room was impersonal again. The bed where passion had flared—now cool, indifferent . . . the wardrobe inviolate, hugging close its secrets once more. Elizabeth Knowlton was as a stranger here, less than a memory. . . .

But there was no Elizabeth Knowlton; now, only Elizabeth Wyndham, wife to the master of Wynds . . . to Robert . . .

I slept only fitfully that night: The air was oppressive, heavy with the threat of rain. . . .

For hours earlier I had prayed for Robert's return . . . craved his arms to hold me close, his lips on mine, raising me to that glorious realm of love. . . . He did not come. . . .

Long in vain I had waited for the dream, for the vibrant path that lighted my way to the golden room . . . For the whisper: "Elizabeth . . . Elizabeth . . ."

Without success my tired eyes had strained to pierce the void of the starless night, seeking the light in the tower . . . To watch it flicker, sway back and forth, an uneasy captive in the window . . .

Nothing . . .

Fulfilling its promise, the rain came: a summer spray, warm and steamy and depressing.

As if caged, I ranged about the suite of rooms, pausing now and then to stare through rain-specked panes. I could not ride, loose this wild urgency in a race through grassy fields . . . let it fly with the winds on Smugglers' Peak . . . Restless, I paced . . . Looked out. Strode. Stared . . . The tower rose in fluid lines against the sky. The tower! I could explore the tower . . . I was mistress here now; I could go anywhere I pleased.

I drew myself straight: In fact, I would see the entire house today. As yet I had not been permitted a proper tour; Auntie Maude had considered my position as companion to preclude such an expedition as both imprudent and a glaring breach of etiquette.

Not now.

I dressed quickly and ran down to the great hall where, lips thin and eyes glittering, Mrs. Clyde was upbraiding a young housemaid. The housekeeper's voice, sharp and cold, slashed at the girl, whose blue eyes were swimming with tears. At my approach Mrs. Clyde ended the objurgation, and the girl hurried away, snuffling. "Lady Elizabeth." The woman trained on me a fawning smile.

"What was that scene about?" I asked.

Mrs. Clyde dismissed the matter as trivial: "Only the simplest housekeeping detail, Lady Elizabeth."

"Send Judd to me at once."

An ugly stain spread over Mrs. Clyde's face. "Lady Elizabeth, the girl was crying over nothing—"

"I am not concerned with the girl," I advised her tartly, "only with Judd."

She relaxed. "I am afraid that he is not here, Lady Elizabeth."

"Not here?"

"He is out with a Mr. Ward, I believe Mr. Judd said . . ."

"Wade?"

"Ah, yes—Mr. Wade."

"Whatever for?"

"On an errand of Sir Robert's, I believe."

I sighed. "When will he return?"

"I really could not say, Lady Elizabeth, except that Mr. Judd informed me that he might be away most of today and was anxious that perhaps I might not be able to carry on successfully in his absence—"

"And why shouldn't you?" I asked coolly.

Her smile was smug. "Of course, Mr. Judd's concerns are entirely without foundation. I have a perfect control on the Wynds Method—even this early in my position." Jingling the ring of keys as she did so, the woman reached into the enormous pocket of her black dress and extracted a well-worn paper. "I have here a map and full description of every room in the manor." She unfolded it carefully. "I have committed it to unerring memory already."

"A map? Let me see that!"

"Certainly, Lady Elizabeth."

The map was roughly executed but childishly clear.

"This suits my needs," I crowed. "I shall take this along whilst I have a look round."

"Er—Lady Elizabeth—" Mrs. Clyde hastened to intercept me. "Pardon me, but are you planning to—"

"My plans are hardly your concern," I reminded her curtly.

Again color streaked her face. "It is only, madam, that many of the rooms are locked. And"—a note of triumph crept into her voice—"I have the keys."

My eyes fell to the ring encircling her waist. I could have requested a more agreeable companion on my first real examination of my home—even the dour Judd. But no matter: Obviously I had need, if with reservation, of her services. "Very well," I agreed, "come along. You may conduct me."

"Delighted, Lady Frances! If you will follow me, then, I shall escort you in proper order, which is the Wynds Method."

I was forced to admit that the housekeeper proved an excellent guide. For a newcomer, her knowledge of the house was remarkable indeed. She was well-informed, precise, and energetic.

More extensive than I had expected, the manor afforded palatial accommodations, among these a guest wing consisting of a series of rooms, each flawlessly appointed and all ready for instant occupancy with only a brief airing or a match to the fitted grate. The cellar, a labyrinth, made me glad for both the company and the expertise of Mrs. Clyde, who knew where lanterns and matches were stored and who led me through its intricate passageways, getting lost only twice.

"Whew!" she mumbled to herself after we had chronicled the wines, "that needs a thorough cleaning, I must say!" She brushed a sticky cobweb from her black skirt. "I shall certainly set those lazy chits on their task, tomorrow. . . ." She took my arm. "Careful of the damp, Lady Elizabeth."

"The sea!" I exclaimed in awe. "I can hear the sea!"

"And no wonder!" the woman snorted, "slapping against the walls as it does. A miracle the place has stood all these

years!" She waved the lantern about. "I think that's everything worth seeing down here, Lady Elizabeth."

"Wait!" I stopped her. "What is that?" I wrenched the
lantern from her grasp and held it high. On the far wall,
chiseled in sweating golden stone, climbed a narrow, curving staircase. Dizzied, I felt a strange throbbing sensation
in my temples: It was the staircase in my dream. . . .
"Where does it go?" I whispered.

"What, Lady Elizabeth?"

"The staircase. Where does it go?"

"Outside, to the little tower courtyard."

Walking drunkenly, I followed the lantern's equally unsteady beam toward the winding stairs.

"Lady Elizabeth!" Mrs. Clyde shouted, "let me hold the
lamp!" She took it from my trembling fingers and gasped.
"Your hands! Like ice!" Her eyes searched my face. "Are
you all right, madam, you've turned that pale!"

I shrugged her off.

"My lady, there is a door at the top. And it is locked.
Pray, do let me precede you!" She ran ahead of me, careful to direct the light at my feet.

I did not need a light; I could have climbed these stairs
blindfolded. Trancelike I placed one foot before the other,
my ears straining for the whisper: "Elizabeth . . .
Elizabeth . . ." Only Mrs. Clyde's anxious clucking and
words of caution rose above the sounds of the irritable,
moving sea.

"No need to soak yourself, Lady Elizabeth," Mrs. Clyde
protested as I stepped onto the "tower courtyard," which
was nothing more than a small enclosure with haphazard
grass covering, untrimmed and rife with weeds. My eyes
were drawn immediately to the tower, its rise majestic,
even in this unkempt setting, as it thrust high, daring the
stormy skies; at its base, almost entirely concealed by a
lush growth of ivy: a door. The door to the tower! "The
key!" I rasped at Mrs. Clyde. "Give me the key!"

"What key, Lady Elizabeth?"

"The key to the tower!"

"But, madam," she said, "I do not have it."

"What do you mean, you do not have it? I thought you
had all the keys to Wynds on that bloody contraption!"

Embarrassment clogged her face. She stiffened. "I do not have that particular key, Lady Elizabeth."

"Then, who does?"

"Sir Robert, alone, I believe."

"I shall ask Judd."

"Very well, Lady Elizabeth."

Chapter 62

After an absence of nearly two weeks Robert returned to Wynds one morning, a few hours before dawn. His hands suddenly kneading my breasts, and lips insistent on mine, awakened me. "Robert!" I cried and wound my arms around his neck. He took me immediately. "Robert, you're hurting me," I whimpered, pulling back.

He laughed, "Minx," driving harder, thrusting farther.

"Robert—"

Faster he rode; deeper he plunged. I felt torn apart. "Please, Robert, please!"

Passion spent, he rolled off and fell asleep at once. Tears smarted from behind my eyes and slid down my cheeks. Forlorn, I whispered, "Robert . . ."

Robert slept until noon. Standing by the bed, I watched his handsome face, flushed in sleep, ached to kiss the smile curving his mouth; to smooth the lock of black hair that had slipped at a rakish angle over his forehead. Robert . . . His eyes opened and he grinned. "Lady Elizabeth, if I am not mistaken—" He drew me close in his arms.

"I missed you so—" I was bursting with love.

"I am back now."

"Where did you go?"

He kissed me tenderly. "Away."

"But where?"

"Away." He mouthed my breasts. "Now, an end to the questions."

"I wish I could have gone with you."

He laughed. "Impossible."

"But, Robert, I want to be with you always."

He kissed the hollow of my neck. "Hush."

"I cannot bear it without you."

"Then don't waste precious time with foolish questions," he said, caressing my thighs.

"Promise you'll let me go next time," I begged.

"I am only thinking about right now . . ."

I was trembling with desire. "Robert, love me . . . Now!"

He smiled. "I thought you'd never ask . . ."

I lazed upon the bed, admiring my husband as he stood before the mirror, adjusting his ascot. I reveled in his handsome face, in the figure that stood straight and tall and lean. My heart swelled with love: Robert . . .

"Lady Elizabeth," he teased, "are you never going to stir from that bed?"

"When I have done looking at you," I sighed.

"Are we to go riding, or not?"

"Robert," I said slowly, "what is in the tower?"

He stiffened. "The tower?"

"Yes. Mrs. Clyde said—"

"Who the devil is Mrs. Clyde?"

"Our new housekeeper."

"I see."

"Mrs. Clyde told me that only you have a key to the tower—"

"So?"

"Is that true?"

"And if it is?"

"Nothing . . . but . . . I am ever so anxious to find out what is there—"

"A pile of old masonry," he shrugged.

I sat up and regarded him seriously. "Then who lights the lamp there at night?"

"Lamp?"

"Yes. A light shines from the tower in the middle of the night—"

He frowned. "You have seen this—light?"

Excited, I nodded. "Yes, many times."

"I think you deal in fancies."

"No, Robert," I protested, "I have seen it! Truly, I have!"

He bent and kissed my cheek. "There is nothing here to trouble you, minx," he said lightly. "Hurry and dress."

"Robert," I coaxed, "take me there."

He tensed. "Don't be tiresome, Elizabeth."

"Please, Robert," I wheedled prettily.

"Elizabeth," he said quietly, "I have said no. Now, I suggest that you drop the subject." He turned and left the room.

Robert was not waiting in the great hall, nor was he in his study. He must have gone to the stables, I told myself. . . . Peter, looking up from his task of sweeping Ebon's empty stall, shook his head. "No, Lady Elizabeth, him gone."

"Gone?" My head swam. "Where?"

The boy lifted scrawny shoulders. "Him not say. Him get on Ebon and ride away, s'all. Fast like, seems so."

"Did he carry a satchel?"

The boy's eyes were blank. "I can't recall, ma'am."

Frantically I urged Artemis over the dusty countryside, through meadows shimmering with heat, fording dry, choked streams. . . . "Find him, Artemis," I shouted, "find him . . ." Smugglers' Peak baked under a hazy summer sky. Leaves hung limp and still. The sea grumbled, but only listlessly. Robert was not here. "Oh, God," I prayed, "let him come back to me."

Ebon was standing on the cobbles when I returned to the stable yard, only mildly resisting Hartley's patient efforts to groom him after what must have been a wild ride. The stallion's sleek black coat was filmed with foam, and his eyes showed the white of frenzy. Artemis nickered as we neared, and Hartley hastened to lift me from my saddle.

The bench, crouching in the hushed deserted garden, sleepily drank the sun's relentless rays. The wooden gate, dropping on its rusted hinges, only drowsed. I hurried past.

It was not until Judd guided me to my chair in the dining hall that I was to see Robert again that day. He rose immediately. "Ah, Lady Elizabeth," he bowed. His dark eyes swept appreciatively over the bodice of my lemon satin gown and rested on the full swell of my breasts riding above it. "You are ravishing," he breathed. "Judd, pour Lady Elizabeth some wine." Robert's cheeks were flushed and his hand a trifle unsteady as he raised his glass in a toast. "To my charming bride!"

"Robert—" I swallowed the words that would have asked why he had ridden off without me.

He took my hand in his. "What is it, my love?"

"I missed you," I said simply.

"Have you finished with this ridiculous meal?" he whispered suddenly.

I nodded.

"Let us, then, retire. . . ."

Chapter 63

For over a week Wynds was caught in a pocket of dizzying summer heat. "We should take to the water," Robert suggested one blistering afternoon as we trotted the horses leisurely over the parched moor.

"I don't know how to swim."

"I shall teach you, then."

"But Robert." I held back. "I am frightened of the water."

"Frightened? With me?" His dark eyes challenged mine.

"Robert—"

"Come along, love, I shall race you there—"

The sea moved lazily before us, absently licking the narrow beach. "See, minx," Robert crowed as he shed his clothes, "La Mer is a fraud. Nothing more than an enormous bathtub!"

My eyes were drawn to the cliff jutting out above; traveled slowly down the ragged rocks . . . Where had she lain . . . Which had stayed her flight to the sea . . . Which had become her stony bier . . .

Robert was splashing boyishly in the water. "Come in, love!" he invited.

"Robert—"

"Take off your clothes and jump in. Don't be frightened, I'm here."

Icy water bit into my feet as I gingerly dipped a toe in the feathery froth; hot sun seared my naked back.

"Walk out to me," Robert coaxed.

"No—I—"

He swam toward me and took my hand in his. "Come, nymph, I shall be your fins!" As he clasped me around the waist, drawing me into the deeper water, I threw my arms around his neck in pure fright. "Easy," he soothed. "Easy, now. What did I tell you—not a bit bad—"

"Don't take me out any farther, Robert, please!" I implored.

He laughed, "Just a little way."

"Robert, please!"

"Only a mite." Already his feet were kicking in the water.

A gentle swell washed over my face. "Robert!" I sputtered. "I'm drowning!"

He laughed.

"Robert!" I shrieked. "Take me back!" I was sobbing now.

With easy grace Robert swam me back to shore. I fell on the beach, shivering in the torrid summer sun.

Chapter 64

A subtle presage of autumn drew off the sultry air late one afternoon. Gray clouds, driven in from the sea by a suddenly chill wind, dulled the glassy skies and banked the fires of the sun. Sharp gusts lifted the horses' tails and whipped their coarse manes. Reined up high on Smugglers' Peak, I watched in fascination as the restless mass gathered and swirled, submerging the sun and then permitting it to escape briefly in iridescent shafts.

Robert was exhilarated. His handsome face turned full on the horizon, his dark eyes danced as the lustrous colors played over the struggling sky.

"It is so exciting here!" I breathed.

Robert did not speak.

"To think," I sighed happily, "that this beautiful place is mine now, too!"

"Yours?" Robert swung toward me. "All this is mine, Elizabeth. Wynds belongs to me." His eyes were flat. "Remember that. Always, remember that." He wheeled his horse sharply and with his whip struck the sleek rump a stunning blow, and as a molten ebony streak they galloped down the precipice and disappeared from sight. He did not look back.

That night Robert rode me hard. "Please," I cried out, "you're hurting me . . ."

Exultant, he laughed.

Chapter 65

My husband escorted me to the dining hall on his arm the next evening. His dark eyes were tender as he murmured, "Have I told you that you look enchanting tonight?"

My heart swelled with love.

As the meal progressed Robert became preoccupied. Frequently he signaled Judd to refill his wineglass, and his eyes grew too brilliant, and his manner oddly excited. His gaze was drawn to the window almost as if he were monitoring the darkening sky. At last he rose abruptly and suggested, "You go on upstairs, love."

"Aren't you coming?" I asked.

"Not yet," he said, "I have a business matter to resolve."

"Don't be long," I begged.

He tilted my chin upward and gently kissed my lips. "Run along, minx," he whispered.

I waited for him to come to bed. Only disappointed, at first, I tossed from side to side; after a while I grew anxious. Where was he? Why didn't he come? I rose and began my restless pacing the length of the room, stopping now and then to look out of the window at the soft summer night. Suddenly I saw it: the light. The light in the tower. I knelt by the sill and, mesmerized, watched the uneasy beam sway back and forth. Back and forth. I waited for its sudden little death, making the tower once again an eyeless monster menacing the sky.

Who held that lamp?

Robert did not come to my bed that night. I lay still, knowing dully that he had gone away again.

Where? Why?

Chapter 66

Mrs. Clyde, it appeared, was waiting for me as I descended the stairs to the great hall. She stood precisely where Lady Frances had lain in state. "Madam," the woman's greeting was brisk, efficient, "if I might request a moment. There are a few particulars concerning the staff I feel require immediate attention."

"Later, Mrs. Clyde," I delayed her request. "First I should like the key to the tower courtyard."

"The key?" The housekeeper was surprised. "Er, of course. I shall be happy to guide you myself."

"That will not be necessary, Mrs. Clyde," I refused. "Simply ready a lantern for my use and give me the key."

"Very well, madam." She rushed off obediently.

As I waded through the shaggy grass matting the small enclosure odd clumps of weed spears rippled, stirred by a timorous breeze. Protected from strong sea winds by the tower's bulk and its high wall, the diminutive courtyard augured sweltering heat, even in the mild sun of a mid-morning. The tower door was narrow, arched, and had been constructed of heavy oak, cut in a thickness of at least two inches. Its hinges were completely concealed by a plenteous growth of ivy, which clung and climbed by means of a tenacious root system and provided a covering of dark green leaves that whispered their brittle message to the faint breeze. The handle was rust-coated and . . . my heart thrummed: The lock bore the clean scratches of recent use. I tore at the ivy: If only I could pry loose the hinges. Yanking at a sturdy vine I snapped it unexpectedly, hurling me backward and onto the ground.

Probing a severe bruise on my hip, I sat for a moment. . . . What in the world was responsible for that, I wondered, massaging the injured area. . . . I righted myself and threaded inquisitive fingers through the shaggy turf. They struck a resisting object. Still kneeling, I brushed the strands of grass free: There lay a stone; on it, letters, feathery and crudely scored: K - a - t - h - e - r - i - n - e, 1832–1854 . . .

Rocking back on my heels, I looked again. The markings were faint but distinguishable: K - a - t - h - e - r - i - n - e, 1832–1854.

A house pet? Dog? Cat?

Not likely: This Katherine had lived for twenty-two years, an improbable life-span for a domestic animal . . .

What, then?

Who, then? . . .

I must learn the answer. Who? Who would tell me? A servant: possibly. A servant: surely. But which one? Annie? I laughed sourly: not that one. Judd: ridiculous! Sarah? No. Mrs. Clyde had only just arrived. Ian: no longer; Ian was lost forever. . . . Hartley, Peter . . . They were ever unresponsive. . . . Who, then? As companion to Lady Frances, I had made no friends amongst the staff; could boast no champion. And as mistress of Wynds, I must not betray uncertainty; exhibit curiosity; encourage familiarity.

If only Auntie Maude were here. As housekeeper, she could have penetrated the secret of the stone. . . . The secret of K - a - t - h - e - r - i - n - e . . .

Auntie Maude . . . Where had she gone? Where was she now?

Robert would know. But, Robert was away. . . . How could I wait until he returned? . . .

As I reentered the cellar, descended the narrow, curving staircase so known to me, I listened for the whisper . . . "Elizabeth . . . Elizabeth . . ." and was rewarded only with the bawl of the sea as it struck against the walls of stone. . . .

With Robert gone, the tower, its wayward light, its neglected courtyard, now token cemetery, became my obsession. At night I crouched by the window, my eyes straining, eager to track its restless beam as the lamp swayed back and forth . . . back and forth . . . Before my morning ride I made a daily pilgrimage to the enclosure, as though through my fidelity its secrets would lie exposed. . . . There, I stood before the solid tower door, grasped the rough handle, traced my fingers over the network of fine scratches marring the ancient metal of the lock. . . . And the stone. Carefully I swept the grass from its rough face: K - a - t - h - e - r - i - n - e, 1832–1854 . . . The letters were there; I had not imagined them.

With Robert gone, I waited for the shimmering path. For the elusive dream. Yearned for a glimpse into the gold room. For a glimpse of—them. Not since I had become Robert's wife had I been led to that door. Not since I had become Robert's wife had I seen—them.

Why had the dream vanished? . . . Where had it gone? . . .

Where had Robert gone? . . .

Chapter 67

A spraying shower put a premature end to my ride one afternoon. It was ten days after Robert's departure. Reining up in the stable yard, I permitted Peter to lift me from my saddle and take the mare to her stall. He was alone. "Peter," I said, carefully casual, "does 'Katherine' mean anything to you?"

He scratched his head. "It be a girl's name, Lady Elizabeth."

"Yes, Peter, I know." I smiled. "Have you ever known a Katherine?"

"Yes, ma'am."

My heart leapt. "Who?"

"Me sister, ma'am. Her be three." He pulled on the mare's bridle. "That be all, ma'am?"

"Yes. Thank you, Peter."

A thin layer of moisture clung to the bench in the garden. The gate swung sluggishly on its noisy hinges. At the side of the dirt path the broken body of a small wren lay stiffening, its feathers damp with rain and streaked with drying blood. I gave a little cry and stood, transfixed. My legs began to tremble violently, and a film of perspiration formed over my face and neck. Saliva soured in my mouth. It was some moments before I was able to summon the strength necessary to walk the short distance remaining to the house.

Mrs. Clyde was standing in the great hall, exactly where the coffin had lain. "Lady Elizabeth!" she exclaimed. "You are ill!" She stared. "You are pale as a ghost!"

Chapter 68

Late one afternoon I returned from the stable yard and, eyes averted, passed quickly through the garden where the bench squatted, idle, and the gate lounged, lazily ajar. Once in the great hall, I was waylaid by Mrs. Clyde, who rushed over from her customary niche (the corner in which the bier had reposed) to greet me: "Lady Elizabeth, you have guests!" She made it a pronouncement.

"Guests?" I was surprised.

"The Reverend Smythe and Family," she informed me. "I suggested they wait in the inglenook. Er—Lady Elizabeth—" She paused. "I have taken the liberty of ordering tea—"

I sighed, "Tea!" then turned. "Thank you, Mrs. Clyde."

The Reverend executed an elaborate bow at my entrance. "Ah! Lady Elizabeth!" His smile was ingratiating.

"Reverend," I murmured a polite response.

"Lady Elizabeth!" Mrs. Smythe positively gushed.

Even Miss Caroline was disposed to be particularly pleasant.

"How nice to see you," I managed.

"In the neighborhood," the Reverend was bluff. "Just thought we'd stop by."

"Yes!" Mrs. Smythe gurgled.

Miss Caroline smiled agreeably.

"I have ordered tea," I said.

"Oh!" The Reverend feigned dismay. "You should not have troubled!"

"No bother," I assured him wanly.

"I understand from the housekeeper that Sir Robert is away—" he remarked conversationally.

"Yes."

"Is he to be gone long?"

"I—well—he had some business to attend to—"

"Of course!" the Reverend nodded his head briskly.

"Mrs., er—Clyde—is it—is a new addition to the household," observed Mrs. Smythe, "replacing Miss—ah—Treadway, I believe?"

"Yes."

"Miss Treadway was your blood relative, if I am not mistaken?" The woman was dogged.

"Yes."

"Why did she—" Mrs. Smythe persisted, but was silenced at last by a murderous glance from her husband.

A flustered housemaid, directed every step of the way by the imperious Mrs. Clyde, appeared then with the tea, placing the tray on an awaiting table. "Is everything satisfactory, Lady Elizabeth?" The housekeeper hovered anxiously.

"I shall ring if not, Mrs. Clyde," I dismissed her.

"Delectable!" The Reverend noisily smacked his lips in hearty appreciation.

"The pastry is light as a down feather!" Mrs. Smythe complimented effusively. "Not so, Caroline?"

"My, yes!" The girl's enthusiasm was promptly obedient.

Mrs. Smythe fastened adoring eyes on her daughter. "You had best commit this crust to memory, darling!"

Miss Caroline blushed.

"Especially now!" Mrs. Smythe added with pointed emphasis.

"Oh, Mama!" the girl giggled.

"Our Caroline has 'plans'!" the mother confided cryptically. "You know—"

"Tut, tut, my dear," the Reverend chided fondly, "how can Lady Elizabeth find concern in our daughter's personal 'arrangements'!" His remarks, too, were coyly punctuated.

The stain of delicious embarrassment suffused Miss Caroline's plain face. "Oh, Mama, stop—"

"She is so shy!" Mrs. Smythe confessed, settling a loving gaze on Miss Caroline, who dropped her head on her breast in girlish protestation.

"Now, now, Mother," the Reverend objected again, this time with a roguish wink. "I am certain that Lady Elizabeth does not wish to hear our 'news'!"

"Pshaw, you two!" Mrs. Smythe's scolding was coquettish. "Lady Elizabeth"—she fixed a triumphant smile on me directly—"our little girl is about to take an 'important step'!"

"Oh, Mama!" Miss Caroline tittered a rapturous denial.

"Darling, Lady Elizabeth will surely be delighted to share with you this common bond—such a new bride herself!"

Miss Caroline's eyes glowed.

"Our darling girl, Lady Elizabeth"—to Mrs. Smythe the disclosure was a conquest—"is about to be wed!"

"Oh?" I affected interest. "And who is the fortunate groom?"

Mrs. Smythe settled back smugly in her chair. "Dr. Briggs! Dr. Jonathan Briggs!"

Dr. Briggs! I was dizzy. Dr. Briggs! My head reeled. Dr. Briggs marry Miss Caroline? How could that be? ". . . I love you," he had whispered, "remember that: I love you . . ." ". . . marry me and what I have will be yours . . ." He had pulled me close: "Dammit, Elizabeth, I love you . . ." ". . . marry me and I shall make you safe . . . I love you . . . love you . . . love you . . ."

Marry Miss Caroline? How could that be?

"It will, of course, be a small wedding—with Sir Robert in mour—" Mrs. Smythe bit her lip.

Dr. Briggs! Marry Miss Caroline!

"The wedding itself doesn't matter," the girl simpered, "only the bride and groom. . . ."

Dr. Briggs and—you?

. . . go . . . please, go . . . now . . . go . . . I cannot hear any more of this . . . go . . .

"If you will excuse me." I stood unsteadily. "I am suddenly not well. The heat, I expect . . ."

"Of course, my dear." Mrs. Smythe was instantly sympathetic. She rose, but not before stealing a surreptitious glance at my abdominal region and in turn casting a knowing eye at her husband. "We were just going anyway . . ."

"Forgive me," I murmured, running to the stairs, "forgive me . . ."

Mrs. Clyde, stationed as usual where the coffin had lain, watched with surprise and curiosity my rapid ascent. . . .

Chapter 69

The winds had shifted, and faint markings of frost stiffened the browning meadow grass, before Robert finally clattered into the courtyard at Wynds. Dusk had fallen early on that September night, and I was already in my suite, awaiting my dinner tray. The commotion outside drew me to the window, and I saw my husband, black cloak flying, leap from his lathered horse and bound into the house. The door to my room burst open and he swept me into his arms, kissing me hungrily. "Robert!" I cried, "you're back!"

"None other, minx!" he chuckled, kissing me again.

"I thought you would never come!" I sighed.

"I am here now and famished!"

"I was about to dine in my room—"

"I shall join you. Judd!" he shouted from the upper hall. "Food! Enough for a small army! And wine! Red and chilled!"

He ate quickly, washing down the meal with great gulps of wine. He was exhilarated: face flushed and eyes bright. He pulled me down on the bed beside him. "Well, minx," he asked, slipping the gown from my shoulders, "how have you been occupying your time in my absence?"

"Riding, mostly," I said, adding shyly, "and exploring the house."

"Judd take you around?" he asked, blowing in the hollow of my neck.

"No. Mrs. Clyde."

"The new housekeeper?"

I nodded. "Robert," I said slowly, "who was Katherine?"

I felt him stiffen. "How do you know about her?"

"I was in the tower courtyard—"

"What were you doing there?" he asked sharply.

"I wanted to have a closer look at the tower—and I found the stone—with her name scratched on it—"

"I see."

"Who was she, Robert?"

"My first wife."

I jerked upright. The bed spun wildly . . . His first wife . . . The room whirled . . . Robert's first wife . . . Moments passed before I was able to speak. "But I thought—"

Robert was silent.

"I thought—M-Margaret—was your f-first wife," I managed at last, recalling her grave in the churchyard cemetery.

"No."

"Who was Katherine?" I whispered.

"I have told you, Elizabeth." His tones were measured.

"Why," my mouth was dry, "is she not buried in the crypt where—Margaret—" My voice trailed away.

"She could not be placed in consecrated ground."

"Why?"

"She killed herself."

"Killed herself!" I gasped. Oh, my God. "Why?"

"She neglected to tell me," he said coolly.

"Was Katherine—"

"Enough about Katherine," Robert said abruptly, pulling me down again, "you are my wife now. . . ."

Chapter 70

Katherine dominated my every thought, sleeping and waking. . . . Killed herself . . . Why? . . . The crude little marker recorded that she had been only twenty-two at her death. . . . Why would a woman, so young, mistress of Wynds, married to Robert, who was handsome, wealthy . . . take her own life . . . Why? . . .

"Was she beautiful, Robert?" I asked him the next morning as his hand reached for the bell cord to summon the breakfast tray.

"Who?"

"Katherine."

"Yes."

"Was Margaret?"

"Was Margaret what?"

"Beautiful."

"Yes. Of course."

"How did she—die?" I tried to appear offhand.

"An internal ailment."

"Internal ailment?" I recited his words dumbly.

"Stomach, I believe," Robert said smoothly. "Dr. Mondale was never able to pronounce a definitive diagnosis."

. . . And he—Dr. Mondale—was dead; Jonathan Briggs had told me that. . . .

"Was Frances—beautiful?"

"Yes. And," he said evenly, "you know how she died. . . ."

. . . I knew how Frances had died . . . Of course I knew: I killed her. . . . Oh, God . . . I killed her. . . . I killed Frances. . . . .

. . . But, Katherine had taken her own life. . . . Why? . . .

"Why, Robert?"

"Why what?" he replied shortly.

"Why did Katherine take her own life?"

"I have said, Elizabeth, all I intend to on the subject of my first wife."

"But—"

He sighed. "This is an impossible inquisition, my dear. One which I can no longer countenance." He rose abruptly. "I shall take my meal in the dining hall, after all." The door closed quietly behind him.

Exhausted, I fell back on the bed. . . . Oh, God . . . Tears slipped from behind my eyelids. . . . Katherine, a suicide . . . Frances, a murder . . . My murder, for I killed her . . . Hot tears scourged my eyes. Savage sobs constricted my chest. I began to retch cruelly; my stomach heaved; the saliva in my mouth thickened as clabber. . . . I have killed. . . .

. . . and deliberately . . .

The spasm quieted at last and I managed to doze briefly, although tortured alternately by Katherine, the shadowy unknown, and then by Frances, wraith, clawing the empty air, hurtling to death's perch . . . I awoke with swollen eyes and a throat raw from gagging . . . I must visit the grave again . . . perhaps the stone could tell me something . . .

Mrs. Clyde commanded her customary post in the great hall. . . . Why must she always stand there: directly where Frances's body had reposed . . . The housekeeper nodded respectfully, "Lady Elizabeth."

"I should like the key to the tower courtyard," I announced immediately.

The woman's level brows elevated slightly, but she withdrew the key from the ring promptly and again extended her services as guide. "That will not be necessary," I declined, "I shall manage alone."

"Very good, madam."

Although the air was sharpening with the bite of early autumn, the tower enclosure remained balmy, its covering of brittle weeds ruffled only slightly by a tempered breeze. I knelt, brushed a truant spear of fragile, dying grass from the rough face of the stone, willing the clumsy letters to reveal something—anything—of their buried secrets. . . . Katherine: Why? Tell me, why? . . .

I did not see Robert for the rest of the day: He did not

come to my bed that night; nor did I meet him in the house or on the trail, the next day. It was not, in fact, until a late hour of the afternoon, following, that I was informed by Annie that my presence was requested at seven o'clock in the dining hall, at which time and place I was to join my husband. Nervous, I dressed with punctilious care and with a sudden eye for modesty, selecting a gown that was prim, almost maidenly.

He stood immediately upon my entrance and deflected an amused glance from my costume. "Ah, my dear!" he bowed graciously. "May I offer you wine?"

"Not just now, thank you." I permitted Judd to seat me.

"And how has my lovely bride been occupying herself today?" His speech was slurred. "Been busy unearthing new specters?" he chuckled broadly.

"It has been a quiet day," I murmured, suddenly uncomfortable.

"Judd!" Robert motioned to the butler. "More wine— and fill the Lady Elizabeth's glass—"

"Er—no—" I declined again.

"Ah, my dear," smiled Robert, "but I insist."

Judd complied. Robert lifted his glass, indicating that I should do the same. "I feel it incumbent upon me to propose a toast. But, quite properly, to whom?" He trained his eyes on the ceiling. "To whom?" he mused. "Ah!" he crowed, "I have it: a toast to the Chevalier Raoul!"

I could feel my face blanch; I stood abruptly. "If—if you will excuse me, Robert," I swallowed hard, "I—am not feeling well. I—" My voice faded. "I should like to r-retire—"

Robert rose politely. "Of course, my dear. I shall summon your maid to assist you."

I shook my head. "N-no," I stammered, "let me go alone, p-please—"

In my room I sank by the bed, trembling . . . Help . . . Help me . . . Someone help me . . .

Auntie Maude . . . Where are you? . . .

Chapter 71

A magnet, the little homely gravestone drew me again and again to the tower courtyard. Again and again I knelt in the grass and stared at the face of the marker with its simple tribute. Willing her to disclose the secret, I begged: "Katherine, why? Tell me, why?"

One afternoon, when the graying skies hung low and the air was heavy with mist, I entered the enclosure, prepared to complete my daily ritual. Only absently, at first, I noticed that the door to the tower did not seem properly secured. Breathless with excitement I pulled hard at the rust-coated handle; the door swung forward slightly. I tugged with all my strength. Squawking in protest, the ancient hinges released their hold, allowing a hazy view of a staircase that curved sharply upward . . . To that very window from which the light had shone so often? Yes, surely . . .

I managed to slip through the grudging opening and began the dizzying ascent. Steadily I climbed. Tireless. Undaunted. What was here? . . . I had to know. . . .

Attaining the highest reach—the topmost steps—I found myself nearly overpowered, suddenly, by a strange odor. It was sweetish, decaying. Blood drummed in my temples as I reached the head of the stairs and passed over the threshold of a round and doorless room; there, in its center, teetered a small table barely able to support its solitary burden: a lantern; there, on a chair that was untidily shedding its scrubby broom, sprawled my husband. Cloying smoke clogged the air; I coughed.

He looked up. His eyes were black, appearing so dark as to be unseeing. His lips curved in a lazy smile. Slowly he rose and with easy grace glided toward me, bowed deeply, and kissed my hand. "Ah! Is it not the inquisitive little cat!" He chided himself softly. "No! Not cat! Cat was Katherine . . . This one is Elizabeth. I shall start anew." With ceremony he bowed again and announced, "Is it not the inquisitive little Elizabeth!" His words, oddly, seemed to slide together. "Welcome to my tower, Inquisitive Little Elizabeth! Welcome to my den!" His hand gentle on mine, he led me into the room and seated me on the derelict chair. "There," he murmured, his voice a caress, "much better. Much better!" He swayed almost imperceptibly.

"Robert"—I was frightened—"what is the matter?"

"The matter!" His laugh was rich, fluid. "Enfolded in euphoria's embrace, soothed by the panacea of kings, and you ask what is the matter! Ah, Little Elizabeth," he sighed, "you have much to learn. . . ."

"What is that smell?" I grimaced.

"The breath of the gods!" he smiled. "Drink deep, Little Inquisitive Elizabeth, and soar up to Paradise!"

"What is it?" I whispered.

"The beneficence of the poppy . . . stolen from the Elysian fields . . ."

"I don't understand—"

"Opium, my dear: heaven's brew!"

"Opium!" I gasped.

"Opium! Eden's royal messenger," he drawled, "zephyr from the kingdom of eternal happiness . . . Opium." His smile was dreamy.

"Opium," I repeated dumbly.

"Join me," he invited, "and together we shall fly above the world. . . ."

I shrank from him. "The light in the tower—was it—you?"

"Intelligent, as well as inquisitive!" he drawled. "I confess," he laughed, "to the perplexing light in the tower."

"But why?"

"How better to signal a ship at sea, my dear"—his voice was mellow, persuasive—"to alert that purveyor of glorious dreams . . . that merciful angel bearing her cargo promising immortality. . . ."

"You mean that ships bring—opium—to you?"

"Not just to me," he explained with boundless patience, "but to share with any and all who wish to taste the pure poetry of life . . . to rejoice in the miracle of forgetfulness. . . ."

"Any—all?"

"Those who frequent my gaming tables—"

"Gaming tables!" What was I hearing? I looked into the tranquil depths of his eyes. . . . "Gaming tables—where?"

"Let me see, now . . . There is an establishment in Torquay, another in Exeter . . . Taunton . . . Glastonbury . . . and other modest stops along the route to the most profitable table of them all—in London . . ."

I sat appalled. "How could you!"

"How, indeed! My dear, why do you think the estate has remained intact?" he asked softly. "Do you possibly imagine Mr. Wade's contribution—and that of his fellows—revenue equal to all this?" His languid gaze shifted to the window.

I stared at him. "Smugglers' Peak . . ."

He grinned. "Touché, my dear. Touché."

"My father died because of the gaming tables!" I cried.

He shrugged. "They are not for everyone . . ."

Destroyed, I smothered a sob and stumbled from the room. As I ran down the curving staircase, eyes drowning in their tears, I could hear his careless laughter follow me. . . .

Once in my room, I crept into the bed and huddled there, shivering with fear and dismay. Was that really Robert in the tower, or some conjured spirit playing in horrific fantasy? My husband, or an alien shadow? . . . Would I awaken soon and laugh at my foolish imaginings . . . or was this, indeed, reality . . . Opium. Gaming tables . . . Tears spilled down my cheeks. My father, gambler: the ultimate degradation of a man, the pitiful annihilation of a life. How vividly I recalled the frenzy of his final years. How clear the memory of his last long and painful struggle. I could see still Auntie Maude, grim defender in the desperate stand against the victorious forces of death . . .

Auntie Maude . . . Where are you now? . . .

I did not stir from my bed the rest of the day, nor did I rise for meals. I had no appetite for even the small glass of tea and slice of hot bread all but forced upon me by a worried Annie. "You gotta eat some, ma'am," she clucked, "else you'll be goin' all sickly, like—" She colored.

I knew what the girl was about to say: like Lady Frances. I smiled wanly. "I shall be all right tomorrow, Annie."

. . . Like Frances . . . Oh, God. Wretched and frail. And now, dead. Dead: because I had killed her . . .

Far into the night I heard Robert moving about in his room next to mine . . . Please, God, do not let him come near me. . . . Please . . . He made no overtures, however, and once again the house was still. Still, except for the dull throbbing of my head, echoed in the beating of my troubled heart . . .

Morning dawned bright and clear, and at midday a tap on the door admitted Annie, bearing a tray laden with delicacies selected to tempt the most recalcitrant appetite. "La, ma'am!" Her grin was cheerful. "Half the larder's right here!"

"Oh, Annie," I sighed, "I am not hungry—really—"

"Tush! For shame!" she cajoled softly. "You'd best be eatin' some before you go out on the trail, seems so . . ."

"I don't think I shall be riding today—"

"But, ma'am, 'tis a day mindful of spring!" She was surprised. "You'll not see its like much again before the set of winter!"

I murmured, "I am not feeling up to it—"

"Well, then," she capitulated, "just eat what you can. I'll be back in a bit for the tray."

"Thank you, Annie . . ."

Chapter 72

For two days I remained closeted in my room, lying hunched in the bed or crouched at the sill, looking toward the tower, my eyes trying to pierce the golden stone. . . . Was he there . . . even now? Handsome head swirling in the sickish haze; dark eyes blank; speech obscured . . . Was this Robert? My husband . . .

For two days Annie had stubbornly tried to encourage me to "Eat a little some, ma'am—"

And for two days Robert had made no effort either to approach or to communicate with me in any way, until the evening he sent Annie with a request for my immediate presence in the dining hall.

"Oh, Annie—" I whimpered, "I couldn't—"

"But the master—he ordered it—" The girl's eyes were wide with worry. "Just put somethin' on that's nice." She tried to smile. "I know you'll feel the better for it."

"No, Annie." My refusal was firm. "Tell Sir Robert that I am not well." I looked away. "Perhaps tomorrow."

Her expression remained doubtful, but she withdrew. "All right, Lady Elizabeth. As you say."

Only moments passed and the door burst open: Robert lounged on its threshold. "What is it, my dear?" he asked softly. "Why was the simple favor of the companionship of my wife at the evening meal not granted?"

"I—I am unwell," I whispered.

"I see." His eyes slid up and down my person. "It was not long ago that this bed was engaged for purposes far more inviting than malingering."

"I—I must have caught a r-rheum—" I stammered.

"Is a chill also a fitting excuse for the unbecoming garb?" A disdainful hand plucked at the long sleeve of Auntie Maude's flannel nightdress.

"It—it is warm," I explained lamely.

"I see." He fingered a tangle of my hair. "And your crowning glory. What of it? Suddenly a witch's broom?"

"I—I am sorry," I breathed.

He strolled to the dressing table. "I suggest, my dear"— he placed the mother of pearl hairbrush in my hand—"that you start to rectify your appearance without further delay."

"Y-yes, Robert." Obediently, arms weak and trembling, I began to brush my snarled hair.

"My dear," Robert remarked idly, "at the rate of progress you demonstrate, your coiffure cannot possibly be presentable until late next summer." He took the hairbrush. "Allow me."

Briskly he attacked my hair. My scalp tingled and then began to burn. "Robert," I pleaded, "not so rough."

"See, my dear!" he crowed. "Even the most prickly knots are beginning to yield!"

"Robert, please!" Tears stung my eyes.

"Ah!" He stood. "Your hair has been restored to its rightful beauty! We must now attend the rest of you—" He strode to the wardrobe and flung wide the drawers. Rude hands swept through the layers of filmy creations, drawing out a nightdress of flesh-pink chiffon. "Remove that abomination, at once," he ordered, "and put on this—"

"B-but, Robert—"

"My dear," he smiled, "I insist." He watched as the awkward flannel dropped to the floor, and the chiffon cloud floated over my breasts and clung in gauzy folds at my hips. His dark eyes were eloquent. "You are a luscious wench, my dear." He stepped toward me and pulled me roughly against him. "Luscious indeed." He was breathing heavily. His lips on mine were coldly demanding. He pressed me down onto the bed. With one savage stroke he tore the chiffon from my body and threw it from him. His teeth on my breasts were sharp; hands on my thighs, harsh.

Pinned under him, I begged, "Robert, please . . . no!" He was mounting me. "Robert . . . No!" I was sobbing now.

He smiled. "But, my dear, I insist . . ."

I screamed as he entered, brutally.

"Luscious," he laughed.

After Robert had disengaged himself and left the room,

I cradled my body and rocked, lulled by the slow, elemental rhythm. Dull tears eased from behind my closed eyelids, softly bathing the offended flesh on which they fell. . . . Help me, God . . . Help me, please . . .

After a time, shivering with cold and despair, I pulled the flannel nightdress over my quaking shoulders and wrapped it tightly around me. I crawled under the blankets and hugged myself close, sobbing quietly. . . . Auntie Maude . . . Oh, Auntie Maude . . .

For a week there was no sign of Robert. No effort was made to invade my sanctuary. Not once did I hear him moving about his room late at night; not once did I see him touch his whip to Ebon's back, urging him over the cobbled courtyard by day. For a week I remained free. Free in fact, perhaps. Ever, I was enslaved by my thoughts . . .

Towards dawn of the eighth day after the bestial act, I lay in disquietude on the bed; my legs were unmercifully cramped, and my head ached dully. For some reason I felt drawn to the empty darkness of the window. I rose quickly and squatted beside the sill. . . . It was there: the light in the tower. Robert was in the tower, signaling a ship at sea, a ship hauling its freight of oblivion and phantom glory . . . Oh, God, Robert, how could you . . . ?

Hypnotized, I watched the glow as it swayed back and forth. Then stopped . . . Robert would be gone soon. Off to his gaming tables . . . Which now, Robert? . . . Taunton . . . Glastonbury . . . Or perhaps the more elaborate establishment in London . . . How long your absence, this time, Robert? . . . How long will I be free . . . Really free . . .

I returned to the bed and permitted myself the first sound sleep in weeks.

Chapter 73

Patiently, Annie stood over me while I ate a token amount from the breakfast tray she had carried to my room. Although the portions consumed were less than marginal, the girl seemed well pleased at my performance. She beamed. "You'll do even better tomorrow! And," she assured me, "once you get some red glow in your cheeks, you'll be a fit sight for the master when he comes back!"

I paled.

"Would you be wantin' else?" the girl added, gathering the dishes for removal.

"Annie," I tried to ease casually into the question. "Who was my Auntie Maude's chief confidant when she was here?"

"Con–" The girl shook a puzzled head. "I don't ken that word, ma'am—"

"Chum, then. Someone she talked to—frequently—"

Annie screwed up her forehead. "Talked to . . . Talked to . . . Let me see . . . Cook—Cook, ma'am," she grinned. "Aye, Cook! They was always with their heads together. Seems so!"

I smiled. "Thank you, Annie—"

An extravagant pigeon: breast blooming with powder down (nothing, actually, more than a liberal film of baking flour), Cook's enormity was plumed by a scanty half-head of tufted hair and broken only by a brilliant smile. The voice that managed to escape her pendulous wattle was, itself, powdery. Her buried currant eyes regarded me kindly. "A wee bit of a thing!" She cocked her dusty head. "And missin' your Auntie Maude, I'll wager!"

Tears stung my eyes.

"Is there some special dish I can stir up for you, ma'am?" she asked pleasantly.

"No," I managed. "I am looking for some—information—"

"Oh?" The woman's gaze strayed to the batter lazing on the board. "If you wouldn't mind, Lady Elizabeth, I can work the dough whilst we talk. It gets out of hand, else."

"Certainly," I said quickly.

"Now then, what is it, ma'am?"

"What do you know of—Katherine?"

"Katherine?" She sucked in her breath, a harsh sound. Her hands were suddenly still. "Who do you mean, my lady?"

"Katherine," I swallowed hard, "Sir Robert's first wife—"

The woman averted her eyes, busying herself with the pasty mass on the table.

"Cook?"

"She has been dead for some years now, ma'am—"

"I know that," I hastened to inform her, "I have visited her stone in the tower courtyard."

The woman showed surprise.

"What happened to her?"

"She was young," the cook evaded.

"I am aware that she took her own life," I said bluntly, "I am anxious to find out—why—"

The woman sighed, "I don't know, my lady." She shook her head sadly. " 'Twas a tragic thing. Leastwise, one so young—"

My heart sank. "You can't tell me why?"

"No, ma'am."

"Please," I entreated earnestly, "who would know?"

Massaging a fleshy forearm, the woman relented. "She had a maid onct, name of Tessie . . . Tessie Caldwell." She mused, "must be all of seventy and more, by now." Her eyes wandered. "Poor soul, badly crippled up with the rheumatics. But devoted to the first missus, seems so . . ."

My heart thudded. "Where can I find her?"

"In the village, seems so."

"Here? In Drewsby?"

Cook nodded. "Seems so . . . Unless she—died . . ."

"Would you know her address?"

The woman's massive shoulders lifted. "Little street. Myrtle—Ash—Cedar . . . Some such like," she finished vaguely.

"Who might know—precisely?" I asked carefully.

"Angus, most like. That one knows the village right and proper, every inch, seems so . . ."

From the first Angus displayed a courteous reluctance toward his assignment—that of squiring me to Tessie Caldwell's village quarters. "Lady Elizabeth, ma'am," Angus objected, "it be not fittin', seems so . . ."

"I am determined to visit this woman, Angus," I told him firmly, "with or without your help." The old man shrugged his bony shoulders; I interpreted the gesture as grudging acquiescence. I smiled my thanks.

The weather had remained unseasonably balmy, and so the journey into the village was as a pleasant outing. Saucy clouds bounced merrily across the sky, fanned by the wings of gulls soaring high above the horizon. We rode steadily but with no attempt at speed, Angus's tacit method of impeding the expedition, I guessed. Still, in good time he reined to a halt before a tiny cottage: The deep gray of its rough, weathered shingles was overlaid with a gnarled creeper, now leafless. Angus slipped down from his perch, opened the door to the carriage, and handed me out. "This be the place, Lady Elizabeth," he announced, unable to conceal his disapproval.

"Oh, my!" I murmured, suddenly without confidence. "Do you think she will be at home?"

"Not to fret about that, ma'am," the old man muttered, "her be that palsied."

I followed a ragged dirt path and approached the front door, which was painted a flat yellow and ornamented by a solitary tin plate; on it was scratched rudely the number 3. I rapped timidly and waited; after a lengthy interval the door slowly opened. Before me hunched an old woman bent nearly double, joints swollen to twice their normal size—indicating cruel and unrelieved pain. "Yes?" Even her voice was harsh.

"I am Elizabeth Wyndham," I introduced myself, "wife to Sir Robert. May I come in?"

She hesitated for a long moment, then with difficulty moved out of the way to let me pass. The modest room was warmed by a cheery fire. "Here, lady, sit." She pointed to the sole upholstered chair, one that she had obviously just vacated. "No," I refused with a polite smile, "I would prefer this one," choosing instead a stiff ladderback. Tessie Caldwell resumed her seat with gratitude. Her eyes, robbed of their once bright blue by age and habitual suffering, were guarded. "M'lady?"

"I am here," I began somewhat awkwardly, "to inquire about—Lady Katherine Wyndham."

The woman's deformed hand shot forth and traced the Sign of the Cross.

I swallowed. "I understand, Tessie—that you were in Lady Katherine's employ—"

She continued merely to stare at me.

"Er—" I proceeded, "I am anxious to learn something about Sir Robert's first—er—wife . . ."

The old woman struggled to her feet. "You go now, lady—"

"Go!" I cried.

"You go," she repeated, "take care of yourself and the heir."

"The heir!" I rasped.

"The heir."

"T-there is no heir—"

"One be comin'. Seems so—"

"But—"

She nodded emphatically. "Take care of yourself and the heir."

"I-I am not—" I started to protest.

"You be. Seems so." Her proclamation was absolute. "Can tell by your eyes."

This was ridiculous. "Tessie—"

"You go, now," she insisted, "can say nothing more. The eyes tell . . ." She was resolute. "It's always in the eyes . . ."

I stumbled out of the cottage, staggered down the path, and leaned heavily against Angus as he handed me into the carriage. "You be all right, ma'am?" he asked in immediate concern. "What that old biddy say to you—"

"Yes, Angus," I murmured, "only, take me home, please."

. . . Why should the visit have proved so disturbing?

. . . Simply becuase an old woman had pronounced, and without hesitation, that I was pregnant? Is that not the indulged obsession of the old: as if they, now with faded eyes, could see clearly into the womb of the world . . .

. . . Pregnant . . . Why should I be surprised, after all . . . And why should the news—even if true—upset me . . . What more normal project for a healthy young woman . . .

. . . Frances had been pregnant . . .

. . . Tessie Caldwell had told me nothing frightening; she had herself been frightened . . . Yet her eyes, clouded with pain, had seemed to see into mine . . . to penetrate through my woolen cloak . . . to pass beyond the shadows of my mind . . . How . . . What did she know? . . .

. . . Whatever her secret, she had managed not to tell me. . . .

I remained in my room almost entirely now; even though I had looked to Robert's protracted absence as release, the old woman's unsettling proclamation lingered to imprison me. Why did it distress me so? . . .

. . . Frances had been pregnant . . .

. . . A child: the heir . . . Why should I be terrified at the prospect? . . .

. . . Frances had been pregnant . . .

Food became abhorrent to my increasingly rebellious stomach. Annie was frankly beside herself. "I am that worried, ma'am!" she confessed. "You never eat nothin' no more!"

"I can't," I sighed, "I am simply not hungry."

"And them pretty new clothes," the girl scolded, "they'll but hang from your bones, should you keep on like this—"

"I shall feel better tomorrow," I promised.

"That, you keep sayin'," Annie frowned. "Let me send for Dr. Briggs—"

"No!" I refused quickly.

"And your face, ma'am, growin' all pinched and small-like," she clucked. "Doctor could put you right in no time, seems so . . ."

"Please, Annie," I begged, "let me rest now." I turned my face from her. "I shall be better soon . . ."

At last alone, I stood before the mirror. Annie was right:

flesh, once milk-white and now only wan, was rapidly falling from my limbs; my face was haggard; my hair hung lank and lifeless; and my eyes, once provocative, stared hollow and pursued . . .

. . . Oh, God . . . what was happening to me? . . .
. . . Take care of yourself and the heir, she had said . . .

Chapter 74

A scattering of frost, which flecked the ground, sparkled in the path of the wintry sun. " 'Tis that beautiful!" exclaimed Annie. "Now, ma'am, you should be outa doors on that horse of yours, suckin' up the clean air, 'stead of lyin' in this room!"

"I know, Annie," I smiled wanly.

"Sir Robert's bound to be home soon!" she chided. "And you—all peaky-like! What'll he be thinkin'!"

. . . Robert . . . bound to be home soon . . . "Perhaps you're right, Annie," I said slowly, "you may help me dress."

"You mean it?" The girl was delighted.

"Yes. I shall ride today."

The flame-red habit was no more than a shapeless, gaudy rag as it drooped on my gaunt frame. "Tch, tch." Annie's eyes were reproachful . . .

Predictably I found Mrs. Clyde directing her staff from her usual vantage point in the great hall; I found myself all but cringing as the woman joined me at the foot of the stairs to relinquish her key to the tower courtyard. Soon I was kneeling in the makeshift cemetery before its solitary gravestone. "Tell me, Katherine," I begged, "tell me . . ."

If Hartley experienced feelings of surprise, or even curiosity, at my dramatically altered appearance, he managed to disguise them admirably; Peter frankly gawked.

"May I have Artemis saddled, please?" I made my request, at which Hartley hesitated. "Her not ridden for some time now, ma'am. Her be pretty frisky."

Peter's head bobbed in automatic agreement.

"I think I can handle her," I smiled.

"There be a fine spotted gelding—older and some settled," the stable master suggested kindly. "Maybe—"

"No, thank you, Mr. Hartley," I declined firmly, "I am used to Artemis."

Although she nickered softly when led into my presence, patiently allowed me to stroke her velvet nose, and stood docile as I was lifted into the saddle, the stable master's assessment proved all too accurate: The chestnut mare was wild, taxing all the strength commanded by now frail arms to keep her under even minimal control. As if pursued, we raced along the main road to the village; still she did not seem to tire.

Annie was right: The air crackled. Crisp cold penetrated the warm wool of my cloak, and I reined up before the little cottage on Shell Street, hoping that the fire would be ablaze and that I could warm my hands and feet, which were by now almost without sensation. I tethered Artemis to a low shrub and followed the dirt path to the yellow door with its single tin plate, crudely marked. I rapped smartly. There was no response. I knocked again. Still I detected no movement from behind the door. I was frantic. . . . Please, God, do not let her be dead. . . . "Tessie!" I screamed, "let me in! I- beg of you!" The door creaked open slowly, and the old woman leaned against the frame. "I say you go, lady," she chanted, "go and take care of the heir . . ."

"I must speak with you! Tessie, please . . ."

Her gaze lifted to my face. An expression of awe filled her eyes, supplanting for the moment the pain that habitually rode there. She sighed deeply and moved aside to let me pass. She then made her own arduous journey across the short expanse of the tiny room, to sink gratefully into the soft, upholstered chair. I noticed that the exertion had spread a fine film of perspiration over her face. Tessie Caldwell looked at me sadly. "Lady, lady . . ."

"Tessie, I need to know—"

"About Lady Katherine . . ." The old woman nodded. Pity traveled over her face. "Aye, lady, you need to know." She shifted her legs at a spasm of pain and began to talk: "I was maid to Lady Katherine . . . I come with her when her was bride to Sir Robert." She sighed. "Her was beautiful and sweet, was my girl. And I loved her." A tear trickled down her cheek. "Aye, I loved her." She was silent for a long moment.

"Go on, please."

"Her and Sir Robert . . . her was wild for him and," Tessie added grimly, "so he seemed for her—"

"Seemed?" I caught my breath.

"My girl grew sickly-like. Pshaw! No more'n what should be in her time. Not wantin' to eat and upset in the stummak. Sir Robert—him fret. I tell him it be natural and will pass. But him—all time fret. Him want a woman for her. A nurse-like." Her tone grew bitter. "My girl—her don't want nurse; her want Tessie. But Sir Robert—went to hire companion." She spat, "Companion! I could do all for my girl. All . . . Except read to her—" Her voice fell to a whisper. "I can't read . . ." The old woman's eyes clouded. "So—her come: the companion." Her voice trailed away.

"Tessie?"

"And then it began. Aye," she said, "it began . . ."

"What, Tessie—what began?"

"Her stay in the room near to my girl. All the time, near to my girl."

Rancid fluid rushed into my mouth. "What room, Tessie?"

"It be some kind of yellow—" The woman nodded to herself. "Aye, yellow . . ."

I swallowed.

"My girl—still sickly-like, stayin' in her room, mostly . . . I am there. Always, I am there. And companion—her there too. At first. Reading. All the time, reading. Then—"

"Then—"

"Companion—her not there so much. Not read so much. Out, mostly." Her eyes narrowed, "With—him."

"With whom?" I hissed.

"Him. Sir Robert."

I could feel the blood drain from my head.

"My girl not know. Long time, my girl not know. But," Tessie said, her voice flat, "I know, long time, I know . . . Then, one night, my girl find Sir Robert and *her*—" she underlined the word—"in the yellow room."

My hands clutched the arms of the chair for support.

"Her heart broke then—my girl. Her come to my arms and cry. My girl. Aye," she said, "her heart be broke." The

old woman's lips began to quiver. "Then, her die. My girl
. . . My girl die . . ."

"How?" I whispered.

"My girl go to the yellow room. With knife. I find her
on the bed, her red life spillin' all over the white sheet. Her
not dead. Not yet." She was weeping now. "I take her in
my arms and rock her back and forth like baby. Back and
forth. Her tell me that her make curse on the room. And
curse on all who live in it . . . And curse on—him . . ."

"Him?"

"Sir Robert. Him never to have heir. . . . Never . . ."
Eyes streaming, the old woman looked me full in the face.
"Them be deathbed words. Deathbed words . . ."

"Deathbed words?" I echoed stupidly.

"Aye, deathbed words . . ." The old woman bobbed her
head up and down.

"Tessie," I spoke fearfully, "what—what was the name
of the companion?"

"Name of Margaret."

I gasped.

"And after her—be Frances." She stared hard at me.
"Deathbed words, lady, deathbed words . . ."

I sank to my knees on the bare wooden floor and began
to retch violently. When the virulence of the spasm eased, I
lay spent, my clothing sodden with cold sweat, and tried to
quiet the irregular beating of my heart. At last I struggled
to my feet and pitched drunkenly toward the door. With
my hand uncertain on the latch, I glanced back at the old
woman: She was alseep, the tears still wet on her crumpled
face.

Somehow I managed to cling to Artemis as we sped back
to the stable yards at Wynds. Wind whipped my face and
stiffened my damp clothes. Somehow I heaved my way up
the great staircase, reeled across the upper hallway, and
reached my room, collapsing, once there, promptly on the
bed. Annie was cross. "Lady Elizabeth!" she scolded. "Now
you've done it for sure!" She began to strip me of my clothing. "Ridin' like some madwoman through them moors—
and not hardly enough food for one of the Reverend's pet
mice in your belly to warm ye!"

I shivered uncontrollably.

"A hot bath's what you need, and a bowl of steamin' soup!" Annie decided. "You lie there in them blankets and I'll be back to fix what ails ye."

"What ails me," I groaned.

"Lie still, ma'am," she commanded, "you jest lie still. . . ."

Chapter 75

Now I seldom left my bed. Annie fed and bathed me as she would a small child. My meals consisted mainly of gruel and weak soup, and I could almost feel the sensation of flesh actually melting from my bones.

. . . A curse . . . on the yellow room . . . and on anyone who lived in it . . . Margaret had lived in it; Frances had lived in it; and—I . . .

. . . A curse on Robert . . . never to have an heir . . . Katherine had been pregnant. Frances had been pregnant; I, too—I knew positively now. . . . Margaret?

Katherine died by her own hand; Margaret of an obscure intestinal ailment; Frances . . . I had killed her . . . And I—

Was I to die? . . .

And how? . . .

. . . I must get away. Escape. Who would help me to escape? . . . Auntie Maude was gone. . . . Dr. Briggs? Would he help me now? Whatever had happened between us, he was a physician, after all. He would help me. . . . I must escape . . . leave Wynds . . . I could be safe then . . .

"Annie," I questioned the girl one morning as she patiently spooned hot cereal into my resisting mouth, "was Lady Margaret expecting a child when she died?"

"Aye, poor thing," admitted the girl sadly, "more than six months along when she was took." She stirred the creamy mixture thoughtfully. "But with her so puny and all from the start of her time, I can't think the babe would have been much—"

I began to shake without control.

"La, lady! You have need of more care than I can give you—"

"Perhaps you are right," I agreed slowly. "I think I should visit Dr. Briggs."

Annie's face cleared. "And glad I am of that!" she exclaimed. "By the good glory, that is fine news!"

"Yes," I made the decision a firm one, "I shall go today."

"Lady Elizabeth!" Annie protested sharply, "and why can't the good doctor call here—as is fittin'!"

"No—" I declined quickly, "I would rather be attended in his surgery—"

"To his surgery, then," she conceded, "but not ridin' that horse, you won't!" the girl declared hotly. "Angus will bring the carriage round!"

I did not argue; I knew that I no longer had the strength to sit a horse.

Mrs. Clyde was positioned as usual as Annie carefully guided me down the staircase; she watched with open curiosity as Judd hastened to hold the door and hand me into the carriage.

"I should be goin' with ye—" Annie frowned . . .

We had trotted halfway to the village when feathery flakes of snow began to drift across the road. I pulled the fur rug around my knees more securely. Angus reined before the surgery. "We be here!" he sang out. Then, poking his head through the carriage window, he asked, "Want I should rouse the doctor, ma'am?"

I was tired. "If you please."

He returned a moment later. "Him don't answer. But there be a note on the door."

"What does it say?"

Angus hung his head. "I can't read, ma'am."

"Let me have a look."

"But, ma'am," he objected, "Annie'll have me head. She said I was not to let you go muckin' about—"

"Just help me down, Angus," I said listlessly, "I can manage the rest."

The note was penned clearly, printed in large letters and composed in a language easily understood by the simplest village folk: "Dr. Briggs has gone away. He is not coming back." Under the brief message, the hastily scrawled initials: "J.B."

I sagged against the door frame. Gone . . . Where? I must find out. How? The Reverend would know. Surely

Miss Caroline and the doctor were married by now. His only daughter's whereabouts: Without question, the Reverend would know them. . . . I hurried to the carriage. "Take me to the vicarage," I ordered Angus breathlessly, "and quickly, for God's sake!"

The snow, until now only a fragile dusting, had thickened measurably by the time we pulled up before the tiny vicarage. In the cemetery, directly adjacent, the gravestones were mellowing under a film of white; my troubled thoughts wandered to the courtyard beneath the imposing tower, host to a simple marker: Katherine, 1832–1854 . . .

Angus, stamping his feet and brushing vigorously at the snow that had collected on his woolen hat, helped me from the carriage and managed to lead me without mishap up the short path to the door. He waited gallantly until it opened, affording me entry, before resuming his seat atop the carriage.

"Lady Elizabeth!" Mrs. Smythe's uttered cry revealed both surprise and dismay.

Thoroughly chilled, I asked, "May I come in?"

"Oh, my! Certainly!" Mrs. Smythe's face reddened; quickly she backed away from the door to permit me to pass. "To what do we owe this honor?" She fluttered about, all the while training an astonished eye on my appearance, as well as an inquisitive one, contriving to determine the nature of my business there that day. "It is the Lady Elizabeth!" Mrs. Smythe warbled to someone somewhere in the shadows. Miss Caroline, surly of countenance, materialized dutifully and stood staring at me with a loathing that was ill-concealed.

I was frankly exhausted. "May I sit?"

"Sit?" gushed Mrs. Smythe. "Of course, dear lady! Of course . . . Caroline—" she directed her daughter, "pray, push that—er—padded chair closer, so that Lady Elizabeth may visit in comfort." She plumped a flowered cushion. "There! That's better!"

Miss Caroline sniffed in overt disapproval.

Mrs. Smythe, waiting in polite anticipaton, asked after a silent moment, "May I—er—serve tea?"

"Er—no, thank you—" My smile was wan.

"Ah—"

Miss Caroline initiated an ungracious move to withdraw, but was thwarted immediately by an unmistakable, if tacit, signal flashed by her mother.

I began earnestly, "Mrs. Smythe, I am inquiring as to the present address of Dr. Briggs—"

Mrs. Smythe paled; her daughter shrieked.

I looked from one to the other in complete amazement. "Surely, you of all people should know how Dr. Briggs may be reached!" Miss Caroline buried her face in her hands. Her mother, keeping an anxious eye on her daughter as well as a courteous one tracked on the lady of the manor, murmured something totally unintelligible. "Mrs. Smythe," I begged, "it is imperative that I learn the doctor's whereabouts. And," my tone was urgent, "quickly!"

Mrs. Smythe swallowed audibly. Her eyes darted anxiously from the squire's lady to her daughter, who was by now hopelessly distraught. "Lady Elizabeth," the woman managed, "it seems that you have not heard—"

"Heard what?"

"Dr. Briggs"—the woman choked on the words—"has—sailed away—"

I was shocked. "Sailed away!"

At her mother's pronouncement Miss Caroline began to wail loudly. Mrs. Smythe's frantic attentions were necessarily divided. "Yes, Lady Elizabeth . . . Australia." She stole a look at Miss Caroline before adding, "He has been gone some weeks, now—"

I sat in utter bewilderment. "But," I protested, "it was my understanding that the doctor and Miss Caroline were to—"

Miss Caroline collapsed on the divan and abandoned herself to a noisy paroxysm of weeping. Her mother frowned. "That, er—that was our hope, too," she whispered to me. "But—" Her hands fluttered in defeat.

"What—happened?"

"Well—" Mrs. Smythe plucked at her plump fingers. "The doctor—er—he—" she hedged. Suddenly she took in a deep breath. "It seems that Dr. Briggs never actually asked for Caroline's hand, after all," she hissed. "She—er—misinterpreted his—attentions—"

At her mother's words Miss Caroline sprang from the couch and proceeded to stalk me, much as a predacious animal its prey. "It's all because of you!" she snarled. "You!" Her teeth were bared. "Before you came here Jonathan was mine! Mine . . . Do you hear me: mine!"

I stared.

"You enticed him . . . used him . . . lured him with your sluttish wiles . . . and then—discarded him as so much trash when something better came along!" Her voice dropped dangerously low. "It was you . . . you slut . . . you . . ."

"Caroline!" Mrs. Smythe rasped. "Stop that filthy talk, at once!"

"Slut!" Caroline screeched. "Slut! Slut! Slut!" She ran from the room, sobbing hysterically.

"Lady Elizabeth." Mrs. Smythe was frankly perspiring. "Forgive the girl. She is—she doesn't know what she is saying—"

I did not move. . . . Dr. Briggs, gone. My last bastion . . . Gone. Where? . . . He had loved me. I was sure. If he knew of my danger he would come to me . . . If he knew . . .

"Did he leave an address?" I asked quickly.

"Er—no," the woman sighed, an ear cocked to her daughter's shrill lamentation, "er—nothing—"

"Are you sure?" I was desperate now.

"No, my lady, not a word."

Miss Caroline's convulsive outburst finally subsided, permitting her mother to return the attention due her estimable guest. "I hope that you will—er—understand Caroline's—" She forced an uneasy smile. "Lady Elizabeth—" she began again, "I know that you will find it in your generous heart—"

I rose without speaking and headed for the door.

The woman put a nervous hand on my arm. "Please," she implored, "please . . . Lady Elizabeth . . . Please . . . Caroline was—it is just that—" Her eyes were terrified. "Do not feel that she—that I . . . that—her—father—"

I did not answer, but walked unsteadily down the path to the waiting carriage and to Angus, who lifted me carefully inside. Whipped, the horses jerked forward. I lay back, drained.

All was hopeless. There was no one. . . . Auntie Maude? Gone . . . Ada? Molly? Where were they? . . . I had tossed their letter into the fire. . . . Dr. Briggs . . . Who would help me now? . . .

The snow blustered in frenzied swirls; even under the thick fur rug I shivered. I could hear the muffled commands as Angus urged the horses to still greater speeds, feel the skittish carriage dance on the slippery road. We were approaching the listing house; standing before it, the solitary sentinel: Amos Childer. But . . .

"Angus!" I cried, rapping sharply against the roof of the carriage. "Stop a moment!"

Snow was falling on horned hands that rested on the ancient scythe; a white film dulled the tangle of yellow hair; vinca-blue eyes stared, owl's eyes . . . I gasped: Ian . . .

Annie put me to bed as if I were an infant, rubbing my hands and feet to warm them and wrapping me tightly in a bunting of blankets. The soup she had brought was fast cooling on the tray. "I have no appetite, Annie," I whispered, "let me sleep . . ."

Ian . . . Oh, God. Ian . . .

Chapter 76

Despite Annie's dogged entreaties, no longer did I leave my bed; even the short distance to my adjacent sitting room proved an exertion too arduous to hazard. "Ma'am," the girl urged me to my feet, "just a few steps now, that'll do it—"

Always I fell back. "I can't, I can't, I can't . . ."

One morning Mrs. Clyde requested formal audience. "Annie, I can't," I whined, "tell her—another time . . ."

"You had best see her, ma'am," the girl advised, "it may have to do with the master—"

The master! Oh, God . . . Robert . . .

Notebook in hand, Mrs. Clyde planted herself importantly at the foot of my bed, the epitome of energetic efficiency. Dramatically she cleared her throat: "Lady Elizabeth, there are vital matters concerning the Christmas festivities I think we should discuss."

"Christmas festivities . . ." I echoed wanly.

Smiling briskly, she declared, "That time of year is fast approaching!"

"I—I didn't realize," I murmured.

"Mr. Judd," the woman announced, "has already arranged for all decorative materials and is supervising the staff in their dispersement, accordingly. Why, the tent in the courtyard is being secured this very afternoon!" she boasted, adding crisply, "Cook has negotiated all the particulars pertaining to the kitchen. . . ."

I nodded helplessly.

"The celebration can be rather elaborate, or so I am told."

"Yes," I whispered.

"What I need from you specifically, m'lady," Mrs.

Clyde continued, "are your preferences concerning the gifts for the personnel."

"Er—personnel—" I repeated, suddenly chilled.

"I understand that it is customary for the household staff to receive certain—ah—gratuities appropriate to his or her individual station—"

I made a feeble gesture with my hand.

"If you have a moment at this time, Lady Elizabeth"— Mrs. Clyde wetted the tip of a pencil with her tongue—"I should like to compile that list of selections immediately." Pencil poised, she waited.

I turned my head away.

"Since Christmas is but thirteen days hence, you must be as anxious to get under way as I," the housekeeper spoke with supreme confidence.

. . . oh, God . . .

"I, for one, Lady Elizabeth, cannot operate under procrastination! Although I will acknowledge"—her mouth was pursed—"that my predecessor was only too willing to let things slide."

. . . her predecessor: Auntie Maude . . .

"Why," the woman elaborated with relish, "it is my information that last year the tent for the—er—laborers was not erected until the actual day of the event! Not in keeping, surely," she waved a censorial forefinger, "with The Accepted Wynds Method!"

"Please," I moaned.

"It is my firm intention to have everything under absolute control before Sir Robert returns for the holidays."

. . . Robert . . . Oh, God . . .

"Please go," I whimpered.

Mrs. Clyde's eyes darted from my face to Annie's in consternation. "Does this mean that the squire may not be present for the ceremonies?"

"Please," I implored.

"Best you leave the lady now," Annie motioned vigorously to the housekeeper, "her is not well."

"A civil tongue, my girl," Mrs. Clyde warned.

"Please," I groaned, "for the love of God . . ."

Mrs. Clyde turned and strode angrily out of the room.

I was weeping softly now. Taking me in her arms, Annie crooned, "There, there, ma'am, the master'll be home soon to care for you. . . . There, there . . ."

. . . The master . . . I began to sob without control . . .

Chapter 77

Exactly one week before Christmas, on an afternoon menaced by the threat of snow, Robert rode into the courtyard at Wynds. The household staff, upon hearing the compelling clatter of Ebon's hooves on the cobbles, was plunged into a sudden flurry of activity befitting the master's return.

"And what can all that blather be—" Annie frowned, running to the window. "La!" Her expression cleared. " 'Tis the master," she cried, "come home for the holidays!" She turned to me, her face radiant. "You'll be all right, the now!"

. . . All right, the now . . . If Annie only knew . . .

I could hear him move quietly about his room; still, my husband made no effort to approach me until early in the evening. Annie was applying a belated brush to my snarled hair and I was submitting to her ministrations with only abstracted protestations—"A pity to let the stuff go to ruin, m'lady," she scolded, "so beautiful it was, and all"—when I heard a soft knock. Robert sauntered through the doorway.

With easy grace he crossed the room and sat beside my bed. He took my brittle hand in his. "What is this, my dear?" His voice was gentle. "You are not well?"

"N-no."

Annie curtsied politely before her master and turned to withdraw. "Stay," he ordered the girl, although his dark eyes never left my face. "How long has this been going on?" he asked me quietly.

"I—"

"For months, it is now—" Annie contributed shyly.

"Has Dr. Briggs been summoned?"

My eyes filled . . . Dr. Briggs . . .

Robert's dark brows lifted in concern. "Are you in pain, my dear?"

I shook my head weakly.

"The doctor?" he asked Annie.

"Ah—no, sir. Him not come here—"

Robert's mouth was stern. "And why has not Dr. Briggs visited my wife?"

"Him—gone," Annie replied uneasily.

"Gone! Where?"

"Sailed somewheres, seems so . . ." Annie was vague.

"My dear," Robert turned to me impatiently, "what is this girl blithering about?"

Although my mouth was parched, I felt compelled to swallow. "Dr. Briggs has gone to Australia."

"Good God! Permanently?"

I nodded bleakly.

Robert stood. "The omission will be remedied at once." He inclined his head toward Annie and drew her to a far corner of the room. "What precisely is wrong with your mistress?" he demanded.

"Her be—you know—" Annie was flustered.

"I know what?" Robert was growing testy.

"Her be about three months—"

"I see. And yet no doctor has been called into the case—" Robert's face was grim.

"Her wouldn't hear nothin' of it." Annie became defensive. "I tried—nearly every day, Sir Robert—" her voice quavered, "I tried."

. . . I tried . . . As God is my judge, I tried . . .

"She is pitifully thin—"

"I know, sir. Like bones, sir—"

"Has she no appetite?"

Annie shook her head. "Her eat nothin' hardly at all—" Her eyes rolled. "It be some to-do, gettin' the spoon near to her mouth—seems so!"

"The room is stifling—"

"Aye, sir. Her likes it this way, sir."

"It should be aired."

"No, sir, her won't have it, sir—"

"Lady Elizabeth's condition cannot be permitted to deteriorate further." Robert was emphatic. "I shall obtain the services of a physician as soon as possible—"

"Oh, sir! Aye, sir!" Even as tears filled her eyes Annie

managed a grateful smile. "She'll get better the now, sir! Just that quick, sir! You'll see, just that quick!"

. . . Just that quick . . .

"Oh, God!" I began to sob. "Oh, God!"

"La!" Annie fretted. "She gets that upset, sir!"

"We must not tire her," Robert whispered. "Comfort your mistress now, and leave the rest to me."

Every evening thereafter Robert made a brief visit to my room, pulled a chair alongside my bed, and, taking my lifeless hand in his, inquired, "How are you feeling, my dear?"

I could only turn my head away.

"I have sent to Torquay for a physician. He should be here within a day or two—"

. . . To Torquay . . . To one of his gaming houses?

After regarding me with tender, searching eyes, Robert took Annie aside for their ritualistic muffled consultation: "Well, what has she eaten today?" ". . . A little light soup, s'all, sir . . ." "Nothing more than that?" ". . . No, sir—exceptin' a few spoons of gruel. Hardly enough to keep a bird . . ." "She is failing rapidly—" ". . . Aye, sir, and a pity, sir . . ." "She seems to worsen a little every day . . ." ". . . Aye, sir. Every day, sir . . ." "The doctor should arrive shortly—" ". . . I hope so, sir . . . I'm that scared, sir. That scared . . ." From far across the room I could hear Annie's deep sigh. . . .

. . . That scared . . . I began to weep softly, although my eyes were dry . . .

Two days before Christmas, Robert was followed into the room by an elderly man, quite stooped and with a startling crest of stone-white hair. He carried a battered leather satchel, badge of the physician. Behind thick spectacles, Dr. Erskine's tired eyes were kindly and direct, making no attempt to conceal their shock upon first viewing their patient. "My word!" he muttered. "What have we here?"

"As I indicated previously, Doctor," Robert explained stiffly, "my wife has not been well for some time."

"You say that she is a young woman?" the doctor whispered.

"She is my wife," Robert answered coldly.

"By Jove!"

"Her condition has deteriorated considerably in the last few months—"

"I should say!" the doctor agreed roundly. "Now, sir, if you will leave me alone with my patient; I need to make a preliminary examination." When Robert had closed the door behind him, the old man circled my wrist with his dry fingers. "Mmm, pulse thready," he murmured. "Well, Lady Elizabeth, is it? I am Dr. Erskine." His hand was scratchy as it touched my cheek. "What seems to be the trouble?"

I shut my eyes.

"Ah, now, dear lady," he chuckled, "your eyelids ain't going to reveal much to an old man, now, are they?" He patted my head. "You must help me, if I am going to help you . . ." I did not speak. "You don't want to go on like this, now, do you?" I submitted listlessly to his probings and pressings, which were unfailingly gentle and not without skill. "Yes," he was positive, "about three months along—"

I groaned.

"You are feeling pain, or discomfort?" he asked quickly.

I shook my head.

"If you continue on this course, you cannot possibly carry the child to full term," he warned.

I began to shiver.

"Cold? It is an inferno in here—"

Tears squeezed past my closed eyelids and slipped down my cheeks.

"Tears?" The doctor was puzzled. "What is it, dear lady? What is it?"

Still I wept.

"Not pain," he mumbled to himself, "not cold . . . Fear!" He took my hand. "Fear! Dear lady—are you afraid?"

I began to sob violently.

"Afraid!" He leaned close and peered directly into my face; his breath smelled faintly of stale tobacco. "Afraid! Of what? What?"

. . . Afraid of what . . . Oh, God . . . Afraid of what . . . Could I tell this old man of the curse placed on me . . . on my unborn child? . . . Could I tell this old man that I had killed . . . That I had killed my lover's wife . . . deliberately. Ruthlessly . . . And exulted in the deed . . . Afraid of what? I could have laughed; instead I cried, "Go away! Please, go away . . ."

"Not before I have given you something to make you sleep. You are in sore need of rest, dear lady." Dr. Erskine extracted a packet of powders from his ancient bag and mixed them carefully in the glass of water that stood on a nearby chest. "Drink this." Gently he put the glass to my lips. "We'll talk again after you have rested . . ."

Exhaustion, in league with Dr. Erskine's magical potion, induced an oblivion that lasted well into the afternoon of the next day, which was Christmas Eve. It was not until early dusk that my eyelids fluttered and I glimpsed Annie sitting beside my bed, watching me. "Ah!" she grinned, "'tis refreshed ye must be, the now!"

I stretched and then—remembered . . .

"The master says that I'm to pretty you up for tonight's party—" she bubbled.

"Party!"

"Aye!" Annie could not contain her excitement. "'Tis the Christmas do—and glorious it is in the great hall!" Her eyes twinkled. "Wait until you see it, ma'am! The wreath's that big!"

"No," I begged.

"Sir Robert says you're to wear somethin' bright. Now, ma'am," the girl smiled, "what's it to be—the red velvet or the green satin?"

. . . The red velvet . . . her dress . . . "Annie, please! Let me be," I pleaded.

"I brung some nice hot water," she ignored my protests, "so's I can wash you up some, before puttin' on them fancy doodads."

"Annie—no! Please, I can't!"

She began to bathe my hands. "After that sleep and a little scrub, you'll be sure to be dancin' all over the hall! Wait and see!" Having selected the red velvet because of

its warmth—"The hall ain't cozy like up here, ma'am"—
she tackled the real hurdle: that of trying to dress me.

"What on earth is the girl doing!" exclaimed Dr. Erskine
as he burst through the door, followed by Robert.

"She is outfitting my wife for the traditional Christmas
festivities at Wynds."

"Outrageous!" sputtered the doctor. "A woman in her
state of health! Whatever are you thinking of, sir?"

"I am afraid that my wife's appearance tonight is mandatory," Robert replied coolly. "The squire's lady must always be in attendance on this occasion."

"Pray, look at her, sir! She can barely hold her head on
her neck!"

Robert sighed. "Regrettable, Doctor, but," his smile was
rueful, "I cannot ignore the age-old customs of my family.
And," he added, "since she is not obliged to converse with
the tenants, or their wives, the ordeal cannot be extraordi-
narily taxing, I assure you."

"She does not have to participate?" The doctor scratched
his chin.

"No," Robert explained, "Lady Elizabeth simply must
preside there, if only for a portion of the evening. These
are, after all," Robert's voice was smooth, "my people."

"And this, I shall remind you, Sir Robert"—the doctor's
old eyes hardened—"is your wife."

"Doctor," Robert said stiffly, "I do not need you to remind me where my duties lie. Lady Elizabeth will attend
the affair, be it for a short time. And that, sir," Robert
finished, "is final." He strode from the room.

Chapter 78

Leaning heavily on my husband's arm, I managed, although unsteadily, to negotiate the broad staircase and reach the great hall without incident. Dr. Erskine trailed close behind, ready to treat a spell of severe weakness, sudden vertigo, or the dread aftermath of a possible misstep. It was at Robert's thoughtful suggestion that we made the descent early, affording me an opportunity to rest in the inglenook and regain my strength before the onslaught of the arriving guests and avoid the accompanying noise and confusion.

From the enormous wreath hanging high over the master's dining chairs to variegated ribbons and lush greenery festooning the walls, the great hall was extravagantly bedecked. The scent of mulled cider and of fresh-cut pine spiced the air. Multibranched candelabra graced the long tables already laid with snowy napery and brilliant with crystal goblets and a silver service that glittered in the dancing light. As squat centerpiece, the wassail bowl, brimfull, waited to dispense its liquid treasures.

I had no thought for all this: I pressed on to the refuge promised by the inglenook and the fire stretching tall on its hearth. Once safely there I sank gratefully onto a bench and began to rub my hands, clammy with perspiration, and mop at the fine beads of moisture that dressed my upper lip and ran along my hairline.

"Doctor—" Robert was preparing to withdraw. "Would you be good enough to stay with Lady Elizabeth for the moment. I must approve the final preparations for the festivities—"

The doctor nodded.

I sat huddled before the fire, trying to transfer some of its comforting warmth to my own starved limbs, conscious the while of the doctor's compassionate yet quizzical gaze. It was not long before formal announcement of the first arrival was intoned, followed by another, and still another, until the hall soon vibrated with gaiety and laughter. Hands working and body tense, I stared into the wild yellow flames, waiting in active dread for the awful moment when I must appear as Mistress of Wynds before her loyal tenantry. . . . Oh, God, grant me the strength . . .

"Are you all right, dear lady?" the doctor regarded me anxiously.

. . . All right . . . all right . . . would I ever be all right again . . .

"My dear," said Robert softly as he reentered the inglenook, "would you honor me and our guests with your presence at this time?"

I turned my frightened eyes away.

Robert took my hands in his. "Our company has arrived, my dear. All that is needed now is the Mistress of Wynds."

I shrank from his touch.

"My dear"—Robert raised me to my feet—"the festivities cannot commence without you—"

"Please, Robert," I begged him, "let me stay here—"

He laughed. "What would the village folk think of the squire's lady then?" His face sobered. "Can you not display sufficient interest in their welfare to wish them felicitations in the Yuletide season? Come now," he prodded me across the small room, "surely you would not be so ungenerous or unkind . . ."

"Perhaps, Sir Robert—" the doctor moved to intervene.

"Sir." Robert's eyebrows lifted with surprise. "You outreach yourself, I fear."

Every eye of the group standing silently expectant in the great hall was directed toward the doorway of the inglenook; fastened on the newest mistress of Wynds. . . . "Smile," Robert muttered in an aside, "these are your people. You owe them that small courtesy." Wearily I allowed Robert to guide me to the chair properly assigned to me and I sat, dropping my gaze immediately to my lap and my tortured hands. Timid murmurings began then, increasing gradually to the volume more normally associated with a social gathering. Any prolonged fascination with the mistress of Wynds was drowned in the wassail bowl.

I made no effort to sample the infinite assortment of

foodstuffs: The first entrée was removed untouched; its
successor, boasting still different varieties, remained un-
tasted. Transported to another day, another time, my mind
was a whirlpool of memories. . . . Was it only a year ago
that I had paused on the broad staircase and looked down
to meet the dark eyes of the man in my dream . . . only a
year ago that he had strolled to the bottom step, taken my
hand in his, and kissed it with cool, firm lips . . . only a
year ago that he had murmured: "Miss Knowlton? I am
Robert Wyndham . . ."

Perfectly I could recall the smile lighting his handsome
face, the look in those eyes shadowed under their mocking
brows. . . . They told me that I was beautiful . . . that
my hair was a golden stream, my eyes liquid amber
. . . my body ripe and promising under a girlish, no
longer fashionable gown. . . .

Tears spurted from behind my eyes.

"Sir Robert," Dr. Erskine whispered, "I think perhaps
your wife should be permitted to retire—"

"I prefer that she wait until the dancing begins," Robert
replied smoothly. "Her departure will be far less conspicuous then—"

"Sir Robert—" the doctor persisted, "Lady Elizabeth is
close to the breaking point."

"It will not be long now," Robert smiled, "the musicians
are due momentarily—"

. . . Ah, how we had danced that other night . . . I
had melted against him . . . thrilled to the warm pressure
of his arms . . . to the message in those dusky eyes . . .
I was consumed . . .

I was young then: beautiful, passionate, reaching for
life . . .

Now I was cursed . . . doomed . . . waiting for
death . . .

Tears were soaking the bodice of my gown.

"Sir Robert!" Dr. Erskine hissed. "Have pity on the poor
soul!"

"It will not be long now," Robert repeated coolly.

. . . The guests had observed Frances as she cowered in
her chair, gaunt body trembling, eyes blank with fear

. . . begging for release, pleading for the refuge of her room . . .

. . . Now they watched me, hunched in that same chair, tears wet on my pinched face, praying for the safety of the same room . . .

At last the troupe of musicians filed in, their appearance greeted by an immediate roar of delight from the noisy, crowding guests, who were by this time more than a little tipsy. At a signal from Judd the houseboys pushed back the tables and chairs so as to increase the floor area for dancing. And, at a signal from Robert, the music began. He stood; bowed before my chair. "This is a waltz, I believe, my dear, your favorite." He smiled. "Would you join me?"

Almost blind with terror I slumped further in my chair. "No," I moaned, "no, no . . ."

"Sir Robert!" insisted Dr. Erskine.

Robert sighed. "As you say, Doctor." He lifted me easily and, followed by the doctor, carried me upstairs, leaving behind the screech of violins and the scraping sounds of wildly dancing feet.

Chapter 79

"Lady Elizabeth . . ." Annie was trying to coax me out of a drugged sleep. " 'Tis Christmas Day, mum—"

I did not answer.

"I cannot wake her, Sir Robert," the girl whispered.

"Your wife should be permitted to come out of this naturally," I heard Dr. Erskine's voice.

"Out of what, sir?" my husband demanded. "What preparation have you administered, Doctor, that she cannot be roused?"

"Merely laudanum," the doctor replied easily. "She was exhausted."

"I am afraid I do not understand, Doctor. Did she not sleep the clock around the day previous?"

"Yes," Dr. Erskine admitted, "but the poor woman must restore her strength in some manner. Since her body will not accept food," he explained, "it must substitute sleep."

"What precisely is your diagnosis?" Robert asked.

The doctor cleared his throat, "Your wife, Sir Robert, is suffering from a hysterical condition, which is causing aversion to food and an inability to eat."

"You are implying that her condition is mental?"

"I think," the doctor spoke slowly, "that an abnormal attitude may be the underlying cause of her debilitation. However—"

"However?"

"Her situation is complicated by the accompanying symptoms of deficiency and emaciation—and jeopardized still further by the pregnancy."

"What is the nature of this—as you phrase it—abnormal attitude, Doctor?"

The old man sighed deeply, "I don't know. I confess that I am completely baffled."

"Then you can offer no course of treatment?"

"Course of treatment?" the doctor mused, "I will say, Sir

Robert, that ideally medicine treats the cause of the disease as well as the disease itself. In this case," his voice was low, "I am in total ignorance as to a feasible diagnosis of what is almost psychotic fear."

"What do you propose, then?" Robert's tone was curt.

"Treat the symptoms," the doctor said simply. "When she is suffering from inanition, try and feed her. When she seems nervous and teary—let her rest. Above that," he admitted wearily, "I can recommend nothing." His remarks fell suddenly whisper-soft, "I fear for the foetus. If your wife's state of health remains precarious, I am convinced that she will abort."

"Will you remain with her?"

"Ah, Sir Robert." The doctor's reply became instantly regretful. "I can commit only a few more days here—perhaps as much as a week. No more." He added sadly, "I have other patients requiring my attention in Torquay."

"I see." Robert appeared satisfied. "I am in the process of engaging a physician to serve the village on a more permanent basis. His arrival should coincide with your departure."

"Splendid. For," the doctor sighed, "I have great fears for the child."

Tears spurted from the sides of my eyes. "No," I moaned.

"Ah!" said Robert, "she is awake at last. Annie, see to your mistress. I shall return in one half hour to escort her to the great hall."

"Escort her to the great hall?" exclaimed Dr. Erskine.

"Yes," replied Robert easily, "the traditional Christmas celebration for the household staff is to commence shortly." He smiled. "The village was entertained last evening—today: the servants."

"Lady Elizabeth must be excused from the festivities." The doctor issued a flat statement.

"I beg your pardon?"

"I cannot permit my patient to attend such a function, meritorious though it may be," the doctor declared firmly.

Robert's voice was cold. "As usual, Doctor, you presume." He turned to Annie. "One half hour."

* * *

Leaning heavily on Robert's arm, I placed one uncertain foot before the other and thus slowly, haltingly, descended the broad staircase. As we neared the bottom step two footmen rushed to place a chair at my immediate convenience, and I sank into it, exhausted, lowering my gaze automatically to the hands clenched grotesquely in a lap of shimmering green satin. The staff stood in respectful silence, subduing an undercurrent of almost childlike anticipation, while Robert offered his traditional felicitations for the season and extended his sincerest gratitude for a year of loyalty and devoted service.

. . . Was it only a year ago that I watched Frances, sunken eyes averted, head drooping low, cower in her chair; cringe at a word directed at her; recoil from the touch of a square, tanned hand . . .

Robert was saying, "As a measure of our warm esteem, Lady Elizabeth has selected a few remembrances for services so expertly rendered." He smiled at me. "My dear?"

I slipped deeper in my chair.

. . . Was it only a year ago that I, barely able to conceal my own excitement, unwrapped a gaily beribboned parcel, uncovering its offering of earth-brown bombazine . . . Only a year ago that I dropped the drab swath from my hands, letting it slide carelessly to the floor . . .

My hand reached to my throat: the amber drop—it was still there . . .

Chapter 80

The ordeal of Christmas has been over now for a little more than a week. Spent, I have lain these days in bed, as if suspended between alternating visits from Annie, patiently bearing her trays of gruel and soup, and Dr. Erskine, mercifully extending his packet of powders with their pledge of blissful release . . .

The doctor left Wynds at dawn this morning. Dimly I heard the carriage clatter over the frost-flecked cobbles of the courtyard. The arrival of his replacement is imminent, I have been told.

. . . Dr. Briggs?

. . . Jonathan . . .

After repeated urgings—"Come, Lady Elizabeth, just one more bite"—Annie, anxiety clouding her face, has finally left the room. Now I am alone: warm and drowsy, listening to the uneasy lullaby of a fire sputtering on the hearth. A hesitant knock sounds on the door. "Annie, please! I cannot eat another thing—"

"Lady Elizabeth?"

My eyes jerk open. She is standing at my bedside. With a slender hand she sweeps heavy auburn hair away from her face, revealing smooth pink cheeks. Shining curls tumble carelessly over the shoulders of her drab gray gown, which is discreetly patched, irrevocably faded, and cannot veil the rich promise beneath. Deeply jade, her eyes as they regard me are merry under feathery golden brows. She is glorious.

"Lady Elizabeth—my name is Jane Landry. Sir Robert has engaged me." Her voice is low, husky. "May I read to you now?"

I am paralyzed.

"Not now? Well, then—" she suggests gaily, "perhaps later? You have only to call if you need me—" Her smile is dazzling. "I am staying in the pretty yellow room . . ."